When You Dance with
Rabbits

When You Dance with Rabbits

MARSHA WARSAW

Pleasant Word
A Division of WINEPRESS PUBLISHING

© 2006 by Marsha Warsaw. All rights reserved.
© 2006 Cover Illustration by Matthew Archambault. All rights reserved.

Pleasant Word (a division of WinePress Publishing, PO Box 428, Enumclaw, WA 98022) functions only as book publisher. As such, the ultimate design, content, editorial accuracy, and views expressed or implied in this work are those of the author.

No part of this publication may be reproduced, stored in a retrieval system or transmitted in any way by any means—electronic, mechanical, photocopy, recording or otherwise—without the prior permission of the copyright holder, except as provided by USA copyright law.

Unless otherwise noted, all Scriptures are taken from the Holy Bible, New International Version, Copyright © 1973, 1978, 1984 by the International Bible Society. Used by permission of Zondervan Publishing House. The "NIV" and "New International Version" trademarks are registered in the United States Patent and Trademark Office by International Bible Society.

Scripture references marked KJV are taken from the King James Version of the Bible.

Scripture references marked NASB are taken from the New American Standard Bible, © 1960, 1963, 1968, 1971, 1972, 1973, 1975, 1977 by The Lockman Foundation. Used by permission.

ISBN 1-4141-0673-4
Library of Congress Catalog Card Number: 2006901035

Dedication

This is dedicated to:
My husband, Steve, and our family for
their love and support,
Our parents and grandparents for showing
us how to live a life of love and
To God, our Father, for seeing us
through all things.

Foreword

I have written this book during sleepless nights after the loss of my father-in-law and mother-in-law, and then my mother, in a nine month time period. It is my hope that those struggling through the pain of loss will be encouraged by connecting with these characters and seeing God's daily blessings in the little things of life. I want whoever reads this to know that, though they are totally wiped out physically and emotionally, there is healing as they let themselves rest in the arms of Jesus, while the world goes on around them. Grieving is a long process. Be patient with yourself and others, and let those around you give you their love. God bless you.

Acknowledgements

Amy Munson and Mary Ellen Leonard for their support and literary expertise.

Blake & Camille Munson for their prayer support and unconditional friendship.

Family and friends for loving support and prayer.

Orlando Bloom (unknowingly) for helping me grieve through wakeful nights by his remarkable portrayal of the confused and grieving elf, Legolas, in *The Lord of the Rings, Fellowship of the Ring*.

All of the fine folks of Pleasant Word Publishing for seeing me through this project.

Thank you all!

Chapter 1

Early morning sunlight filtered through the treetops, scattering the shadows clutching at the simple cottage nestled near the forest east of the horse barns. The golden rays seeped through the small bedroom window then burst into wide streaks, providing stages for the myriad dust flakes dancing in the air. The sun's blanket settled upon Shale's shoulder. She opened her eyes and drew toward its soothing warmth.

Across the room, her younger sister was sleeping peacefully. Piper's strawberry blonde hair surrounded her cherub face like a halo. Her cloth doll nestled securely in her arms, its blonde braids resting against her cheek. Shale's heart filled with love and pain at the same time. Momma had made the doll for Piper, and she was never without it now that Momma was gone. Gone. How could it be true? Yet, it was. Shale closed her eyes until the wave of despair passed. She tried so hard to comfort her brother and sister, but nothing seemed to help. Again last night, she had rocked Piper as she wept—deep, heart wrenching sobs that tore at Shale's heart. Truth be told, she had wept too.

Fighting back new tears, she rose wearily and went to the kitchen. She heard the early morning birdsong welcoming the new day, but she did not join the song. Momma would have been up singing and already have breakfast made. Shale sighed, peered into the cast iron pot filled with fresh water, and set it over the fire to heat. She must remember to thank Samuell for preparing the water and the fire for her. He was a thoughtful brother, despite his tendency for mischief.

Shale hurried back to the bedroom and shed her night gown. They must not be late today! She picked up her brother's shirt, pushed her arms through the sleeves, and quickly buttoned it. Papa's brown tunic slipped easily over her head and settled over Samuell's shirt. She tugged impatiently at the shirttail to straighten it. It was so uncomfortable wearing the layers of clothing to disguise herself as a lad, but Papa insisted. Since the death of their mother, Papa had been adamant. He said he did not want anyone mistaking her for Momma. She did not understand. Momma's death had been an accident.

Shale leaned down and tucked the hems of her father's pant legs into her boots. At least Samuell and Piper had not seen the fear and anger in Papa's eyes when he told her this. They did not need to know how great his concern was for their safety. They needed life to go on as normally as possible. She jerked the laces of her boots tighter and vowed to be strong for them again today.

She sat on the edge of Piper's bed and gently touched her shoulder. "Wake up, little bird. Our new day is here."

Piper stirred and sat up rubbing sleepy eyes. "I am still sleepy, Shale," she yawned.

"I know. Kelly will be waiting for you," Shale encouraged. "You are baking today, are you not?"

"Yes." Piper yawned again. She stretched her arms over her head and crawled onto Shale's lap. "I hear the birdsong. Are there carrots for my rabbits?" She looked up at her sister with bright green eyes. Shale nodded and Piper rushed off, her silky hair streaming behind her.

Shale returned to the kitchen, tucking an annoying strand of strawberry blonde hair behind her ear. She measured out the oatmeal for their breakfast and added wild blackberries, honey, and walnuts to the bowl.

Bouncing branches of bright blue and pink flowers drew her attention to the window, as Piper parted them and darted toward the lush garden in the side yard. The beauty of the new day did nothing to cheer her. *I must still gather herbs and seeds before the frosts come. Maybe there will be time after the sale is over.* She sighed. *There is so much to do. So much.*

Piper hopped into view, dancing among a troupe of little brown rabbits dotting the lawn. Shale watched as Piper twirled and blessed each little rabbit with a tender touch and delightful smile. Skipping toward Momma's flower bed, she led the playful bunnies on their morning tour of the yard.

Shale bowed her head with relief and prayed, "Thank you, Father God, that Piper is able to find joy among the creatures you have made. Please help me to take joy in your creation. Let it remind me that you are with us and love us so much. Please help us through this day and bring Papa home soon. We need him, Father God."

Shale turned resolutely back to the matter of breakfast. She picked up the blue bowl and dumped the oatmeal and seasonings into the boiling water. Her thoughts turned to her father again. He was three weeks late in returning. It was lonely and frightening without him. They were still reeling from the loss of their mother, and his absence was difficult to bear. Perhaps today Papa would return with the new brood mares he was sent to purchase for the farm. He should be here. The sale was tomorrow. Biting her lip, she remembered arguing with him before he went.

"Surely someone else could go this time, Papa," she had begged.

"You will be fine here. Follow the plans we have made, and look to Eli for help," he had snapped. "You know that I must go. The foreman insists."

Her forehead creased at the thought of the foreman. She did not like the man. She did not trust him. He barked orders at the workers like a snarling old dog and did not treat the horses any better.

Angrily, she stirred the oatmeal, sending some of it slopping out into the fire. It hissed at her in protest. She stirred all the harder.

The foreman had no compassion. He had snapped impatiently at Samuell when he asked about the delay in Papa's return. He cared for no one, and little for the horses, except what price they would bring. Many of the new stable hands copied his rotten attitude. The original owner of the horses would not have allowed this. He loved the horses as much as Papa did.

Shale brushed her hair back from her face and let a soft smile grow about her lips as she remembered the kind, old man who had owned the farm. She missed his twinkling brown eyes and the laughter they had shared watching his horses learn under the skilled hands of her father. The old man especially loved the newborn colts and fillies that arrived each year. Often, he had appeared at the door of their cottage to take them to meet the new arrivals. This, too, had changed.

He had been taken to live with his family in a village far away, after an illness of man had left him unable to care for himself. How he had begged Papa and Eli to help him stay at the farm. Her mother and Kelly offered to care for him, but his family wanted him near them.

Shale shuddered as she remembered his gaunt face. His lips turned up only on one side, as he gave them a brave smile the day they carried him to his carriage and drove away.

The farm had been sold within a moon of his departure. Of the original workers only Papa and old Eli remained. Eli knew the herd so well, he had made himself indispensable at least for now. He and his wife, Kelly, were their dear friends. *What would we have done without them when Momma died?*

Shoving aside her thoughts, she ladled the bubbling oatmeal into three bowls. While she waited for her brother and sister, she hurriedly wrapped slices of Kelly's fresh brown bread and thick chunks of the yellow cheese she had sent for their lunches and tucked them into small woven bags.

"Here!" Piper cried, dropping shiny red apples into each bag. "I shined them with Momma's apron."

Shale's heart constricted at Piper's words and the sight of Momma's apron in her small hand, but she smiled and stooped to hug her. "Thank you, Piper. They are so shiny I can hardly see. Are you ready for your lessons today?"

"She practiced with me and is doing poorly," Samuell answered with mock dismay on his young face. Piper rushed at him, and he scooped her up and swung her in a circle. "You are doing very well indeed, little sister," he laughed.

They sat down at the table and bowed their heads.

Samuell prayed, "Father God, thank you for our food. May it give us strength for today. Help Piper with her studies and us with our horses. Please protect us and help Papa to return soon. And Father God, please teach Shale how to make good jam like Kelly does. Amen." He winked at Piper and reached for his milk.

Shale wrinkled her nose at her brother and quietly began stirring her oatmeal. Her thoughts drifted to the day ahead. Piper would go to be with Kelly, while she and Samuell would be in the south meadow training the weanlings and yearlings. It was her favorite part of the day. For a time, she was able to put aside her fears and concerns. She loved the sweet smells of the grasses and wild flowers growing in the meadow and the woodland at its border. Together, she and Samuell would laugh at the antics of the young colts and fillies. They would run hard and stop quickly, only to turn and jump as high as they could for the affections of their trainers.

Slurp! The sound brought her attention back to breakfast. Piper giggled at Samuell, who fixed Shale with a pitiful look of utter innocence.

Choosing to ignore them, she took another bite of oatmeal and let her thoughts wander back to the day. At least they would be away from the stables and the crude men that worked there. She did not want to see which horses would be sold. She loved them all and dreaded their loss. Prospective buyers had been coming to view them for the past two weeks. She and Samuell were praying that their favorites would stay at the farm or go to kind owners who would lovingly care for them.

"You are not eating much, my sister," Samuell said, nodding at her bowl.

His comment snapped her thoughts back to the kitchen. "It is enough," she answered sharply.

Samuell's eyes reflected his hurt. He looked down at his bowl.

"Samuell, I am sorry. Thank you for starting the fire and bringing fresh water this morning. It is a great help to me." Noting Piper's worried expression, she added, "Anyway, I am not an old badger stuffing myself for the winter now, am I?" She smiled and raised her light eyebrows at Piper.

Samuell gave her a small smile and took his bowl to the washbasin. Piper did the same and dashed out the door to the garden.

"I am worried about you, Shale," Samuell said quietly. "You are not eating. Please take care of yourself. Piper needs you." He did not wait for her reply. The back door closed quietly behind him.

Shale sat still for a few moments. He was right. She must pay more attention to what she did and said. They did not need more worries.

Samuell entered the kitchen with an armload of firewood and set it by the fireplace.

Shale smiled her thanks and rose to wash the dishes. Peering out the window, she smiled softly. There was Piper, squatted down in the grass, talking earnestly to the cluster of small brown rabbits. Shale began washing and looked out again to see Piper dancing and twirling across the lawn amidst the hopping rabbits.

She blinked and stared out the window. It almost looked like the rabbits were twirling, too. "Samuell," she said, "look at the rabbits!"

Samuell leaned over the basin just in time to see the dance conclude. "Were they twirling?" he asked with amazement.

"You know Piper and her way with animals."

"Yes," Samuell answered. "She is much more gifted than we. Here she comes, and she is not happy."

The door to the cottage banged open and Piper stomped in. "Samuell!" she demanded. "That dog wants to come into our yard again. He scares my rabbits. I told him to go home or you would shoot him with your arrows!" She stood before them with her arms folded across her chest and her small mouth in a fierce scowl.

Samuell struggled not to laugh at the ferocious look on his little sister's face. "I will get my bow and warn him," he said. He took up his bow and cast a wink at Shale.

Shale did not see him. She had turned back to the washbasin. She must not let Piper see the tears of unreleased laughter spilling down her cheeks.

After Samuell had rescued the rabbits, the three children of Connor pulled their headbands down snuggly on their heads and left the safety of their home. Shale walked Piper to Kelly's small cottage, then hurried to join Samuell leading the young horses to the meadow.

A few miles away Henicles, the wizard, approached the farm. He laughed heartily as his companion Avian, an elf from Cambria Forest, finished a merry song full of mischief.

Placing his hand on Avian's shoulder he urged, "Sing another one, my friend—then it shall be my turn."

Avian smiled broadly. He was pleased Henicles had arrived before he left on an errand for his father. It was good to have company on the trail, and he was enjoying time with his old friend.

He took a breath to begin his next rhyme, but before he could begin his song, a wagon rounded the corner ahead and sped toward them. The horse pulling it was wide-eyed with fear. Flecks of white foam dotted its rough coat.

Avian called clearly to it and stepped toward the horse. It stopped and quieted under his gentle murmurings and touch.

"Get away from my horse, elf!" Suspiciously, he glared at Avian.

"Greetings, friend," Henicles soothed. "We only mean to help."

Scowling, the man did not reply. He slapped the reins on the tired horse and hurried the poor beast down the road.

Henicles leaned on his staff in thought. He had purposely sought Avian for this quest. His gift of perception was immense, his valor great, and his heart true.

"A gruff fellow," Henicles spoke at last.

Avian nodded and stood staring grimly after the man. "That poor horse will not survive long under such care."

"I have noticed many regarding you with unfriendly eyes as our journey has brought us closer to the farm of my friend, Connor," Henicles said thoughtfully. "This concerns me. Connor is of your race, although he has chosen to live here among men and train horses for a respected breeder. He is highly esteemed for his skill."

Henicles thrust his staff forward and resumed walking, deep in thought. Avian fell in step beside him.

"You have said that you are concerned by the sudden sale of these horses and their placement throughout the realms. What are these horses like, Henicles, that men would seek them so earnestly?" Avian inquired.

"Not only the horses themselves, who are exceedingly agile, intelligent, and strong. It is their training and their trainer, I fear, that is sought. His grandfather knew the Presage. Some believe Connor does as well." He looked meaningfully at Avian. "It is not only men who seek this."

"The dance of death. I have heard of it. In a time long past, many were cursed for it. It is banned among my people," Avian responded, a frown creasing his brow.

"Indeed, my friend," Henicles shook his head in disgust. "There are rumors it is being practiced again." He paused, studying the land ahead of him. "I would have you leave me now and travel through these woods to the meadow south of the farm, for it lies ahead. Await me there. I may be returning with some fine horses. Find a safe place to conceal them, should the need arise. Your father's business may have to wait." Using his staff to propel him, he strode off down the road.

Avian, too, had felt the disquiet settling upon them. Silently, he moved through the cool woods in search of the meadow.

Henicles approached the gate of the Munson Horse Farm and paused, leaning heavily on his staff. His eyes widened as he read the sale bills posted on the gates. He entered and saw no familiar face.

Across the lane Eli straightened from brushing a tall mare's sleek coat. He gently patted her withers and blinked in surprise when he heard a familiar voice call his name.

Henicles skirted the busy stable hands and approached Eli with a smile.

Eli's expression darkened when he saw the foreman staring at them. As he turned and untied the mare, he tossed Henicles a warning glance. "M'lord, did ye wish ta be alookin' this 'un over?" Eli asked. He led the mare toward Henicles.

The brusque foreman approached them and addressed Henicles suspiciously. "You there, what is your business?"

"I am told you have fine horses here, my lord, taught by a skillful horse master. I represent a buyer interested in breeding stock. Also, I am seeking a mount for myself, for I travel far in my journeys. What have you to show me?" Henicles replied eagerly. He examined the mare with a shrewd eye.

The foreman regarded the tall wizard and answered proudly, "It is true that we have the finest horses of any you would find."

"Eli! Show this wizard our best." With a smug look the foreman sauntered off, yelling instructions to another worker.

"Come 'is way, m' lord, and I be a showin' ye our mares first." Eli led Henicles to a beautiful mare tethered furthest from the stables. With his voice low he spoke, " 'em children be not safe 'ere."

"What has happened?" Henicles whispered, then called out, "Walk her for me." He studied the mare's movements as they walked her further from the stables.

"Little un's with m' wife. T'others be in the south meadow. Do not be a callin' 'em by name. Shayna be dead." Eli fixed Henicles with a look of grave concern and turned the mare.

"'ey say 'twas a huntin' accident. I be not believen' 'em. A strange man come 'ere. 'e were rough lookin' and mean. 'e and Connor 'ad words. Next day, Shayna be found, shot in 'er 'eart by a arrow while she was arunnin' in the woods." The large man's shoulders slumped. "The younguns, 'ey be a hurtin' somethin' awful."

Eli's voice became louder as the foreman approached, "Ye can see sir, 'is mare be a fine 'un. She runs like o'wind itself, an she'll be a bringin' many fine little 'uns to your 'erd. Some of 'ers be in the south meadow now, m' lord."

"There is no time for him to see them. Take that mare to the red barn for the next customer," the foreman barked impatiently.

"I will buy her now," Henicles stated firmly. "This is the finest mare I have seen in my travels thus far."

"Well! Now that you have seen for yourself, you know we have the best." The foreman's chest puffed out with pride.

"Indeed you have, and I would see more. Your man here tells me some of her offspring are in a meadow," Henicles replied, stroking the withers of the mare.

"They will be in soon enough for you to see. Show him the other mares and the geldings," the smug foreman bellowed at Eli.

Turning to Henicles, the foreman instructed him, "Settle up with me at the house when you are finished." After a moment's hesitation, he added, "If you like, stay for the celebration to begin the sale tonight." He left them, strutting like a peacock toward the barn and another prospective buyer.

Henicles turned to Eli, "I need four horses. Which ones are the children's favorites?"

"'ey'll be ready for ye." Quietly he added, "Tell me na more. Just keep 'em young 'uns safe. 'ey be not safe 'ere." Quickly, Eli scribbled the names of four horses on a scrap of paper and handed it to Henicles.

Henicles studied the activities and men about him as he approached the main house where preparations for a celebration were in progress. A prim maid showed him to the office where the foreman was in conversation with a tall, well dressed man, whose brown hair was tied back neatly.

As Henicles entered, their conversation abruptly ceased. The foreman peered around the customer, who did not turn to look at Henicles.

"A moment and I will be with you. Wait in the drawing room," the foreman spoke impatiently. He waved his arm for the wizard to leave them.

Henicles nodded and retreated from the room. He studied the customer carefully, but could not see his face. The tension in the man's shoulders alerted Henicles. Had he seen this man before? He settled down on the comfortable sofa and closed his eyes. He listened intently to the conversation, but the well dressed man spoke no more.

Henicles looked up in surprise when he was summoned. The other customer had not passed him.

The foreman was all too eager to take his money. "Come in, come in. You have your papers in order?"

At a nod from Henicles he continued, "And your money? Good." He greedily took the gold coins from Henicles's hand.

"I do apologize for interrupting you before," Henicles spoke apologetically.

The foreman handed Henicles a bill of sale and turned back to the many papers scattered across his desk. When Henicles didn't leave immediately, he looked up with a scowl and demanded, "What do you want?"

Henicles took a step backwards and answered, "Nothing more, my lord. I was not sure we were finished." He had seen nothing to indicate where the man had gone.

"You have your bill of sale. Leave. Or stay for the celebration, as you please."

"Thank you." Henicles's eyes lit up as if he were anticipating the foreman's good ale. "Alas, I must hasten on. Perhaps another time, when my buyer bids me return. I am sure he will when sees your fine animals."

The foreman turned back to his work, a smirk distorting his grisly face.

Eli waited in the courtyard with the four horses Henicles had purchased. "Leave quickly! Some of 'em was not ta be sold. Godspeed." Eli turned abruptly and returned to his work.

Henicles mounted the tall gelding easily and led the three mares down the road in the opposite direction from which he had come. He traveled five miles before those following him turned back toward the farm. He continued on another mile and paused. He listened carefully and scanned the area before he stealthily entered the forest to his left. He led the horses deep into the woods and circled back to approach the meadow.

Avian reached the meadow south of the farm and crouched behind a thick myrtle bush. Two lads were working a group of young horses. He admired the beautiful conformation of the colts and fillies before him.

A magnificent mare watched attentively nearby. The taller lad called upon her to demonstrate new commands to the young horses. Avian watched, enthralled as the mare trotted forward, stopped, backed up three paces, and leapt lightly to the side each time the taller lad signaled with his hands. Avian had never seen a horse stride with such grace and agility. Suddenly, the mare nickered loudly and tossed her head up and down.

Immediately, the lads signaled the colts and fillies to perform simpler tasks. The young horses responded eagerly. They stopped and started with each whistled command.

The mare lowered her head and began to graze on the thick grass. She swished her tail in a lazy manner and ignored the activity beside her.

"Move over, Willow. Hah!" called the shorter of the lads.

The mare lifted her head and slowly sauntered several paces away where she resumed her feast. She appeared unconcerned with her surroundings, but Avian was not deceived. The wise mare was carefully observing the approach of a stout, blustery man accompanied by a well dressed man with a sheaf of papers in his hands.

The blustery man shouted to the lads, "Bring them closer, now. Move them on!"

The lads obeyed, and their charges performed the simple skills perfectly. The neatly dressed man agreed to purchase three fillies. Nimble fingers wove red ribbons into their manes, indicating the color of the buyer. The lads continued to work the horses until the men disappeared over the hill on the lane leading back to the barns.

Avian's sharp ears heard the sound of horses walking in the woodland long before Henicles drew near to him. He turned his attention from the bright meadow and hastened silently toward the sound.

"Ah, Henicles, they are truly beautiful." Avian ran his hands over the mare nearest him. He spoke softly in Elvish; the horses lowered their heads and began nibbling at the scant grass growing beneath the thick trees.

"The children, are they here?" Henicles questioned impatiently.

Turning away from the horses, Avian answered, "Two lads, yes. They are very skillful with the horses."

Henicles frowned, "Two lads?"

"Yes. Come, they are near," Avian replied. His long, blonde hair drifted back over his shoulder as he led Henicles through the woods. Holding back a branch, Avian allowed Henicles to pass before him to the large myrtle bush. Kneeling down for a better view, Avian nodded toward the meadow. Shale and Samuell were teaching the young ones to respond to hand signals.

"They also teach them whistled and verbal commands," Avian whispered to Henicles.

Henicles nodded but did not take his eyes off the meadow. His frown grew deeper while he contemplated the lads and their methods of instruction.

The training turned to fun and Henicles watched as the two lads stood on the back of the mare. Willow cantered through the meadow with the young horses racing behind her.

Suddenly, the lads dropped into the tall grass. The young horses racing behind the mare followed her example and leapt over their trainers or dodged away from them. The lads sprang up and began running, only to dive out of sight in another spot. The colts and fillies snorted and jumped over them again, tails held high in the air as they leapt. Laughing, the lads praised the young horses with encouraging words and vigorously rubbed their necks.

Henicles' frown melted to a faint smile. He was sure now. These were the children of Connor and Shayna. The litheness of their movements and the music in their laughter revealed it.

The game ended abruptly. Willow neighed an alarm and Shale swept upon her back, followed quickly by Samuell. The mare cantered forward and the young horses gathered about her.

They resumed the training session with easier commands again. The foreman approached, bringing another customer to the meadow. Willow pawed the ground restlessly.

Samuell spoke angrily, "I wish Papa were here. He would put a stop to this!"

"Hush, Samuell. There is nothing we can do now. Please do not anger him, or he may not let us work with them any longer." Shale quieted the mare with her hands.

"Put them through their paces, lads!" the foreman bellowed. He smugly crossed his arms over his thick chest and nodded to his customer.

The well dressed man's scowl turned to a sly smile while he watched the yearlings obey Samuell's commands. Shale cringed when he selected several young ones. She reluctantly wove the man's grey ribbons into their manes. The foreman and his customer left, debating price and further training of the yearlings.

"Samuell, work them a little longer, please." Shale sat down in the tall grass and absently picked a few strands, weaving them between her fingers. She removed the wide band from her head and ran her fingers through her short hair, tucking loose strands behind her ears. She fought back the tears threatening to spill down her cheeks.

"She has cut her hair!" Henicles gasped in astonishment. "Things are more amiss here than I feared."

"What do you mean, Henicles?" Avian asked, looking at the two again.

"The slighter one is a maiden, not a lad. The other one is her younger brother and there is a younger sister as well. I must speak with them."

In a specific sequence he made the cry of the whippoorwill. Shale looked up, but not toward the sound.

Noting the foreman was out of sight, she carefully signaled back.

"Samuell, run them around the meadow, please, and then take them in. Come home as soon as possible," Shale quietly spoke.

"Is it Father?" Samuell's bright, gray eyes were large with hope.

"No, but a friend." She pulled the wide band down upon her head and leapt up onto the mare.

"Don't tarry," Samuell urged. "It is not safe to be alone in the meadow anymore."

Shale guided the mare to the woodland's edge. From time to time, she would dismount and look closely at the shrubs. When she drew near the myrtle bush, she dismounted and began picking the abundant wild raspberries.

"Peace, child," Henicles greeted her from behind the myrtle bush.

"There is only the peace of God in my heart, Henicles. There is no other peace here. My mother..." Shale's tears choked her words.

"I know, child. I know," Henicles spoke softly to her.

She turned her face toward them then, and Avian saw her tears and the empty expression of grief pouring from her eyes. His heart was moved to sorrow, for the sadness he had felt coming from them was now magnified before him.

"How ...?" she began.

Henicles cut her off. "You must leave tonight."

"But Papa is not here," she agonized. She stepped toward them and picked more ripe red berries.

"I will leave immediately to search for him. I will find him. Do not fear," Henicles assured her. "You must flee tonight. You can wait no longer. I have horses for you."

Shale swallowed the lump in her throat and slowly nodded her head. She continued to study the berry bushes in front of her.

Henicles hurried on. "Cast a glance here. This is Avian of Cambria Forest. He will take you safely from here. Be ready," he instructed.

Shale's green eyes grew large. He was an elf. She glanced questioningly at Henicles.

"He is my trusted friend. I would leave you with no other," he reassured.

Taking a deep breath, she answered, "I will trust you, Henicles, as my father does."

Shifting her gaze to Avian, her expression changed to one of grim determination. "We will meet you beneath the tall willow tree to the east, three hours after the sun sets."

"The moon is full this night. Do not delay," Avian cautioned her.

The mare lifted her head from grazing and nudged Shale's back. She turned from them and tucked her berries into a cloth pouch tied to her waist. The mare nudged her again. "One moment, Willow." Shale bent as if to tie her boot laces and gathered her courage. She nodded at Henicles and galloped across the meadow to catch up with Samuell.

Avian's keen eyes located the reason for her haste. At the top of the knoll a man quickly slipped into the shadows. "They are watched. A man, there in the birch thicket. Henicles, there is much you have not told me." Avian looked questioningly at the wizard as they stealthily made their way back to his horses. His thoughts were on the maiden he had just met. She revealed her grief to them briefly, but beneath that many emotions swirled. She kept them tightly concealed in the depths of her soul. He could not read them.

Henicles' deep brown eyes took in the tall elf before him. He was secure in his decision. Avian would not fail him, and during this task he would learn much—much about his charges, much about himself, much about life. Placing his hand on Avian's shoulder, he instructed him, "Be wary of all. Take them to Pennsyl by whatever path is safest. Their knowledge of this area is great. I have no time to tell you more. Make haste." With a look of warning, he mounted and quietly guided the gelding through the woodland. He prayed for guidance and safety for them all.

Avian spoke briefly to the mares and returned quickly to the myrtle bush. The man was following the children to the stables.

Swiftly Avian ran through the woodland along its northern edge. It led to within twenty feet of the stables. From here he observed the activity of the stable hands. Some spoke eagerly of enjoying the ale supplied for the celebration that night. The less fortunate complained that there would be little ale left for them when they had finished stabling the horses readied for the sale tomorrow.

Good. They will be distracted tonight. Avian's keen eyes caught the movement of the man slinking in the shadows of the far stable. From the opposite direction the chatter of a child carried on the breeze. The man straightened and moved into the stable.

At the other end, the lad from the meadow emerged and spoke to an old man leading a fine mare to the grooming area. After a moment, they parted and the lad jogged off hurriedly over a rise where Avian could see the top of a cottage and a short dark chimney. The sound of childish chatter led in that direction. Soon a narrow trail of smoke curled from the chimney.

The man reappeared and slunk along the side of the stable toward the cottage. Avian crept silently past the stables, appearing as a shadow. Spotting the man near a small thicket to the side of the cottage, he crouched, observing.

Dusk thickened about them and another man approached the first. Gesturing casually toward the cottage he spoke, "Why do they have you watching stable boys and children? Will you not miss the celebration this night? I had hoped to arm wrestle you again."

"I will miss nothing. They will sleep as they do each night. I will have my share of ale." The man in the shadows eyed the other. "What do you care?"

"It seems to me foolish to be watching over children when such priceless horses are about," the second man replied, shaking his head.

"The horses are well guarded. Fear not for that. As to these," he waved his hand in a gesture of dismissal, "they are the horse master's and when they are tucked in their beds, I will find you and win back my knife. You caught me off guard is all, Knox."

"We shall see, my friend. Tonight then." The man bowed mockingly.

Avian watched as the mocker returned to the main house and the guard settled into the shadows. No one else approached the cottage, and the smells and sounds of cooking reached him.

A small child walked from the cottage to a low rope stretched across the neat yard and hung two towels upon it. She went to the edge of the cottage and looked about the yard. "Come little bunnies," she called softly. "I have treats for you."

The maiden stepped to the doorway and called, "Piper, come in now. Supper is ready and I am sure the rabbits are eating theirs."

Reluctantly, the child turned toward the cottage. "I don't know why they go home so early in the evenings now," she lamented.

"Because the darkness comes earlier, now that it is autumn," the maiden reassured her. They stepped inside and the door closed behind them.

Good. They are presenting the appearance of a normal evening. Avian hastened back to prepare the waiting horses. *At least the older two could ride well. That would not be a problem*, he thought as he ran. The age of the younger child concerned him. How would they manage with such a young child, should they be pursued and have need to fly with great haste over the many miles to Pennsyl?

He pictured in his mind the rough terrain they would travel to arrive there. He frowned and searched his sharp memory for places to harbor them from their enemies. Two places came to mind, and he set his thoughts on how best to approach these.

The sun was setting quickly, spreading its golden, rosy colors into the shade of the woodland. It was beautiful and peaceful. He loved the contrast of light and shadow when evening settled into the woods. Avian thought of the beauty of the woodlands of his home as he led the three mares to the large willow tree.

"May the remainder of this night be as peaceful," he prayed. His gaze searched the area around the willow tree for a secure place to observe the approach of the children.

Henicles cantered down the road away from the horse farm until he reached the fertile grasslands northwest of the meadow where he had left Avian. There he urged the horse on, rapidly covering the distance between the farm and the nearest village. The innkeeper here was known for his loose tongue and rich ale, both of which flowed freely among the customers. Here he would seek lodging for the night and begin his quest for information of the whereabouts of Connor.

Henicles admonished the stable boy, "Guard this horse with great care, lad." He slipped the lad a silver coin and entered the inn.

Good, he thought. The room was full and noisy. Many tongues would be wagging tonight. He settled himself in a chair near the fireplace and listened intently to the many conversations about him.

In the house of Connor, Shale helped Piper put away the clean dishes. She sensed the presence of the watcher. He had come every evening since Papa left.

Piper chattered happily about her day with Eli's wife. "We made many loaves of bread today. I stirred and stirred the eggs and butter until they were creamy smooth. Kelly said I am a good helper. The cook needed our help because there will be a celebration tonight." Piper brushed a wayward lock of strawberry blonde hair back from her face. Her smile faded as she remembered the sale. "Will they sell Willow, Shale? I love Willow, and she loves me." Her lower lip trembled at the thought.

"No, Piper, of course not." Shale knelt beside her little sister and wrapped her small frame in a warm hug. "We need Willow for training the little ones. She is very important to the farm. They will not sell her." Shale tucked the wayward lock under Piper's headband and smiled reassuringly.

"Good. For I will ride her when Papa comes home," she announced.

Samuell grabbed her under her arms and swung her around on his way to the door. Giggling, Piper curled her legs up under her body so she would spin faster. Samuell set her down and reached for the latch.

"Where are you going?" Shale asked with alarm.

"To get my rope from the stable." Puzzled by her tone of voice, he continued, "I need it to compare with the new rope I am making." He studied her face then replied, "I will return quickly."

"See that you do," Shale replied, turning back to the dishes on the drain board.

Samuell shook his head and winked at Piper.

"May I go with you, Samuell?" Piper asked. She held tightly to his hand.

"No, little one. I will not be visiting the horses tonight," Samuell assured her. "I must work on my rope."

Shale watched the pout form on her sister's lips and soothed, "You need to relax after baking bread all day, little bird. I do not know how Kelly would have managed without your help."

Shale listened intently and heard what she expected. The watcher followed Samuell. Touching Piper's nose with her finger she added, "You have flour on your nose." The pouting lips were quickly replaced with a smile. Rubbing her nose, Piper hurried off to wash her face.

Shale stood by the window and listened intently. The horses at the first stable nickered a friendly welcome. "Good," she whispered, "Samuell has arrived at the stable safely." They needed no attention drawn to them tonight.

A few minutes later the nickering was heard again. "Thank you, God. He has not dallied," Shale spoke softly to herself.

"What did you say, Shale?" Piper entered the kitchen in her long white nightgown. Her fine hair, freed of its headband, floated wildly about her face.

"I was just thanking God for his gifts of today," Shale said, scooping Piper up in a hug.

Samuell slipped in the door, a finely braided horsehair rope in his hand. Reaching up, he dropped the latch in place and spoke to his sisters, "Eli thinks the brown mare will foal tonight." Looking at Shale he added, "There are extra men watching them."

Stepping closer to his sisters, he tickled Piper, then hurried past them to the fireplace with Piper in hot pursuit. She reached out to tickle him as she ran. The nightly tickle fight began.

"God bless you, Samuell," Shale murmured gratefully.

When Momma had died, the tickling had stopped. Samuell had renewed the playful ritual for Piper while Papa was gone. Shale dropped her towel and rushed to join the fun. Finally, they collapsed on the floor. Piper's hair was a mass of tangles.

Samuell placed a small log on the fire. Picking up a brown basket, he sat on a stool near the hearth and began braiding a white horsehair rope.

Shale sat in a chair near him and called, "Come, Piper, let me brush your hair and Samuell will tell us a story."

Piper dashed back from their room with her hairbrush. Her delicate face was still flushed from their game. She crawled onto Shale's lap and clasped her small hands in front of her. Her doll rested in her lap.

Shale brushed and nimbly braided Piper's fine hair into one long braid. She smiled with relief when Samuell chose a funny story. Maybe Piper would not cry for their parents tonight. There was much to prepare after she was in bed.

Piper wiggled down from Shale's lap and galloped around the small room imitating the little horse in Samuell's story. Neighing and prancing, she tossed her newly braided hair about. Shale let her play longer than usual, hoping she would fall asleep quickly. Soon Piper settled on the hearth rug near Samuell and drew her little doll to her cheek.

"Come, little horse. You will sleep on warm, sweet grass tonight in a secret meadow with bright stars and a glowing moon above you," Shale said. She lifted Piper, already nearly asleep, and carried her to their bedroom.

"There, little filly, close your weary eyes and dream of shining stars." Shale tucked the light coverlet around her and kissed her forehead.

"Sing my song, Momma," Piper murmured. She curled onto her side with the soft doll snuggled against her. Already her eyes were closed. Her lashes formed twin lines of fringe across her cheeks.

Shale quietly sang, imagining her mother there, singing with them. When she finished, Piper was playing in the meadow of her dreams.

Shale dried her tears before she went to talk with Samuell. She worried about Piper calling her Momma, but it was only when she was exhausted or very excited. Piper must not lose her memories of Momma. She must not forget.

Samuell had gone to his small room off the kitchen.

"Goodnight, Samuell. Rest well, for tomorrow we must begin the next phase of their teaching. It will be a long day." She spoke in a normal voice, then whispered, "Tonight, Samuell. Henicles has sent a friend for us. He has horses. Stay in bed. We must not arouse suspicion. What can I bring to you?"

"My knife—I left it on the mantle," Samuell whispered, barely audible. "I did not get to say goodbye to the horses," he moaned.

"Nor did I. It may not be for long," she whispered back hopefully.

Shale retrieved Samuell's knife and leather bound book from the mantel and sat down in Papa's chair. She opened the book and bowed her head. She prayed for God's blessings and protection for all those she loved. She thanked God for sending Henicles to them and the elf who would help them. Surely God had sent him, too. Henicles would not trust them to just anyone. Yet a small doubt disturbed her thoughts, for she had overheard her father tell Eli to be cautious of any elves that came to the farm, as well as the strange men.

Closing her book, she rose and set the kettle near the fire for the morning. She blew out the candles and retired to her room.

Shale stretched out on her bed and listened intently. The watcher was staying later than usual this night. Why did he not leave? Sliding her hands beneath her pillow, she felt for her mother's ribbons. Her fingertips found the satiny smoothness, and she gathered them in her hands and entwined them through her fingers. They would be late meeting the elf who awaited them, but they could not leave now.

At last, she heard the sound of footsteps moving away from the cottage. She did not move until she heard the nickering of the horses in the nearest stable, telling her the watcher had passed by. He should not return, for she was sure the ale would be flowing freely tonight.

Shale rose and went quickly to the pantry. She removed four bags of dried fruit and the six small loaves of bread Piper had brought home. If only there were more. She packed these and filled three canteens with water.

Returning to her room, she pulled out a vest with many pockets and checked their contents: a slender knife, a small coil of lightweight rope, and a variety of herbs. Quickly she added her barrettes, another headband, more packages of herbs, and her mother's comb.

She knelt beside her bed and lifted the mattress. Her searching fingers found the small pouch and drew it out. She opened it reverently. Inside was her mother's wedding necklace. Furiously brushing tears from her eyes, Shale placed the ribbons in the pouch and tucked it securely into her vest.

She opened the lower drawer of the dresser and pulled out a smaller vest identical to hers. Carefully, she slipped Piper's blanket from her loose fist and added it to the vest with her barrettes and headbands. Lastly, she fastened the vest on the sleeping child and tucked her little doll securely inside. Carrying Piper, she entered the darkened kitchen lit only by the light of the stoked fire.

Samuell was up with his vest on, quietly packing his treasures: horsehair ropes, his knife, and something Shale did not see. Slipping his quiver and bow on over his vest, he picked up their food supplies and canteens. Nodding at Shale, he silently opened the back door of the cottage.

Avian waited impatiently near the willow tree, ever alert to the sounds and feel of the night. Sounds of revelry drifted down from the farmhouse. No other unusual sounds reached his sharp ears, but there was an ominous feel to the air about him. The horses moved restlessly in the shrubbery a stone's throw from the tree, and the children were late. The full moon would rise above the tree tops soon, illuminating the earth below it.

Disturbed by these things, he left the willow tree and approached the farm. Nearly 30 feet down the path he heard the soft rustle of leaves, followed almost immediately by the whirr of an arrow flying to its mark. His own bow was armed before the thud of the body hit the ground. Swiftly he moved toward the sound. Again he heard the soft rustle of leaves. This time the sound of a body being dragged and hidden in the woods.

A dozen paces further down the path, Avian watched the children emerge from the woods. The maiden hastened down the path carrying the younger child. The lad ran with his bow drawn. They froze, staring wide-eyed as Avian revealed himself with his bow aimed toward them. Silently, he motioned with his head for them to hide behind him.

After a moment of silence, Shale asked urgently, "Quickly, where are the horses?"

Avian silenced her with a glare and stood listening intently.

Despite the glare from the tall elf, Shale continued, "Please, my lord, we must not delay."

Avian stood his ground, focusing all his senses on the woods about them. He maintained his silence and demanded theirs.

"My lord," she began again, her intense eyes challenging his inaction. Killing the strange man was not to their advantage, but there had been no choice. They could not risk being discovered. They must flee now.

"There is no one else. Please, take us to the horses now!" Shale's whisper was sharp with impatience and growing fear. Her wide eyes pleaded with him to move.

Hearing no one else in the wood, Avian turned and led them swiftly to the clearing. Shale thrust the sleeping child into his arms.

Avian protested, "I cannot defend you with a child in my arms." He held his arms out for Shale to take back the sleeping child.

Shale ignored him and rushed to where Samuell was quickly loading their few belongings onto the horses. They were overjoyed to see some of their favorite and swiftest friends.

Piper stirred, reaching her small hand up to pull the collar of Avian's shirt to her cheek.

Shale mounted in one fluid move, then reached out for Piper. Avian impatiently lifted the child up to her. Shale held Piper securely and nodded to Samuell.

He spoke softly in Elvish to the horses and started down a narrow hunting trail to the east.

"We go north," Avian instructed.

Shale's fear rapidly turned to anger. She whirled around to face him. "East. My brother knows these woods better than anyone, save my father. Do not hinder us."

Furious, she turned and guided her mare through the opening where Samuell had disappeared silently into the woods. They had practiced this countless times with her parents. She would not risk the lives of her brother and sister, nor would he. He had done nothing to help them, except show them where the horses were and slow them down. She stopped fuming long enough to duck beneath a low branch.

Reluctantly, Avian followed. He could not protect them if he was not with them, and he could not risk the noise and time of arguing. What foolishness this would lead to he could only imagine. "Indeed, there is much you have not told me, Henicles," he muttered to himself.

As the lad led them unwaveringly on the twisting trails throughout the night, Avian pondered his charges. These did not seem to be the same children he had watched in the meadow earlier that day. He had been surprised by their stealth and ability to defend themselves. Their green elven cloaks covering their many pocketed vests, and the surety with which the lad now led them, told him they had been prepared for flight. The maiden's subdued manner had been replaced with a fierceness that reminded him of a she-bear protecting her cubs. Even the young child seemed to sense the urgency of their flight and did not fuss when she awakened during the long ride. Yet, he would set things straight as soon as they had put some distance between themselves and the farm.

Connor settled back against the tree and feigned exhaustion. He carefully noted where the horses were tied, where the sleeping men had laid their weapons, and the position of his one guard. The guard was not concerned about him escaping with his feet and hands bound.

Over confident and arrogant, Connor thought. He maneuvered the pear-sized chunk of rock behind his back to a position where he could rub the old rope binding his wrists. It was tedious work, but effective. He moved his wrists up and down while pushing against the sharp edge of the stone. *He must get home to his children. They must escape.* Again, he lifted his prayers to God.

The fraying rope loosened against his wrists with each thrust against the sturdy rock. He studied the guard. Yes, his head leaned down and to the side, his jaw slack. Connor freed his hands of the slack ropes encircling them. He leaned forward cautiously and withdrew his knife from his boot. Quickly he cut free his ankles and crept into the trees. The horses turned toward him but made no sound. He sprang upon the fastest one and led them rapidly through the forest.

He was three days of hard riding from his children. He must reach them and warn them to flee, as they had 'played escape' many times before. They would not be playing this time. He would never teach the Presage. After seeing his children were safe, he would go into hiding.

Chapter 2

Sollen, second son of King Corsac, ruler of Brainerd Wood, lifted the letters concealed in the bottom drawer of his desk. His pulse quickened as he carefully unfolded the dry, yellowed papers. He read again of the feelings of power and control his great-grandfather felt during the Presage. He relished the graphic description of the final moments when the opponent's life was snuffed out.

His great-grandfather had written it all: the sounds of the body being crushed by the raging horse spurred on by its rider, the smells of blood and deep wounds to the body, the feeling of his opponent's blood splattering his face, the sight of the red stain growing in the sand of the arena. It was depraved, but Sollen did not see this. He was intrigued, drawn in by the evil and his own lust for power.

Following his great-grandfather's notes, Sollen worked with the horses himself. For six years he had personally trained his horses, now numbering 24 with the addition of four foals this spring. His prize possession was the eight year old stallion. To think his father had wanted the animal put down because of its aggressive behavior! It was just what he had been looking for, and his father had reluctantly given the animal to him.

Soon his father would see. Soon they would all see the mastery of Sollen, horse master and warrior. He smiled thinking about it.

Slowly, he had aroused interest in the sport. Elves and men had begun purchasing horses for him to train. Thus, Sollen had discovered the location of a horse master whose horses' early training was perfect to lead them on into the Presage. Beautiful animals, they were much like the ones his father raised. Sollen hated to admit it, but their training was far beyond his ability. These horses, however, had been taught to protect and be devoted to their riders. Could this be undone? Sollen did not know. He did not care. Let his competitors try. He and he alone had the training manual and diary. No one remained who had actually seen the Presage. What, if anything, this horse master knew would be determined when he was delivered by the men Sollen had hired. His arrogant smile twisted to disgust. *How had the horse master escaped them? Idiots! But they would find him. He would go back for his children and they would capture him again. If they did not, Knox would pay with his own blood.*

Sollen folded the letters carefully and secured them in his desk. He stepped to the doorway and observed his younger brothers and the stable hands working with the horses. He tightened his boots and strode from the building to the arena where the stallion waited for him.

Near dawn, Avian and the children of Connor approached an area where the woods thinned and large rocks protruded above the ground. Silently, they waited at the edge of the wood. Many minutes passed. Finally, Samuell led down into the outcropping of rock, following the forest's edge. Near the second boulder he turned between two overgrown bushes and disappeared from sight. Avian passed between the bushes and ducked his head. They were entering a small cave.

Inside, Samuell dismounted and Piper slid off Shale's mare into his arms. Setting her down, Samuell patted her head and gave her an encouraging smile. "You have done well. Help your sister now," he encouraged her. He brushed past Avian and left the cave.

Dismounting, Shale shook her arms. She did not understand why they ached so. Many times before she had carried Piper through the night without this discomfort. She reached up to remove a pack from the mare and winced. She rubbed her arm then tried again. Lifting the pack from the horse brought a sharp twinge and she set it down beside Piper.

"Please set out our breakfast while I care for the horses," Shale said. She smiled encouragingly at the small child. Piper glowed up at her in return and tugged at the leather string securing the pack.

Shale took the horses and approached Avian. "I will care for your horse, my lord," she said calmly.

"I will care for my own." He patted the mare's sleek neck. There was no defiance in the maiden's eyes, nor was there apology or trust.

"It is not necessary, my lord. I am quite able to care for them." Shale stood before him, blocking his entrance into the deeper part of the cave.

Perhaps cooperation would help. They were all on edge, he thought. "Indeed you are, but many hands make light work, and we are all hungry and in need of rest." He smiled kindly and began walking toward the back of the cave. "This is an excellent sanctuary," he observed.

"It isn't very big, but big enough for us. We would come here every summer and..." Catching herself, Shale paused, looking down at the clay floor of the cave.

I should not have said that. I must not reveal too much. Can he be trusted? she wondered. She sensed no deceit in him, and he no longer seemed angry. He was very calm and handsome, but appearance did not reveal the heart. Quickly, she prayed for wisdom and protection.

Shale turned and faced him again, the calm in her voice leaving abruptly. "You would do well to listen to us. We will soon be trusting you with our lives. Trust us now." She reached for the reins of his horse, then pulled her arm back and rubbed the muscle just below her shoulder. Determined to take his horse, she tried again.

Avian moved his reins from her reach, puzzled by her reaction. He studied her defiant face and saw also weariness and fear. Calmly, he moved on into the recesses of the cave.

Sighing, Shale followed him. She felt so very tired.

In a silent truce, they took the packs and tack off the horses and let them drink at a small pool with a flowing current. Shale led them back toward the front and gave them hay stored on a ledge carved into the rock.

Samuell had a small fire going. Its flames flickered and reflected off the crystal walls of the cave. Piper sat quietly, watching them approach. She stared shyly at Avian and clutched her doll to her cheek.

Their breakfast of bread, cheese, and apples was set out neatly on a cloth. Quietly they began to eat—all but Avian, who stood watching them.

A small mouse scampered toward Piper. She held out a piece of cheese for it.

"He is not really hungry," she informed them. "He just wants to say hello. He says there have been men about by the river. Maybe Papa is with them," she said hopefully.

Quickly, Shale spoke to Avian, "Eat, my lord. They are not missing us yet. We are ahead of them and well hidden."

"You have proven very resourceful," he replied evenly. "I will check to be sure we have left no tracks and that no men are about as the little mouse says." He gave the small child a quiet smile.

"I have already done so," Samuell said tensely.

"Even so, I will have a look around," Avian replied.

Shale's eyes met Samuell's, hoping to ease his indignation. He turned away from her.

"Piper, finish your food and let the little mouse go to his bed. You may not mind sleeping by him, but I do," Shale said crossly.

Piper's eyes widened and began to tear.

Why did I say that? Shale chided herself. "We would not want to squish him," she added in a lighter tone.

Piper wiped at her eyes. "Oh, no. Hurry home, little mouse. Thank you for telling me," she added in a whisper. She bid the small creature farewell and it scampered back towards the hay.

Shale called Piper to her. "Come and sit with me."

"What did it tell you, Piper?" Samuell asked. He stood facing the entrance to the cave. His hand rested on the hilt of his knife.

"He said we are safe here, he likes our hay, and that he is not bad." Piper pointed at Avian's uneaten food.

Samuell paced a few steps toward the entrance of the cave. He turned to Shale, who sat quietly rocking Piper. The child's eyes were already closed. "What do you know of this elf?" he asked.

"I know only what Henicles told me. He said he is his trusted friend. From Cambria Forest, I believe," she replied. "He does not know you, Samuell. Do not take offense at his caution. You have led us well. Papa will be pleased."

"Does he know Papa?" Samuell straightened and glanced at the entrance of the cave.

"I think not. I do not even think he knows we are of his race. Perhaps it is best not to tell him?" She looked questioningly to Samuell.

Samuell shrugged his shoulders and walked to a rock near the horses, where he could see the entrance of the cave more clearly.

Avian returned as Shale was covering Piper with a soft woven blanket. He gave no indication of having heard their conversation, but his eyes were full of thought.

"I will take first watch," Samuell informed them and went to the entrance of the cave.

Shale rubbed her aching arms. It was odd to feel this way. She could not remember ever feeling this way before. She had no further energy to ponder this or their guardian. God would care for them. She stretched out beside Piper and fell asleep quickly.

When they all awoke, they ate again. Samuell and Avian went to feed and water the horses.

"You covered our tracks well," Avian commended him. "Your woodcraft skills are great, especially for one so young."

Samuell considered the tall elf beside him and glanced protectively at his sisters. "Our father taught us many things, and we have learned them well. I will lead again tonight." He cast a defiant glance at Avian and strode back to his sisters.

Confident, prepared, afraid, and very quiet, Avian thought to himself. They were all very quiet. They tired easily, unlike other elves. Something was wrong and it gnawed at his mind, yet he could not name it.

They waited for twilight to start off again. To pass the time, they played quiet games with Piper, often drawing them in the dirt and clay floor of the cave.

Avian remembered a few of them and joined in. Piper stared at him timidly, her doll secure in her hand. In unguarded moments he received a glimpse of a smile from her.

"You will not beat me again, will you, little bird?" Samuell pouted his lips and stared at Piper with sad eyes.

She giggled and made her mark on the game.

"You have taken the best position," Samuell exclaimed, "but I will not lose this time!"

Shale's eyes sparkled while she watched Samuell play with Piper. After many games, he had only been victorious once.

At dusk they left the cave. The woods grew thick again and pine needles silenced the sound of the horses' hooves. Around another twist in the trail, Samuell suddenly disappeared. Ducking thick branches, the others followed.

After riding a fair distance down the new trail, Samuell dismounted and went back to cover any evidence they may have left. Avian accompanied him.

"Look for broken or bent branches," Samuell said. He scattered pine needles over a hoof print. "The pine needles make a natural cover and provide silence."

Avian glanced up sharply. He did not need instruction in covering his trail. At least the lad had spoken to him. He nodded in reply.

They rode on until they came to a swiftly flowing river. Samuell led them to a spot where a rockslide had occurred.

Shale explained the plan to Avian. "Samuell will release the rock pile into the river, briefly slowing the current. We must cross quickly. I do mean quickly, for the rocks cannot hold back the water for long."

She moved her mare to an area sloping into the water. "See the two birch trees? Aim for them," she instructed.

Gripping Piper tightly, she waited for her brother to release the rocks. As the first rocks avalanched into the water, Samuell raced his mare to a nearby tree and jumped from her back into its thick branches. A second later he swung to the ground.

Shale urged her mare back from the water and whirled around. Avian sat straighter in his saddle. He caught a glimpse of the child's wide green eyes as they flew past him toward the tree. Samuell whistled for his mare and mounted her at a dead run. Shale sped toward him. They slowed briefly as they passed, handing Piper from mare to mare. Samuell raced with her for the crossing.

Shale crouched upon the rump of her mare and raced to the great tree. Standing now, she jumped up into the tree as the mare gave a small buck that tossed her higher. She grasped a slender branch wound with rope and let her weight pull it down.

Above her the great tree shook. A long branch reaching over the river shot upward, releasing more rocks into the river's flow.

Shale's mare spun around and waited under the tree. Shale dropped down upon her and they bolted for the river.

Samuell and Piper were already midstream in the knee deep water. Avian looked back to see Shale flying toward him.

"Go! GO!" her mind shouted to his.

Seeing she was right behind him, Avian guided his horse into the frothing water. It now reached the belly of his mare. He could hear Shale's horse enter the river behind him and urged his mount on.

Samuell and Piper were already out of sight, hidden in the dense forest. The river was rising rapidly. It now touched the saddle blanket on his horse.

Behind him Avian heard a splash. He turned in his saddle and saw Shale in the river. She was swimming to reach a pouch floating rapidly away from her. She lunged again and snatched it from the strong current.

The mare had waited for its rider. Now frightened by the water swirling around its neck, it raised its head and fought to reach the shore. The weary mare heaved itself up the bank, turned and searched the rushing water for Shale.

A sharp bird call ripped the air. The mare tossed her head and passed by Avian into the security of the woods. The call came again and Avian melted into the forest.

Samuell was standing within ten feet of him. Piper sat within reach of her brother, the ever-present doll clutched tightly to her cheek. She looked up at Avian bravely.

He winked at her and cautiously shifted to his right. His piercing eyes found Shale struggling in the still rising water. "Father, save her," he prayed. *I should have gone back for her*, he silently berated himself.

The tumultuous river alternately thrust Shale forward and pulled her under. She desperately grasped at a large branch wedged in a cluster of boulders. The waters swirled her around and crashed her against the rocks. She surfaced, gasping for air. Her white knuckles gripped the branch, and she pulled herself hand over hand between two boulders and clung there.

Out of the woods on the far side of the roaring river came three riders. They scanned the area carefully. Two dismounted and searched the ground near the woodlands edge.

One of the searchers addressed the man on horseback, "I hear nothing. I see nothing. I smell nothing. It was those rocks that you heard splashing into the river. He did not come this way."

The other man on the ground replied, "Connor used to hunt here. It was a hunch. That's all."

The man on horseback growled, "He is very clever and a skilled woodsman. Keep looking!"

Ten minutes passed and the searchers reached the riverbank. Samuell sighed in relief. Their tracks were washed out by the river. "Please, Father God, don't let them look under the tree," he silently asked.

Ten more minutes crawled by. The trackers approached the man on horseback again. "We have found nothing. There is nothing. It was only a rock slide you heard."

"Rock slides do not whistle," the rider reminded them. "Look again."

The two men turned back to the river and searched from there up the hillside. "There are tracks of several horses coming down the hill. They must be some of ours for they are well shod," one of the trackers called.

The rider angrily jerked his steed around and galloped back into the woods. The others mounted, muttering under their breath, and followed him.

Avian watched Shale until the men were out of sight and the quiet of the woods was filled with night sounds again. She had managed to lift herself partially out of the water and was leaning on the branch. Her body shook in the cold water. Avian frowned. She should not be so affected by cold. Quickly, he made a decision.

Turning to Samuell he said, "Find a safe place for a fire. Your sister will need its warmth."

Samuell hesitated, his gray eyes puzzled.

"Make haste." Avian took a coil of thin rope from his pack and threw it across the river to Shale. She slipped it over her head and under her arms, then pushed herself free of the boulders.

Samuell took Piper and the two horses. They hastened silently into the darkness of the forest.

Avian begin pulling Shale through the wild water. She kicked her legs to help. Once she was upon the shore, he hurried her into the forest and lifted her onto his horse. Shale did not protest. She buried her fingers under the horse's warm mane and clung there.

Samuell waited along the trail and guided them through dense brush to a small clearing. Piper was carefully piling sticks near a small fire with one hand, while she held tightly to her doll with the other. Three small rabbits sat a short distance from her in the shadow of the trees.

Avian pulled Shale off the horse and carried her near the fire. He set her down and began pulling off her boots and socks. "Lad, help me get her clothes off. She must be warmed."

"I'm all r-right," Shale chattered. She grabbed her boot from him.

"You must be warmed," Avian was adamant. He had seen the effect cold could have on humans. Was she only half elven?

He grasped her ankle firmly and tugged off her other boot, then reached for her sock.

Shale drew her knees to her chest, removed her sock and threw it at him.

Samuell stared at the two glaring at each other. He did not understand what was happening to his sister, but he had come to respect Avian's knowledge.

"Wait," he called. He stepped to his horse and removed a blanket from his pack. He held it up in front of Shale and turned to Piper. "Help her get out of her wet clothes. Hurry!"

Avian stalked to the horses and stared into the forest. "Something is drastically wrong, Father God. What is it that unnerves me so—that escapes my thoughts and taunts me?" He reviewed all he knew of his companions. They were well prepared and had excellent wood skills.

They knew exactly what to do and where to go. They were courageous, but not strong. They tired easily and slept much, unlike other elves. Now this.

Their parents. That was it. He feared their grief. He did not know how great its effect could be, but he did know that elves could succumb to grief and die.* This was what had eluded him and left him feeling so uneasy.

Turning to Samuell he repeated urgently, "She must get the wet things away from her to be warmed."

"Do you almost have them?" Samuell asked quietly.

"Al-almost," Shale chattered in reply.

Piper was trying so hard to help her. She had even laid down her doll. Shale managed a grin for her. "Th-thank you. I will need another b-blanket, please."

Piper ran out from behind the blanket. Avian held out his blanket to her. She snatched it from his hand, giving him a peculiar smile.

He glanced at Samuell.

Samuell turned his head, trying to hide his own smile.

Shale emerged wrapped in his blanket and sat down near the fire, still shaking.

Samuell stirred a mixture of herbs and tea leaves into the water heating over the small fire. The smell of mint and another herb Avian did not recognize rose fragrantly from the kettle. When it had brewed, Samuell handed Shale a steaming mug full.

---

*"The Complete Guide To Middle Earth" by Robert Foster, page 148.

Just holding the warm mug in her hands made her feel better. She closed her eyes and breathed in the soothing fragrance of the herbs. It reminded her of her mother.

Piper sat close beside her, holding her little doll securely. From time to time, she would glance at Avian and the peculiar smile would play about her lips.

Avian watched them from across the fire and wondered again who these children were. He knew now that if the maiden were not weakened by grief, she would not be reacting to the cold this way. For so long now the elves had lived in peace. No grief had come to them. He wished for more of his mother's knowledge of healing. He would need to observe them all more carefully.

"Lad, give the child some of the tea you have made and drink some yourself," Avian said.

"I am fine." Samuell stopped warming his hands over the fire where he crouched and stood to pour Piper some of the tea.

"We have time now. We will need to ride far and fast when we leave here. Please drink," Avian urged him quietly.

Samuell filled two mugs and handed one to Piper. "More?" he offered Shale.

"Yes, please. It is very good, like Momma's. I am feeling better already." Her shaking had stopped. She took another sip of the warming brew. "Isn't it good?" She smiled at Piper.

Piper dutifully sipped more tea with a horrid grimace.

Samuell smiled at her saying, "Drink up, little bird, so you can fly." He crinkled his nose at her.

"Way up high in the sky," she answered him, crinkling her nose, too.

"Do you want more, little bird?" Samuell coaxed her.

"No. He needs some," she announced, pointing at Avian. "Mine is almost gone."

"Not quite," Shale said, leaning over and peering into Piper's mug. "Keep going."

"Would you like some?" Samuell turned to Avian. "Forgive me for not offering it sooner."

Piper's green eyes grew bright with interest, and Avian began to wonder what this brew tasted like. If it would help the child to finish hers, he would try it.

"If the rest of you have had enough, I will have some." He looked at each of them to see if they needed more.

No one said a word as Samuell filled a mug for Avian. Shale did not look at him. Samuell handed him the warm mug. Piper leaned forward, eager for his reaction.

"It smells very good," Avian commented. He breathed in the intense fragrance of mint and something he should remember.

He took a large sip. His eyes widened, but he looked directly at the small child and said, "Oh, yes, very good."

Piper's anticipation turned to disappointment. Her brow creased and she frowned. "Doesn't it taste like...?"

"Piper!" Shale cut in quickly then cringed. She had not meant to say her sister's name.

Piper put her hand over her mouth to stop her words. Her eyes were large and round.

"I will race you, little one. I have just a little left," Samuell challenged her. His dancing eyes peered over his mug. He raised it to his lips and she quickly did the same.

After many such drinks, it became obvious to Avian that Samuell was not really drinking his so that Piper would win the contest. Even so, he drank with great enthusiasm, gulping loudly.

"I am almost done. Oh, it is going down fast. I am going to win." He lifted his mug to his lips again.

Shale watched quietly. She said nothing when Avian stepped away from the fire and poured most of his out. The anise flavor was very strong if you were not used to it.

Finally, Piper jumped to her feet. "I am done, Samuell! I beat you!"

"No, you did not. Let me see." Piper tipped her mug upside down.

He shook his head in disbelief. "Beat me again. How do you do that? Now I must finish alone." He pouted his lips in a woeful expression and swallowed all that was left in his mug. Breathing a long sigh, he turned it upside down.

Piper turned to Avian, who pretended to swallow the rest of his and turned his mug upside down also.

Shale did the same, then asked for her pack. "We need to go. Those men were not looking for us, but..."

She stopped, seeing Piper's eyes grow large. "We need to ride under this beautiful moon, don't we, my sister? We love the moon."

Samuell brought her pack and again held up a blanket for her.

"I will bring the horses," Avian said. Turning to Piper he added, "Little one, would you ride with me awhile under this beautiful moon? We will count all the stars through the treetops."

Piper looked at Samuell.

He nodded and gave her an encouraging smile. Shale needed to rest and he had to watch the trail carefully. He nodded his thanks to Avian.

"Come child, we will ready the horses. Which one shall we pick first?" Avian consulted her. It had been many moons since he had spent time with children. He was being charmed by this little one with her shy smile and expressive eyes.

"I pick Misty, for she likes me best. Your horse is fastest and thinks you ride very well. I like her, too. She is brave and protected Papa when the bad man came. He wanted Papa's book, but Papa would not give it to him."

Avian considered this information but did not pursue it.

Piper bubbled on about the horses, telling him their likes and dislikes, "Willow is my favorite. She is going to have a foal. She is never stubborn." Piper looked up at him with the peculiar smile nearly bursting from her.

"What is that smile for, my lady?" Avian asked her.

Glancing behind her, she whispered, "My sister said you were as stubborn as an old gray mule!" She covered her mouth with her hand and giggled. Her green eyes sparkled at him.

"Oh, did she?" Avian grinned. He swung the giggling child up onto his horse. Throughout the ride that night, quiet whispers and occasional muffled giggles could be heard from the two star counters as they followed Samuell through the thick forest.

They rode on until noon the next day before stopping for a brief rest. They were making good time and Shale seemed to be holding up well enough to continue. While Piper and Samuell stretched their legs running and playing quietly, Avian laid out the food rations.

Shale sat with her eyes closed, resting her back against a tree. Piper ran to give her the yellow and blue flowers she had picked.

Samuell approached Avian. "What is wrong with my sister?"

"She is fine now." Avian reached for an apple.

"She was not fine last night," Samuell persisted.

Avian turned to face Samuell and met his eyes. "You have all been through much. Grief affects everyone differently. It is especially difficult for elves."

Samuell drew in his breath sharply. "How did you know?"

"That you were of my race? Henicles told me when we met you in the meadow. What is wrong?" Avian asked.

"Father told us never to tell. He made us cover our ears. He made my sister cut her hair." Looking into Avian's eyes, he asked, "Will she be all right?"

Gripping Samuell's shoulder Avian answered, "Your bond is strong. It gives you strength. Your sister will be fine."

Samuell looked back at his sisters. They were smiling, sharing the flowers and making them into small bouquets. Five rabbits sat near them.

Turning back to Avian, he said, "If I had been riding my own mare it would have known what to do, as my sister's mare did. I would have been the last to cross the river. My sister would not have been swept off her horse into the water." His sorrowful eyes fought back tears.

"She did not fall, Samuell. She swam into the water to retrieve a pouch that was washing down the river. It is not your fault. You kept your younger sister safe. That was most important," Avian stated firmly.

Samuell's hand quickly brushed his cheek. "I have no knowledge of the land before us."

"You have led us well. I will need your skills on our journey. You must be ever alert for anything unusual or any feelings that bring you concern." Avian handed Samuell his food with a look of respect.

"Be assured of it," Samuell answered. He hesitated a moment. "I am Samuell."

"I am honored to know your name, Samuell." Avian nodded to him. "I am Avian."

"My sisters are Shale and Piper. Thank you for helping us." His words did not reveal the effect of Avian's words upon him, but his countenance shone and he stood taller and prouder.

Samuell walked to his sisters. "Nothing we have is more important than you are."

Shale looked up at him, startled by his statement. He did not explain but stood a little apart from them, watching protectively and eating his apple.

At nightfall, Avian carefully hid them and left to scout the area. Piper ate and soon fell asleep. Samuell and Shale joined her.

Avian studied them when he returned. Piper was curled up against Shale, cradled there by her sister's arm. They looked so peaceful now.

Samuell lay near them, but the peace they displayed did not reach his young face. The need to protect his family lay heavily upon him.

Before the dawn, Avian woke Shale and Samuell. When they were nearly ready to travel, Shale awakened Piper and gave her fruit and bread to eat.

"I want to ride with him," Piper announced. "He is funny."

"Not today, Piper. He will lead today. Ride with me and we will make up silly songs to sing tonight," Samuell coaxed.

Piper frowned but went to her brother.

Funny? He is demanding and arrogant, Shale told herself. Curbing her angry embarrassment, she reconsidered her sister's comment. The warrior had shown genuine concern for their welfare. He could have hurried them on and not offered to help with Piper. He treated Samuell with respect and actively involved him in planning their flight. He had only been concerned with her welfare last night. Sighing, she turned her attention to following him through the remainder of the thick forest then onto a long plain, where they traveled near the forest edge as far as they could.

All that day, they rode fast and far. Avian was very alert and ever watchful of their surroundings. Shale noticed Samuell often consulting with him as they rode. It troubled her, but she said nothing.

By evening, Piper was tired and fussy. While Samuell and Avian tended the horses, Shale busied Piper with preparing the simple meal. Piper whispered to her sister, then watched excitedly as Shale sliced apples into pieces for her. Carefully, Piper sprinkled each slice with a little cinnamon, then seated herself beside Avian.

Shale hoped he would not mind the child's attention. It was very hard for Piper to be quiet and still for so long. If it pleased her to sit near their guardian, then all the better.

"Thank you for the apples. They are delicious," Avian said and popped a slice into his mouth.

"I made them for you," Piper explained.

Piper spent most of her mealtime staring at Avian and making silly faces at him. His response was a gentle smile with a bit of mischief mixed in. Soon he was telling her she looked like a lovesick gopher, or a tree frog, or a baby bird about to hop from its nest.

He quieted her when she began to giggle. "Shh, little one, we must be quiet baby birds." After cleaning up and playing quiet games with her brother, Piper began to give in to sleep. She sat in Shale's lap and asked Shale to sing for her.

Shale looked to Avian who nodded his consent. Quietly, she sang several songs to Piper. She rocked the sleepy child back and forth. Piper relaxed in her arms. Nearly asleep, she asked for Momma's song.

Samuell lay down and turned his face away from them.

Slowly, softly, Shale began to sing. Near the middle, choked with tears, she could not go on. Piper stirred in her arms.

Beside them Avian's quiet voice continued the song and Piper quieted again. Avian took her from Shale and laid her down.

Gently touching Shale's shoulder, he pointed to where Piper lay, indicating she should rest, too. Shale blinked back her tears and gave him a small smile of thanks.

While he stood watch, Avian again gave thought to his companions. If only Henicles had told him more. There were so many contradictions. They didn't dress or act elvish, except when unaware, as when Samuell had spoken to the horses, and now with Shale singing to Piper. Samuell obviously had great skill of woodcraft, but tried hard not to reveal it. Great grief engulfed them all. He saw it in their solemn eyes. Their mother was dead, their father missing. What had happened to them? Why had they not lived among their own people? What had Piper meant about a bad man arguing with her father about a book? Who were they? The night wore on and no answers came to him. He prayed, "Father God, thank you for our safe journey. Thank you that they trust me now. Please guide us and keep us safe. Give me wisdom to help them."

In the morning they set out again, and the day passed much as before. Avian continued to observe them. Their riding abilities were great. They were as one with the horses—even little Piper, before weariness took hold of her. Shale's patience with the child impressed him. He remembered the love in her eyes when she held Piper and sang softly to her.

In the afternoon, they stopped in a copse of maple and oak trees and ate their apples and bread.

Piper shyly went to Avian and felt his ears and face. "You have ears like me!" she cried whipping off her headband.

"Piper! Put it back on!" Shale blurted out in alarm.

"Do we really have to?" Samuell asked, mounting his horse.

"Yes, we do. Someone might see." She looked searchingly at Avian as she slipped Piper's headband down over her ears.

"It is best for now," Avian answered thoughtfully. He lifted Piper to his saddle and lithely sprang up behind her. Shale did not complain, but he knew her arms grew weary holding Piper as they rode.

Smiling at the frowning child, he said, "Let us go, my fair Lady Piper." He turned his horse and cantered off. Piper spread her little arms out wide like a soaring bird.

Shale sighed as she mounted. Piper did that when she rode with Papa. *Where is he? Maybe Henicles has found him and they are on their way to us now*, she hoped.

On the next night, Avian asked Samuell's opinion regarding their camp for the evening. Samuell was quick to give his advice, and they settled in a thick grove of white birch.

There would be no fire again tonight, for Avian and Samuell were on edge. Several times that day, they had left the maidens to scout the area surrounding them.

Shale was uneasy, too. She quizzed Piper on her animal lore, hoping she would not notice their apprehension. They sat on a large rock quietly sharing an apple.

"There are no rabbits tonight," Piper commented. Her green eyes were round and she scooted nearer to Shale. Shale put her arm around Piper and squeezed her shoulder. "Perhaps they will reveal themselves when Avian returns. We are not settled in yet," Shale responded.

Avian had already left them to circle the camp. Samuell was with the horses, for they were restless.

Tonight Avian was not assured. He ducked a branch and moved beyond the boundary he usually set for camp. Unease had been growing within him all day. Deep inside, he could feel the danger. It was near. It was deadly. He must find it before it found them.

His ears heard nothing. No birds, no animals. He turned his head and caught a faint scent of smoke. Someone had been smoking a pipe nearby. Was that where the danger lay? He stood motionless, intently concentrating on bits of information brought to him through his keen senses and awareness.

To his right he heard a bird call. It was Samuell's signal of warning, yet he hesitated.

There was more than that and it was near, very near. He could feel it approaching. At the sound of Samuell's birdcall it had paused and now moved stealthily toward the sound. Avian held his position. He blended perfectly into his surroundings.

Men. Four surly men moved past him with great stealth. Stopping to listen often, they moved steadily toward the camp. Slipping in behind them, Avian followed them and cut to the right. He would ambush them at the hollow ahead.

At Samuell's signal, Piper fled into the woods clutching her little doll tightly. Shale slipped into the woods near her and drew her knife from the sheath fastened to her lower leg. The forest remained silent.

"Save us please, God," the sisters prayed silently. They waited in silence. Shale made eye contact with Piper and motioned for her to stay down.

The first of the four men entered the open area of the hollow, searching the area visually before the others followed.

To Avian's surprise he spoke, "It is clear. You are sure these are the children he wants?"

"It is probably nothing ahead but wild dogs to tear our throats out," the third man growled apprehensively.

"They were dressed like Knox said. Move on," the second man angrily answered.

"Who else was with them?" The first man spoke again.

"It does not matter, and if you don't shut up it won't be wild dogs tearing out your throat," the second man threatened them.

The fourth man emerged from the forest, silencing them with a deadly stare.

Avian's brow creased sharply at the sight of this man. He recognized him, and the third man as well. While traveling with Cameron a year ago, they had found a man cruelly beaten to death and had seen these men fleeing on horseback.

They would never touch his charges. Avian's arrows flew swift and true. The men dropped where they stood in rapid succession, never nearing the safety of the forest or firing an arrow of their own.

Again the birdcall came. Samuell! Avian raced toward the camp. Nearing the place where he had left them, he paused and whistled the nightingale's call. He thought he heard a cricket call but was not sure; it was so faint. A tiny hand reached out and touched his leg.

Avian pounced and Piper's wide frightened eyes met his. Bowing his head to hers, he lowered his knife, thankful he had heard her tiny cricket call. With a finger to his lips he left her, warning her to stay hidden with his eyes. He scanned the area, meticulously searching for Shale's location. She would be near her sister.

In the stillness, a cricket chirped to his left. A slight movement caught his eye. Shale had seen his encounter with Piper. Subtly, she revealed her position to him.

Shale raised five fingers to Avian. There were five hunting them. She wished for her bow and arrows, but the horses had slipped deeper into the forest at Samuell's signals.

Again, from a different direction, Samuell's call came. He was attempting to lead them away from his sisters. The whirring sound of an arrow filled the air, followed immediately by a sharp thud. Whoever shot had hit a tree. Another arrow flew, and then another, and the sounds of them meeting their marks immediately followed. A voice cried out, then another. Neither voice was Samuell's.

Avian glanced back to where Shale was hidden. She was not there. His heart pounded within him. Piper remained in place. Again he signaled her to stay. She pointed to the left and sank low to the ground.

Avian saw Shale at the edge of the trees with her bow. Suddenly, she dropped to the ground and let loose her arrow. The thud of her arrow striking its mark was heard and Shale disappeared into the forest.

Silence engulfed them. Avian could neither see nor hear an enemy, but his senses told him someone was behind him and to his right. Silently he moved in a circling pattern, cutting off the escape of the two remaining enemies. Listening carefully, he focused on his surroundings. They were moving toward Piper.

Avian feared she would come out of hiding too soon and moved to protect her. He was not alone. The man nearest Piper dropped with two arrows and a knife in his heart. The other hit the ground immediately after. His own arrow ricocheted off a tree and narrowly missed Shale.

Shale and Samuell stood staring. Avian had drawn and released his second arrow so swiftly they could hardly believe their eyes.

Silently, Avian held up his hand with five fingers stretched out. Samuell nodded. All were dead.

"Call Piper out now," Avian ordered. "We must flee."

Shale tried to whistle the signal but her mouth was too dry. She looked to Samuell who managed to make the notes. Piper crept out of her hiding place. She flew into her sister's arms and they clung tightly to each other.

"Samuell, get the horses. Now," Avian commanded. He must keep them moving.

"Shale. Shale!" he demanded. "Gather your things. Make haste! We are leaving now!"

She slowly turned to him, still clutching Piper tightly in her arms. She blinked her eyes and stepped toward the rock.

Seeing her move to obey, he retrieved her knife and all the arrows he could find. He glanced over at the two sisters. Piper clung tightly to Shale as she stuffed the apples into the brown pouch.

Samuell brought the horses. He pried Piper loose from Shale and pressed her doll against her cheek. "We are safe, little one. God is with us." He kissed the top of her head and lifted her up to Shale.

Avian led them swiftly from the gruesome scene. He prayed they would not be overwhelmed by what had happened. Swiftly they rode throughout the night.

At one point Piper asked for Momma's song. Shale glanced at Avian.

He shook his head from side to side.

Shale began to hum softly in Piper's ear. The small child whimpered and clung to her sister. Gradually, she relaxed and the rocking motion of the horse soon lulled her to sleep. When Shale was sure that Piper slept, she unwound her wide cloth belt. She rewrapped it, securing Piper to herself lest she also drift off during the long night ride.

In the moments before dawn lit the sky, they paused long enough to give each a piece of bread. Piper awoke only long enough to munch a piece of bread and drink a few sips of water from their store.

"Can you carry her still?" Avian whispered. "I would have Samuell free to arm himself."

Shale lifted her eyes to his and nodded, stroking her sister's soft hair. She managed a small smile but spoke no words. Words were not needed. He could see it in her eyes. She trusted him.

Nodding, he turned to Samuell. "Let us move on."

They continued as they had through the night, Avian leading and Samuell guarding the rear, with Shale and Piper tucked safely between them.

The small child remained withdrawn and clung to Shale. She grew restless and cried from time to time while they rode. Shale tried shifting her to sit facing her in the saddle. Piper would quiet and sleep, then awaken crying again.

Avian stopped briefly to let her walk. She clutched Shale so tightly they could hardly take a step. After a few minutes Avian had them mount again. He felt an urgency to hasten on.

Shale and Samuell did not protest, and even the horses seemed to sense the need to keep pressing ahead. Three days after the attack they stopped for a night's rest.

While Shale and Piper prepared to sleep, Samuell opened his pack. He removed his most prized possessions and said, "These were my grandfather's and his father's before him." He handed them to Avian for inspection.

Two slender, silver knives lay across Avian's palms. He admired them, noting their fine balance and the secure fit of the handles to the palm. The larger one had much Elvish engraved upon the handle. The symbols were familiar to him, but there was no time to read it, for the maidens returned. Samuell quickly slipped his knives into his pack. As he did so, Avian noted a small leatherbound book tucked deeply inside.

Samuell held his arm out to Piper and she came to him. He lifted her up in his arms and patted her back. Smiling, he whispered to her, "Tonight we must play the quiet game again, little bird. I notice that you are very good at it. I am proud of you."

She peered up at him with tired eyes.

"Come, Piper, let us sleep now," Shale spoke tenderly to the child. Together the sisters stretched out on their blanket.

"I will take first watch. Rest, Samuell, while there is time." Avian rose and left them. He prayed for their rest to refresh and strengthen them. He longed to see the light of life in their eyes again. He must get them to Lord Cale quickly. Some way God would help them, he knew.

During the night, Shale awoke to see Avian staring deeply into the woods. He was listening intently to the sound of elvish song that had awakened her from dreaming of her parents. She rose and stood near him.

"Stay here yet," he cautioned.

Silently, he slipped into the woods. Soon she heard sounds of greeting and laughter that stirred her heart. Samuell was awake now, amazed at the voices he was hearing.

"Yes, Samuell, they are elves. Avian has gone to speak with them. He bid us stay here yet."

Together they listened intently, a hunger for their kindred growing in their hearts. The voices grew quieter and spoke rapidly for a time. Gradually they resumed their melodic rhythm, and Samuell returned to sleep with a sweet expression on his young face. Shale lay down by Piper again and soon was sleeping amidst the feeling of security brought by voices so much like her parents.

Light was dawning ere Avian returned to them with a glow of rest and relief upon his countenance. "I see by your faces that you rested well. That is good. The elves are ones who live near Pennsyl," he explained. "They have no news of Henicles, but Lord Cale is expecting us. We will be meeting his people in a few days' time."

Piper awoke and lay securely in her blanket watching Avian and her siblings. Seeing them relaxed and talkative, she turned her attention to the squirrels playing at the base of the tree beside her. Making a chucking noise to them, she sat up and welcomed them to her lap. Soon she was following them and returned with her pockets full of walnuts for their breakfast.

"Here, Samuell. The squirrels have shared with us. Will you crack them, please?" Piper pleaded.

"Gladly, my sister. Thank you, squirrels." He bowed slightly to them.

Piper handed the nuts to Samuell and placed the nutmeats into a fold of her dress. She left them with Shale and walked to the pretty blue flowers growing beneath the edge of the trees. She picked a bright bouquet and raced back, presenting them to Avian.

He took the blue flowers and smiled. "You honor me, Piper," he whispered and glanced at Shale. She was distributing their rations for breakfast. Her gentle spirit was reflected in even this small task.

Shale continued setting out their fruit and cheese. She was lost in thoughts of her own. *The elves' singing must have given Piper a sense of peace and security.* She silently gave thanks for Piper's peace that morning. She handed Samuell his portion and placed the nuts he had cracked on a cloth in the center of the rough, fallen log they were using for a table.

Piper joined them, pulling Avian with her. "It is my turn to give thanks," she said. "Thank you for the squirrels and their nuts they shared with us, and that the singing people are good. Amen."

"How do you know they are good?" Samuell asked. He popped a walnut half into his mouth.

Piper spoke emphatically, "Samuell, Squirrel knows everything about everyone for five miles from here."

"I beg your pardon, Squirrel," Samuell said solemnly and bowed slightly to the closest squirrel.

"I have been thinking about your headbands," Avian began. "Perhaps we would look more like ordinary travelers if you did not wear them. Do you have different clothes to wear? Something more elvish?"

Sadly, Shale shook her head. They had only one change of clothing with them, and it was the same.

Samuell turned to Shale. "The headbands could go," he agreed. "I know I would not miss mine."

Shale shrugged her shoulders in response. Samuell reached up with both hands and tugged off his headband. He rubbed his head vigorously and grinned at Piper.

Piper giggled and whipped off her headband. Her fine hair flew in all directions. She grinned at them and, shaking her hair about, did a little dance.

Avian was relieved by her behavior and smiled widely at her antics. Her withdrawal after the attack had concerned him greatly. He was eager to reach Pennsyl, for surely Lord Cale would have knowledge of healing for their grief.

Catching up Piper, he swung her into the air. "We will ride at a slower pace this day, for our kinsmen are nearby. My Lady Piper, will you ride with me again this fine morning?" he requested.

Piper laughed merrily and patted his cheeks.

Avian glanced at Shale. She was smiling strangely at him, remembering the look on his face when she had handed him the sleeping child the night of their escape.

"What is that smile for?" he asked.

Shale only smiled back, leapt upon her mare and said, "Lead on, Avian the Merry." She still wore the band about her head, but had pushed it back from her ears. This and the twinkle in her eyes enhanced her delicate features.

Avian rode next to her and encouraged questions about Pennsyl and the elves living there.

He told them many things about elves that day, and of Lord Cale and Pennsyl.

"Why are we going to Pennsyl?" Samuell inquired.

"It is Henicles's counsel. He is to be trusted, as is Lord Cale. They are very wise," Avian informed them, watching closely for their response. Shale and Samuell kept their thoughts to themselves. They knew little of Cale.

Piper started singing silly songs and Samuell joined her. When they finished, Avian sang a silly one for them. Laughing, they all nearly fell off their horses.

They stopped by a small river, and Shale ran to it. Tossing off her boots and socks, she slipped her feet into the cool water and sighed loudly. Avian led the horses to her and stood near as they drank.

Samuell and Piper, still full of silliness, slammed against Avian, pushing him into Shale and sending all of them plunging into the winding stream. Avian sprang up laughing. He splashed water at Samuell and Piper.

Piper shrieked and ran to Samuell.

Avian turned to Shale and took her arm. He lifted her up out of the water effortlessly.

Samuell and Piper charged into Avian again. He held tightly to them and pulled them into the water with him. Shale laughed and pulled her soaking clothes loose from her body.

Piper giggled and crowned Avian with a golden leaf as he sat in the middle of the stream. Samuell stood and bowed, "Hail, Lord Avian, King of Leaves."

Their fun was interrupted by an elvish voice, "Ah, King Avian of the golden leaves, I greet you and your fine company." There was laughter in his voice, but it did not reach the eyes of the warrior Avian had spoken with the night before.

Shale hurried Piper to the horses for dry clothes. She did not want her little sister frightened by their words. Grabbing dry clothing from their packs, she led Piper behind a thick myrtle bush.

"You are indeed pursued as you suspected, by six riders. Two turned back, two will trouble you no more, and two we have lost due to the valor and speed of their horses, which look much like your own. I have not seen such as these in a long time." The fair elf regarded the horses and Samuell. Nodding towards the bush, he asked, "Who is with you? You have fair companions."

"My mother's kin," Avian responded casually. "Thank you, my friend. We will hasten on."

The rest of the day they rode swiftly without speaking. At nightfall they stopped to quickly eat and rest the horses.

Avian approached Shale and Samuell. "I am sorry. I should not have let my guard down. We should not have tarried. Forgive me."

Shale spoke quickly, "My lord, you did not tarry or let down your guard alone."

She began walking beside him and added quietly, "It was good for the children." She tucked a strand of hair behind her ear.

"I am not a child," Samuell asserted from behind them.

Both turned to look at him, and Shale stood appraising her brother.

"Indeed, you are not. Forgive me, Samuell. I have noticed your wisdom and skill. It is just that...that you are... my little brother," she finished lamely. She handed him her reins and hurried after Piper.

Uncomfortable, Samuell looked at Avian and sighed, "Maidens." He shook his head and grinned.

"Indeed, they are a puzzle," Avian laughed.

They continued riding through the night, though at a slower pace. At midmorning they were met by several elves who greeted them warmly from Lord Cale.

Samuell rode near Avian, carefully noting how his answers eluded topics and questions that might affect their safety. He joined in the conversation only when asked a question.

Shale and Piper rode together quietly, observing the Elves and listening intently to their conversation. Piper fidgeted in the saddle. She turned to Shale and said, "Why do they...?"

"Listen and you will learn much," Shale instructed her. She did not want to draw more attention. Already the elves had been admiring their horses and casting inquisitive glances at their clothing.

Piper's eyes, alive with questions, darkened in disappointment. She slouched against Shale, pushing her back in the saddle.

Shale hugged her and whispered, "We will ask Avian later."

Piper smiled faintly.

"Listen," Shale urged. "They are talking about a feast tonight."

Piper sat straighter and leaned forward in anticipation. They listened eagerly and exchanged excited glances. Self-consciously, Shale brushed her fingers through her short hair. It was no longer than Avian's or Samuell's.

"Father God, thank you for our safe journey. Should I pretend to be a lad while I am here? The clothing the elves wear is not as baggy as that of the stable hands. Please guide me," she prayed.

Upon arriving at Pennsyl, they were taken to Lord Cale, who greeted them warmly. He dismissed the elves attending them and summoned his sons and daughters. "Come with me to my study," he directed.

The weary travelers looked longingly at the table laden with fresh fruit, nuts and tiny cakes. Cale said, "Why have you come to me?"

Avian explained, "Henicles bid me bring these children to you for protection, my lord. Henicles himself is seeking their father, who is missing."

When You Dance with Rabbits

Shale drew Piper closer to her and looked at Avian with alarm.

"My father is on a trip to buy horses," Samuell corrected. "He is late in returning, but he is not missing."

Two agile Elves and two graceful maidens entered the room. All had the same flowing red hair as their father.

"I see," Lord Cale replied. "You and your sister may go and find rest and refreshment." He signaled to one of the maidens, who stepped forward and smiled at Samuell and Piper.

"I desire to remain, my lord," Samuell replied. He did not understand. It was the duty of the eldest son to hold counsel in his father's absence.

"Please, Samuell, she will be afraid alone," Shale quickly urged. She was still unsure about revealing her identity.

Avian nodded in agreement. He would seek guidance from Lord Cale on how to handle this matter. The children were under his protection now.

Samuell hesitated. Piper looked at him with frightened eyes. He bowed to Lord Cale and departed with her. He would protect her and leave Shale in Avian's care for now.

They followed the tall maiden to a sunlit room. On the small stone table refreshments awaited them. The maiden seated herself and beckoned them to do the same.

Shyly, Piper sat near Samuell and tasted the fruit the maiden placed on their plates. Politely, she thanked her and said no more. She had not missed Samuell's look of warning.

Lord Cale directed the others, "Please sit and enjoy these gifts."

The tall elf with blue eyes seated his sister. Shale hesitated, waiting for someone to seat her. Avian bumped her arm as he pulled out his chair and she followed his example.

The son with green eyes left momentarily and returned with his mother. She smiled warmly at them.

Cale filled their goblets with a cool, sweet drink. It was refreshing, and Shale felt the fatigue melt away from her.

Lord Cale began the conversation. "Avian, tell me of your journey."

"We fled with great haste, my lord. The safety of my charges was threatened throughout our journey," Avian began. He paused and glanced about him.

"You may speak with all confidence," Cale assured him. "Please go on."

Avian explained the need for escape and described their journey to Pennsyl. Lord Cale asked Shale many questions about her family and the state of the farm.

Of Avian he asked word of the world about them. Shale was amazed by Avian's knowledge—and to discover that his father was King of Cambria Forest. She had heard of the great forest, but knew little of it or its inhabitants.

"Kendra, please take our guest to her chambers and see to her needs," smiling Cale nodded to Shale. "We will take counsel now. When it is time for the evening meal, you will join us.

Shale looked questioningly at Avian and pushed back her chair. He rose and took her hand as she stood. "Rest well, my lady," he said. His warm smile was reassuring.

"Thank you, my lord," she politely replied. Turning her attention to Lord Cale and his wife she said, "I thank you for opening your home to us."

Kendra smiled and led the way from the room down a long bright hallway decorated with colorful vases. Delicate weavings hung from the walls, adding dimension and interest.

Shale followed her silently. Lord Cale's questions probed deeply and unearthed fears and hurts she had suppressed. "Where are my brother and sister?" she asked tensely.

"Fear not. They have eaten and are resting in the chamber next to yours. You may see them if you wish," Kendra soothed.

"Yes, please," Shale replied quietly.

The hallway widened and opened into a secluded area. A beautiful garden filled with tall ferns and blooming plants greeted them. Kendra softly opened a slender wooden door to an airy chamber.

Piper reclined on a pale blue couch. Her eyes were closed and a peaceful expression rested on her young face. She loosely held her doll against her chest. Across the chamber, Samuell also rested. Shale nodded at Kendra's gentle touch on her arm. Softly, she closed the door.

Kendra led Shale to a slightly smaller chamber decorated in shades of violet. Fresh fruit, water, and clothing awaited her. "Welcome to Pennsyl. Everything in this room is for you. Please feel free to rest or walk in our gardens. I will be there if you have a question or wish to have a companion." Kendra smiled and left her.

Shale chose not to walk in the gardens or have companionship. She stayed in her chamber and pondered their situation. Henicles trusted their lives to Avian, who had proven true. He also was entrusting them to Lord Cale. He had treated her graciously, yet his probing questions troubled her. *Surely Lord Cale knew her father. Perhaps he did not speak directly of him for their protection. Were they not safe, even here?*

She paced to the dressing table and picked up the silver-handled brush. Absently, she brushed her cropped locks and continued pacing around the chamber. She paused before a picture of a lad and a maiden in a pleasant meadow. A gray horse grazed in the background and blue, yellow, and white flowers dotted the landscape.

She thought of the meadow at home where they trained the young horses. How many remained there after the sale? She carefully placed the silver brush on the small table by her couch and lay down. Her troubled thoughts became troubled dreams. Blessedly, these were interrupted by Kendra's soft knock on her door. "Shale, it is time to share our evening meal. May I enter?" she asked.

"Oh, you have not changed," Kendra said. "Please let me help you. This pale green gown will be lovely on you. There is no need to dress as a stable boy here."

Shale hesitated. Was it wise to let others know?

Sensing her concern, Kendra spoke, "If anyone were looking for you, they would not look for a lovely elvish maiden, would they? You will blend in well with the other maidens here. Samuell and Piper have already changed for the evening and are in the garden with my sister. They look no different than the other elvish children who live here. My father feels it is best to allow you to resume your normal appearance. He is responsible for your safety now."

Still unsure, Shale consented. It would feel good to wear a gown again.

Kendra's smile was real and engaging. Shale smiled back at her. Self-consciously, she brushed her fingers through her short hair.

"May I help you with your hair? If we pull it up on the sides here, it will look longer, and this silver band with the veil in back will conceal its length," Kendra offered. Her nimble fingers lifted Shale's hair to show her how it could look.

"It must have been very hard for you to cut it. There. Do you like that? You look so lovely, Shale. Let us join the others." Kendra led the way through the gardens where Samuell and Piper joined them.

Samuell looked so much taller and mature in his elvish attire. He took his place standing beside Avian, who was staring at Shale and Piper. His gaze was warm and appreciative.

Samuell nudged him. "It is only my sisters." He rolled his eyes and shook his head.

Shale felt her cheeks flush. Piper was twirling around in her new blue gown, making the skirt swirl around her ankles until she saw Lord Cale. Quickly she hid behind Shale and announced that everyone there had ears like hers.

Glancing to their left, Piper saw one of Cale's sons. His hair was braided like Papa's, and he was standing with his back to them, talking animatedly with his brother.

Piper flew toward him crying, "Papa! Papa!"

The brothers turned to her and smiled warmly. Piper's jubilant smile abruptly left her face. She burst into tears and ran blindly across the courtyard, dropping her doll.

Shale rushed toward her, but Avian was closer. He scooped her up safely into his arms. "Hush, little one. It is all right."

Samuell patted her back. "Hush, little bird. I am here. You look so lovely in your pretty blue gown," he soothed. "Do not ruffle your feathers."

Piper hid her sweet face against Avian's neck and peeked out at Samuell's encouragement. Shale reached them and found Piper's smile back on her lips. Her green eyes sparkled through her tears.

Lord Cale approached them with Piper's doll. He patted her head and gave it back to her with a gentle smile. His rich brown eyes glowed warmly when she gave him a shy smile of gratitude.

Avian spoke quietly to them, "My Lady Piper, may I have the honor of your company and your sister's at supper this evening?"

Piper whispered, "Yes." She clung tightly to his neck.

He turned to Samuell. "Will you assist me? Two such lovely maidens may be too much for me."

Samuell stepped to Shale and offered his arm. She was thankful her parents had taught them proper manners.

"Thank you kindly, my lord," she replied. She resisted the strong urge to take Piper.

Avian spoke in a low voice, "Lord Cale requests that we use your names as little as possible. Currently, you are to be known as my cousins on my mother's side."

"We know nothing of your family," Shale whispered, alarmed. "What will we say if someone questions us?"

"Stay with me. I will help you." He smiled at Piper and set her feet on the floor. "You are both so lovely I will have to defend you from all of your admirers as it is," he said merrily. He twirled Piper around and bowed to her.

"Now take my arm as well," Avian instructed Shale. He stepped closer to her and she took his arm.

"Now you are engaged with Samuell and me for the evening," Avian announced as if it solved all of their problems.

Shale and Samuell stared at him in bewilderment.

"No one else may seek your attention, though they may make your acquaintance, if they are bold enough," Avian explained.

Seeing she was still puzzled, he added, "No one will ask you to dance without my permission, and no one will engage you in private conversation because you are with Samuell and me." He smiled his most gracious smile and scolded her lightly, "Smile, Shale. You are safe here. This is a time for lightheartedness. Be merry." He nodded politely to a passing maiden.

"If we are to be introduced, yet we are not to use our names, what names are we to give?" Shale smiled graciously as Samuell seated her at the table.

"As your elder relative and escort, I will answer all the questions. Pay attention to what I do and say," Avian answered in the same formal manner in which she had asked her question. *Was she going to be difficult now?* He had been looking forward to being with her in a relaxed atmosphere and receiving her smile—a real one.

He seated Piper and took his seat beside her.

"I think you are enjoying this far too much, Lord Avian," Shale replied crossly. She smiled sweetly and leaned toward him to smooth Piper's dress. She noticed the small smile playing about his lips had now vanished.

She was on edge and she knew it. They had remained unnoticed at the farm, but this game was entirely different. None of them was accustomed to large parties. The perceptive abilities of her people were far greater than those of stable hands. She felt the curious eyes of many upon them. Surely, Lord Cale often had visitors. Why, then, did they attract so much attention? Perhaps she was overreacting. She sensed no animosity.

She sat back in her chair and glanced at Samuell. He was easily conversing with one of Lord Cale's sons.

"Indeed, we are to enjoy this evening of celebration and welcome in Pennsyl. Aren't we, little one?" Avian said, smiling down at Piper seated between them. "I love your cinnamon apples, but I am looking forward to something different tonight. Are you also?" He winked at the small child.

"Yes," Piper smiled up at him and winked back.

Avian turned his infectious smile to Shale.

Nervously, she smiled back at him.

"Look at the lovely flowers, very much like the ones in your garden. You can always converse about plants," he suggested.

He reached across Piper and squeezed Shale's hand reassuringly. Piper placed her hand on top of theirs and grinned.

Sitting at the feast with Lord Cale's family around them, the conversation turned to pleasant topics. Shale relaxed and ate the delicious food. Many of the dishes were unfamiliar, but the apples tasted like the ones Momma had served them at home.

"Try the apples." She smiled at Piper.

Piper took a bite and her eyes lit up. Quickly she scooped in another bite.

When they had finished, Lord Cale stood and announced it was time for singing and storytelling. Piper gasped with delight and her eyes danced.

Shale smiled. Piper loved music very much. There had been little of it since their mother was gone. She turned to observe Samuell. His eyes held a spark, but he remained controlled with his response.

Avian cleared his throat and she turned to him with a smile.

"That is much better, my lady," he smiled mischievously. A real smile at last.

As they gathered to go down to the river for entertainment, a tall man approached them.

"Cameron!" Samuell called. "Have you seen my father or Henicles?"

Cameron gripped Samuell's shoulder in friendship, but his eyes held a warning. "We must not speak of them openly," he whispered. "It is good to see you and your sisters as well," he added in a normal tone as Piper rushed to him and grabbed his hand.

"Our journey was perilous," Samuell said quietly.

"You will be safe here," Cameron said confidently. He swung Piper up into his arms for a hug. "How are my rabbits?" he teased.

"They are my rabbits," Piper announced. "They can dance now."

"Surely not as well as you?" Cameron teased.

Music started playing near the river. Piper wiggled down from Cameron's arms and clasped Samuell's hand tightly. "Come, Samuell. Come!" she cried.

"Let us walk with the others, little bird," Samuell replied.

The children of Connor enjoyed the stories and songs. Slowly, they relaxed and entered into the festivities. They asked Avian about the songs unfamiliar to them, for many they had not heard. He was happy to explain. It brought back the wonder of them to his own heart.

The jovial atmosphere turned to sweet songs and ballads. Lulled by the quiet music, Piper and Samuell settled into a pile of fluffy pillows that had been provided for them. Avian nudged Shale and looked in their direction. Both had given in to sleep and the peacefulness of Pennsyl.

A few songs later, Shale felt herself growing sleepy.

Avian took her hand and rose, pulling her to her feet. "Come, we will walk in the gardens. The moonlight will awaken you. If Piper were awake we would count the stars." He smiled down at Shale.

"We may count them, anyway," Shale returned his smile. She grew quiet as they walked. He had not released her hand.

"Here we may view them well," Avian said, stopping near the rose garden, where the trees did not block the view of the brightly twinkling stars.

She looked up from the roses and gasped. "I have never seen them so bright before." In her excitement she moved closer to Avian. "What is that star? There to the left of the moon. I do not remember it." She looked up at him eagerly.

Avian tore his eyes away from hers and answered. "It is Mara, the scout. She leads Orion on the hunt, now that fall has come."

"Mara...she is truly beautiful." Shale sighed and studied the sky. She felt whole and safe there with Avian.

He leaned down and whispered in her ear, "How many have you counted? I have one thousand."

"What? I have not been counting, just drinking in their beauty." She felt herself lean against him and shifted back. "You cannot have counted so many." She started walking again.

When they stood upon a small bridge with a slow moving stream lazily meandering toward the river, she plucked a small orange leaf from a bordering tree and tossed it into the stream. Silently it floated off, turning and swaying upon the ripples. She faced Avian and said, "I wish to thank you for your kindness to us on our journey. You were especially patient with Pi..I mean my sister."

Smiling at her, he replied, "She was very brave and remarkably well behaved."

"She had to be. We practiced our escape often, pretending it was a game," Shale explained. "Piper was not surprised to find herself on horseback when she awakened."

They talked about the journey, laughing at their differences of opinion and Avian's reaction to having the sleeping Piper thrust into his arms at the onset of their flight.

Shale laughed. "If you could have seen your face! You were so flustered! But serious," she added, hoping she had not offended him.

"Am I doing better now?" Avian took her hand again. "Come, we will hear more songs and merriment to teach Samuell and Piper."

Turning back toward the festivities, he watched her as they walked. She was relaxed for the first time since he had met her. There was a quiet gentleness about her, a quiet strength. Yet, she was vulnerable. He felt the trust flowing from her hand.

Remembering the fierce protectiveness she had shown for her siblings when they had fled the farm, he reconsidered that thought. No, it was true. She was vulnerable. Still, he did not release her warm hand cradled in his own.

Chapter 3

Connor disappeared into the forest, thanking God for the safety of his children and for true friends. Remembering what he and Shayna had taught their children, he thought through the steps they would have taken to escape.

If Samuell were leading them, he would go first to the cave. But where would Henicles take them? To Pennsyl most likely. He ran soundlessly through the forest thinking, *I will begin looking in the cave. They may have left a message. There is food, water, and safety. I will have time to think.* To think. He had avoided that for so long, forcing himself to focus only on his work and his children.

Getting to the cave was not easy. Small groups of men on horseback or afoot were patrolling the area. He was forced to lie hidden for hours and take alternate routes to get there. Two days of precious time were lost.

Connor entered the cave just after dusk. Yes, they had been here. The ground was disturbed inside the cave and some of the supplies used. It appeared there were three horses and four riders.

He recognized the small footprints of his little Piper. But these tracks were not Henicles's. They were the faint tracks of an elf, and a warrior at that. Who was with them? Were they safe? Surely Henicles would choose carefully who he entrusted them with, but how much did Henicles know?

Connor shook his head. He was not sure who could be trusted even among his elven kinsmen now. His captors seemed to know little about why they held him. He had overheard enough of their talk to know that elves were at the heart of the desire for the Presage.

His thoughts turned to his children. Samuell would lead them well. Quiet and strong, a quick learner, Samuell reminded him in many ways of his wife—though in appearance Samuell resembled him. Piper was still just a baby to him. He hoped she had her doll. It was constantly in her possession since Shayna had died. The thought of his wife brought fresh grief to his soul. He bowed his head and let the tears, so long contained, pour from him. Deep, agonizing sobs overwhelmed him and he buried his face in his hands. His grief flooded through him, leaving him drained of strength and completely exhausted.

Several hours later, Connor brushed his wayward blonde hair back from his face. He needed to braid it again so it would not interfere with his vision, but he had lost enough time already. Why had he slept?

He noted the ground next to him bore markings of a childish game. Shale's writing. So like her mother in appearance, he had made her cut her long, blonde hair, tinted with red as when the setting sun glazed the meadow with its rays. He hated making her do it, but he would lose no more of his family. He had heard her crying softly in her room that night. It had pierced his soul.

"Enough!" he told himself. Quickly, he ate and drank. Surely they had made it across the river. He would check to see if the rocks had been tripped to allow safe crossing on horseback.

It was another day before he was able to leave the cave. Searchers were everywhere! At midnight, he slipped soundlessly away.

Near the river, Connor paused briefly and listened. Nothing disturbed the sounds of the night around him. No men were about. He hurried on and came to the riverbank. Yes! The rocks had been tripped. His children were safely across. From across the river the sound of elvish singing reached his ears. *Friend or foe?*

Connor jumped and clutched the lowest limb of a tall oak whose branches leaned far out over the riverbank. He swiftly climbed the strong branches and found the fine elven rope hidden there. He skillfully tied a secure knot, ran down the long branch, and jumped. The rope swung him far out over the river to the other shore. One foot landed in the water. The elven singing stopped and the wood grew quiet.

On the riverbank, he was stopped, as he expected, by the elven guard.

When You Dance with Rabbits

"Why are you so stealthy in your travel?" asked the guard. "I have watched you since you left the tree line, yet you did not answer my call."

"One traveling alone at night is always cautious," Connor answered. *What call had been given?*

"Walk ahead of me," the guard ordered. Connor walked until he came to a glowing fire where a group of a dozen elves sat. One stood and studied him as he approached.

"Sit," the guard spoke again.

Connor sat near the fire and looked about him. He did not recognize any of the faces. "Greetings. Thank you for sharing your fire with me," he said. He held his hands out to the warmth. "There are many men about on the far shore today. What do you know of this?" He regretted the words as soon as he had spoken them.

"It is you who crossed the river in haste. Tell us." It was the elf standing who had spoken. *Apparently, their leader.*

"Alas, I do not know. It is curious. When I heard your merry song, I was eager to join you," Connor answered congenially. "I wish only to continue my journey."

His questioner took a step toward him.

"What is your name, friend," asked an elf hidden in the shadow of the trees.

"Gildor," Connor replied calmly.

"Sit with us, Gildor, and share our meal. Tomorrow we will travel on, though perhaps not across the river. Where will you venture?" Again it was the one hidden who spoke.

"To Pennsyl," Connor replied, stretching his legs out near the fire. He did not wish to appear secretive or unfriendly.

"Seeking what?" The elf stepped forth from the shadows.

Connor sighed. "Rest and new song. I am in need of both." He peered into the eyes of this new elf, sensing an interest in his quest beyond mere curiosity.

The other elf moved away and joined the others. They began singing softly again.

"I am Perry." He sat and tossed Connor a piece of bread. "We have met others seeking Pennsyl." He studied Connor carefully.

"As do many," Connor replied.

"Our brother, Avian, was leading them." Perry glanced at him and took a bite of bread.

"I have not heard of Avian."

"He is a skilled warrior from Cambria Forest."

"The travelers should be in good hands then." Connor smiled. He did not wish to seem overly eager to hear more.

"Indeed." Perry continued, "I know you from somewhere. You work with horses such as they were riding."

"The less said the better, my friend." Connor's eyes locked on Perry's, but he could not bring himself to confide in him. Looking back to the fire he considered this. He needed help. No, he could not risk harm to his children. He must go on alone.

Perry considered this comment and the intent look with which it was given. His quick mind flashed back to his encounter with Avian's group. One young elf with Avian greatly resembled the one he was talking to. What danger lurked that Gildor, if that was indeed his name, could not confide in his brothers and seek their assistance? Perry sensed no evil in his companion; great concern and need of secrecy, yes. He made his decision. "The travelers I spoke of earlier were pursued by men on horseback, on this side of the river. We assisted them."

Connor made no reply, but his eyes widened slightly.

"Those traveling with Avian wore strange head coverings, and one was very young. Because of their horses, their travel should be swift. Lord Cale was alerted and sent warriors to meet them." Perry stretched his long legs out toward the fire and settled in to listen to the story begun across the way.

After the story he spoke again, "I have heard of spies in Pennsyl. Be wary. As I informed Avian, I inform you." Perry studied Connor for a moment. Connor met his gaze and nodded his thanks.

Before dawn the next morning they parted company. Connor wished for his horse, but he would make good time running. He would not slow down. His children needed him.

Truth be told, he needed them. He could feel little Piper's arms around his neck and see Samuell striding beside him to keep up. Shale would be quietly observing them as she always did, picking up on their feelings and trying so hard to make everything all right for them. Why hadn't he realized this before? So stricken with his own grief, he had not noticed how his children suffered, too. He hastened his pace, longing to hold them and know that they were safe.

Connor sought safety in a large oak tree for the night. Three times he had eluded parties of searchers. Some he recognized from visits to the farm. Were they looking for him or for his children? Fatigued settled in on him and claimed his weary thoughts.

Chapter 4

Two weeks after Avian and his party arrived in Pennsyl, Lord Cale called a council. "As you know, we have had no word from Henicles. It is time to seek more information. There is more to this than an elf and a wizard missing."

Turning to his sons he said, "Search among our own peoples. Listen carefully for anything concerning the training of horses for sport, and of those we search for."

"Cameron, Avian. Seek Henicles and discover what you can." Gazing at all of them, Cale continued, "Return in two month's time. Hopefully, Henicles is even now approaching us. You will leave at first light. Go with care."

When You Dance with Rabbits

Cameron and Avian made good time the first two weeks out. No news was found as yet. They purposed to return to the area of the farm. Perhaps Eli could tell them where Connor was sent to purchase mares for the farm.

When they neared the farm, they separated. Cameron went to spy at the Inn and Avian to find Eli.

In the stillness of the wood near the stable door, Avian's sharp hearing caught the conversation between the foreman and an affluent customer.

"I cannot tell you who I represent, but I can assure you that you will be paid well. Very well." The man withdrew two gold coins from his pocket and handed them to the foreman. He smiled, pleased to see the glint of greed in the foreman's eyes. "When will the horse master return? I am expected to view his techniques."

Turning from the gold coins growing warm in his hand, the foreman answered, "Soon, soon, I assure you."

"That is not what I have heard," the man commented, staring pointedly at the foreman.

"What do you mean?" the foreman growled. He stared at the man uneasily.

"Word has reached me that your horse master is held captive. Perhaps by a competitor of yours," the man replied calmly.

The foreman fixed him with a shrewd look. "He has escaped and will return here any day. He works for us and no other."

"It is said he will not teach certain things," the man nodded knowingly, "and that his children were taken from under your very nose."

Furiously the foreman exclaimed, "There was sorcery involved! They will be found and returned very soon, I assure you." His fingers flew through the forms in his hand. "As it is, only our horses have begun training under his direction. Only our horses have the strength and light-footedness to enable them to perform the maneuvers easily. It will take years to bring other horses to their levels. They have been trained from their birth."

"Indeed, my purchaser is well aware of this training. It is the future he is concerned with. Are there others who know this training? Anyone whom the horse master has trained to assist him?" the buyer pressed.

"No one. He works alone," the foreman barked.

"What of his children? Is there a son?" the buyer persisted.

The flustered foreman scowled. "Why do you care about that?

Shrugging his shoulders the buyer replied, "A father may teach more to his son than to a stableman. A family tradition perhaps."

The foreman became thoughtful. "His two young lads work with the young ones. They do nothing beyond the basics."

Eli entered the stable for the final check before ending his day.

The buyer spoke, "I look forward to seeing your fine horses tomorrow. I will be here at eight o'clock." Nodding, he left.

"You heard him, Eli. I expect you to have them looking sharp, and I want you to show them. They respond better to your handling." Pausing to consider this, the foreman continued, "You have watched their training, Eli. Has our horse master taught you his techniques for training?"

"'Um, the caretaker, m' lord. Nothin' sa fancy as a trainer be in me," he replied, quietly soothing the mares as he moved about them. "I only know 'ow ta care fer 'em."

"Do his lads know his techniques?" the foreman pushed.

"'ose youngun's? Ye 'ave seen that yer own self, m' lord. 'ey just gentle 'em."

Eli patted the last mare, satisfied they were all settled for now. This mare would foal in a day or two. "I be back ta check on 'is 'un t'night," he informed the foreman. "She be restless and it be near 'er time." Eli smiled gently and stroked the mare's neck.

The foreman spoke gruffly as he stomped out the door. "See that you do. We need a healthy foal." As he left, he made up his mind to keep a closer eye on his best stableman.

"'at Piper gal would love ta see yer baby, Willow. 'er eyes would light up like the mornin'. We miss 'er, ma' missus 'n me."

The mare nickered and raised her head. Eli turned and stumbled back a step. From there he assessed the tall, lithe figure before him. Was he a friend of Connor's, or someone to be wary of? "Who ye be? If ye've come ta buy horses, ye'll have ta wait till the mornin'."

"Be at peace," Avian said. "I seek word of the children's father. They are safe now, and they send their greetings to you and your wife." He looked steadily into Eli's eyes.

"Na' 'ow da I know 'at?" Eli stepped from the stall. He noted the mares remained calm in the elf's presence.

"Piper told me she calls you wooly bear, and your wife smiley bear. She misses you both," Avian replied.

Eli considered this. What the elf said was true. "What be 'er favorite food?" he questioned, eyeing Avian suspiciously.

"Apple cake made from apples at this farm, and her favorite color is blue," Avian answered, still looking directly into Eli's eyes.

Eli shifted his weight from foot to foot, considering Avian's knowledge of Piper, the calmness of the mares, and the demeanor of the elf himself. Finally, he spoke. "Come ov'r 'ere. The guards be 'round soon for 'eir checkin' time. Go back 'ere into 'em shadows by me. The children be safe and well, eh?" He studied Avian's face and eyes for his reaction. Avian held Eli's gaze and nodded, smiling.

"Praise be ta God! 'ank ye for takin' 'em. I tri…" Eli began.

Two of the mares snorted. Eli began singing at the same volume he had been speaking, motioning Avian into the shadows. "Praise be ta God. Praise be ta God. All creatures be a singin' praise be ta God."

"What are you doing out here, old man? Who are you talking to?" The young guard studied the stable carefully.

" 'is un be foalin' soon, Rolly. Jus' keepin' a close eye on 'er. Singin' calms 'em ya know, even singin' poor as mine." Eli chuckled softly and began humming.

The guard relaxed and moved to Eli's side. "They are beautiful. Is this not the one that belongs to the horse master himself? I hope he returns soon, for he is looking forward to the arrival of this little one." Gently touching the mare's shoulder he continued, "Do not stay up too late, Eli. You will work yourself to death. I will check on her for you and summon you if anything changes." He turned and left.

Eli continued singing awhile, carefully listening for sounds from the other stables. The horses always snorted as the guards moved about. Without turning to Avian, he moved to the mare's side and spoke quietly.

"Connor be 'ere 'bout a month ago lookin' for 'is younguns. I told 'im Henicles 'ad taken 'em. I told 'im ta be aleavin' right quick, an' 'e did. Many be seekin' 'im. I da not na' why. Ga 'round 'a east stable ta leave. 'Tis near the woods 'ere an' the guards 'ill not go 'ere for 'ey be afearin' 'ose woods. Take care of 'em younguns, ma' friend." He continued softly singing.

"I cannot leave you yet. You must help me. What do you know of Connor's captors, and where was he going when he left you? We fear for him and are trying to find him before others do."

In a singsong voice Eli replied, "'e be travelun' north ta bring new mares for our 'erd. 'e did na' say where 'e be goin' ta. 'ere be a place 'ey used ta take their younguns—a cave I be thinkun.' I be not knowin' where 'twas."

"What else can you tell me?" urged Avian.

Eli continued humming as he considered this for a time. "I 'ear bits and pieces. 'Tis 'ard to piece 'em together. Many 'orses we trained be bought fer somethin' far away. Some place called Kambee Woods? Be 'ere such a place?"

Avian's brow furrowed and his expression grew grim. "Cambria Forest. You are sure?"

Eli nodded as he patted the mare.

"You have been most helpful. Be wary, my friend. I may yet return to you, or send a messenger who will bear the passwords: "blue apple." Trust only him. Do you have a place to escape to?"

Eli looked up at Avian. "If it comes ta 'at."

Moving past him, Avian patted the mare's smooth neck and spoke to her in Elvish. She nuzzled his arm and nickered quietly.

To Eli he said, "She will deliver by morning. You must not allow them to sell her or the foal. They are very special, for her understanding is great, and she will protect you in your time of need."

Puzzled, Eli looked from Avian to the mare. He had witnessed many foalings, and she did not appear that close to her time. He looked up again, only to find that Avian had silently disappeared, leaving him alone with his questions.

At a nearby inn, Cameron sat by himself, listening intently to the talk around him. Two tables over, a wealthy appearing man with a brown pony tail was deep in conversation with a stern, less refined man. They were discussing plans for purchasing several mares in the morning.

"The foreman has not seen the escaped horse master, and indeed, confirmed the children have been taken, much to his frustration. Our purchaser will not be pleased with our lack of information, but he will be well pleased with the mares we purchase. You must move them slowly, for some are with foal."

"'Tis a long way to go before winter." The stern man's voice rose. "We lose no foals. 'ey are priceless to our purchaser and we receive a 'efty bonus for delivering 'em safely. What is 'e going to do with 'em, without this special training he speaks of constantly?"

The buyer lifted his drink and lied, "You know as much as I do about that."

"Some dark thing 'tis, I fear, and such fine animals too." He stared hard at the man beside him. "I will deliver the mares, but I do not want to know what is to be done with 'em."

"They are for breeding purposes, you know that." Seeking to distract him, the well-dressed man turned the conversation to the matter of the journey. "You are right to consider the time needed to move them. Perhaps we will need to arrange for a place for them to stay in route, should winter weather come upon us with young ones. It is indeed a long road to Jaden. After the last sale, we stayed at a farm by the river. Perhaps they will welcome us again. Still, we will hope the weather will hold and try to get them to Jaden as quickly as possible." He finished his drink and pushed away from the table.

Cameron was greatly disturbed at this news. Quickly his mind thought back to the council when Avian had told of Henicles's suspicion that the elves were somehow involved. This now proved to be true. In the southern regions of Cambria Forest, the royal family raised prize horses. He had not known they were now raised in Jaden's kingdom as well. Perhaps the sons of Cale would have more information from that area.

The hour was growing late. The two men rose from their table and went to their lodgings. Cameron waited, listening for any comments concerning the two men or their quest. Comments were made about the changing conditions at the farm, but nothing of more use was said. After the last patron went out, he spoke with the owner.

"I know nothin' bout that place. They say it is looking run down a bit since the old man left. The new workers have been good for business. I hope they have many more sales. 'Tis good for my business as well. Do you need a room?" the owner asked Cameron hopefully.

"Not this night, thank you." Cameron nodded and left the Inn.

Avian met Cameron a mile east of the crossroads south of the farm. They traveled several more miles and made camp.

"I want to go to the sale tomorrow," Cameron said. "I have my eye on two buyers. They mentioned taking horses to Jaden."

Avian's face grew grim. "In Robin's Wood. The elves there are either seeking good breeding stock, or they are involved."

"Or both," Cameron added. He looked into the woods at the sound of rustling underbrush.

"Can a weary traveler find rest here?" It was Henicles.

"We are relieved to see you, my friend," Avian welcomed him. "Come and sit with us."

"What have you discovered?" asked Cameron.

"All will be known in due time," Henicles replied. "The night is restless."

"Would you like some roasted rabbit?" Cameron offered.

"Do not tell the little…"Avian began.

"Ahh, do not forget me when it comes to meat roasted over a fire such as this one," Henicles interrupted. "It smells wonderful. Tomorrow we will return home," he said quietly.

Avian and Cameron nodded in agreement. There was reason not to talk openly. They would save their questions until later.

Avian began a hunting tale while Cameron handed food to Henicles. They became engrossed in Avian's tale. It ended dramatically, and they retired for the night.

Piper and Samuell were kept busy learning the history of their people and sharpening elvish skills. Piper was an adept student at music and loved the harp, while Samuell's archery and riding skills improved daily.

When they were alone, the children of Connor shared memories and feelings of their parents and prayed for the safety of their father and the friends seeking him.

Shale often found herself brooding. The days, even in Pennsyl, grew dreary and long. She no longer had to prepare their meals. She did not have to constantly watch to see that Piper had her headband on and did not speak with the workers or strangers at the farm. She did not worry about them returning to their chambers as she had at the cottage. She had tried so hard to care for Samuell, Piper, and her father.

She jumped at a sudden noise and peered deeply into the woods as she walked by them. She quickened her pace. She had no energy, no desire to eat. Her stomach was in knots. As tired and weary as she was, sleep would not come until well into the night. Her thoughts tumbled about. *Where was Papa? Why did God take her mother from them? Why had all this happened? Were they truly safe?*

"Yet, you love us, God," she whispered. She was sure of this truth. As sure as the starlight each night. As sure as the wind on her face. The one thing that had not changed in her life was God's love.

"What now, Father God, what now? If Papa is away a long time, where will we stay? Surely Lord Cale will not let us stay indefinitely." Perhaps she could find some work to do here. She was skilled in herbal medicine, horses, and average at sewing. Maybe an apprenticeship in the healing arts.

Healing...she wondered if even Lord Cale could have saved her mother. The fatigue and weariness of the last months weighed down on her. Her pace slowed and the appeal of the woodland faded.

As she had promised, Kendra took them all riding one day. Their faces shone with joy to be riding again.

The feel of the wind rushing through her hair as the horse cantered across the meadow refreshed Shale's soul. She laughed when Samuell stood on the back of his mare and waved his arm, urging her to do the same. Quickly, she stood and they let their mares move close together. At Samuell's short whistle they each jumped to the other's mare. Back and forth they played, lightly leaping from one mare to the other.

When they stopped, they lay in the sweet grasses, laughing. Piper slid off her pony and jumped on them. Her small fingers dug into their sides and the tickle fight began.

Samuell lifted Piper up onto his shoulders and cried, "The tickle beast is coming for Shale!"

Piper roared with all her might, waving her arms in the air. Shale shrieked and dashed off through the tall grass.

The tickle beast pursued her and bore down upon her. Shrieking again, Shale succumbed to the attack and became the beast in return.

Kendra sat upon her steed and laughed with them. When the tickle beast was caught in a fit of giggles, she dismounted and unpacked their lunch. They ate their sandwiches and cookies under the draping branches of a tall willow.

"Look at all the butterflies, Piper." Shale pointed to the myriad of butterflies flitting about the wild flowers.

"They are every color of the rainbow," Samuell added quietly.

"My rabbit said there are ten different kinds," Piper informed them. She tossed a piece of her bread to a chubby brown rabbit sitting by her feet.

"What else does your rabbit say?" Kendra asked her.

"She says that many who come here stay a long time. Will we stay a long time? I like it here, but I miss my Papa." Piper's lower lip trembled.

"You may stay here as long as you like, Piper. It is our joy to have you with us. As for your Papa, he may stay, too. You remember that my brothers, and Avian, and Cameron, and Henicles are all looking for him, don't you?" Kendra consoled her. "We all pray they will return soon. It takes a long time to travel far though, does it not?"

Piper nodded and lifted the fluffy rabbit onto her lap. "OK, I will see you this evening," she said. The rabbit hopped into the tall grass and disappeared.

Samuell stood and took up the reins of Piper's pony. "Are you ready to return for your music lesson, little bird?" he asked.

Piper rose and skipped to her pony. "Bye, Shale. Bye, Kendra. Thank you for lunch," she sang.

Samuell held her pony while she mounted, then gained his own saddle and turned for the stables. "I will be with the horses," he said to Shale.

"Come, I will race you, Piper." He winked at Shale and Kendra. Piper bent low over her pony and urged it on.

"They are remarkable children, Shale. I have enjoyed getting to know all of you." Kendra smiled warmly, then began gathering the remnants of their lunch.

Shale smiled and looked up as a horse and rider approached them.

"My Lady Kendra," the messenger called, "your father bids you come and bring the lady with you to the greeting field. A horse master from far away has asked for a meeting there."

Kendra and Shale exchanged glances and quickly mounted their horses. They galloped to a ridge above the greeting field and observed someone approaching Lord Cale from across the way.

"Alas, he does not stride like my father," Shale lamented after the messenger left them. "I had so hoped it was Papa." The wind blew his cloak about and Shale noted a flash of silver beneath it.

"Did you see that?" she spoke in alarm to Kendra.

"What? What did you see?" Kendra asked.

Shale did not answer. She leaned forward and spoke softly to her mare. Commanding the mare's movements in the patterns taught by her father, Shale crossed the meadow and drew nearer to the man. He stopped walking toward Lord Cale and hesitated, staring intently at the horse in front of him. The mare's careful pattern of maneuvers brought her ever closer.

The man clenched his fists and released them. He glanced furtively to the left. The mare sensed his fear. She snorted and tossed her head up and down. This was no horse master.

Shale quickly shouted, "He is an impostor. He is armed!"

The two guards near the man drew their weapons. They seized the alleged horse master and searched him. Finding a long knife beneath his cloak, they took him prisoner.

Shale turned her mare and rode back to Kendra.

Kendra looked at her father, turned her mare and galloped away. Shale followed. They rode swiftly to the stables and left the horses with the stablemen.

"Come," Kendra said to Samuell.

Samuell frowned and left his horse in her stall.

When they had reached the privacy of their gardens, Kendra asked Shale, "How did you know he was an impostor?"

"Anyone familiar with horses would not have been intimidated by these maneuvers. They are basic. He is no horse master," Shale explained.

When You Dance with Rabbits

"Tell no one we were riding today. We must change quickly. Samuell, get your bow and arrows and wait for me here. Come, Shale," she commanded.

When they reached their chambers, Kendra instructed, "Wait here. My father will summon you. I cannot explain now. Remember, tell no one we were riding."

Within the hour, Shale was summoned to Lord Cale's study.

"Explain yourself," he commanded.

Shale swallowed and began, "My lord, I hoped he might be my father, but he did not walk as my father does."

"How did you come upon us?"

"We were summoned, my Lord." Shale's brow furrowed with confusion.

"By whom?"

"By the one you sent to us. He said a horse master was to meet you. I had so hoped it was Papa."

"Had you seen this elf before, the one who summoned you?"

"Yes, my lord. I have seen him often about Pennsyl."

Cale considered this. "Why did you ride out into the Greeting Field?"

"I saw a flash of silver beneath his cloak so I purposed to test him." Shale sat tall in her chair. "He did not recognize the maneuvers my horse performed. These are basic maneuvers. Anyone training horses would know this, anticipate each step, and be not at all frightened. He was afraid."

Cale continued, "You entered the Greeting Field unbidden. This is not allowed. You must understand; even here we must be careful. Your father does not teach as other horse masters. The maneuvers that you performed are known to few."

Shale shifted uneasily, feeling her cheeks flush.

He walked around the small table and stood looking down at her. "I did not summon you to the greeting field."

Shale shuddered involuntarily.

"I am concerned, for many saw your skills today. In seeking to protect me, you may have endangered yourself and your siblings. This I must decree for your safety. Until I am assured that you are secure here, none of you may go near the stables. You are not to be alone except in your chambers, and you must stay in the gardens when you are outdoors."

His voice softened as he watched her face grow pale, "I am grateful for your desire to protect me. Do not fear, but be cautious. Go now and rest, for you are weary. Your healing will come with time."

Shale bowed her head and left Lord Cale. She wished they would stop saying that. She was fine.

Oh, yes, I am fine, and what a fine mess I have made. I am a fool. She wished for Avian to return. She felt safe when he was near. Her mind raced, and she lengthened her steps as her frustration grew. Behind her she heard the quickening of light steps. She turned and saw a familiar warrior following her. Behind him, Lord Cale nodded approvingly.

He smiled pleasantly and approached her. "You are not to be alone, my lady. May I walk with you, or are you intent to dash this path to death as I follow you?"

Shale stared at him belligerently, and then felt her spirit soften. He was sent to help. "I will walk with you," she answered quietly, "but I do not wish to talk." She trudged on a moment, then asked, "Where is my sister?"

"Since you do not wish to talk, I will be brief." He looked for her smile but received none. "She also has an escort. She is singing with two other children in her teacher's garden. I am to appear as your escort, my lady."

Shale did not answer but slowed her pace to meet his leisurely one. As they neared the garden, she saw Samuell and Kendra speaking quietly together. A dark-haired warrior stood a fair distance away holding a long bow. He appeared to be near Samuell's age.

Samuell approached Shale rapidly. "I can no longer work with the horses. I do not understand." Samuell's voice was edged with frustration.

"Lower your voice." Kendra said firmly. "Alas, it is true. Your skills must remain hidden for now, and also your sister's. Your identity must be protected." In a normal voice she continued, "Here, try my bow. I would have another contest with you. May the best shot win." She grinned at him in challenge.

Samuell took her bow and examined it. He aimed carefully and released his arrow. It hit the mark dead on. Turning to Kendra, he bowed. "My lady, it is your turn." He held out the bow to her.

Shale watched, amazed. When had her little brother become such a gentleman? She excused herself and returned to her chambers accompanied by her disappointed escort.

"I will await you here, my lady," he informed her.

"Thank you," she murmured and softly shut her door.

The events of the day had shaken her. Thinking at last she would see Papa, then to find someone armed to harm Lord Cale. The heaviness of fatigue slipped over her. Grief and worry left her exhausted.

For so long she had fought it off—denied that it followed her like a shadow day and night. There had been so much to do, so much to be alert for. At the farm, she had Samuell and Piper to care for, to ease their sadness, to keep their world as sane as possible. And always they were on their guard to watch what they said, how they did things. They were never to draw attention to themselves, not ever. Their lives may depend on it, Papa had said. Samuell and Piper's lives.

Shale wrapped her arms around herself and dropped onto the couch. She missed her mother. She longed to feel her arms around her. She longed to hear her mother's voice and pour out her heart to her.

The deep pain of loss welled up inside her. It poured forth, rushing to surround and drown her. Hot tears coursed down her cheeks in torrents and she smothered her cries in her pillow. "Oh, God help us!" she cried.

As the sun began to set, Kendra entered the chamber and gazed kindly at the crumpled form on the couch.

She did not want to awaken Shale from her much needed rest.

Henicles had asked how Shale was faring, and Kendra had told him of her fretfulness, poor appetite, and restless nights. Time for grieving her losses had come.

Reluctantly Kendra spoke, "Shale, it is time to awaken." Shale awoke, startled, and quickly sat up. Kendra's heart melted when she looked at Shale's red eyes and tear streaked face. "Do not hold back your tears, Shale. Let them flow for your healing. You have lost so much and are weary with grief. Lie down again. I will get us refreshment." Kendra touched Shale's shoulder and briefly stepped out of the room.

Returning with tea and fruit, she asked, "Shale, if you would like, please tell me about your mother."

Shale looked into the eyes of her friend and sipped some of the tea. Slowly she began, "My mother was beautiful, with the sweetest smile God ever made. She was witty, always making us laugh. She worked very hard and taught us many things. She loved plants and herbs. She grew all kinds indoors as well as in her gardens. Even Henicles was surprised at the plants she could grow." Shale sipped more tea and added quietly, "She loved us so much."

Shale paused and bowed her head. "Momma loved being outdoors. That's where she died, at the edge of the meadow. The arrow pierced her heart."

"I am so sorry for your loss," Kendra said. She took Shale's hand and held it.

Tears streamed down her face again, and Shale wiped them on her scarf. "After that, Father became more and more distant." Shale looked out the window as she spoke. "Oh, he tried to comfort and encourage us, but he was hurting so much himself that he could not see our pain. I tried to make up for it, for Samuell and Piper."

Shale looked up from her cup. "They seem better here with other children. Still, they cry at night. But that is good, is it not?"

"It is, and for you also, Shale. You have had little time for your own grief." Kendra stood and moved to the balcony, leading Shale with her. "My father bids you peace. You may rest here as long as you desire. Pennsyl is a place for healing. Fear not, you are welcome here. Come and see! Father himself is with Samuell and Piper. He delights in them." Kendra smiled and Shale joined her. Together they observed the three in the garden.

Kendra touched Shale's arm and told her, "I have news. Cameron, my brothers, and Avian have returned. Henicles is with them."

"Is there news of Papa?" Shale asked hopefully.

"I do not know. They have just arrived and will take counsel with my father," she answered. "Now, tonight we may be asked to dine with our guests if their council is not too late. You have missed Avian, have you not?" Kendra smiled at the blush stealing across Shale's cheeks.

"Let me help you with your hair, and you with mine. We will put gold and blue flowers in yours. I happen to know Avian likes them. Piper told me." They both laughed. Piper was always trying to put flowers in someone's hair.

Shyly Shale spoke, "He is a prince among his people, Kendra. I do not even know where I come from in regard to the elves. My parents did not talk about their heritage." Looking up at Kendra, Shale confided, "I would not disgrace him."

"There is much you will learn about yourself, Shale. Fear not. Avian is beyond such thoughts. We will hope to see them tonight," Kendra encouraged.

"Tomorrow is Piper's birthday. I hope they will be able to come and be with us. Piper would be so happy. It is her first birthday without Momma. And Papa is not here," Shale paused. She tucked a strand of silky hair behind her ear and looked down at her hands. "It will be very hard for her."

"We will love her and make it as fine a celebration as we can," Kendra exclaimed. "How can I help?"

"She likes apple cake. Mama would always make that for her." Shale smiled gently, remembering.

"Then we will have apple cake. We will put yellow flowers in her hair. They will compliment the new dress you made for her. I admire the embroidery you did," Kendra said, encouraged that Shale was coming to life again.

"Momma taught me. I am trying to make up for their loss. I feel I fall short so many times," Shale confided. Her voice caught in her throat.

"I see how hard you try. Samuell and Piper love and trust you. They are doing well. Do not be so hard on yourself."

Kendra stepped behind Shale and gathered up her hair. She twisted it up on the sides. "Your hair is growing quickly. Do you like it this way?" she asked.

Shale allowed herself to be distracted and joined Kendra in preparation for the evening. While they were dressing, they received word that the council had ended and would reconvene in the morning.

They waited in the gardens for the evening meal to be served. Shale was pleased that the council had ended in time for visiting. Avian was nearby talking with Samuell and Piper. His eyes grew bright when he saw her, and his smile warmed her heart. She turned as Henicles greeted her warmly and took her arm. They strolled down the path a short distance from the others.

"Tell me of your father, Shale. Was his behavior different prior to this last trip?" Henicles studied her, gently urging her to confide in him.

Shale thought carefully, then responded, "He became much more secretive and very wary of the new owners and workers at the farm. We were not allowed to speak with them, except about the training of the horses. I had to dress and act as my brother did, even cutting my hair." She touched it self-consciously. "We were no longer allowed to go freely about the farm, or roam the woods without Papa. At least once a week we would check supplies and go over our plans for escape. Thus you found us so prepared for flight. But right before this trip he did not seem especially concerned. He said he was going to select mares for the new breeding program. That is all. What are you thinking, Henicles? What news do you bring? Where is my father?" Her anxious eyes searched his for answers.

Just then they were summoned to the meal. Avian and the children stood waiting for her.

"All in good time, my dear," Henicles replied and patted her hand. "We will speak before the night is over."

Avian offered his arm. "You look beautiful, my cousin," he said loudly enough for her escort to hear. "It is a joy to see you again. You must tell me all you have done while I have been away."

Shale smiled warmly and took his arm. "I am glad to see you again."

After the meal, Henicles took Samuell and Shale into a secure room. "It is determined that your father was taken captive during his journey. He escaped, but we have not yet seen him. He refused to comply with his captors' wishes; therefore they still seek him, and they are seeking you to force his cooperation."

"Is he safe, Henicles? Why have you not found him?" Samuell spoke sharply.

"There is no one more skilled in woodcraft than your father, Samuell. He will be found only when he wants to be," Henicles replied.

Avian came and stood beside her chair. Shale turned searching eyes to him and he took her hand.

"He is safe, for they need his skills to perfect their evil plan. Have you heard of the Presage, the dance of death?" Henicles asked.

Shale and Samuell both shook their heads. The puzzled looks upon their faces confirmed the truth.

"It is well that you haven't." Henicles shook his head in disgust as he explained. "It is an ancient battle performed on horseback, in which the horses are trained in specific movements and skills. These are used against the opposing rider, somewhat like unto war maneuvers, but far more detailed. The riders become nearly entranced with the precision of it, culminating in a fight to the death. It is an evil ritual used as sport, creating a blood lust among its participants."

"What has that to do with Papa?"

"Some believe he can teach the Presage."

"That is foolishness." Samuell jumped to his feet. "My father would never teach anything evil."

"I believe you," Henicles assured him. "That is why they seek to force him. That is why they seek you."

Shale stood in alarm. "Those at the farm—are they involved? Henicles, my mother? Did they...did they kill her?" Seeing the possibility in his eyes, she covered her face in horror.

Avian put his arm around her. "We do not know for certain."

"Thank you for saving us that night. I cannot, I cannot even..." Shale's words were lost in her tears. She turned herself to Samuell's embrace and sobbed.

Henicles placed one hand on her trembling shoulder. "Go and rest now. God be with you and give you his peace. Tomorrow is Piper's birthday. You must be brave another day, but tonight know that your sorrows are shared by your friends."

Chapter 5

Piper's party was in full swing when the men joined them from the council the next afternoon. Piper danced around in her new dress with yellow flowers bouncing in her hair.

She and Samuell were spinning the blindfolded Shale around. It was her turn to see if she could find the golden cord of the suspended pouch and release the gifts inside. The children began the song and circled around Shale giggling at her attempts to find the soft cord.

As the song neared its end so did Shale's turn and Avian, with his finger to his lips, slipped into the circle. Holding the end of the golden cord, he tickled Shale's nose. Crinkling her nose, she reached out quickly for the cord. The children roared with laughter as Avian easily dodged aside and tickled her again. With the third tickle, she caught his sleeve and spun around.

"I have you now, Samuell," she shouted taking hold of him.

"It is not me, my sister," Samuell shouted from behind her.

"Who then?" Shale cried releasing her hold. She tore off the blindfold causing a yellow flower to fall from her hair.

"Hug me, Avian! It is my birthday!" Piper's little voice sang out. She hugged his legs tightly.

Avian swung her up into a hug and watched Shale's blush deepen. "Happy Birthday, Piper. Now it is your turn to seek the golden cord." Avian set Piper down, and Shale tied on the blindfold and stepped out of the circle. Samuell spun Piper around and around and the song began.

Avian stepped near Shale with the yellow flower in his hand and tucked it into her hair. "I have missed you," he whispered. He took her hand and they laughed together as Piper sought the golden cord.

That evening Shale sat on the balcony watching the elves gathering near the river for the singing. A tired little Piper came to be tucked in for the night.

"Did you have a nice birthday, Piper?" Shale asked, lifting her sister onto her lap.

"Yes," Piper answered quietly.

"Only yes?" inquired Shale.

"I wished for Momma and Papa to come. Papa always helps me blow out my candles and dances with me high up in his arms. Momma's cake is so good with apples from our trees at home." Piper yawned.

"They love you very much, Piper. I miss them, too," Shale whispered, fighting back tears. They slid from her eyes anyway.

"When will Papa come?" Piper rested her head against Shale's shoulder, yawning again.

"I do not know yet. We will pray it will be soon." Shale laid Piper on her bed and tucked the covers under her chin.

Piper's eyes were already closed, and she clasped her doll close to her face. "I smell Momma."

"Dream sweet dreams of her, Piper. I love you." Shale sat by the bed and watched Piper's sleep deepen.

She returned to the balcony and looked up at the stars. She had made Piper's dress using her favorite colors for the embroidery. Samuell had helped her blow out the candles. Lord Cale and Avian had danced with her high up in their arms. They had all tried so hard to make her day special.

As gratefulness and sadness mixed upon her, Shale turned her heart to God and prayed, "Thank you, Father God, for the many blessings of this day. Please bring Papa to us soon. Bless Piper with sweet dreams and keep us safe."

At the sound of soft footsteps she turned. Kendra's maid was there with a message to join the others on the verandah. Shale thanked her, and with another look at Piper, slowly made her way down the stairs. She wondered if the men had returned to the council again. The world was so much more alive when Avian was there. Fresher, cleaner, the colors more brilliant. Catching her thoughts, she hurried down the stairs.

Only Avian waited for her. He smiled, and for the second time that day the cloud of worries lifted from her.

"Is our birthday girl sleeping?" he asked.

"Yes, with sweet dreams. Thank you for making today special for her," Shale said sincerely.

As they walked, they talked about the party and the children's antics. Shale laughed and it sounded almost strange to her.

Avian took her hand and pulled her gently close to him. She wanted only to stay there forever. Everything around her became more alive—the stars so bright, the breeze soft and cool, the water singing softly. Just to be near him filled her with joy.

Joy endures and sustains, Momma said, she thought. *Maybe I am only happy.* Happiness depended more on circumstances.

"What are you thinking?" Avian whispered to her.

"That I am right now so very happy."

A rustle to their left drew their attention, and Avian moved on toward the singing. "Is something wrong?" Shale asked, her eyes large with concern.

Avian looked deeply into her eyes and replied, "I do not think so. I do know that I have requested a special song for you, and I do not want you to I miss it. Besides, Lord Cale will be having words with me for being so late escorting you here." He smiled warmly and quickened their pace.

The music and singing were beautiful as always, but tonight seemed especially so, Shale thought as they settled near Kendra and Cameron. Avian nodded at

Lord Cale, who nodded back. Sitting so their shoulders touched, they shared sweet apples and grapes.

Lively music introduced the next song. Avian turned to her and spoke intently, "This is my song for you. You must trust me, Shale."

She returned the intensity of his look, troubled by the urgency in his voice.

"It is a funny song," Avian smiled to ease her concern. "Listen carefully with me." He sang the verses for her.

She had heard this ballad before; a children's song of a rabbit's adventures to find his home. She joined him on the chorus, "Dance little rabbit! Dance till you are home! Dance little rabbit, be careful where you roam! Dance little rabbit...."

The next song was joined with much singing and dancing and Avian drew her onto the dance floor. He glanced at Lord Cale as they began.

"Come with me, Shale. Piper and Samuell are already safe. Remember the song. There are spies among us." Avian smiled and his eyes urged her to be brave.

She smiled brightly back at him lest anyone know their topic was so serious. They moved to the refreshments and Avian smiled and whispered, "There are two horses behind the right fountain. Walk with me."

They paused to applaud the last song and meandered toward the fountain, hand in hand. Avian picked a flower and gave it to her.

Her eyes searched his and she wondered if they would be together if escape were not necessary. But this was no time for such thoughts.

When You Dance with Rabbits

They slipped away during the applause for the next song and let their horses pick their way quickly out of Pennsyl.

Chapter 6

The rest of the night and all the next day they rode far and fast. Coming upon a forested area, Avian helped her into a tree for the coming night. There a flat-boarded area was concealed with supplies at hand.

"I am going to see if we were followed. Be very quiet," Avian spoke quietly.

Her eyes pleaded with him to be careful.

He returned after an hour and found her waiting with her knife drawn by her side.

"I saw nothing. Rest now. We will talk in the morning." He squeezed her hand and sat to rest. After a few moments, Shale saw him relax and let herself sleep.

She awakened to the sound of bird songs. Avian was not there. She listened carefully. Someone was talking in a low voice. "We found where the horses were. Their tracks lead south."

A second voice continued, "They have gone on foot then. You were too slow."

"Why would they go on foot when they could ride?" the first voice spoke again.

"Because horses are easier to track than elves on foot," a third voice added.

"Well, they can't go through those thickets. Look this way first," suggested the first voice.

"Get on with it," the second voice ordered.

When she could hear them no more, Shale slowly sat up. *Thank you, God. They had not found Avian. Maybe he would come soon, now that they had gone.*

Near the supply pouch words were carved into the platform: "remember the song." She thought back to the first verse, then the second. Something about a rabbit going through a thicket to its home so the fox could never find it. But rabbit didn't go there for a whole day. Then the rabbit hopped to the end of the thicket and through a bright red berry hole. She moved quietly until she could see the thicket more clearly. It was covered with deep burgundy berries, not one red one. The rabbit waited a day; so would she.

The day passed slowly. Twice she heard the sound of horses' hooves. She thought often of Samuell and Piper. Where were they now? Were they pursued also?

"Please, Father God, keep them safe and at peace and give wisdom to those who protect and guide them," she prayed. "Please keep Avian and Papa safe too, and bring them safely to me."

Weariness came upon her again and she slept. When she awakened it was dusk. She concentrated on the verses of the song. There was something about a ride down a river, through the rainbow, and into darkness without a glance.

"Dance, little rabbit. Dance till you are home. Dance little rabbit, be careful where you roam ...."

Nightfall came and still Avian did not.

He hated leaving her. He hoped she remembered all of the song. He had known it since childhood, and used it as did all the young elvish children to find their way home when tested. Did Shale know it? Had her parents taught it to their children? He hoped she had not been as distracted by their nearness as he had been. She needed to remember the song. He thought back to their time on the trail fleeing her home. She had shown good judgment and had knowledge of the woods. She was intelligent. She would make it to the Raven Tree. He shook the thoughts from his mind. He had to get back to Pennsyl.

Avian crept toward the thicket where he had hidden their horses. His sharp hearing picked up the sound of three men on horseback. They were moving slowly, trying to track them. Their search led them away from the horses and Shale.

Avian waited to see if they returned. He pondered his next move. *I could make good time running, but we will need the horses eventually.* There was no sign of the men. He could hear them moving further away.

Silently, he started toward the horses. Using hand signals he instructed them to follow him. He led them quickly to a small clearing and mounted his horse. He gave the hand signal to Shale's mare to trail him. If the men followed, they would not see the dawn.

In Pennsyl, Avian reported the pursuers. He shifted restlessly in his chair, then stood and paced to the window. *Shale should be through the thicket and on her way up the river by now.*

"Avian," Henicles called. "Come and join me. I have a question of concern."

He returned to his seat. "Yes, what is it?"

"How far is the bridge of Robin's Wood from your kingdom?"

Avian frowned. Henicles knew this. He answered anyway.

Beside him Henicles whispered, "She will be fine."

Shale awoke to the pale light of early morning. Avian had not come. She prayed, "Father, God, please keep Avian safe, and Samuell and Piper and Papa. Thank you that you are with each of us."

She removed a biscuit from her vest and took a bite. To her surprise it was moist and sweet. She bent to study the thicket again, and a strange sight met her eyes. There on the thicket, low to the ground, was a ring of red berries. Of course, these berries turned red when they dried. Yesterday she could not see them, for they were not dry yet. Avian had marked her path. Listening carefully for any unusual sound, she crawled to the thicket. A small pathway was there. Being careful not to leave a piece of torn cloth or other sign near the thicket, she crawled into the narrow passageway.

Once through the broad thicket she could hear a river nearby and made her way to it.

"By the log, old rabbit found a bit of cord upon the ground,

"and to the cord a raft was tied. Upon it old rabbit did ride,

"up the river, it is told, to the rainbow and the gold."

Carefully, she searched each fallen log for a rope. There. Tied to the oldest, largest log was a fine elven cord, thin as a spider web. It led to a very small raft, but she would fit.

The grass and trees were tall by the river. Still, she hoped she resembled the rabbit and not a sitting duck. Crouching on the raft, she drew her gray elven cloak over her head and poled up the river.

Toward evening the sound of water grew louder. To her right was a pool with a broad waterfall. The remaining sunlight played upon it, reflecting luminescent colors. The rainbow! Poling to the side, Shale nimbly climbed off the raft and made her way cautiously to the falls. She studied it carefully and finally saw the entrance on the side near her. Cautiously, she slipped behind the curtain of water, carrying the raft with her.

A small cave was there. The rock at the entrance was wet, but back a little further was a dry place to sit. "Your Song" was scratched on the rock floor. Avian had been here sometime. He was safe, then. "Thank you, Father God," she breathed.

When You Dance with Rabbits

Avian set off with Henicles and the sons of Cale before daylight the next morning. Their hope in leaving together was to confuse any spies. Those suspected of spying in Pennsly would be taken and questioned within the hour.

The company traveled together for several hours, then bid each other safe journey and set out on their own paths: Henicles to seek Shale's father, the brothers to seek information among the elves, and Avian to rejoin Shale on their flight to Cambria Forest. He hoped she had made good time.

Shale angrily threw a rock into the waterfall. *How did that verse go?* "Dance little rabbit, dance till you are home. Dance little rabbit... a tree straight as a lance... a..." something. What was it?

Frustrated, Shale rose to her feet and stepped toward the falling water. The solid rock floor was wet and slippery. She stepped carefully towards the entrance. *Maybe if I study the trees outside it will help me.* Near the entrance she paused. *Are those voices?* Her pulse quickened and she stepped closer to the entrance. The sound of men's angry voices filled her ears.

Shale traced her steps backward. From this spot she could peer out through the water. She saw two men on horseback shouting at a third man on foot. "They are definitely looking for something. No, they are tracking. Looking for me?" she whispered.

Quickly, she thought through her actions before entering the cave. She had hidden the raft in here. Had she covered her tracks well enough? She had walked along the edge of the pool and stepped up on stones to get to the cave. Carefully, she returned to the entrance and peeked out. On one stone lay dried mud from the river. It must have dripped off the raft.

Her peripheral vision caught a slight movement to her left. A large gray rabbit twitched his nose at her. He hopped onto the stone and began scratching off the mud. She could not believe it. Perhaps Piper had prayed for her rabbits to watch over her. "Thank you, rabbit," she whispered gratefully.

Shale turned her attention to the contentious men. One turned toward her and she gasped. She had seen him at the farm with the foreman several times. The third man moved into view and she recognized him as well. Yes, he had argued with Papa about the training of a horse he wanted. She remembered the hateful look in the man's eyes that day and shivered.

The men dismounted and began unloading their packs and gathering wood for a fire. They ceased their arguing and attended to their tasks. As night fell, they gathered around the fire and did not set a watch.

Silently, as she had been taught, Shale slipped from the cave into the shadows of the trees. The men were arguing again.

"Why have you not found the trail, if this is the way they came?" the leader demanded.

The man who had been on foot answered, "I tell you they did not come this way. They are going down river, not upstream!"

"They are headed for Cambria Forest—I know it," the second rider announced.

"Who in their right mind would go there? They say it is haunted and full of foul beasts," the man on foot responded.

"The elf is from Cambria Forest," the second rider insisted.

"And elves travel everywhere. Anyone knows that," the leader growled.

"The maid said he was in the council two days ago. He could not be with the children," argued the third man. "She said he left with the wizard and those other elves."

"The maid has been wrong before," the leader spoke with distain.

"But Cyril saw them leaving together, too. The elf is not with them. He is not taking them to Cambria Forest," the third man insisted.

The man who had been on foot rose and threw a stick into the fire. "Aye, Cyril said the lot of them headed south. He was with them all right, not here."

"And where are the lads? That is who we must find!"

The leader held up both hands and snarled at them, "Quiet both of you. We leave at first light and head down river."

Shale crept back to the darkness of the cave, and pondered all she had heard. *Avian had gone back to Pennsyl and left with Henicles, or so it appeared. They spoke of a maid. What maid? Were the children safe? Were they safely taken the same night she was? Why had they been separated?* Shale bowed her head and prayed for protection for her family and all those trying to help them. "When will we be safe, Father God? When?" Weariness fell upon her like a heavy cloak. She felt so tired, so very tired.

When she awoke the men were gone, and the sun was well into the sky. Silently, she chided herself for sleeping so long. *Now what? Should I wait here? Will Avian return for me?* Her eyes focused on the floor where the words "Your song" were scratched on the rock.

She wished she had been more attentive. She remembered Avian commenting on certain parts, making jokes. Thinking back to that night, she searched her memory and slowly sang,

"Oh, little rabbit, when the sun shines
through the ancient tree,
"away with you and hasten—don't wait for me—
"to the northeast swiftly flee, until you
find the Raven Tree."

Shale watched as the sun moved slowly through the sky, until it was behind the oldest tree she could see from the cave. The sun now shone fully onto the falls, causing them to glisten and sparkle so brightly she could hardly look through it.

It is the perfect time to leave. No one can look at the waterfall for the brilliance blinds the eye. How far to the

Raven Tree? What is a Raven Tree? A roost for ravens? A black tree? A dead tree?

Shale's feet flew through the woods. She wanted as many miles between herself and her enemies as possible. Near sunset she saw ahead a heavily forested area. One tall, dead tree bore its black branches high above the green of its companions.

The Raven Tree? Surely—and then what? The next verse—how does it go? She could not remember. Did Avian realize how distracted she was, being so near to him?

"Don't be silly," she chided herself. She raced on toward the forest.

When she entered the tree line, Shale was surprised to find a dozen gray and brown rabbits gathered. They twitched their pink noses and hopped together down a narrow pathway to her right. The thicket they led her through scratched at her arms and face. She pulled her hood and cloak about her and hurried on. The rabbits clustered near a bramble bush beside a fallen log and watched her. One hopped a little further into the woods, and she followed it. There was the Raven Tree.

She turned to thank them, but the sleek rabbits had disappeared. She regretted the many times she had shooed Piper's rabbits away from her lettuce.

At the enormous base of the black tree she paused. It was indeed dead, its trunk smooth, with thick vines running up it. The dark color of the trunk and branches began to blend into the darkness of the forest about her. The sun had set.

Shale scanned the branches of the tall trees surrounding her. She shuddered. Uneasiness crept upon her as if someone or something were watching, waiting. The ancient forest grew ever darker.

She walked around the huge base of the tree. On the northeast side a woven ladder was secured six feet above her head. She rolled a log over to the tree and stood on it. *Maybe if I jump, I can grab it and pull it down.*

Shale sprang up and stretched for the ladder. She felt its smooth fibers against her fingers and grasped them tightly. The log beneath her feet slipped away and she tumbled to the ground.

Springing up, she winced. Why did her left ankle not bear her weight? *Why did it hurt so?*

The ladder was in easy reach now. Shale gripped it tightly and pulled hard, testing it. Slowly, she let her full weight come to bear upon it. It held without creaking. Using her arms and right leg, she began to climb.

Suddenly, she froze in place. Something was running toward the tree. She relaxed when three deer rushed past, their large brown eyes wide with the joy of the run. She sensed no fear in them. Nothing pursued them. Still, she felt a need to reach the safety of the haven above.

Up and up the ladder led her. Finally, she reached the wide platform near the top and pulled herself onto the firm wooden floor. The platform was large enough for five elves to fit comfortably. The leaves of the surrounding trees hid her and gave shelter.

Peering over the edge, she shuddered. She did not like such great heights. Hand over hand, she pulled the woven ladder up and fastened it high above the ground below. Her ankle throbbed with each beat of her heart, and her boot felt very tight.

Shale positioned herself halfway between the outer edge of the platform and the entrance hole in its middle. She leaned up and removed a length of rope from her pack. Securely, she tied the rope to a branch above her and wrapped the other end around her waist. She had never slept so high before.

Carefully, she lifted her left ankle and placed it on the pack. She removed her boot and lay back to rest. Fatigue crept upon her. The leaves danced around her, moving in blurry circles.

The aroma of the herbs tucked safely in her vest relaxed her. If only she could make some tea. The cool night air settled about her and eased her throbbing ankle.

What was that skittering sound? Were those eyes that blinked at her above in the branches? She studied the area again, but saw nothing.

"Don't be foolish," she scolded herself. "It is only the branches and leaves rustling as a squirrel passes on its way to its nest."

That is what she would have told Piper. Thinking of her siblings, she prayed for them—for their guardians, for her father, for Avian, and for herself, that she would not be afraid.

The night sounds became familiar and soothing. Just before she slept, she thought she heard fair voices singing from afar. Her dreams were full of little lost rabbits.

Shale awoke with a start, and cried out in pain. Her bruised and swollen ankle had slipped off her pack, thudding on the hard wood. She fought off the nausea and lay still until the throbbing eased.

What was wrong with her? She had never felt this way before, never fallen before. Where was her sense of balance and her strength? She had never seen her parents like this. Is this what it felt like to die? Eli's mother had died, but she did not know how it happened. Did you just fade away, or was it suddenly that you left your body?

Her body ached from being in the same position for so long. But it hurt too much to move, and the nausea persisted. She reached into a pocket of her vest and removed a peppermint leaf. She chewed it, and the nausea subsided. Carefully, she lifted her ankle up onto her pack again and eased herself down onto the platform.

She turned her head to the left and stared. It was misty and shiny looking. She forced herself to study the branches and leaves above her head. Nothing shiny or misty here, just the swaying of the leaves with the gentle night breeze, nothing to be alarmed about. God was right here with her. Right here. Right here... slowly she drifted into sleep again. *Avian. Where was Avian?*

Avian urged the horses on. Shale had called to him in his mind, but it had disappeared quickly. He had been aware of tree branches and something about her pack. *If she is not at the Raven Tree, I will need to backtrack to find her. She should be there. She is smart and knows the ways of the woods.*

He galloped on. Soon he would be able to see the Raven Tree among the green of the forest. By the river, he had seen the tracks of three horses. They were going downstream. Shale should not have been followed.

Avian entered the forest and was met by a cluster of gray and brown rabbits. They looked like a group of warriors on patrol. He rode on by them and reached the great black tree.

The ladder was higher than the elves left it for the training of the young ones. She was here. He called up to her eagerly, "Shale, lower the ladder."

There was no answer or sound of movement. Avian began to call again but sensed a presence to his right. He blended into the forest silently. Two of his kinsmen stealthily appeared, arrows ready.

"I know I heard horses before the voice called," said the first.

"I smell them. They are sweaty," his companion agreed.

Avian whistled and revealed himself to them.

"Avian! Welcome! You have been gone far too long," his dark-eyed friend greeted him excitedly.

"It is too long, Jamie. All is well here?"

"Indeed, and better now that you are back. We are in need of a celebration, are we not, Dracy?" Jamie spoke to his companion.

Avian called up into the tree again and received no answer.

"There have been no training sessions this week," Dracy informed him.

"I have sent a friend here," Avian explained.

Quickly, he climbed the tree nearest the Raven Tree and crossed over by its branches. Catching the rope ladder, he pulled it free and raced up to the platform. His eyes grew large as he saw Shale lying with her ankle elevated. He knelt beside her and touched her ankle.

Jerking away, Shale raised her knife, and then fell back with a cry.

"Don't move," he cautioned. "I am sorry." Her ankle felt hot to his touch. It was badly swollen.

She opened her eyes and whispered his name. Her voice was dry and small. Avian lifted her head and gave her a small drink. The liquid was sweet, and she reached for more.

"Wait, not too much. How long have you been here?"

"I do not know," she whispered. "There are eyes in the trees and strange noises."

"Be still. We will get you down."

Avian called down to his kinsmen. Quickly they made a sling to lower her and tossed it up to Avian.

"Shale, eat this. It will give you strength." He gave her another small drink and a piece of bread. She leaned against him and slowly chewed it.

"I am sorry," she murmured.

"For what?" he asked.

"I could not remember the song. I did not know where else to go," she whispered sadly.

"There is no where else to go. You did everything you needed to do," he said reassuringly. He smoothed back her hair. "You are very brave."

She looked up at him. "No more verses?"

"No more verses," he smiled softly and let her head rest against his shoulder.

"Avian, we are ready," Dracy called up to him. They had brought the horses.

"Here, I will help you into this sling and we will lower you. Slowly now. There." He supported her ankle and helped her ease into the sling. She was stronger now, but the effect of the drink would soon wear off.

"How does this work?" Shale asked in a shaky voice.

"Very easily. I will slip you over the side and then lower you down," he explained.

"We are very high up!" Shale gripped the rope tightly.

"Do not look down. Look at me." He continued securing her in the sling.

"I do not like this."

He swung her off the edge gently. Her ankle dropped and she stifled her cry.

"Look up at me. Watch me. Good. You are fine. You are nearly down now."

Eager hands gripped the sling and set her on the ground safely. "Here, my lady, we have you. Rest now. You are safe," Jamie assured her. He looked with alarm at her ankle.

Avian glanced again to where she had tied herself to the tree. She really did not like heights. He took up her pack and rapidly descended.

"Ride on and tell my mother to prepare a healing room. She is in need of secrecy and protection. Do not announce our arrival. I will celebrate with you later," he added lightly.

"I will await you at the gate to the west garden," Jamie called. He turned her reluctant horse into the forest and cantered away.

Avian gave her another drink of the sweet liquid and she drank it eagerly. He took the saddle and reached out for her.

Dracy set her on the horse in front of Avian. They swathed her ankle and secured it to the saddle horn. "Godspeed, my friend," he called. He watched them canter away and set out to continue his watch on the borders of Cambria Forest.

Avian knew each jolt caused her pain, but there was little he could do about it. He slowed the horse to a walk and gave her another sip of the medicine.

"That is good. I want more, please." She reached for the vial again.

"Not yet. It is enough."

"I feel warm all over." She leaned back against him.

Avian held her with his arm around her waist. He let the horse pick its way down the path.

"I think this is very nice," she said, snuggling back against him.

"I think you are very drunk," Avian replied with a smile. "But it is nice," he whispered into her hair.

"I don't like squirrels. I don't like rabbits either," she announced without opening her eyes.

"I love rabbits," Avian answered.

"I love you," she sighed, placing her hand on his arm. They rode a short distance before she spoke again. "Rabbits have lots of babies," she mumbled.

"What did you say?"

"Rabbits have lots of babies," she repeated, leaning her head against his shoulder. "Let's have lots of babies."

"Shh, go to sleep," he whispered.

"My leg hurts."

"I know. It will get better."

"Do bunnies' legs hurt?" she rambled on.

"Yes. Sleep now." Avian listened carefully, but heard no one approaching. He hoped the drink would put her to sleep. *Should I give her more? No, it is too soon.*

"I want more. It tastes very good." She answered his thought.

"Not yet. You must wait."

"Do the bunnies wait?"

"Yes, for a long time. Rest here with me. Sleep now."

"I love you."

He smiled. The horse walked on steadily and Avian relaxed. She was quiet at last.

"I am waiting for the bunnies."

He did not answer her.

"I love you," she murmured.

"I know...shh. Rest now." He began to quietly sing in her ear. Finally, she remained silent.

Avian breathed in the scent of her hair and felt the warmth of her hand on his arm. He longed to hear her laughter and see her eyes sparkle again. She had been so beautiful at Piper's party, trying to find the golden cord. Her cheeks were flushed pink, and then when he had teased her they grew pinker yet. He shifted in the saddle so her head could lean against his.

He loved her. He knew he did. Did she really feel the same, or was she completely overtaken by the medicine? Was it just all they had been through together? Would they both feel the same when life became ordinary again? Would life ever be ordinary with her?

She was so unlike the other elvish maidens he knew. She was free of pretense. She was real and alive, and... hurting. He must not forget. Shale had many things to work through: the loss of her mother, the disappearance of her father, leaving her home, being separated from Samuell and Piper.

He frowned. The council had decided the children of Connor would be safer separated and unidentified. He dreaded telling her. It would break her heart.

He longed to give her joy—to love her as no one else could, to take away her sorrow and see her happy and free again. His arm tightened around her waist. He envisioned running through the woods with her hand held tightly in his own.

"Father God, help me and I will do this for her. I will give her my life."

Chapter 7

Sollen fumed over the lack of information his spies reported. The horse master remained free, and his children had disappeared. It was rumored they were in Pennsyl under the care of Cale. This was no longer true, and no further information was available yet.

"All in good time," he consoled himself. He would continue his plan. The training was going well. His future competitors would be pleased with the progress he was making. Soon the competitions could start. Of course, he would have to provide some training to the opponents, not just their horses, or it would be no challenge at all. He had that yet to plan. Yes, he had time. All the time he needed.

"Sollen, good news!" Bairel called to his younger brother.

Sollen turned and regarded Bairel striding toward him. It must have something to do with the coming festival. Bairel could hardly talk of anything else, and it was still months away.

"Avian is back in Cambria Forest. The competitions will be much more challenging now." Bairel slapped Sollen on the back and went on his way to the practice field.

"Avian," his sister welcomed him warmly as he entered the chamber just off the room where she was caring for Shale.

"How is she today?" Avian asked. He began sorting through the bowl of fruit on the table and chose a yellow apple with a blush of pink on one side.

"She cries in her sleep. She cries for her parents, for her siblings, and for you," Crystal answered. She watched her brother closely for his response.

Avian looked at her sharply. "No one can know of her family."

"I know that, my brother. Why do you think I care for her myself?" Crystal answered defensively.

He shifted uneasily. "I am sorry. I know you and Mother have not left her side."

Crystal sighed. He was so on edge since his return. "She is better, but she still reacts strongly to medicine." She could not resist teasing him.

"Tell me about it." He shook his head.

"She likes rabbits—and then she does not." Crystal giggled at his discomfort. "Come. She is awake and lucid now."

Crystal steered him toward the inner chamber. She detected a slight flush of color on his cheeks.

Crystal opened the door to the healing chamber, and the scent of arnica reached him. He noted the compress draped across Shale's ankle to reduce swelling, and remembered the bouquet of wild daisies Piper had given him on their flight to Pennsyl.

Shale smiled when he entered, bringing a pink glow to her pale cheeks. Her strawberry blonde hair spilled onto the pillows surrounding her.

Avian returned her smile.

"My lady, I bring you a visitor. My brother. See what you can do to improve his humor." Crystal gave Shale an impish grin and left them.

"Crystal is your sister then. She is very kind and a skillful healer, but I fear I am a bother." Shale sighed, then added hopefully, "I hope to be up tomorrow."

"Her knowledge of healing herbs is great. She has insisted that she alone provide your care, though my mother has helped."

"I must thank your mother, too. I do not remember her being with me." Shale frowned. "Thank you for helping me, again." She shifted her ankle on the pillow. "When can I see Samuell and Piper? I long for them."

He saw the gleam of hope sparkle in her eyes. He wished not to tell her, but she had to know. "They are safe, Shale."

"Please bring them to me. I am much better. I do not want to worry them any longer. They will see for themselves that I am well."

If only I could. "I cannot bring them to you."

"Are they hurt?"

"No, they are safe and well." He looked down at the apple in his hand. "I cannot bring them to you because they are not here, Shale. Cameron and Kendra have taken them to the land of Bellflower." His eyes did not leave hers.

"Why? Why are they not here? They need me! I must go to them. You must take me, now." She threw off the coverlet and began scooting to the edge of the bed.

"Wait." He put his hand on her shoulder and tossed the coverlet back across her lap. "You cannot travel now. You must…"

"My Lord, Avian?" A strained voice called from the outer chamber.

Avian put his finger to his lips and strode quickly to the doorway. What stranger would enter a healing room without invitation? "Who enters here unannounced?"

"I come on behalf of my Lady Charleen, my lord." Just inside the entrance of the outer chamber stood a young maid nervously twisting the corner of her scarf.

Avian advanced toward her. "You have entered ill advised. These chambers are for healing only. Your lady's needs can be provided for by others. Depart."

Charleen's maid blushed furiously and bowed. "I was only to make known her arrival to you, my lord." She turned and fled the chambers.

Shale searched Avian's face with alarm.

"It is nothing. A misplaced messenger." He sat down near her.

"There is no news of Piper and Samuell?"

"No. When there is I will tell you immediately."

"Where is this place? This Bellflower? Why are they there?" Shale held the coverlet knotted up in her hands, and scrunched it together.

"The council felt you would all be safer if you were separated. I did not agree, but it is decided. Samuell and Piper will not be separated. They will be under the watchful eyes of the Lord Aaron and the Lady Audrey. There they will grow in knowledge and grace. They will be safe and will learn many things." Avian's eyes did not lie.

Shale stared at him. He made it sound as if they had been given the greatest gift in the world, but what of that if they could not be together? Tears traced little paths down her cheeks.

He wanted to kiss them away.

She wiped at her tears, and drew in a ragged breath. Would this nightmare never end? *What next, Father God? Please be with them, and let me come to them soon.*

"I am sorry, Shale." He touched her hand and she grasped his tightly. Avian's heart melted inside him. He reached out and gathered her into his arms.

She was determined not to cry, but his compassion released her tears of loss and helplessness. "W-Who w-will help Piper go to sleep at n-night?" The sobs shook her and she clung to him.

Avian held her and bowed his head to hers. He had no words to comfort her. *Please help her, Father God.*

What can I do? What can I say to help? He waited until the sobs became little shudders, then leaned over to the bedside table and handed her a soft cloth.

Shale pressed it to her face. She could not stop the trickle of warm tears flowing down her cheeks.

"I am thankful Samuell and Piper are safe." She leaned back against the pillows, exhausted.

"I know."

She drew a deep sigh and handed him the cloth. "I am sorry. I have drowned you." She pointed at his shoulder.

He laughed. "A goal of your family, it seems. At least you have not pushed me into a stream as Piper and Samuell did."

She remembered Piper crowning him with a leaf as he sat in the middle of the stream on their journey to Pennsyl. She could not hold back the tiny smile. *Oh, Piper, I long for you. Are you playing with your rabbits now?*

"What has brought that tiny smile?"

"The warriors of Bellflower will never hunt rabbits again. Piper will tame them all."

Avian grasped quickly at the opportunity to cheer her. "I can see the rabbits following her now. You said that she teaches them to dance?"

Shale nodded. She could see Piper leading the rabbits in a merry dance as if she were their queen. "Maybe she will dress them in little gowns." She managed a small smile.

Avian settled back in his chair. "My sister tells me you like rabbits again." There was a mischievous twinkle in his eyes.

"What?"

"You do not remember what you said to me when we were riding here?" He picked up the apple and passed it back and forth between his hands.

"No, I am sorry. I remember little of that. I remember being so relieved that you were safe, and you had found me. What did I say? Was it important?" Her eyes grew large.

He held her gaze a long time, and then took a small silver knife from its sheath. He sliced the apple and lay half of it on the silver tray beside her. Its sweet scent was tempting and she took a slice. He was avoiding the answer.

"What about rabbits? What did I say?" she persisted. He seemed disappointed that she did not remember.

"Silly things. Probably just dreams you had from the ballad and the medicine I gave you for the pain in your ankle," he replied. He shifted in his chair and took a bite of apple.

"Is it about Piper?"

"No, not at all." He raised his eyes to hers, surprised.

Shale looked down at the apple slice in her hand. She looked up at Avian. "You will take me to them?"

He nodded.

"Soon?"

"When it is safe." He wanted to reassure her, but he did not know when it would be safe.

Shale leaned back against her pillows. She must be patient. "I long to see the woodlands." She sighed and looked up through the high window in the room where the treetops waved in the wind.

"You long to mount your fine mare and flee to your siblings." He shook his apple slice at her. "I said I would take you, and I will."

Shale tilted her head and frowned at him. *Was he scolding her? No, his smile lit his face.* "When may I go outdoors, then? I do miss the flowers and the trees."

Avian opened his mouth to answer, but did not get the chance.

"When I feel you will not harm yourself more by being up," Crystal answered. "I hope it will be soon, Shale. You should rest now. May I give you some tea?"

"I am fine, thank you," Shale answered. She turned her face toward the window. *You cannot give me what I need. I need my family.*

"Come, Avian. You have tormented my patient long enough. She must rest." Crystal started toward the door.

Avian sighed. *If only she knew the truth of her words.* He touched Shale's shoulder and she turned to him.

"Rest well and do not fret. Father God is to be trusted."

Shale nodded and gave him a brave smile.

He could hardly bear the forlorn look in her eyes. He hesitated, then bent and kissed her forehead.

In the outer chamber, Crystal caught his sleeve. "Charleen is here."

"I know." Avian ran his hand across his forehead.

"You know? How?"

"She was rude enough to send her maid in here!" Disgust filled his voice. "What pretense does she use this time?"

"She wishes to learn the healing arts. I have no time for that, and mother is leaving soon. We should put her with the apprentice group and have her gather herbs."

"There will be few fresh ones at this time of year."

"Exactly. She will tire soon and leave. If her interest was sincere and she came at another time, I would try to teach her. It would benefit her to have such knowledge."

Charleen was here only to see Avian and they all knew it.

"That is an acceptable plan under the circumstances, but it will not be needed." The voice was calm and gentle.

In her chamber, Shale turned her head toward the whispers. The voice was familiar to her.

"Mother, I do not know what else to do with her," Crystal anguished. "I think she needs to learn, but not now."

"I have explained to Charleen that it is best to send a messenger first to arrange for such instruction. As she did not do this, she has arrived at a most inopportune time. In three days she will begin her journey home. I have told her that she may seek the opportunity for instruction in the spring. She is most unhappy," Bethany informed her children.

She turned to her son, "Avian, please—at least greet her, before you must leave on whatever errand you dream up this time. We must be polite."

"Very well, Mother, but I will not dance with her."

Whoever Charleen was, she was not welcome. Shale wondered what she was like and pictured the foreman from the farm. A smile played upon her lips at the thought of a grumpy female version of the stout man.

"How is our patient?" Bethany asked.

"I have wounded her heart with the news of her siblings, Mother." Avian turned back toward the chamber.

Bethany laid her hand on his arm. "It cannot be helped, my son. Their safety is vital. In time, she will understand."

Avian nodded and left with their mother. Crystal quietly opened the door and peeked into the healing chamber.

Shale closed her eyes. She wanted time alone to think and pray. *Who would tuck Piper in at night and comb the tangles from her hair? Who would tease Samuell and correct him when he carried his mischief too far? Who would care for them when they were tired and grieved? Who would sing Momma's song?* Tears squeezed out beneath her lashes and rushed down her face. She pulled her pillow closer and cried. *Lord, I do not want to be away from them, not now! Not now! Please help us, Father God.*

Wait.

Wait? For what, Father God? I need to do something now.

Listen and learn and love. Trust me. I love you.

"Momma always said to be grateful," Shale murmured. Taking a deep breath, she began, "I can see the tree tops tossing in the wind. Avian said Samuell and Piper are safe. I do not think he would ever lie to me. Their guardians are kind and skillful. I am well cared for." She sighed wearily and let herself fade into the fuzzy realm of sleep.

A week later the King himself came to visit Shale. Avian had his smile and tall, lithe figure.

Crystal welcomed her father and introduced Shale.

"Welcome to Cambria Forest, my lady. I trust you are feeling better under the watchful eye of my daughter?" His manner and voice were kind and reassuring.

Shale relaxed her grip on the pillow she was holding. "Yes, my lord. Thank you for your kindness to me. Crystal has taken very good care of me, and I am up more each day. I shall not be a burden to you much longer."

"You are hardly a burden. We look forward to guests to brighten our days. We only regret that you have arrived so troubled. I am told that your body is healing well. How is your heart?" The King peered steadily into her eyes.

Startled by the direct question, Shale drew in a slow breath and answered carefully, "I am finding comfort and kindness here, my lord. I hunger only for my family, and then I may be at peace."

"In due time word will arrive, and I will see that you are informed immediately. Tonight, my family and I would have you join us for our evening meal and music.

Are you feeling well enough?" He smiled encouragingly at Shale.

"Yes, my Lord, if it is not too much trouble," Shale answered hopefully. She looked at Crystal.

"Of course we will go. It will do you good to be out of here for awhile." Crystal smiled eagerly.

"I noticed you in the garden with my son yesterday," the king said. He leaned toward her and spoke in a quieter tone. "Although, I hear my daughter was quite upset with her brother." He laughed and stood to leave.

"It was wonderful to be outside among the plants again, my lord. It was very kind of Avian to take me there." Shale looked at Crystal for forgiveness. Avian had snuck her out while Crystal was away.

Before the evening meal, Crystal began fussing over Shale. "Use my barrettes for your hair. I have others. Here is a lovely gown. Let me help you with it. We will have such fun tonight."

"Is it a special celebration? I do not wish to interfere," Shale said. She admired the gown laid out on the foot of her bed and reached out to feel the soft material.

"We are celebrating because you are better, my aunt's time is near for her baby to be born, and we have guests from Robin's Wood, who have come to counsel with my father. Come, let us dress. I long for music and dancing. I wish you could dance, too."

Shale noted the excitement shining in Crystal's eyes and let her assist her with the gown.

"It is beautiful on you. Come, Avian will be here any moment to assist you. I do not want you to put your full weight on your ankle yet."

Avian seated her and sat down across the table from her. A dark-haired elf seated Crystal beside her. He crossed to the opposite side of the table and took his seat across from Crystal, smiling. Shale had never seen anyone look as radiant as Crystal did right then.

When they were all seated and ready to begin their meal, a messenger approached, announcing the arrival of Henicles. Shale looked hopefully at Avian. He gave her an encouraging smile, but his eyes were guarded.

"Bid him come and share our meal," the King answered good-naturedly.

Henicles crossed the room with his blue robe flowing behind him. "Greetings to all. Thank you for welcoming me to your table."

"Henicles, what brings you to me this time? No doubt to assure yourself of the well being of our guest." Corey smiled kindly at Shale.

"Yes, yes, and you are looking well, my dear, especially after your adventures." Henicles's smile was caring, but she needed more from him.

"Is there news of my father? What of Samuell and Piper?" she questioned earnestly.

"We should speak of this later." He glanced about the room taking in the positions of the servants, who disappeared at a nod from the Queen. He cast a troubled look at Avian.

"Is there nothing you can tell us?" Bethany asked. Henicles again glanced about for any who might overhear, then began quietly, "No further news of your father. I have had word that Cameron has taken the others into the wild, for the way was guarded to their destination."

"Into the wild?" Shale spoke with alarm. "Samuell will fare well, and Piper, until it is no longer a game to her."

"I will go and search for them," Avian said. Quickly, he rose from the table.

"I will go with you," Shale announced. She stood up on her strong ankle.

"I can travel faster alone."

"I will not slow you down, even with this ankle. It is much better, and you know I am a good rider," she insisted.

"No. You must stay here."

"I will be safe with you. We must find them, and I am a good tracker."

"I do not doubt that, but you do not know Cameron's signs." Avian voice was firm.

"You can teach me," she challenged him.

"Wait, wait," Henicles counseled. "There are many ways into Bellflower, and Cameron knows them all. Please, sit down, both of you. Besides, they are expected; help will be sent for them. They will arrive safely. We must wait for word." Again he looked about the room.

Shale was not so easily appeased. She leaned over the table toward the wizard. "Who thought it so wise to separate us in the first place, Henicles? Don't you understand?! They need me! I am all they have!" Shale's voice rose in her frustration.

"Shale…" Avian began.

She whipped around to face him. "And you! You helped them! You took me away from them. How can I help them if I am not with them?"

"Peace, child!" Corey spoke with authority.

Frustrated and embarrassed, Shale sat down with flaming cheeks. "Forgive me," she quietly responded.

Looking down at her plate, she sat very still as the conversation began around her. *Henicles was right.* She knew it. It was just so hard. They needed her, and she could not go to them. Fighting back tears, she glanced up briefly and met Avian's gaze. He did not appear to be angry. She looked down at her plate and nibbled a bite of food. In fact, what was that in his expression? Pity? Empathy? Amusement? She glanced up again, only to find him engaged in Henicles's conversation.

When they moved into the courtyard for music and storytelling, Avian assisted her to a seat near the flowers she had enjoyed yesterday. He moved another chair near enough for her to rest her ankle on. Without a word, he smiled and went to join his father and Henicles in private conversation.

They had all been so kind to her, and what did she do? Make outbursts at the table in front of their guest. She wished she could go to her room, away from everyone. Her ankle throbbed with each beat of her heart. No, if she asked to go, then Crystal would leave too. Crystal had been looking forward to this evening's festivities. She would not spoil it for her.

Glancing up, she saw Henicles' kind gaze upon her. He rose and began the evening with a tale of foolishness that soon had everyone laughing. Crystal and her mother settled near her.

Others told tales, and then the songs began. There were jolly ones, ballads, love songs, and sad songs. "Dance Little Rabbit" was sung with great enthusiasm, and Avian watched her singing with it.

Crystal's apprentice brought Shale a cup of herbal tea, and she gratefully accepted it.

Avian left the group of singers and sat beside her. "When your ankle is well enough, I will dance with you," he whispered. Shale looked up at him with questioning eyes.

"The Festival of Golden Leaves comes in four weeks' time. Perhaps then you will feel like dancing with me," Avian informed her.

Shale gave him a sad smile. Why would he want to dance with her, when she had just accused him of trickery in front of his family? "Avian, I must ask your forgiveness for my outburst at the table. I was thoughtless and unkind. I truly am grateful for all you and your family have done." She looked down at the cup in her hand. "It is hard to feel so helpless."

"You are forgiven—and you are not helpless, Shale. You made it to Cambria Forest by your own skill and strength. Your preparation and wood skills amazed me the night we fled your home. You are too hard on yourself."

He paused and lifted her chin. Looking deeply into her eyes, he said, "It is said there is a time for work, a time for rest and healing, a time for forgiving, and a time for dancing." Did she not understand his meaning?

"I want to dance with you, Shale. Not to be kind to a guest, but because I want to be with you."

She stared at him. His large hazel eyes drew her to him. What was he saying?

They were interrupted by Crystal, again. Her cheeks were flushed from dancing, and her hazel eyes shone with excitement. She grabbed her brother's arm with both hands and pulled him toward the singers. "Come on! It is time for the tale of the hunt. You must play your part." Avian protested. Not now. He had just gotten his courage up.

"Watch us, Shale," Crystal cried.

"Go on," Shale urged him. She gave his shoulder a push and laughed. He looked back at her while Crystal dragged him across the floor.

Shale smiled. It was good to see them lighthearted. She sipped her tea. She must ask Crystal how to make it, for it was very soothing. She laughed as Avian acted out the part of the unfortunate hunter who managed to miss each opportunity to impress his companions.

A gentle touch on her shoulder caused her to look away from the actors. Queen Bethany was bending near her.

"I am retiring now, Shale. Tomorrow, I begin my journey to my sister's for the birthing of her child. Perhaps you are ready for rest as well?" Avian's mother spoke quietly. Her warm brown eyes and endearing smile reminded Shale of Avian.

Looking back at the story still being portrayed, Shale hesitated. Avian's eyes met hers and he smiled.

She returned his smile and carefully stood. His smile dimmed, but he nodded in understanding.

Shale graciously accepted the Queen's offer. "Thank you, my lady. Crystal is enjoying herself far too much to be disturbed. If you would only see me to my room, I am sure I can prepare myself for bed."

"Come along then. We will depart, for long will be their merriment tonight. I am pleased with your progress, but we must balance all things." Taking one last look at the others, they slowly made their way inside.

Shale began, "I must ask your forgiveness for my behavior tonight. After all you have done for me I…"

The Queen laid her hand on Shale's arm. Smiling, she replied, "It is already forgotten. Sleep well tonight."

Shale looked up, surprised.

Bethany's eyes were filled with understanding and acceptance.

"I will my lady. May you also be blessed with rest and peace.

Kendra knelt beside Piper. "We are going to play a new game, Piper. We are going to pretend that she is your momma." Kendra smiled encouragingly.

Piper shyly looked at her pretend parent and clung to Samuell's hand.

"Just for awhile, Piper, until Shale and Papa come for us," Samuell said. He did not like this, but he knew they must do it to be safe. He had already questioned Cameron thoroughly regarding his new "parent."

Piper continued staring at Raina with wide green eyes.

Raina did not push the children, but slowly interacted with them and their protectors. Samuell made himself do things with his new "mother," who welcomed his attention and help with the campsite.

Gradually, Raina drew nearer to Piper and asked her to set out the eating utensils. Gentle and empathetic, Raina soon had Piper following closely beside her. Raina had no children of her own and welcomed this time with Samuell and Piper. By bedtime Piper had climbed into Raina's lap for singing.

Samuell watched cautiously. He would never let anyone hurt Piper. He sensed no deceit in them. Cameron said that Lord Aaron and the Lady Audrey had selected Raina to act as their parent. He knew they were very wise, and he chose to trust their judgment. Still, he would be on his guard.

After a few days together in the forest, Cameron and Kendra continued on the journey to Bellflower. Samuell and Piper would come a few days later with Raina.

Arriving in Bellflower went well, for it was abuzz with the excitement that the Lady Kendra had returned. The new little family settled into their home with little notice.

Samuell sighed. Everyone accepted them as a family, but then—why would they not? He must remember to remind Piper to keep playing the game.

After a month of travel and eluding his pursuers, Connor was finally nearing Pennsyl. About midday, he heard a group of travelers to his left and carefully moved nearer to listen for information.

"There has been trouble in Pennsyl," one spoke up.

"Pennsyl! What trouble?" asked his companion.

"Someone tried to attack Lord Cale. He was armed with a knife. A maiden rode her horse between them and would not let him near Lord Cale. He had lied about whom he was, to try to get close to Lord Cale. The maiden recognized him as an imposter."

"Who did he say he was?"

"They are not saying, but I heard he is a horse master."

"From where?" his companion asked.

"It is not known."

"Tell me more about this brave maiden," the companion queried.

"She was brave, indeed, to enter the greeting field unbidden." The elf shook his head and continued. "They say she was an excellent rider. She and the horse moved as one. Look! There is the song master. Come, I must speak with him about my daughter's wedding."

At this news, Connor's heart was filled with both pride and alarm. What treachery was afoot that someone would attack Lord Cale in Pennsyl? His children. They were after his children.

He ran on. By nightfall he was within one day's journey of Pennsyl. Tomorrow he would see a friend, the berry grower who made fine wine for Pennsyl. Perhaps he would take a message to Lord Cale to arrange a meeting with him. Connor knew he could not enter Pennsyl as a normal traveler because of those who sought his children.

Three days later, Connor waited in the quiet of early dawn for the berry grower to escort him to see Lord Cale. They entered the side door and followed the hallway through the wine cellar, then up a flight of stairs to an outer courtyard. Cale awaited him.

"Connor, it is truly you. Welcome." Cale greeted him and placed his hand on Connor's shoulder.

"Thank you, my lord. It is good to see you again. Much time has passed," Connor answered, returning Cale's sign of friendship.

Cale observed Connor's fatigue, accentuated by grief and worry. "Let us sit here and take counsel together." He indicated a small table set with fresh fruits and breads.

Connor did not move. He wanted so much to ask about his children, but this issue must be addressed first. "I wish you well, my lord, and I loyally offer you my service. I do not want my loyalty to you questioned. I heard you were nearly attacked."

"I do not question your loyalty," Cale assured him. He gestured toward the table. "The circumstances of your coming, however, do greatly concern me. Where did you receive this news?"

Sitting down, Connor replied, "A party of travelers four days ago passed me in the woods. Some were very talkative."

"We have made the right decision then." Cale spoke more to himself than to Connor. He looked with care into Connor's eyes. "You are wondering about your children."

Connor answered anxiously, "Greatly, my lord. Are they safe? Are they here? I would see them."

Leaning toward him, Cale quietly said, "They are safely away from here. After the attacker came, we feared for their safety here. I have sent them away. They are wonderful children, Connor. I am grieved at the loss of your wife. Shayna was a joy to all who met her."

Connor nodded and sighed deeply. He had so longed to see his children. Better that they were safe. "Thank you, Lord Cale, for protecting them. May I go to them?"

"Do you think that wise? Are you followed? I need you here, Connor. We must take counsel with Henicles and Cameron. There is much evil at work in this. I fear it may run deeply among the elves. I will send word to your children that you are safe. It will bring them joy and comfort."

A long week had passed slowly for Shale. She looked up from stitching the new pattern Crystal had taught her, as Crystal burst into the room.

"Shale, there is news! Your brother and sister have safely arrived at their destination." Crystal embraced her. "Our prayers are answered. Avian will tell you more later, but he bid me give you this news."

Shale nearly collapsed in Crystal's arms. "Thank you, Father God. Thank you!"

Shale waited in the courtyard that afternoon for Avian to come to her. She stood and gingerly took slow dance steps to the wall and back. Feeling someone watching, she turned around.

Henicles clapped his hands quietly for her and joined her on the stone bench adorned with flowers." You are as graceful as ever," he remarked." I am proud of you Shale." She looked at him questioningly.

"You are making the most of a very trying time. Most of us are good givers, helpers to others. It is much harder to be a good receiver of others' gifts. Think of what joy you have received when helping someone, such as an old wizard who visited your family one cold night. You loosened my shoes and brought me warmed cloths to wrap my feet in. Do you remember that from many years ago?"

She nodded, remembering the visits Henicles had made to their home.

"Now you are the receiver for a time, as we all must be. You will give again. Learn everything you can while you are here. King Corey and his people can teach you many things," Henicles counseled. "Time well spent is never wasted. We must trust, Shale. Trust and hope. Do not despair."

Stretching his long legs, he continued. "Grief is a process, my dear, a very strenuous process. It is as exhausting as working all day digging hard dirt. You now find yourself with time to think through your losses. Let yourself express the feelings and emotions you are experiencing. In time you will be able to face the realities and become involved with life again."

"It is often a back and forth experience, somewhat like a dance. One step forward and two steps back. You have been taking small steps forward. Do not be dismayed when backward steps come. It is all a part of your grief journey. Take time now for the healing of your heart." The old wizard reached out and put his gnarly arms around her, as her eyes filled with tears.

When she quieted he added, "Crystal is happy for your friendship. She does not care for the foolish attitudes of some of the young elf maidens at court, who think more of their attire than others' cares and concerns."

"What do you mean by 'at court', Henicles," Shale asked.

"Ask Crystal that question. You will see soon enough. I will advise you with these words, though. Hold true to what is precious to you, Shale. Fear not what others might say or believe. Continue to keep your identity secret. It is vitally important." Patting her hand, he looked up. "Ah, hear comes Avian now. You have been waiting for him, have you not?" Henicles's eyes twinkled at her. He greeted Avian heartily and left them.

"You have been visiting with Henicles, then?" Avian asked, smiling.

"Yes, he is a wise and dear friend, but he did not tell me what I most want to hear." Reaching out she took his hand. "Avian, please, tell me of Piper and Samuell."

Pleased by the excitement shining in her eyes and the spontaneity with which she grasped his hand, Avian sat with her in the healing warmth of the afternoon sunshine.

Smiling into her upturned face, he began, "As you might expect, Piper is charming everyone she meets and befriending all the woodland creatures. Samuell is often seen in deep conversation with Lord Aaron. For now he must hold back his questions for the horse masters. I believe his archery skills continue to improve as well. I will challenge him to a match when next we meet." Avian's eyes glowed with anticipation.

Shale thought surely it would not be long until she would see them again.

He paused, studying her hopeful face. "To protect them, Shale, they are living as someone else's children. They are bonding well with their new parent. They are brave children, Shale. They send their love and miss you very much. I will take you to them as soon as it is safe enough."

"That will not be soon, though, will it?" Her eyes sought his, already knowing the answer. "I feel so empty without them, Avian. I miss hugging Piper and brushing her hair. I miss Samuell's quiet strength and humor. You have not seen his humorous side, have you?" Shale asked as she brushed away a tear.

"At times I have seen that, Shale. He can be very clever." Avian laughed at her questioning look and held up his hands in defense. "Do not ask me about that. I cannot tell you. Now, a little bird tells me you have been practicing your dancing. Come, will you practice with me?"

His eyes held so much mischief she could not help but smile up at him. Still she said, "And why would you wish to dance with a grouch such as me?"

"I see no grouch today. If she appears, I shall duck and run. I believe I am still faster than she." Becoming serious he continued, "I wish you had shared your worries, Shale. Burdens are more easily borne when shared with ones we can trust. You can trust me."

"I know," she interrupted him. Already she was fighting back her tears. She quickly stood and, because of her haste, teetered slightly.

Steadying her, Avian asked, "Which dance shall we start with?"

She crinkled her nose at him and began humming a merry tune. They began the steps of her favorite dance. Avian supported her with his strong arm around her waist. They smiled and talked as they moved about the courtyard.

Henicles watched from the corner of the garden. Considering all things, Connor's children were adjusting well. Still, his forehead creased with concern as he watched the two dancing across the garden. At any other time he would be pleased to see them so. Now danger was still near at hand, and he was not so sure. Turning, he went on his way to consult with Corey.

Chapter 8

"Shale, try on these gowns with me," Crystal called, entering with her arms full of gowns. "They are for the festival. I am so glad you will be there. It will be so much fun with you there."

"Was it not fun before?" Shale asked.

"Oh, parts of it were. I love watching the competitions. Avian will be in the archery and knife throw again this year. Those are my favorites," she enthused. "I love the gowns and the flowers and seeing my family." She laid the gowns out neatly on the bed.

"What part was not fun?" Shale persisted. "I want to know, Crystal."

Crystal stared at her new friend for a moment. "It is just that some of the maidens act so foolishly, and sometimes just so mean to others." She plopped down on the bed and fingered the sheer sleeve of the pale blue gown beside her.

"Why would they behave so?" Shale asked with concern. Her friend wore a hurt expression on her pretty face.

Crystal stood up and dramatically slunk across the floor fluffing her hair. "They are seeking husbands of stature and status and have their own competition. I do not join their foolishness. If I marry, I will marry someone I love, whose heart is true. It is sickening to watch them. Avian would dance with each one and then escape to some duty he would think of. That would make some of them angry."

She flounced back onto the bed and grinned at Shale. "This year I hope he only dances with you. Oh, but I am being spiteful now. Come, let us forget that and try on these gowns. I want to see you in this one." She held up a dainty white gown with lace trimming the long sheer sleeves.

Shale stood and let Crystal slip the soft gown over her head. It felt so feminine. She remembered the many times she had worn the clothes like the stable hands had worn at home. She was again aware of how very much Crystal and her family had given her. How could anyone treat Crystal unkindly?

"Turn around and let me see," Crystal cried. "It is beautiful, Shale." She picked up the blue gown and let it slide over her. Grabbing Shale's hand, Crystal cried, "Let's show my mother!" Giggling, the two hurried down the long hallway in search of the Queen.

The day for the beginning of the Festival of Golden Leaves arrived with a flurry of activities greater than the day before. Shale had never seen such hurried activity, with maids rushing here and there, directing the arrivals to their respective quarters. Shale was impressed with the calm demeanors of Crystal and her mother as they greeted their guests and saw to their needs.

Early in the afternoon, Crystal and Shale moved from chamber to chamber, seeing that the guests were well cared for and had received everything they needed to make their stay pleasant and comfortable.

Shale began to see first hand how demanding some of the elven maidens could be. Crystal remained calm and smiling, gently assuring them all would be well and seeing that the maids of her court fulfilled their requests.

They entered one of the larger chambers, where a very tall maiden was being attended to by her many maids. Beside her a shorter maiden with auburn hair was having her hair combed out. "Greetings, Charleen," Crystal said warmly. "And Muriel, how wonderful you could join us this year. I am pleased that both of you have arrived safely to celebrate with us."

Turning to Shale, Crystal continued, "Next year the festival will be held at Robin's Wood, Charleen's home. Smiling at Charleen, Crystal introduced Shale, "This is Shale, my dear friend."

Charleen briefly regarded Shale as if she were acknowledging a bug.

Muriel gushed, "We are greatly pleased to join you and your family. I trust all of your family will be here to celebrate this year. I am eager to see them." She smiled waiting expectantly for Crystal's response.

"Yes, we are all here. My aunt's birthing went well, thank you," Crystal replied sweetly. She blinked at Shale, knowing full well that Muriel had asked only to see if Avian would be attending.

"Do you have need of anything at this time?" Crystal asked, looking about the room and meeting Charleen's eyes, thus cutting off further questions from Muriel.

Charleen responded with an arrogant toss of her pretty head. "Greetings to you, Crystal. Thank you for your kindness in asking. As you can see, we have many maids and will require more linens and another mirror."

"I will see that you are provided with more linen. As for another mirror, they are all in use. Did you not bring enough for your extra maids?" Crystal answered, glancing at the three mirrors already arranged at their table.

"It is you who must do the providing this year, Crystal, daughter of Corey," Charleen shot back coldly.

"Indeed, and we shall see to that now. Are there further needs?" Crystal asked, looking at Muriel, who shook her head no.

"Not at this time," Charleen answered for her cousin.

"Very well. May your rest be peaceful before our celebration of thanksgiving begins." Crystal smiled and led Shale from the chambers.

She said nothing about the exchange, but continued down the hallway where she spoke to a very busy maid concerning linens for Charleen's chamber. The maid rolled her eyes and smiled at Crystal, who was called to attend to the matter of some late arrivals.

"Let me take them for you. You are very busy," Shale offered.

"Oh, no, my lady. You must rest your ankle. I will do it." The maid squared her shoulders and stared at the doorway down the hall.

"I don't mind, really. I am waiting for Crystal." Shale reached out to take the linens from her. "Let me. It will only take a moment," Shale persuaded her.

Taking the linens, Shale walked back toward the chamber, glad she could lighten the maid's load. As she entered their chamber, Shale was appalled to hear the two maidens speaking unkindly of Crystal.

"She is so unfair, but I must be nice to her, for Avian is her brother," Muriel was saying.

Charleen's stony glare silenced her cousin. With a haughty voice she replied, "Crystal deprives us intentionally, for she is jealous. This whole place is disgusting and she…"

Shale gasped. How could they say such things?

Charleen turned and stared coldly at Shale.

Gripping the linens firmly in her arms, Shale spoke, "How can you say that? Crystal is kind and generous. You have more items in this room now than any others do. I have observed this, and I know it to be true. You are most unkind to accuse Crystal of unfairness. She is my friend and is very caring. You should not speak this way about her."

"Who are you?" Charleen regarded her with narrowed, flashing eyes. "I will not be corrected by a maid. What is your name?"

"I was introduced to you moments ago. I am a friend of Crystal and her family. I have brought your linens out of kindness, so you would not need to wait. Be thankful for your hosts. They are gracious." Cheeks flaming, Shale held her ground.

"And who are you to speak to me in this manner?" Charleen demanded again.

"She is a guest of my family and is serving my guests to honor and assist me, Charleen, daughter of Corsac. I see that your room is well prepared with all the necessary items. Perhaps some forethought on your part would have been helpful to you." Queen Bethany's stern gaze was uncompromising. "What further needs do you have?"

A grim faced woman hurried into the chamber. "Charleen, let us finish unpacking your things, to be sure you do not already have what you are requesting." If her daughter sought to marry Avian, she must not be offensive to his mother. She rushed on, "Thank you, Queen Bethany. Your graciousness is greatly appreciated."

Bowing slightly to Bethany, she turned to her daughter. "Come, my daughter. Let us prepare for the banquet." She hurried Charleen further into her chambers.

Bethany nodded to the pair. Turning toward Shale and the maid who had joined them, she spoke quietly, "Come with me, please. My gracious maid will deliver the linens to the appropriate chambers. Won't you?

Thank you." She bestowed the slight maid with a sweet smile.

"Yes, my Queen." The wide eyed maid looked respectfully at her Queen and hurried down the hall.

They turned and walked together down the long hallway. When they had entered the family's private area Bethany spoke. "You handled the matter fairly, Shale. Charleen is a trial to all she meets. I must ask you to avoid her completely during the rest of the festival. She can be very spiteful and, as we must remember, we do not want to draw undue attention to you."

Sitting, she patted the ornate bench beside her, and Shale sat next to her. "I want you to enjoy this time, but do be on your guard. You will be introduced as a visiting friend of our family, which you most certainly are. Stay with Crystal or Avian or myself. We will help you, and more importantly, we enjoy your company, my dear." She smiled brightly and patted Shale's hand.

At the look of discomfort on Shale's flushed face, Bethany spoke again, "Be at peace. You have done nothing wrong. It is only for your protection and happiness that I am concerned."

"I ask your pardon, my lady, and I thank you for your concern and kindness..." Shale hesitated, searching for the right words.

Bethany smiled patiently at her.

Crystal entered the room, and her face lit up. "Shale—there you are! I have been looking for you. Come. I have thought of a different way to wear our hair this night. Come, Mother, help us." She pulled her hair up and twisted it to show them her idea.

From the garden entrance Avian entered, holding his head in both hands. "Oh, my aching head," he moaned as he approached them. "Even in my own home there is the constant chattering of maidens."

Crystal stooped and pulled a pillow from the bench. She threw it at him and pulled Shale along with her to her chambers.

Bethany laughed and bid her son sit with her.

Avian kissed her forehead and sat beside her. "How are you this busy day, my mother?"

"Well, my son. It is good to see your sister so happy." She reached out to take his hand.

Smiling he nodded. "I would like you to make me happy as well."

"And what do you need, my son?" Bethany looked steadily at him, wondering what he was up to this time. "You hardly look forlorn. Would you have me make coverings to stop the chattering from entering your ears?"

"Would you?" he begged in mock desperation. Becoming more serious he continued, "It is nothing so difficult, my mother."

"Then what is your request?" she asked again.

"I wish to escort Shale during the festival. Since she is under the protection of our family, I accept this responsibility. Will you grant me this?" He waited for her response with eager eyes.

Bethany considered this. She also wished it, but perhaps for different reasons. Cautiously she answered, "I was thinking the same, Avian. I am glad it will not be a burden to you, especially since the circumstances are as they are."

Avian's brow creased in a frown. "What do you mean?"

Bethany became more serious, "Shale has already drawn undue attention to herself. She has not found favor with Charleen."

"Who could?" Avian burst out.

Bethany continued, "Shale has done so by defending your sister against Charleen's ravings. We must work hard to keep her safe. I have told Shale that she must stay with you or Crystal or me during the festival."

"Be at peace, my mother. It is done for you already. Crystal and I will take care of her. Thank you." He kissed her forehead again and left with a light step.

Bethany pondered her son's eagerness to escort Shale. She remembered watching them practicing the various dances together. She thought of the expressions on their faces. Would being with Avian only draw more unwanted attention to Shale? She had not had the heart to hide the maiden in her room throughout the festival. All of them would be disappointed.

Bethany could imagine the glow on Shale's face when she saw the great hall decorated with the splendors the forest offered. Boughs of pine, myrtle, ivies, and bouquets of assorted flowers would not only adorn, but fragrance the hall. Gold and silver ribbons, ornamentations, and sashes with brilliant colors would be added to further beautify this place of gathering.

The finery of the elves themselves would be breathtaking. The graceful movements of the dancers would bring a kaleidoscope of color!

Seeing her would be like watching a child discovering the beauty of the gardens. Yet, Shale's safety was most important. She must seek the wisdom of her husband.

In their chambers, prior to the feast that would begin the celebration that evening, Bethany explained her concerns to Corey. "I fear with our son at her side she will be noticed even more. If we hide her, she will be disappointed, as will our children. I know her safety must come first. What are your thoughts, my husband?"

Corey considered these things while Bethany finished preparing herself for their appearance at the feast. "I believe she is safe here. Avian is often called upon to escort our guests. It is nothing unusual."

"Yes, but not as willingly as this time. He himself asked my consent to escort her. Do you remember watching them dance together in the evenings? Have you not seen how they look at one another? This is my concern," Bethany added.

"Yes, I see," Corey said slowly, "but it is a merry time for all, and she is so quiet. We often have guests, my love. Come, do not worry yourself." He gave his wife a knowing look and said, "Our son is very adept at politely turning away those to whom he does not wish to speak." He took her two hands in his. "Come, let us enjoy the feast this night."

The next day dawned clear and bright—a perfect day for the archers to show off their skills. Crystal and

Shale hurried to the competitions, laughing as they went. The conflict of the day before was forgotten. Instead of sitting on the platform with the family, they hurried to find a spot near the archers so they could cheer for Avian and the other Cambria Forest archers.

Already many had gathered, and the archers were taking their practice shots. The sharp twang of bowstrings and whoosh of arrows filled the air. Avian joked with his teammates. He cast a glance about the field and smiled warmly when he saw them. He drew back his arrow for a shot. Just as he released it, the dark-haired friend beside him nudged his arm, and his shot went wide. They laughed merrily together.

The competition began with the younger archers. Shale watched carefully to test in her mind the skill of the competitors against her brother.

So intent was she that she jumped when Avian whispered in her ear a reflection of her own thoughts. "Samuell would do well in this event. He is especially skilled in distance shooting."

"I was thinking the same, except for the one who just shot. He was very skillful." Shale smiled up at him. "I am confident you will do well today."

"Thank you. Come with me for refreshment," Avian invited. "I am thirsty and my events will not be for awhile."

"Which events are you in?" Shale asked as they walked.

"In archery there are distance and moving target, then knife throwing. Not so much this year. I want to have time for other things today." He smiled down at her and offered her a cup of sweet, cool juice. They moved to the edge of the crowd around the refreshments.

"Where do all of these elves come from? There are so many," Shale asked in amazement.

"Not so many as usual," he answered thoughtfully. He had forgotten again that she had not been raised among her own kind. "Some are from Pennsyl, some from Robin's Wood near the river, and some from over the mountain way." He hesitated, then said, "Crystal tells me that you met Charleen." He studied her reaction.

She looked at him and then away, "Oh, yes, we met."

"She is very demanding, Shale. She has no sway here, none over me, or you or Crystal. Do not let her trouble you." He took her hand protectively.

"Avian, come," called Dracy, his friend. "It is nearly time. Leave the maidens alone for a while. They will weary of you soon enough tonight," he grinned at Shale and left.

Avian started after him, still holding Shale's hand.

"Avian, please go ahead. I cannot walk so fast yet. Hurry, you must not be late," Shale urged him.

Squeezing her hand, he slowed his pace. "We have time. I am sorry. I forgot." Smiling into her eyes as they walked, he said, "I want you with me today. I will find you before the meal."

A soft blush covered Shale's cheeks as she clung tightly to his hand and quickened her pace for him.

Crystal smiled warmly and cheered her brother as he entered the contest. She cast Shale an amused smile. "You are glowing, Shale."

Shale's blush deepened. They both burst out in cheers as the event began. Avian won easily at distance shooting. A dark-haired elf tied with him and won the match off during the moving target event. Avian congratulated him heartily.

Shale turned to Crystal. "Who is the one who defeated Avian?" she asked. Crystal did not answer. She was blushing herself as the two competitors approached them, smiling warmly.

"Orrie, may I present the Lady Shale," Avian said, introducing them.

"I am honored to meet you," Orrie replied kindly. His eyes turned back to Crystal.

"He is from Robin's Wood and has requested to join my sister for lunch." In a slightly lower voice to Shale he added, "Poor soul."

"Avian!" Shale exclaimed.

"What did you say?" Crystal demanded.

"That we must join the banquet ahead of you two or there would not be any food left to choose from," Avian answered. He took Shale's hand and led them toward the Second Hall. Their approach led them into contact with Charleen and her maidens.

Charleen smiled enticingly at Avian and offered him her hand. Avian took her hand politely and bowed over it. He took Muriel's in the same manner.

"Good day to you, Charleen and Muriel," he said and nodded politely to their maids. Charleen's eyes narrowed. He did not kiss her hand as she anticipated. He treated her no differently than Muriel. "Lord Avian," she spoke, "your performance was outstanding at the archery contest. Your aim is true." She lifted her light eyebrows and smiled again.

Avian took Shale's hand securely in his own and acknowledged her, "Thank you. I believe you have met the Lady Shale and our friend, Orrie. We bid you good day."

Shale smiled kindly, but she and Crystal were ignored. Avian squeezed her hand and they went on.

Avian and Orrie carried their lunches to a bright meadow near the competition fields. Crystal and Shale walked beside them with goblets of cool juices. Avian nodded and smiled at those who invited them to join their party, but selected a place near the edge of the meadow where a tall oak offered them shade.

Orrie and Avian were in merry moods. They told tales of past competitions and funny stories of today's events. They could hardly eat the delicious food for laughing. Shale was pleased to see Crystal enjoying herself.

Orrie stood and led Crystal toward a patch of yellow flowers a short distance away. He bent down and began to pick them, along with the shorter white ones growing beside them.

Avian spoke loudly enough for them to hear. "Do not fret, Shale. He knows who won the distance shooting today."

Crystal glared at her brother. Orrie took her hand and they walked on through the flowers.

Avian settled back against the tree, pleased he had succeeded in drawing attention away from himself and placing it on his sister. Golden leaves floated to the ground and landed on the thick grass of the meadow. He watched them with Shale, then turned to her. "Tell me, where are your thoughts?" A note of concern touched his voice.

She smiled sweetly, "My thoughts are here. How beautiful this day is, how blessed I feel to be here with you." She leaned her head on his shoulder and looked up to watch another golden leaf glide leisurely to the ground.

Laughter erupted to their right and Shale straightened quickly, conscious of the others enjoying their meals in the meadow. "I am very thankful to have Crystal as my friend, too," she added quickly, glancing in their direction. "She is so happy today."

Avian took her hands. His eyes were intense and shining with emotion. "Are you happy today?" he asked.

She returned the intensity of his look. They both jumped as a long horn trumpeted out the call to begin the afternoon events. From the flower patch they heard quiet laughter.

Flustered, Avian frowned. "Knife throwing is first."

"You must go then. Go and win," Shale urged. Her cheeks were bright with color and her green eyes glowed.

"Kiss me for luck?" Avian asked and kissed her before she could answer. He sprang up and was gone.

Quickly rising, Shale began gathering their things. She could still feel the warmth of his lips on hers.

Crystal joined her and they smiled shyly at each other. They hurried to finish and rushed down the slope to the event. Orrie was also entered.

The competition was fierce, as both teams were quite skillful. Shale was amazed at the accuracy of the competitors. Throw after throw landed fully in the center of the target. She gasped when Avian's throw split the handle of the competitor's knife. It had still been quivering where it was stuck in the thick wood.

In the end, Dracy and Jamie had both scored highly to settle the contest. The Cambria Forest team maintained their title for another year. Orrie greeted Crystal and Shale, and they waited for Avian to join them.

Celebrating a hard won victory, the Cambria Forest team was jubilant. Avian placed his hands on the shoulders of Dracy and Jamie and congratulated them. He grinned over at Shale and waved for her to join him.

"Go ahead," Crystal urged. "We will walk with you."

Shale looked at the happy pair. "I will be fine. You two go on. I will come with Avian." Carefully she began moving through the crowd toward the celebration. Her ankle felt a bit shaky. She should not have hurried down the slope.

"Wait a moment, fair maid," a strange voice called out from behind her. "Wait, a moment." Someone took her arm in a firm grip.

Turning, she looked into the face of one of the competitors on Orrie's team, and with him was Charleen.

"I have not seen you here before," the tall elf said. "I was wishing to meet you. My sister said that she met you yesterday." His gaze was not unkind. A touch of amusement danced in his eyes.

"Greetings," Charleen began smugly. "My brother wanted to meet you and I saw no harm in it, being you are..."

"Being she is a guest of my family," Avian cut in, calmly staring her down. "Greetings, Baierl. Great were your skills today. I must practice more before next year, or we may not retain our title."

"It was a fierce competition today, no doubt, Avian. Will you not introduce me to this fair maiden?" Baierl requested.

Avian smiled down at Shale and took her hand. "This is the Lady Shale, a guest of my family," he emphasized. "We beg your pardon. My mother awaits us for tea, and we would not disappoint her. Please enjoy the hospitality my father has provided for you." He turned to leave.

"I hope, Lady Shale, that you will save a dance for me this night," Baierl persisted. He bowed slightly.

"Her time is taken," Avian countered. "Good day."

Sollen watched his older brother fail in his attempt to take the interest of the unknown maiden and apply it to himself, thus leaving Avian alone for his sister's ploys. Sollen's temper simmered beneath his smile. It would suit his purpose well in the future if his sister succeeded in infiltrating the family of Corey. Working through her, he could gain more power.

He turned away from his siblings in disgust. His brothers were fools. Baierl was lazy and content to seek his own small pleasures. He had no ambition for the throne. Instead, he delighted in hunting and music. Arrogant, capable, skilled in many ways, Baierl was interested only in pursuing what gave him renown and pleasure at the moment. He lacked vision. He was pathetic. His younger brothers would be no problem. They were enamored of horses and hung on every word he spoke. When the time came, they would follow him.

He turned away from the group and trained his eyes on the layout of Corey's kingdom. Located on the river, Corey's people benefited greatly from trade and transport. Yes, somehow he would access this kingdom. It would benefit him when he took over his father's throne.

His father. For years now he had been planting seeds of doubt concerning his father's abilities to rule among the warriors and counselors in his own kingdom. Today when opportunities availed themselves to him, he did the same with Elves of other kingdoms. It would be easy to use this subtle approach against King Corey as well, especially if his sister were to marry Avian. She would be a controlling wife, as was their mother.

Sollen's eyes darkened. No woman would control him. Although he often benefited greatly from his mother's manipulations, Sollen hated her. She whined and complained constantly. How his father stood it, he did not know. He grunted in disgust. His father had grown complacent these many years of peace. He did not desire to expand his kingdom, to use his power.

But Sollen knew he must bide his time. His delight in the ritual of Presage, known by his grandfather and practiced by his great-grandfather, helped him endure this waiting. He relished it. Using it, he increased his skills of war, sharpening his senses until he could nearly hear the heartbeat of his opponent. It gave him power over those around him.

This was his greatest desire: power and control. No one would stand in his way. No one. He would see to that. At the call of his name, Sollen turned and entered the good-natured bantering of those about him.

Bethany had chosen to entertain only her family at the tea this year. They needed this time together. It seemed to her that their gatherings had grown further and further apart. She loved spending time with her siblings and their families. Conversation settled around their families and the day's events.

Avian sat near Shale, and often she turned to meet his warm hazel eyes and share a smile. She felt awkward at times, listening to his family share their stories and jokes. It was difficult not to join in with stories of her own family.

Avian laughed, and Shale turned to him. She loved his laugh. It was like a clear trumpet blending its sound through the forest. Her heart felt as light as the leaves they had watched gliding to the ground in the meadow today. It was good to see him at ease and laughing with his family. For so much of their travel he had been on guard and distant.

Shale looked down at her hands folded in her lap. She longed to hear Piper's laughter mingled with the other children's. Samuell would be enjoying the stories they were sharing. She must guard her thoughts. Thinking too much about her family today would be difficult to handle.

She turned her attention to Avian's aunt. The mother of the new baby sat easily, supporting the baby on her lap so she could look out at her admiring relatives. The child was beautiful, with round blue eyes the color of the sky. Soft blonde hair lay sparsely over her head.

Her mother smiled at Shale and began sharing a funny story about Avian as a child. He protested loudly, which only increased the laughter on his behalf. Shale relaxed and enjoyed their fellowship.

The tea party drew to a close, as mothers gathered their children for rest before the evening's festivities. Many of the young couples wandered through the fragrant gardens, hand in hand.

Avian seated Shale on a bench by the lush ferns. "I notice that you are favoring your ankle. How is it?" he asked concerned.

"It is stiff from sitting. I am fine really," she assured him. "I enjoyed being with your family."

"It is good to be with them. We do not see each other as often as we would like, yet when we are together it is as though we have never been apart." He reached up and tenderly brushed back a loose lock of her hair.

"You are missing your family today," he said with compassion. "I am sorry that you are not able to be with them." He sat down beside her.

Shale's eyes filled with tears and she looked away from him for a moment. Then she said, "Tell me, what is the name of that fern?"

This was a game she had played with Piper on the long journey when Piper grew restless. He did not answer until she looked at him. He smiled into her eyes and answered, "It is the red fern of Orion."

"It is not," Crystal interrupted them. "You know that, Avian."

Avian cast a disappointed look at his sister. "I suppose you are here to tell us that it is time to prepare for the banquet." He stood and looked at Orrie. "Come, we must allow them to make themselves even more beautiful and mysterious."

Avian shook his head with disappointment.

As they left to prepare for the banquet and evening festivities, Crystal talked excitedly about their hair and gowns. She was looking forward to sharing the festivities with Orrie. Shale cast a longing look back at Avian.

While Crystal pinned colorful flowers and ribbons in her hair, Shale's thoughts turned to him again. Tonight he would be her escort. She was honored, thrilled to be with him, and at the same time terrified of embarrassing him. *If only we could just go riding together instead,* she thought.

"I will return quickly and we will go," Crystal called. She hurried to her chambers.

Shale took a deep breath and gazed at herself in the mirror. Was that really her? Her hair had grown quickly with the tender care she had received. It was still much shorter than the other maidens, but styled this way it was not noticeable.

"Father God, I am very thankful for the things my parents and Avian's family have taught me. Please help me to honor them," Shale quietly prayed.

Crystal burst back into the room wearing a lovely jeweled necklace. "Come, let us go. You look lovely." She took her friend's hand and drew her down the hall to the family courtyard.

Bethany took in their excited voices. She was pleased with their friendship. They related well with each other. Crystal had few close friendships, for she had learned that others would try to use her position to their advantage and not be true friends. Shale had revealed no such intentions.

To her husband Bethany remarked, "I really believe Shale is fresh and innocent of the devices endured among the courts of the elves. She and Crystal are good for each other."

"Not all behave in such manners, it is true. I tire of it myself." He looked at his wife's patient face. "You have done a remarkable job of raising our children, my love. They are true hearted and strong," he replied. "Let us enjoy this night, and not be drawn into it ourselves."

Avian approached the courtyard quietly. He paused near the entryway and observed his family. Crystal and Shale were happily chatting and adjusting the flowers in Crystal's hair while his mother advised them. She bid them sit with her, and Avian realized she was gently advising Shale of royal party etiquette. Crystal mimicked behaviors in a ridiculous manner.

He could not resist joining in. Grinning and posturing arrogantly, he approached the ladies, plying them with requests for their attentions.

Crystal and her mother easily rebuffed him, and Shale, having observed their responses, did the same. In merry moods they left together for the banquet.

As they entered the Great Hall, Shale gasped in delight. Alive with light and color, bathed in the fragrance of pines and flowers, the Great Hall was a tunnel of rainbows splashed with the twinkling light of the very stars themselves. No, it was even more. She could not describe it.

Avian squeezed her hand, and she looked up into his glowing face. The warmth of his smile brought joy to her heart, and she felt her cheeks grow warm.

He seated her at a table with Orrie and Crystal, and sat beside her, enjoying her amazement. He glanced at his mother and received her radiant smile. She had been anticipating this moment when Shale would see the beauty of the elves.

Shale turned to him. "Avian, help me remember so I may tell Piper everything!" Her sparkling green eyes glowed with wonder. She was like a small child herself, taking delight in the newness of the world. He could not take his eyes off of her.

Now that the royal families were all seated, the banquet began. Shale watched carefully as Crystal began eating and did not notice any changes in the etiquette she knew. She relaxed in her seat and passed a basket of pastries to Avian. The meal was delicious.

A merry tune and cries of delight led to the movement of many dancers to the center of the Great Hall. Shale began to rise, but settled back in her chair at the touch of Avian's warm hand on her arm.

"We will wait until the crowd has thinned a little. There will be many dances yet this night," he assured her.

Shale settled nearer to him and watched the swirling dancers. So many bright and shining colors gracefully moving in and out before them were a feast for her eyes. "Avian, they are like a field of wildflowers flowing with the movement of a gay summer breeze," she exclaimed. She clasped his hand between her own. "Do you see Orrie and Crystal among the dancers?" she asked him.

"Watch by the pine wreath with yellow ribbons. They will pass by it soon. There, see, they are nearing it now."

Laughing, the pair moved rapidly past them, and Shale turned to Avian exclaiming, "I do not think I could keep up with that dance tonight, but will you teach me some day?" Her eyes were dancing with anticipation and she tapped her foot to the music.

He nodded and leaned close to her, explaining the meaning of the dance and sharing her delight. He had not seen her so excited before.

When the music slowed and many stepped from the center of the hall, he took her arm and led her to dance.

"We will start with a slower one, Shale," Avian directed. "I do not want to tire you."

Her smile faded slightly and her brows drew together as if to protest. Instead she said, "It is probably best." She looked about self-consciously, as they began moving with the music.

Suddenly, the music began a rapid beat and Avian whirled her around the floor, grinning broadly. Her eyes grew large with delight and she held tightly to his arm, no longer able to think of anything but the dance.

The lively music slowed and he led her to join Crystal and Orrie at their table. Her face glowed with happiness. Avian smiled. No more did Shale feel self-conscious. She was lost in the joy of the night.

After many dances with Avian, Shale sat near Bethany with her foot propped on pillows. She had overdone it and her ankle throbbed. Avian must have seen it in her eyes, because he had taken her to his mother and helped elevate her ankle before he left to assist his father. They were setting the loops of rope for a balance demonstration later in the evening. Shale sat watching the participants preparing to entertain them. Her attention was diverted when she saw the tall elf who had stopped her earlier in the day approaching. She turned to Bethany.

The Queen raised her eyebrows and smiled encouragingly. She whispered, "Remember what we practiced."

"Greetings to you, fair lady," Baierl spoke in the tongue of his people.

"Greetings to you this fine evening," Shale replied.

"You speak the ancient tongue," Sollen spoke, feigning curiosity.

Shale gazed curiously at him.

Beside her the Queen laughingly replied, "As do we all, Sollen. Are you enjoying the evening?"

Baierl spoke quickly, "Yes, thank you, my lady. Only one thing is missing—a dance with this lovely maiden."

"I fear this maiden will be dancing no longer this evening," Bethany replied, nodding at Shale's elevated foot. "She has quite overdone it already."

"Alas, it is true," Shale replied, shifting her foot on the pillows and frowning at the swelling that had caused her to loosen her laces.

Sollen turned to leave. He shifted his weight and bumped hard against the satiny stool supporting Shale's foot.

She tried to catch her ankle, but it jarred against the floor. "Ohh!" she cried out in pain. Bethany turned in alarm.

"I beg your pardon, my lady," Sollen's cynical smile turned to a frown. Her pain was real.

"Is there anything I can do to help?" Baierl asked earnestly. He quickly straightened the stool and replaced the satiny pillow.

"No, no thank you," Shale managed to say. Gingerly, she lifted her ankle and settled it on the pillow.

"My brother is an irresponsible..." Baierl began.

Bethany cleared her throat. Her stern gaze halted him.

"I will be fine, my lord, with a little rest. Please enjoy the rest of the evening," Shale said politely.

Bethany forced a smile and bowed to dismiss them, but the anger had not left her eyes. She was sure the bump had been intentional. They were rude and arrogant, the whole family.

Baierl nodded and left.

Thank you, Father God, that Avian did not see this. Bethany motioned for her maid and sent her for healing tea and a small poultice. She patted Shale's arm and gave her an encouraging smile. Shale had handled the situation well.

Bethany turned her attention back to the other guests seated around them. A discussion of Shale's injury was not wanted, and she skillfully shifted their attention to the new baby cooing on her sister's lap. Across the hall she could see Baierl scolding Sollen thoroughly.

As she sipped the soothing tea, Shale smiled. Crystal was aglow with happiness as Orrie guided her through her favorite dance. Shale whispered a thankful prayer in her heart for this kind family. She had noticed how differently they treated their servants, with dignity and respect. Many others did not do so. She was thankful also for Crystal's kindness in sharing her gowns. She felt like a princess herself tonight.

Avian was coming toward her, but was detained by a lovely maiden in a shimmering gown the color of a blushing rose. He bowed politely to her and continued toward Shale.

"How is your ankle, Shale? May I bring you refreshments or would you care to walk to the tables with me?" He sought her eyes for any hint of discomfort.

"I am much better after resting and taking my tea. I would like to stretch it a bit, please." She smiled at him and allowed him to help her rise and test her first step. "See, it is much better. Let us go."

There were so many different things to try. She selected only familiar ones, and they joined Crystal and Orrie at a small table near the dance floor. Together they enjoyed the sweets and watched the dancers twirl by.

Shale turned as an excited cluster of little maidens brushed by her. Their arms overflowing with roses, they scurried around two large tables and arranged the flowers in bunches according to color. There were deep blues, bright yellows, and creamy whites. The lush petals released their rich fragrance throughout the Great Hall.

Shale breathed in the delightful scents and closed her eyes. She was standing with Momma by the flower garden at home, touching the velvety petals of her roses. Piper played nearby with her rabbits, and Samuell and Papa led the young horses down the path to the meadow. Shale sighed contentedly.

"Do you find Orrie's story that interesting?" Avian whispered. "Where are your thoughts, Shale? Not with the hunting of the wild boar, I am sure."

Her eyes flew open. "No, I am sorry," she whispered back.

His eyes encouraged her to continue.

"I was in my mother's garden at home." She sighed again. "The fragrance of the flowers reminded me."

Avian took her hand. He gently rubbed her fingers with his own.

Orrie was still telling his story to an attentive Crystal.

"We are hunting wild boar?" Shale whispered to Avian.

He nodded and entered the conversation.

Shale listened carefully. She did not wish to offend Orrie. She had not intended to drift off in her thoughts.

Jamie and Dracy stopped at their table and joined in the hunting tale.

Shale allowed her thoughts to drift back in memory to Piper placing tiny blue flowers in Avian's hair on the journey to Pennsyl. She smiled gently.

"What has brought such a sweet smile to your face?" Avian questioned.

"A memory of a merry time not long ago," she answered carefully. It was tiring always being on her guard concerning what she said when others were around. She smiled at him and shrugged her shoulders lightly.

Avian gazed into her eyes searching for her memories. He could see Piper picking tiny blue flowers and running toward him. It was the first time Shale had allowed him to share her thoughts.

Crystal and Orrie laughed and Shale's concentration broke. She smiled sweetly at Avian and turned to their companions.

Slower music began and an aura of excitement filled the Great Hall. Many couples rose to dance. Mothers and fathers left their babies and young ones in the care of starry-eyed young maidens and joined those gathered in the center of the hall. Lord Cale and his graceful wife wove their way toward the dance floor.

Orrie took Crystal's hand and asked to have this dance with her.

Blushing, she stood and they entered the dance. Avian and Shale watched as the dancers moved gracefully in rhythm with the beautiful music. Orrie snatched a yellow flower from the table as they passed and gave it to Crystal. Her blush deepened as she smiled up at him radiantly.

Bethany observed Crystal as she danced with the dark-haired elf. What would be her response to his choice of flower? Were they simply lighthearted and showing they would pursue the relationship? She hoped so for now. She would like to keep her daughter with her awhile longer.

Avian's face glowed with joy. He was enjoying time alone with Shale. His hazel eyes were absorbing every detail of delight etched on her face. When should he ask her? Now?

Behind Shale, he saw Charleen and Bairel rapidly approaching them. He stood abruptly and said, "Come dance with me."

Surprised by the urgency in his voice, she rapidly stood and stumbled. Baierl reached out to steady her, but Avian drew her close and whispered, "Please, may I have this dance? It is a very long dance. I was waiting to ask because of your ankle." He was rushing and it flustered him.

Shale nodded and smiled up at him. He ignored Baierl and Charleen and guided her to the dance floor. "I want to dance this dance with you." His eyes were earnest and searching. "I want to be with you. I have waited for this time together." His gaze did not leave hers.

Shale's eyes grew large and sweet with tenderness. She loved being with him. Did he not know this? Did not every fiber of her being glow from within when he was near?

Behind them, Baierl and Charleen stood frowning.

"Alas, I have lost a dance with a beautiful maiden. I see another, rather sad. I shall go and make her smile. Better luck next time, my sister," Baierl announced and strode off.

"Wait. Do not abandon me so. Escort me to the refreshment table at least," Charleen begged.

Sollen sighed in disgust as once again, Baierl failed to take the maiden from Avian, freeing him so Charleen could claim him for the flower dance. Baierl wasn't trying. *Who was this maiden?* Sollen thought, remembering her encounter with his sister. She was courageous as well as beautiful. He swallowed his drink and walked away to avoid a maiden's meaningful glances.

The fragrance of the flowers grew stronger as the dance moved them closer to the table. Impulsively, Shale reached out and snatched a bright blue one from the huge array as they twirled by. Tenderly, she reached up and tucked it into Avian's hair.

At his startled expression, her eyes grew huge and questioning. She stopped moving with the music.

Avian pulled her close again and continued the dance. He looked deeply into her questioning eyes and whispered, "I see you are not aware of this custom, Shale."

She stepped back from him at his direction. He twirled her and drew her back to him. A small smile played at the corners of his mouth. Avian moved on with the music of the dance. He held her gaze and guided them toward the end of the long hall. Her full green eyes were deep pools of emotion. "I will hold you to nothing, Shale."

"What have I done?" she asked apprehensively.

Avian smiled, "Nothing so horrible that you should frown so, my lady." He paused a moment, watching her relax a little. Her eyes were still wide and searching. "Shale, you have just claimed me as your husband."

Shale tensed in his arms, her eyes huge and frightened. She tried to think. "The flower? I did not know. I love blue flowers. I…"

Avian tenderly touched her lips with his fingertip and turned with the music. She could not take her eyes from his.

Bethany's sister tugged at her sleeve, interrupting her thoughts. "My lady, Shale has placed a blue flower in Avian's hair."

Bethany's gaze quickly shifted to her son. Was this deceit? The maiden seemed so innocent of the ways of the court. Had she really known this opportunity would come to her? Who was she really?

But wait, no. As they moved with the dance, Shale's face was revealed to her. The embarrassment upon it, the way she stiffened in Avian's embrace as he quietly spoke to her, gave assurance that Shale did not know what she had done.

"Peace, Peace," Avian soothed, looking intently into her eyes. He nodded toward the other couples around them.

Shale glanced at them, noticing the various flowers they held. Sometimes the colors matched and sometimes not. Her eyes went quickly back to his. His expression intrigued and puzzled her. Wavering between a smile and—what? Compassion? Hope?

The energy flowing between them increased and her eyes grew larger. It was always there, but so much greater now. She could scarcely breathe.

"I have three choices to reply. Being your suitor with a yellow flower, your friend with white…" His gaze grew intensely warm, pouring into her eyes. The smile no longer played about his mouth. "or with a blue flower your husband, as Piper showed us on our journey, with the blue star flowers she gave me," Avian said. "Do you read my mind, Shale? Does your heart feel as mine? I must ask truly for myself, will you accept my blue flower? For I would joyfully accept yours." Earnestly he searched into the depths of her eyes for her answer, seeking a window to her soul.

Never in her life had she felt this way. The feelings were so intense. Her heart pounded within her. She wanted to kiss him forever, to pour out her whole heart and soul to him. But who was she to want him?

Bethany tried to relax and continued to observe her children. Corey came to her with a brilliant blue flower.

"My love, it appears our children are in love. Shall we not join them?" he smiled and held out his hand for her.

Radiantly, the Queen rose and joined her King for the dance. The hall erupted with cheers as Corey twirled her onto the floor. The King and his Queen flowed around the Great Hall to the lively music.

Clinging tightly to Avian, Shale buried her face against his chest and replied, "Avian, I am unworthy of you. You are the son of a King. I am…I do not even know who I am. I…"

He tenderly cupped his hands around her face and lifted her eyes to his. "You are the one I love. The one I would share my life with. The things you feel unworthy of are trivial matters, Shale. It is you, your very soul that I love. Do not be dismayed by things that do not matter. Be assured by the things that matter most, of the love in our hearts."

He watched her closely. Her eyes welled with tears. His pulse quickened as he watched the array of emotions flashing across her face. At last her expression softened, changing from unbelieving to believing. A small smile began and spread over her countenance.

"My heart answers yours," she whispered. Trembling, she touched his face, his lips. "Avian, I love you with all my being."

Gently he smoothed away her tears with his thumbs. Taking her hand, he led her to the table filled with flowers and chose the bluest one he could find. He offered it to her.

Shale's hand trembled. She took the beautiful flower from him and whispered, "I love blue flowers."

Avian drew her close and kissed her slowly.

A shower of flower petals rained down upon them, followed by another and another. Joyful shrieks and cheers accompanied them. Looking around, they found Dracy and Jamie each holding a young cousin of Avian's high in the air while they showered them with petals.

Hearing the excitement of the crowd, Sollen turned casually to see which newly betrothed couple was now being showered with blossoms. *Poor fools, or an alliance formed?* His eyes narrowed and he scowled. He did not like this. He did not like it at all.

Bethany's hand tightened on her husband's arm. "Corey! Avian has given Shale a blue rose!"

Corey drew her attention back to him and kissed her sweetly. "My love, the maiden our son has chosen is pure of heart. It is true that we know little of her. But what we have observed over these months speaks clearly. Would you not agree? I am reminded of our early days together," the King said softly, touching her hair.

One child had chosen. Where was Crystal? Clinging to her husband, Bethany's eyes fell upon her daughter giving a yellow rose and a brilliant smile to Orrie. Bethany closed her eyes and prayed for her children. She opened them and smiled up into her husband's reassuring face.

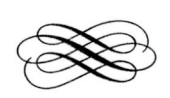

One week had passed since the Festival of Golden Leaves. In the blessed quiet of the early morning, Avian walked with Shale among the trees and flowers in the meadow.

"You are very quiet, my love. Are you questioning our decision?" Avian asked.

Shale stopped and turned to face him, placing her hands on his arms. Her eyes met his. "I fear that perhaps some of your feelings for me may be because you have been my protector and you feel sorry for me."

"No. I have asked myself those same questions many times. I am sad with you, Shale; not feeling sorry for you. Through all these things, you have not given up. You have given of yourself. I have seen you be brave, clever, loving, and kind in very difficult circumstances. I do not love you with pity." He kissed her forehead and they walked on slowly. He led her beneath a tree and they sat in the shelter of its branches. "What other questions trouble you?"

She picked a flower and entwined its stem through her fingers. "When we were dancing, did you want to give me a blue flower? You did not want to dance at first." Her voice was very quiet, but she looked steadily into his eyes.

"I wanted to give you a blue flower more than anything in my life, but I was going for yellow because your heart is already so full. I wanted you to have time to work through things first." He brushed back a strand of hair and caressed her face. "I am very happy, Shale, and I want you to be happy, too. Are you sure? Do you need more time?"

Shale held his face in her hands. "Avian, I love you. I do not need more time to know that. I have come to know you well over these many months. I am sure that you are the one I would share my life with through all time. I find in you kindness and assurance. You are open and honest. I feel safe with you; safe to be myself."

Avian encircled her in his arms and drew her close. "You are safe, Shale." He lay his head against hers. No one would hurt her again. He would not let them. They held each other for a long time, resting in the assurance of their commitment.

"Come," Avian said reluctantly. "We are to be picking the last of the raspberries." He stood and drew her to her feet.

She walked lightly beside him.

"What of Samuell and Piper? You are thinking of them." Avian smiled and gave her hand a small squeeze.

Shale's eyes were large and questioning.

"They will live here with us until your father comes, and longer if they wish. There is no question about that, my love."

"Your parents will not mind having them here?"

"You know they will not."

"Thank you, my love."

They walked on to the brook, and Avian swung her across.

She landed lightly on the other side and waited for him to leap across. "There is one thing that still troubles me." Her expression was very serious.

"Tell me."

"You are very, very mischievous," she said. "I do not know if my brother and sister should be around such an influence." She shrieked and dodged the water he splashed her way as he leapt across the brook.

A broad smile lit his face. "This from the one who yells at me in front of my family and friends." He ducked and let the berry basket sail over his head. "This from the one who does not know if she loves rabbits or not. What influence is she?" He grinned his most mischievously and returned the basket to her.

Shale whispered, "You have never told me about the rabbits."

"Oh, the rabbits. I love rabbits."

She frowned at him.

"All right then, I will tell you." He took a deep breath. "When I found you injured in the Raven Tree, I gave you medicine for the pain, and for strength, for we had a long ride yet ahead of us. You reacted strongly to it and talked. Much." He grinned remembering.

"What did I say?" Shale asked, looking into his teasing eyes.

"Many things. Do bunnies' legs hurt, I do not like bunnies, I love you, and…" He could hardly contain himself, "bunnies have lots of babies; let's have lots of babies." He laughed.

"I didn't." Shale's cheeks were bright red.

"You did. I was so afraid someone would hear you, that I sang to you hoping you would fall asleep. You did finally." He could not stop grinning at her.

"I said I love you?" she inquired.

"Twice," he affirmed.

"Well, I do." She wrinkled her nose at him and kissed him soundly.

Chapter 9

In Pennsyl, Lord Cale held counsel with those he had summoned. His sons and Connor sat to his right, while Cameron and Henicles sat to his left.

"Tell us what you have discovered, Mali," Cale spoke to his eldest son.

"There is an increase in the number of horses in the southern regions of Jaden near the valley area. A growing sense of dread weighs on the peoples of that region. We have noted an increase in King Corsac's herds as well, and his son Sollen has begun a herd of his own."

Henicles spoke next, "There is a growing interest in the lost art of Presage. Among many stable hands in various areas it is discussed, not by name but by description."

"Some are learning the Presage?" Lord Cale asked.

"Attempting to learn the maneuvers and train the horses, yes," Henicles answered. "I learned of this while searching for you, Connor."

"There must be wealth involved for the purchase and care of so many fine horses," Cameron added. "The king of Robin's Woods is arrogant and does not put the welfare of his people foremost in his mind. I believe he may be behind this."

"Or one of his sons," Henicles interjected. "It is long since you have been among your people, Connor. Do you remember any recent contacts or rumors of the elves' desire for more horses? Did they buy horses from your farm?"

"Not directly have they purchased from my herds. Many send buyers to represent them, and many horses have been sold over the last months by the new landlord. It is quite possible."

"We must act quickly. It must be stopped. The Presage was outlawed for its cruelty and the lust for death it breeds. It is a black art!" Henicles exclaimed.

"We must have proof," Cale reminded them, "and we do not. Who among us would he be most likely to trust?"

"I will go," Connor sighed heavily. "The Presage is a beautiful, precise, and intricate dance, although a dance of death. Few riders have the patience for it, and few horses the training or temperament. I believe it is this perfection King Corsac seeks. If so, he has changed little, though many years have passed."

Looking at Henicles, then Cale, he continued, "Corsac is my brother." Here he paused, letting this revelation of his identity sink in.

Looking up at them he continued, "Our father was gentle and loving. He had a way with horses as I have never seen in any other. He taught me many things; to fear the Presage is one of them." He met each one's gaze steadily. "Though my father feared the Presage, he was so enthralled with the unity of motion between horse and rider that he practiced the steps when he thought he was alone. But I saw it. I memorized it all. I heard the sound of the sword cutting the air as the horse danced to the side with quick, subtle movements. I saw them leap and spin and kick. Perhaps he knew I was there." His eyes took on a faraway look, as if he were a young one back in the stable, hiding as he watched. Rousing himself, he continued, "My father never fought anyone. He never killed."

Pausing, Connor looked down at his hands, then began again. "Mother was of a different spirit. I never understood their devotion to one another. Mother was arrogant, self-seeking, and greedy. I fled her whenever I could. When it was clear to her that I would marry Shayna despite her disapproval and her efforts to prevent it, she became furious and forbade my father to grant me my position as his son. I married Shayna regardless of the threats, and in time we fled and began a new life together, far from them. Unfortunately, my brother did not escape the influence of our mother. Now that my parents have crossed over the sea, my brother rules. We shall see how he will treat me. I will find out all I can."

"He will be suspicious of your return at this time," Terrell said.

"I will go to them, seeking help for the finding of my children," Connor began.

"They do not have your children!" Henicles burst out.

"They do not know that I am aware of that, Henicles. The timing is not off enough that they would suspect I have done anything but search for my children."

"We would benefit greatly from spies near to them," Cameron pointed out.

"Go then. Keep us informed by the methods we have discussed. Go with all care and our blessings. May God be with you," Cale bid him farewell.

"Lord Cale, you have not told me where my children are. Do not tell me now, for the less I know, the less I can give away. It is enough to know they are safe. I thank you again for your wisdom and care for them." Connor bowed to the council and left to prepare for his journey.

As the days grew shorter in Cambria Forest, the warriors went hunting to store food for the winter. Avian went with them.

Shale knew he loved the thrill of the hunt. She could see him racing his horse through the trees in pursuit of his prey, his blonde hair blowing behind him and his hazel eyes piercing the area ahead.

She turned as Crystal and Bethany entered the bright room where they sewed together. Avian's family was loving and kind. Already they treated her as a daughter. Shale was grateful for them. She had grown to love them, too.

Still, an empty place lived in her heart. It would be small sometimes, then overwhelm her suddenly. She mourned because her mother could not meet them. She would have loved them so very much. She would have adored Avian.

Shale rose from her seat and went to her chambers to retrieve her sewing supplies. She paused in front of the mirror hanging over the oak dresser, lifting her hair and pulling it to one side. Maybe Avian would like it this way. She wanted to look special for him on their wedding day.

Shale took a soft leather pouch from the drawer and loosened the drawstrings. Carefully she reached inside. Her fingers retrieved soft colorful ribbons of blue, green and gold. She reached in again and removed the silver necklace that had been her mother's. She would wear them for her wedding, as Momma had done.

Shale sat down on the edge of her bed and examined the treasures in her hands. Her mother would not be there to put the ribbons in her hair. She would not be there to laugh and dance with them.

"I miss her so much, Father God. So much. It tears my heart," she cried. Shale fell into her pillow and let deep retching sobs pour out of her. When they stopped, she rinsed her face in cool water and returned her treasures to their hiding place. She retrieved her sewing and joined Bethany and Crystal.

Bethany observed Shale carefully. She was preoccupied with thoughts. During the day, she ate small amounts, and at times her eyes filled with tears unexpectedly; *some thought bringing memories to her.*

She was radiant when Avian came, and their evenings were filled with joy and laughter. Often she and Crystal talked of the wedding. It was unlikely her family would be there. How would it feel to know that? To be planning for a day of such joy and know that your loved ones could not be there with you?

Bethany prayed silently, "What can I do for her, Father God? How can I help her? I thank you for bringing her to us."

A reception! They would have one in the summer to welcome her family and others to share the joy of the new couple. She would suggest it tomorrow. Surely by then the need for secrecy would be over.

They would make Piper a new dress. Shale could use her new embroidery patterns to embellish it. That would help her pass the time this winter.

She would also encourage Shale to speak of her mother and not hide her feelings inside her. That could be done carefully in their private times without compromising her safety. "Thank you, Father God," Bethany whispered. Her eyes glowed with anticipation.

The next afternoon when they gathered to sew, Bethany suggested her idea. "Shale, I have been thinking about your wedding. I wonder if you would like to have a reception in the summer so that more guests may come and share in your joy."

Shale's soft green eyes grew warm and moist. She laid her embroidery in her lap and blinked back her tears. "That would be so wonderful. Do you think we could?" she asked breathlessly.

Bethany smiled confidently. "It will be a fine time for a celebration. Many more could join us."

Shale rose and rushed into Bethany's embrace. "Thank you so much," she cried.

Crystal pushed a tear off her own cheek. "We must make a dress for your sister to wear!" she exclaimed. "What does she like? Long, flowing sleeves? No sleeves? You can embroider the new flower pattern you designed."

"That would be lovely for a summer gown," Bethany encouraged. The maidens' cheeks were flushed with enthusiasm for their project. They began to discuss and draw out patterns for the style of Piper's gown.

Bethany relaxed and picked up her weaving. Soon they would need to begin Shale's wedding gown. It was a mother's joy to do this for her daughter.

The next day as they sat together, Bethany asked, "Shale, will you tell me the thoughts you have for your own gown, your wedding gown? I would like to make it for you. May I?"

"It would honor me, my mother," Shale answered with relief. She had thought to make it herself, but had been too shy to ask for materials. Her eyes shone with joy at Bethany's offer.

Bethany's heart melted. "My child, the honor is mine." She walked to them and laid her hands upon their soft hair. "I am blessed with my daughters."

Crystal took Shale's hand and exclaimed, "Now you are more than my dear friend. I have always wanted a sister. Avian does not stand a chance." Their laughter filled the quiet room.

"Have some mercy on him," Bethany pleaded. Laughter erupted again. "He truly does not know what he is in for." Giggles overtook them all, and the king emerged from his study to see what they were about.

How our emotions have swayed back and forth today, Bethany thought. She quieted herself and asked, "Do you remember the style of gown your mother wore on her wedding day? Would you like something similar?"

"I remember she spoke of flowing sleeves with tiny blue flowers around the hems. She embroidered the same tiny blue flowers on our first baby gowns," Shale answered softly. "I remember Piper's had tiny green leaves as well."

Bethany grew very thoughtful at this. Something tugged at her memory.

Gradually, Shale began to tell them more about her mother. She had loved music, singing, and dancing. One day she told them a story.

"When my sister was very small we were playing in our yard. Momma shrieked and ran to my sister. There was a large worm on her gown. Momma knocked it off and rushed us into the cottage. We did not come out until the next day. That night we had oatmeal at supper, for no vegetables had been picked. Papa did not say a word." Shale smiled. "I think he knew what had happened. Worms were the only creatures that my mother feared."

Crystal laughed and their talk turned again to their sewing.

Bethany considered this story carefully. A strange far away look came upon her face at this tale, but she said nothing.

That night Shale again opened the pouch and took out her mother's ribbons and silver necklace. "I miss you so much, Momma," Shale whispered. "I miss your sweet smile, your laughter, and your humor. What fun you would have sewing with us." She touched the tiny flowers of the necklace. "I miss you. You would love Avian, Momma. You two would make each other laugh."

Shale walked to her small window and turned her face to the twinkling stars. "Please, Father God, let us find Papa soon. Keep him safe—and Piper and Samuell. Heal their hearts and let them know they are not alone. I love them so much. I ache to see them."

She paused and wiped at her tears. "The hole in my heart seems smaller now, but I think it will always be there for Momma. Is it not true? Thank you for the loving kindness of Avian's family. They treat me as their own child, and I love them. I want Papa and Samuell and Piper to be at our wedding, but the reception will be wonderful, too. Thank you, Father God. Please help me be a good wife to Avian. I love him so."

Bethany draped soft flowing fabrics over the table in the sewing room. She had chosen them carefully, considering Shale's coloring and the season of the year. She looked up eagerly as the two maidens entered. "Which ones do you like?" Bethany asked.

"They are all so beautiful!" Shale exclaimed. She touched the soft fabrics and watched the way the light enhanced them when they caught the sunlight filtering into the room.

"I am not sure which shade would look best with my ribbons and necklace," Shale said thoughtfully. "Perhaps this one with a bit of lavender?" She looked up for their opinions.

"You have your ribbons and jewels? Wonderful!" Bethany exclaimed. "Go and bring them to us, please."

Shale returned with her mother's ribbons and necklace. Her green eyes were bright with excitement. Eagerly, she laid the multicolored ribbons across the variety of fabrics. "What do you think?" she asked.

Bethany and Crystal stood beside her, staring open-mouthed at the ribbons.

Bethany spoke first. "April, thank you for your help this morning. Please take these lavender threads and dye them a deeper shade. No one can work magic with colors as you can."

The maid gathered the lavender threads and reluctantly left. She had wanted to see which fabrics the Lady Shale would select.

"Shale, they are beautiful," Crystal softly spoke and touched a soft gold and silver ribbon.

"My dear, they are truly beautiful. I know they are precious to you, for they were your mother's," Bethany hesitated.

"What is it, my mother?" Shale asked, her eyes large and searching.

"These ribbons signify royal birth, Shale." Bethany let the meaning of her words settle over Shale.

"I do not understand. I want to wear them at my wedding as Momma did at hers." She stared at them. "You think they would betray me? I know nothing of them being from royalty." Shale's voice was filled with disappointment and concern.

"I do not doubt that, my child. I want you to wear them." Bethany's forehead creased with her frown. "It is your safety I must be concerned with."

Crystal quickly offered suggestions. "Perhaps they could be worn in your hair with ribbons of other colors mingled among them?" Crystal's eyes searched her mother's hopefully. "If it were a small wedding? With the reception to come in the summer, it could be. Or we could sew them to your gown, or make a sachet for your wedding bed?"

Shale's fingers caressed the silky ribbons then placed them in Crystal's hands. "I do not wish to endanger anyone," she said. Looking up at Crystal, she forced a smile. "You are very gifted, Crystal. Please make something lovely for our wedding."

Shale quickly turned to the flowing fabrics cascading from the furniture. She lifted a soft, shimmering one of pale blue. "I love this. I think Avian will like it, too."

"I knew you would like that one," Crystal enthused. "It will be lovely with your necklace." She cast a glance at her mother.

"How would you like the styling to be?" Bethany quickly asked. She would discuss the necklace with her husband.

Shale shyly brought out a drawing she had made. "Will this be acceptable, my lady?"

Startled by the formality, Bethany searched Shale's eyes. "My child, it is my great joy to give you this. But I have broken your heart this day."

Shale reached out to her. "It is not your fault, my mother." The tears flowed again and again she could not stop them.

On the first day of winter, in the warm light of the fireplaces decorated with holly, ivies, and pine, Avian and Shale pledged their love and their lives to each other before God, his family and a few close friends. The pure joy on their faces outshone the beauty of the ceremony.

To Avian, Shale was as glorious as any sunset he had ever seen. Her pale blue gown illuminated her gentle beauty and brought forth the resplendent color of her now long hair and deepened the green of her eyes. A finely crafted silver necklace with tiny flowers circled her throat. The delicate silver band he had fashioned adorned her head and highlighted the array of multicolored ribbons woven loosely throughout her hair.

Shale could not look away from the love on his face. It dimmed even the majesty of his appearance.

He seemed so tall in his white fitted shirt. It reflected the color of her gown, turning his hazel eyes a beautiful turquoise. Set upon his brow was a golden circlet, and his blonde hair shone as if the sun itself lived within him.

Together with their guests, they feasted with much laughter. Avian swept his mother across the room in an elegant dance while his father and his bride attempted the same steps. Avian smiled broadly. His father hated this dance, but his mother had insisted upon it.

Crystal had slipped from the room and now returned. She stood watching them with a smile. Avian and her mother danced by, and she nodded to them.

They finished the dance, and Bethany went to her husband. "You did very well, my love, thank you," she whispered.

Avian swept Shale up in his arms and announced, "You are all taking far too much of my wife's attention from me. I will tolerate it no longer."

The room erupted with laughter as he whirled her away.

"Don't bother with breakfast. We will leave something at the door," his mother called after them.

Laughter echoed down the hall, and Bethany turned back to her family. Corey took her hand and led her to dance with him.

Avian opened the door to their chambers and Shale gasped with delight. Their room was bathed in the soft glow of firelight and candles. The fragrance of pine, lavender, and roses filled the air. On a small table, fruit and wine waited.

"Oh, my love, there are rose petals on the bed! Where did they find them?" she whispered in his ear.

Avian let her slide gently down until her feet barely touched the floor, then kissed her slowly. He looked deeply into her eyes, and his hands removed the ribbons from her hair.

Shale touched his face and slowly kissed him. Their kiss became more searching and they clung tightly to each other.

Hesitantly, Shale eased apart from him and knelt to remove his boots. She took his hand, led him to a large basin filled with fragrant water, and seated him on a chair before her. Slipping his feet into the steaming warmth, Shale carefully bathed his feet and kissed them.

Avian rose and kissed her tenderly, then seated her on the chair. He lifted her slender foot and eased the light blue slipper off. He smiled up at her, remembering the time she had fought to keep her boots from him.

Shale leaned forward and kissed his head. She did not say a word, but lifted her other foot and placed it in his hand.

Avian removed her other slipper and placed her feet into the scented water. He lifted the soft cloth and gently caressed each foot. He dried them and, rising, took her hands and brought her to stand next to him.

She drew a soft breath as he bent toward her. His warm mouth covered hers, claiming her as his own.

After the marriage bathing was completed, they stood holding each other in the warm glow of the firelight. "You are so beautiful. You fill my heart," he whispered.

Shale's misty eyes looked into his. Her heart was so full, she thought it would surely burst with joy.

At times, she seemed so fragile. Avian had been afraid she would pull away from him when this time finally came to them. With delight, he realized this was far from true. Her warm mouth met his eagerly. With each touch of his lips she blossomed before him like a flower kissed by the sun. Her love-filled eyes opened to his, then closed slowly as her mouth reached for his again. Her warm hands pressed him to her.

He lifted her securely in his arms. She did not stop kissing him. He carried her to their bed and gently eased her down onto the softness. The sweet scent of roses filled their night.

No one was surprised not to see the new couple the first day. After lunch the second day, a bit of joking occurred. When their supper remained untouched in the hall outside their door the next morning, his mother became concerned and knocked. There was no reply, and she knocked louder. Cautiously, she opened the door to find the room empty, the fire cold, and a note on the table that read, "I am taking my beloved wife away with only me for awhile. We will return in two weeks."

Bethany could only smile. His father had given the same gift to her.

Chapter 10

During the days, Avian and Shale walked and raced through the snowy woods, cherishing this time alone together. Sometimes they rode in the snowy meadows and lay in the warmth of the afternoon sun. At night, they would snuggle before a fire and watch its glowing embers fade to tiny sparks, then seek the shelter Avian had prepared for them in his favorite tree. From here they could count the bright stars in the cold night sky and watch the moon slowly cross it. The light reflecting off the snow-covered ground gave a luminescent glow, matching the love in their eyes. They shared their hopes, their dreams and their love.

Often Shale would awaken in her husband's arms and tenderly study his face. She had never felt so complete, so alive. Silently, she thanked God for creating her a maiden that she could know such love and joy as Avian gave her, for he gave his very self.

On the fourth day before dawn, Avian led Shale through dense fir trees. The rich smell of the branches filled the crisp air as their horses brushed against them.

"Where are you taking me, my love?" Shale asked, peering at Avian with curious eyes. He smiled, but did not answer her.

The breath of the horses made misty puffs in the cold air as they breathed. "Misty," Shale said, patting the strong, warm neck of her mare, "that is all he will tell me. We must wait to see this wonderful place."

Turning to her husband, she continued, "Though all of the places you have shown me have been wonderful, for you are there with me."

Avian smiled again and took her warm hand in his. He remembered her reaction to the cold in the river when they had first met. It troubled her no more, and he breathed a prayer of thanks. He had much to be thankful for. "We are nearly there, my love." *At just the right time*, he thought.

He watched her eager eyes search ahead of them, but the thick fir trees continued to conceal his surprise. The sky was becoming lighter, creating a gentle glow upon the snow.

Turning to circle an ancient fir tree, Avian lifted a finger to his mouth for silence. Shale nodded, her eyes glowing with anticipation. When they had circled halfway around the tree, three gentle deer looked up at them with wide brown eyes and dashed gracefully away into the forest as if they knew this moment was for her alone.

Shale gasped in delight as the sun peaked over the treetops, casting its brilliant rays across a glistening meadow. The sparkling snow, twirled into delicate drifts by yesterday's wind, was irresistibly inviting. Casting a challenging glance at her husband, she broke the quiet of the moment and urged her mare into the meadow at a gallop.

Allowing her a head start he watched, holding back his mount. Her hood blew back and her long tresses danced in the wind, a cloud of red in the whiteness of the meadow.

Avian's mount moved restlessly beneath him. The stallion's muscles were tense with contained power. Avian released him and they exploded into the meadow, throwing sprays of snow high into the air.

Rapidly the distance closed between them. Hearing them approach, Shale cried out and urged her mare on. Catching up to her, Avian reached over and snatched her from her mount, kissing her soundly. The horses slowed and he slipped onto a snow bank with Shale in his embrace. She was shrieking playfully at him and he sought to kiss her again.

A gruff voice commanded, "Move away from her. Now!"

Avian quickly turned to find an arrow pointing at his head, the eyes of the archer deadly. Shale stared unbelievingly then shrieked "Papa! Papa!!"

Seeing the dangerous look upon her father's face unchanged, she cried out again, "Papa, no!! He is my husband. My husband, Papa!" Quickly rising, she placed herself between them and repeated, "Papa, he is my husband, Avian."

Bewilderment flowed across her father's face, and Shale rushed to hug him. "Oh, Papa. Papa, it is so good to see you."

He lowered his bow and arrow to hold her. He did not take his eyes off Avian. The two regarded one another, and Shale reached out to Avian and pulled him nearer to her father.

"Papa, this is Avian, my husband. It is our wedding time."

Connor stared at his daughter in disbelief. Understanding came fully to him as he looked into her love-filled eyes and noted the pink blush spreading across her cheeks. "Papa, tell me…" Shale began.

"Not here. We must move to a safer place." He looked to Avian, still appraising him. Avian led them into a sheltered thicket, then called the horses to them. Carefully, he led them back to the safety of the tree.

Connor did not miss the careful preparation of this place. The young elf had thought of his daughter's welfare and joy in preparing it.

"Are you followed?" Avian asked him.

"Two or three men on foot," Connor replied. He regarded Avian again.

"Are they near? They will not pass by our guardians," Avian assured him.

"I did," Connor replied. He stared coldly at Avian.

Avian frowned and said, "Come, the sooner we are safe, the better."

"Lead," Connor said.

Shale waited in the tree and prayed for their safety. Papa was here! He was safe, but still pursued. She trusted God, but it was hard knowing that sometimes His answer was not what she wanted. She feared losing Papa again. And Avian! She could not live without him.

It seemed like hours before they returned unharmed, although the sun showed that not one hour had truly passed. She hugged them both and stood with her arm around Avian.

"You have brought us great joy this day," Avian said to Connor. He placed his hand on Connor's shoulder. He felt the strength but also the weariness in her father.

"Not exactly the best way to meet one's son." Connor extended his arm to Avian's shoulder as well.

Although his greeting was genuine, Avian sensed the concern Connor still held for his daughter. Turning to her, Avian explained, "The men will trouble us no more. We are safe." He sought to assure them both.

"How did you find me, Papa? Have you seen Samuell and Piper? How are they? I have missed you all so much!" Shale's questions tumbled over each other in her eagerness for news of her family.

"I only came upon you today on my journey, child. I have not seen your brother and sister, but I am assured they are safe, as I was assured that you were safe." He passed his hand over his eyes. "Then to see you snatched off your horse like that. How can so much have happened since last I saw you?"

"It is past a year of men since I have seen you, Papa," Shale said quietly. "I am so grateful that you are here. Avian helped us escape from the farm, Papa, and I…"

"Shale," her father interrupted, taking her hand. "I want to know everything, but it is important that I do not, for I would not betray your safety. You must pretend that you have not seen me, my daughter. No one must know."

He looked at Avian, who nodded in agreement. "I would speak with my daughter alone."

Avian squeezed Shale's hand. He descended from the tree, leaving her alone with her father. Connor began pelting her with questions, "Are you safe? Are you held against your will? Are you forced into this? Is this marriage what you want?"

"Papa, I love Avian. I want to be here. I love him and he loves me. His family has made me their own." Her eyes grew large, imploring him to believe her. "This is but our wedding trip, Papa." A blush of pink covered her fair cheeks. Shale's eyes radiated her joy—and unbelief that her father would think such things had happened.

"Forgive me. I do not know whom we can trust anymore." He had studied her face throughout her answer. Connor relaxed and hugged her closely. Drawing back, he said, "So it was love at first sight. Would that I could have been at your wedding."

"But you are here now," Shale spoke quietly as her tears slid down her cheeks, "and it was not exactly love at first sight." She laughed remembering. "Papa, there will be a reception in the…"

"Peace my daughter. I cannot know these things. I must go." He looked lovingly at her and hurried down the tree.

"Avian, be very careful whom you trust. There is trouble among the elves," Connor warned.

"Henicles and Lord Cale have informed me. Would you not speak of this with my father, Corey?" Avian counseled. "We may be of help to you."

A sharp crease formed quickly on Connor's brow and he spoke tersely, "You are the son of Corey, the king of Cambria? What have you done? My daughter's identity must not be known. She cannot appear before crowds of our people with you!" He looked at them both as if they had lost their minds.

"Papa, our wedding was very small, only Avian's family and..." again her father interrupted her.

"And do you think no one will wonder who this strange maiden is, who has wed the son of Corey?" her father was shaking.

"I will protect my wife and her family with my own life," Avian answered. Protectively his arm encircled Shale.

"You had better start today!" Connor spoke angrily. He paced away from them, then back, regaining some composure. Studying the pair before him, he struggled for clarity.

Before him stood his daughter, his child, but not as he remembered. She belonged by her own free will to the tall, confident elf beside her. Their wedding trip. Had so much time passed?

What little he knew of Avian, he must trust. Henicles had trusted him, as had Lord Cale. He hesitated, torn with leaving his child once he had found her. Connor shifted his weight. He had to let it go, to trust her to God and her husband.

At last he spoke. "Do you live at the home of the king? Good, that should be safer. Attend as few functions as possible. You look so like your mother, Shale. You may be recognized. Be on your guard. Be careful of your servants. They can easily overhear things that should not be known." How well he knew this. It had cost him much at one time. "Perhaps you will be safer this way, but I fear for you both. May God watch over you, my children."

He looked to Avian. "The elves guarding you, are they trustworthy?"

He raised his hand, not letting Avian reply. The stern look on the young elf's face said enough. Connor knew he insulted by asking, but he could not help it.

Appraising them both, he urged again, "No one can know that Shale is my daughter. No one must know that I was here."

He clutched her to his chest and said, "My love is with you." He reached out and gripped Avian's arm firmly.

"Let us help you," Avian offered again.

"Later, my son. The time will come, though it may be long," he sighed deeply. "Henicles will come. Trust only he himself, Lord Cale, or Cameron, but only them personally. No messengers."

Watching him disappear into the thick firs, Shale and Avian reached for one another. He looked into her eyes and spoke to reassure her, "The men are gone who sought him. He will travel safely for a time."

"Should we return?" she asked.

"I think not, for we are not yet expected. Your father looked well," he said smiling down at her. "Troubled, but well."

"Yes," she could not say more. She turned and her eyes searched the woods where her father had disappeared.

"We must trust God and do what we can." Avian lay his head on hers and rocked her gently, expecting her to cry.

Brushing away a few tears, she looked up at him and said, "There are blessings. It is a blessed wedding gift to see him, to know for certain he is well."

A small smile hinted at the corners of her mouth. "I am also very thankful he did not shoot you, my love." She crinkled her nose at him, for she could not decide whether to laugh or cry.

Kissing her forehead, Avian held her a moment longer, considering these things. "Come, will you walk with me, my love? There is yet beauty to the morning."

Connor journeyed directly to his brother's kingdom. Memories haunted his steps, both good and bad. He approached the guards at the entrance to Corsac's palace. "I wish to see King Corsac."

"Who requests an audience with the King?" the blonde warrior asked.

"Connor," he replied. He said nothing more.

The warriors studied him, and the dark-haired one turned and entered the building.

Connor did not wait long.

"The King will see you in his private chambers. Follow me," the warrior commanded.

A faint sense of familiarity came upon him as he strode down the long hallways. How long it had been since he had trod them.

King Corsac responded immediately to the news of his brother's arrival. Rising to his feet, he instructed the guard, "Take him to my chambers. Make him welcome."

He turned to his servant. "Bring wine and food."

Corsac hastened down the hallway and considered calling together his family. *No, I must see him myself first. It has been too long.* The last report he had of Connor, things were going well for him and his family. Was Shayna with him, and the children? Eagerly he hastened to his chambers. Yet, a small doubt gnawed at him. Why had Connor come unannounced, when a great celebration would have welcomed him?

"Connor, it is truly you. It is good to see you, my brother, although I would have expected to receive word that you were coming," Corsac beamed. He grasped Connor's forearms in greeting.

"I have come in secret, my king, for I am in need of your help. My children have been taken captive from my home. I believe by the same men who are pursuing me."

"What is this you speak of?" King Corsac replied angrily. "Who would do such a thing to my family?"

Connor was encouraged by his response. "I was approached by one who demanded that I teach the Presage. I refused and was later taken captive. I escaped only to find my children stolen from my home. I need your help, my brother."

Corsac's brow furrowed. "Would that you had come bearing glad tidings. Who were these men? Tell me everything."

"Alas, I can tell you little, my brother. I want my children back safely," Connor spoke cautiously.

"Where is Shayna?" the king asked. "Is she safe?"

The agonizing grief on Connor's face melted the heart of his brother. Corsac had not agreed with the decision of his father, ordering them to leave so long ago.

"She is dead, beyond one year now. They say it was a hunting accident. After I sent the man away, an arrow pierced her heart while she ran and sang in the woods that she loved." Connor covered his face with his hands.

"No. NO!" Corsac said, disbelief crossing his face. In his mind he saw Shayna, beautiful and glowing with love for his brother.

Connor swayed slightly on his feet and Corsac steadied him. "Come, my brother. You must rest. Then tell me everything. I cannot believe this has happened."

He seated Connor and rang a bell, ordering wine and food brought to them immediately.

"Eat, Connor," he commanded. "Then take rest. We are going to figure this out, you and I. We always could, and we will again."

Connor ate and drank some wine, then was shown to a room where he rested. At present, he did not believe his brother involved, at least not directly or with full knowledge. He thought carefully of what he should say. He realized how much he had missed Corsac. Still, he must stay alert to his cause.

Meeting with Corsac, his sons, and Pendott, their counselor, Connor told them of Shayna's death and the changes of farm management. He related his kidnapping, the escape, and returning to find his children gone. "Then I traveled to you, for who else would help me, if not my brother," he finished sadly.

"Did you not inquire of your children on your way?" Baierl asked.

"I was pursued. I could spare little time or exposure. I have come to you as quickly as I could. I did speak with two groups of elves, one near Pennsyl. They had heard nothing." Connor's shoulders sagged.

"How many and how old are your children?" Sollen asked, "And when did they disappear?"

"During the time of blackberries. One is little more than a baby to me. The other four are older," Connor lied. He rested his forehead in his hands.

"What is this Presage that you speak of?" Baierl inquired.

Sollen remained silent. He would let Baierl speak. His brother was hot on the scent of any new adventure.

"A dance of battle upon a horse, very beautiful and deadly," Connor studied the young elf as he answered.

"And you know this dance?" Baierl continued.

"I know of it. It is evil," Connor stated firmly.

Sollen considered this with great interest. Blessing or curse to him? His uncle could be very helpful to him, or be a risk to the secrecy of his plan, for he would recognize training patterns that others would not.

"It was a dark art of the second age. Our grandfather had practiced it, to the shame of our family. It is forever banned in all elven kingdoms," Corsac spoke thoughtfully. "To hear that men are seeking knowledge of it is greatly disturbing news."

Brendell, third son of Corsac spoke. "There are rumors of a large herd in the lower valley of Jaden, many miles from here. The horses are rumored to be a magnificent breed, strong and noble."

Baierl leaned forward in his chair. "I, too, have heard these rumors, but paid them little heed," he said suspiciously. "Now I am concerned. Those in the valley area are a secretive lot, and I do not trust their loyalty to my father's throne."

Sollen did not like the way this conversation was going. He shifted uneasily in his chair. His youngest brother unknowingly helped him by steering the conversation in a different direction.

"We must send out scouts to find word of your children, Uncle," Piperel urged.

"I fear to do that may endanger them further. Be on guard for your own selves. I fear my presence may be a danger to you as well," Connor warned.

"Fear not, my brother. We are well guarded and secure. How can we help you if we send out no scouts?" argued Corsac.

The counselor had remained silent, listening and pondering the needs before them. Now he spoke. "With your leave my King, I have questions."

King Corsac nodded his approval. "Speak, Pendott."

"You believe your children's lives are endangered by these men if they find you, and you do not cooperate with them," the counselor stated to Connor.

"Yes, especially after my wife's death. I was never convinced it was an accident," Connor answered grimly.

"Who knows that you are the King's brother?" Pendott continued.

"I gave my name to the two guards at the entrance of the palace," Connor answered.

"Only the guards and those in this room," Corsac responded, thinking quickly. "The guards will speak of it to no one."

"No servants heard you call him brother?" the counselor persisted.

"I think not," replied Corsac indignantly.

"We must be sure, my King, for the children may be in even greater danger if it is known that they are of royal blood. Your identity may best be kept secret for the present," Pendott cautioned them.

"I have renounced any claim or connection to my brother's throne. I do not desire to live as royalty," Connor stated firmly.

"Even so, your enemies may still see it as an opportunity to further benefit themselves," Baierl interjected, following Pendott's reasoning.

Brendell spoke, "Or as a detriment, for we are a powerful kingdom. It may help us to retrieve the children."

"We cannot show force as yet, for we do not know where they are," Baierl counseled.

"I have a suggestion, my King," said Pendott, "if you would hear it."

"Speak," Corsac said.

"Let him train your horses. Let us brag of his skill and display it. That should draw the enemies' attention and they may reveal themselves and try to take him again. They may reveal more of themselves than they intend, and we will be able to discover who they are and where the children are held." He looked to Connor for his response.

"This will take too much time," Connor exclaimed. "I must find my children soon."

"It may not take as long as you think, for the horse masters are eager and envious. Our horses are coveted, and at the Festival of Golden Leaves many will gather to see them and make purchases. News of the King's new horse master will travel quickly to the valley people and throughout the surrounding kingdoms. Autumn is not that far off, and the festival time will be upon us. It will be a fine place to display your skills, for many will gather here," Piperel encouraged.

"This is true. When they know that you are here, they will come," Baierl added. "Can you teach something that will draw the attention of those who seek the black art? Then they will be especially drawn here."

"I can teach movements that appear like the dance, yes, but it will take time," Connor replied impatiently.

"Peace, my brother. The spring rains do not allow much travel," King Corsac urged. "The festival is to be held in our realm this year. We will hold it early. Soon we will send our most trusted ones to subtly spread the word of my new horse master and seek for any news of your children."

Connor lowered his head to his hands. "What if I am recognized?"

"I have a plan," Pendott assured him. "I can change the color of your hair. Your manner of speech is already altered from ours."

Connor frowned.

"You have an accent of the area you have come from," Pendott explained.

"Are we agreed then? Connor, will you be my new horse master? Will you consent to live here, at least until we have found your children? I would have you close to me again, for I have missed you these many years." The king looked about the circle for agreement, resting his eyes last upon his brother.

All nodded in agreement and Connor raised his head. "Thank you."

The two brothers stood and grasped each other's forearms. Corsac spoke, "You will begin tomorrow. I will see that you have all the help and supplies that you need."

"May I help him, my father?" Brendell spoke eagerly. Looking to Connor, he continued, "I have some skill with horses."

He looked hopefully at his brother. "That is if you can spare me, Sollen."

Brendell turned back to Connor. "Sollen has a herd of his own. Very fine horses. You must see them."

Wishing to stop his brother's prattling, Sollen responded quickly, "Of course, my brother. You can be of great assistance to him."

"Very well," responded the king. "Let us retire to the courtyard for music."

"Please excuse me, my King. I am weary and Pendott must attend to me," Connor reminded Corsac.

"Forgive me. I did not think. Your name. We must change it." He thought for a moment. "We shall call you Wynon."

Sollen did not accompany them either. Inwardly, he seethed. *Another heir to the throne. Others to stand in my way. But they would not succeed. An unknown uncle and cousins would not stand in the way of Sollen. The cousins were missing. Good. Perhaps someone would save him the trouble of dealing with them, should they desire his father's throne. Connor denied interest, but he must be watched closely. Very well. He would learn as much from his uncle as possible. He had plenty of time. His spies would yet find the children of Connor.*

Connor was relieved to find the horses gentle, intelligent, and well trained with basic things. It would take less of his time to teach them his methods.

Brendell learned quickly and became a great asset to him, yet still his heart longed for Samuell at his side. Thinking of Shale and the changes he had seen in her, he wondered how tall Samuell was now. And Piper, his baby, did she still carry her precious doll everywhere? The ache in his heart stabbed deeper. "Brendell, canter the horses," he commanded, and focused his attention on them.

Over time, Sollen slowly began to put the pieces of information together. Here was his uncle, but with his children missing. The servant at Cambria Forest had heard the unknown maiden arguing with the wizard about being separated from someone. Siblings, perhaps? The timing of her presence at Cambria Forest would fit, and she had been injured, healing slowly. Her pain had been real. He had made sure of that himself. What would cause this, but grief? Its effect could be great upon an elf, he had heard. His uncle, though strong, often grew weary as well. Could it be that Avian had wed the daughter of Connor? Confirming the relationship between Avian's bride and his uncle should not be that difficult.

Sollen considered the possibilities this could offer him. Control of his uncle, forcing him to reveal his knowledge of the Presage, and influence over Avian; perhaps putting the aloof Crystal in his grasp and giving him an edge into Corey's kingdom. She would be a boring wife, but a model queen for him. Finding the other children would be his goal now. His ultimate goal was to eliminate any threat to his seat on his father's throne. That should not be difficult either. Not for him.

Chapter 11

As they lay together before falling asleep, Shale turned shining eyes to her husband. "Avian."

He turned his face toward her.

"You have made me so very happy." She took his hand and rested it on her lower abdomen. Her eyes fastened on his. "It is four moons since we wed," she whispered.

He smiled, turned on his side and kissed her.

She put her fingers to his lips and held his hand against her body. "Avian, two moons have passed and my time has not come…" She stopped speaking as she saw the realization of her words fill his eyes. She loved his eyes. As she watched, they widened and looked down to where their hands rested on her abdomen, then quickly back to her. Lovingly, she stared into them, searching for his thoughts.

The sweetest smile came upon his face, and his eyes grew warmer and softer. He kissed her jubilantly, then kissed their growing child.

"You are sure?" he asked in hushed excitement.

Shale nodded, smiling shyly at him.

He kissed her again and laughed, "I thought it was too many teacakes!" He dodged her teasing swat. He jumped from the bed and pulled her up with him.

She stood with him, held lovingly in his arms. They began slowly dancing. He lifted her up. "I want to run through the woods and sing for joy."

"Then let us go, my love."

Instead, he twirled her around the room and gently placed her on their bed. He could look at her forever, for she was fairer to him than even the woods he loved. Together, they rejoiced and dreamed late into the night.

When Shale awakened, Avian was returning to their room. "Have you been running in the woods and singing, my love?" she asked.

"Of course, and I will carry my wife to breakfast." He swooped down upon her and hugged her tightly to him.

"May your wife breathe, please?" she teased him, not letting him pull away. Drowned in kisses, she finally gasped for breath and released him.

"Up, my lady, for I am filled with joy and eager to share our news." He reached for her as if to carry her off that moment.

"Wait, my lord! I am not dressed for breakfast!" she protested.

"They will not care!"

"A moment, please, Avian."

"Just for you. But hurry, my love," he replied, "before I must kiss you again."

Everyone looked up when Avian arrived carrying Shale in his arms and gently seated her at the table, kissing her soundly. She blushed and returned his radiant smile.

Bethany sat up straighter in her chair. Her son was absolutely radiant and Shale was glowing. *She has told him, then.*

"My son, you are in a fine mood this morning," greeted Corey.

"Indeed I am, my father." Avian turned a radiant smile again to Shale and took her hand.

"Mother, you are looking especially beautiful today."

"Thank you, my son," Bethany answered, joining in the merriment.

Crystal had not yet joined them. Avian eyed the entrance like a hawk, but still she did not come. He shifted his feet and flexed his fingers. A rustle at the doorway made him turn quickly and he began, "Crystal…oh, it is the maid with our tea and juice. Thank you." He took the tray from her and set it on the table, then turned to face the entrance again.

He paced until he stood behind Shale's chair and placed his restless hands on her shoulders. He bent down and leaned around to see her face. He received her loving smile and straightened. "My father, is there room here for another to live among us?" he asked.

Puzzled by the question, Corey creased his brow, "What? Who?" He glanced at his wife who was smiling now.

"Your little grandchild!" Avian announced.

Corey quickly shifted his gaze and met Shale's blushing smile. He looked to his Queen and back to his son. "There is room for many to live here," he laughed. He stood and embraced Avian, then planted a kiss on Shale's cheek.

Crystal came into the room, wondering at the commotion. Avian raced to her chair and pulled it out for her. "Allow me to seat you, Auntie Crystal," he whispered in her ear.

"What?" she cried. Immediately her eyes went to Shale's abdomen, then the radiant faces all around her. She jumped up and hugged Avian and Shale. "This is wonderful news! When will the baby arrive?"

"Early winter," Shale's eyes glowed with love and excitement. "Will you attend me?"

Crystal could not clearly see Shale's face for the tears racing down her cheeks. "I would be honored, my sister," she whispered.

At midmorning Shale found Crystal alone in the courtyard. She noticed that, although she was truly happy for them, Crystal had been very quiet that morning. "Are you troubled, Crystal?" she asked. "What is it?"

"I have yet to hear from Orrie, and spring is upon us. I am missing him. I am wondering if he still holds my yellow flower near his heart as I do his." Crystal sighed.

Shale squeezed her hand. "I am sure you will hear from him soon. It has been a hard winter for travel."

"I am so very happy for you and Avian, Shale. I truly am. I am just feeling lonely and left behind in life. But it is not my time yet." She linked her arm with Shale's, and together they walked arm in arm to a sunny bench.

"I think Orrie will be entranced when he sees you wearing the yellow gown you made this winter." Shale watched Crystal's cheeks grow pink.

"Do you really think so?" she asked.

"Yes, but when he sees your sweet smile and dancing eyes, he will not notice the gown. He will see only your true heart for him."

"I wish to see his true heart for me," Crystal sighed. "Have you watched many fall in love?"

Shale contemplated this. "I watched a sweet man and woman courting at the farm. Momma drew my attention to them. They would find excuses to venture near each other during the day. They would glance shyly at each other and their cheeks would turn red. Momma and I were picking berries and saw them hold hands and exchange a kiss. I giggled and they dropped their hands and stepped apart. Momma said to them, 'I think you should kiss her again, Eli.' Then we took our baskets and left. They married in two moons' time. Momma was very happy." Shale smiled at the memory and thought of Kelly and Eli far away from her.

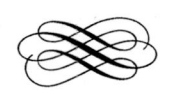

After supper, Kelly joined Eli outside their small cottage while he brushed Willow and the fine colt she had borne the horse master on the night the elf had visited and given Eli assurance that the children were safe. "'e be magical, Eli. Yer work with him be goin' well," Kelly complimented her husband.

"Aye, 'ey both be magical animals," Eli said casting her a gentle smile.

"Fine they are, but not magical. Why is that yearling not in training with the others?" demanded the foreman.

Eli and Kelly both jumped at his voice. He had never visited their home before.

"M' lord, 'e be belongin' to the horse master, as ye know," Eli replied, stroking the colt's withers.

"And who has been feeding him this past year? Show me what he can do." The foreman stood with arms crossed over his chest, waiting for Eli to comply.

"I ha' been apayin' fer 'eir feed and providin' 'eir shelter, my lord. A record be kept at the stables. I be not cheatin' ye."

Eli led the colt through the pasture gate and cautiously gave hand signals to the yearling. The colt tossed his sleek head and moved fluidly across the small pasture to Eli's commands. His conformation was excellent and his alert eyes missed nothing. Eli continued to give basic signals with his hands, but at times the colt appeared confused.

"He would be more advanced if he were training with the others," grunted the foreman. "He would bring a good price."

"I told ye, m' lord. I be not a horse master." Eli reached out to caress the yearling's muzzle. "I be doin' m' best fer 'im till 'is master be acomin'."

"Coming! What makes you think he will return, old man?" The foreman eyed him suspiciously. "What do you know of the horse master? Tell me."

"Alas, m' lord, I 'eard no word of 'im, but I 'ave 'ope." Eli looked fully into the man's face.

The foreman's gaze turned from suspicion to greed. "Many buyers will begin arriving this week. He would bring a good price. Sell him to me."

"'e be not mine to sell, m' lord." Eli frowned.

"You are waiting for nothing, old man. He will not return. He is probably dead." The foreman turned his head, appraising Eli's cottage. "You like it here, do you not? Your house is warm and dry. Your garden soil is rich. Where would you go, old man, if you did not stay here? Think about it. I will not ask you again." Scowling, the foreman turned and strode away, muttering to himself.

Kelly went to Eli's side. "What shall we be doin', m' love? Ye cannot sell 'em."

"Come inside now. The sun be settin'." Eli took her hand and led her through the door into the warm little kitchen. Sitting down at the table across from her he said, "We will be doin' what we 'ave planned ta do. 'ow soon can ye be ready, m' love?"

Kelly smiled warmly at her husband and rose from her seat. She opened the lower cupboard door, revealing several loaves of bread, a jar filled with dried apple slices, and a round of cheese. "When the moon rises this night, I be atravelin' with thee."

Eli and Kelly made good time on horseback and in three weeks reached the plot of land beside a flowing stream. A small brown cottage nestled among a grove of walnut trees. Eli pulled the heavily creased paper from his pocket and checked the markings again.

"'ere we be, Kelly! This be our 'ome." He smiled jubilantly at her. "Thanks be t' Master Evan fer givin' us this bit o' land. I loved ever' minute I worked fer him, all those forty years."

"They be good years, Eli." His wife smiled at him and took his worn hand. "An' we be a 'avin' more of 'em 'ere."

"Aye. I 'ave one thing left to be adoin'." He turned to the mare and colt.

Kelly watched as Eli removed the halters and packs from the mare and yearling. She dabbed at her eyes with her clean white hankerchief.

Eli patted them affectionately. "Thank ye. Find 'im now, lass. Ye know 'ow. Be on yer way and be ye wary. Go on now. Off with ye both."

Together he and Kelly watched as the mare and colt trotted toward the woodland. At its edge, Willow turned and whinnied. She tossed her head up and down and pawed at the earth. Turning into the woodland, she nickered to her colt, and they disappeared among the dense trees.

Kelly wiped her eyes again.

"Don't fret, 'ere, missus," Eli comforted her. " 'ey will be afindin' 'im."

He patted her back and asked, "Where do ye be wantin' yer garden?"

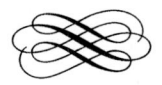

"Crystal! There are travelers arriving! Avian said to tell you Orrie is with them." Shale smiled joyfully at her friend.

Crystal had received two letters from Orrie, assuring her of his desire to see her as soon as he could. First he must complete a task for his King.

The two watched from the balcony as the travelers were allowed in to an audience with King Corey. Orrie looked up and received Crystal's radiant smile.

Shale squeezed Crystal's hand and went to rest before the evening meal together. It would be a festive time tonight. She looked forward to the merriment and dancing with her husband.

Avian did not come to their room before mealtime, and Shale began to feel a little nauseous and shaky. She had eaten her fruit already. Folding the tiny gowns she was making for their baby, she went down the long hall to the dining area. Only Bethany and Crystal waited at the table. Shale exchanged greetings and quietly asked for bread and tea.

Bethany smiled and answered her unspoken question. "They will not be joining us tonight, as they are still in counsel. Tomorrow we will plan for an evening of entertainment."

Turning to Crystal, she added, "Orrie has such a lovely voice, perhaps he will favor us with a song or two." She smiled warmly at her blushing daughter.

It was late when Avian returned to their room. He slipped quietly beneath the blanket. Shale stirred and turned to lie in his arms.

"You have had a late council, Avian," she murmured.

"We will talk in the morning before breakfast. Wait for me to come for you, my love."

"I will wait for you forever."

He kissed her sweet face and held her securely, noting the increase in the roundness between them. Gently, he laid his hand there. Shale resumed sleeping, and Avian pondered the news. It troubled him. Maybe he should take her to see Piper and Samuell now. They would not attend the festival. It was too risky. He would tell his father tomorrow. Still troubled, Avian drifted off to sleep.

In the morning, Avian returned to escort her to breakfast, but decided instead that they would stay in their room. Shale was pale and nibbled a wafer slowly. She smiled as he encouraged her to lie down and rest.

"Our child will think he has the laziest mother in all the kingdoms if I lie around all the time," she mildly protested.

"No, he will know that his mother is the most beloved, because his father cannot stop holding her." Avian eased himself down beside her and held her closely. His slightly furrowed brow did not escape Shale's observation.

"What troubles you, my love? Is it me? Avian, I am fine, really." Leaning up on her elbow, she peered questioningly into his eyes.

"There is to be a festival at Robin's Wood," he began.

"The Festival of Golden Leaves, yes. Crystal cannot stop talking about it. That is where Orrie is from, is it not?" asked Shale.

"Yes," he answered, stroking her hair back from her face with his fingers. "They are holding it early this year. They wish to display the skills of their new horse master, Shale. It will be dangerous, and we are not going."

"Do you mean my father?" Shale spoke incredulously.

"Yes, and there is more." He watched her carefully.

"Tell me. What is it? He is well, is he not?" Anxiety edged her voice.

"Yes, he is well." Avian took a breath and continued, "It is rumored that your father is the King's brother. Do you know anything of this?" he asked.

"King Corsac's brother? You are teasing me now." She studied his face intently. There was no glint of teasing in his eyes. "My parents never spoke of their homeland or their people. I know nothing of such a thing. I do not believe it to be true." She paused, thinking.

"What is it?" he asked, seeing her mind quickly working.

"Remember—for our wedding ceremony, my ribbons had to be mixed in with others? Your mother said that they were royal colors. Surely, it could not be true,

Avian." Shale laughed nervously. "That would mean that Charleen is my cousin."

"It could mean greater danger for you," Avian cautioned.

"Very well, my husband. We will not go."

Avian looked surprised, and leaned up onto his elbow to stare at her. "You are not going to protest! I had all my good reasons ready to persuade you." He frowned, pretending to be disappointed.

"I need not be persuaded when an opportunity to be alone with my husband for three weeks presents itself. Although I will miss seeing Crystal dancing with Orrie." She sighed, and let her fingers trace his face. "I could not acknowledge Papa, anyway."

"I was thinking we might go to Bellflower to see Samuell and Piper," Avian said with a smile. "The rivers should not be a problem at that time."

"Oh, could we?" Her radiant smile lit the room.

"Do you feel well enough?" Avian whispered, caressing the roundness between them.

"We will ride. I will be fine." She kissed him slowly. "Thank you. How soon will we leave?" Her eagerness could not be contained.

"Listen to me first, my love. I may not be staying there with you. Cameron has asked me to help him protect your father." Avian continued as Shale's smile faded, "I have not given him my answer. I want all of this to be over for you. I want you to be safe, and all your family."

Shale put her soft hands on either side of Avian's face and looked deeply into his eyes. "Listen to me, my love. I love my family. I want to be free to see them and be with them. But Avian, I love you more. I want you to be safe." Her eyes rimmed with tears at the thought of him being in danger.

Avian pulled her to him and stroked her silky hair. "I will be fine. There is no need to fear." He remembered when he had first met her. The expression of deep sorrow etched on her face then, masked with grim determination when agreeing to meet him in the woods that night, had shown him her courage. She had lost enough, but she must be brave once more. "I will be fine. I still hold the title of best archer at the festivals, you know." He was teasing her, trying to draw out her courage.

"Only because they do not allow the maidens to compete. You know I would win." She managed a smile for him.

Shale tucked her gifts for Piper and Samuell into her bag and tied it shut. It had been a month ago that Avian had told her they would journey to Bellflower, and she was eager to be off. She selected a yellow apple from the basket on the table and tasted it. She gently rubbed her abdomen and said, "This is sweet, my baby."

Her maid approached. "My lady, your husband has sent a message for you to come to him as soon as you can be ready. He will meet you by the old oak in the far North Orchard."

"That is good, although he said he would come for me here." Shale considered this only briefly. "I am eager to be away with my husband on this pleasant journey and to…" Shale caught herself before speaking of her siblings. "…to be out in the woodlands again and see the wildflowers blooming. Perhaps we will find some herbs to save. Let us go, Cinda." Shale smiled happily and rested her hand over the growing baby. "You will like the rocking motion of the horse, my little one."

Picking up Shale's bags, Cinda started out the door. "We are to find your horse in the orchard, my lady."

"Please call me Shale, Cinda. No one is about to hear you. It will be good to walk to the orchard before we start our ride." Her face shone with anticipation. "You are sure Avian is not coming for me? What did the messenger say?"

"That your husband was running an errand and would meet you there to save time," Cinda answered.

"And a long farewell from our family, perhaps." Shale refused to let the nagging doubt at the back of her mind interfere with her great desire to begin this journey.

She longed to see Samuell and Piper. It would be a brief visit, for the travel would be slow, and they would need to return home for Bethany and Crystal to attend her at her birthing time. Oh, but to see Samuell and Piper again would be so wonderful. She ached to put her arms around them.

Her mare awaited them, saddled and ready in the orchard, munching on the sweet grasses. The aroma of the orchard filled Shale with delight and she hastened to her mount.

"Thank you, Cinda." Shale smiled at her maid as she loaded Shale's bags onto the saddle. "I will see you soon. May God watch over you."

Shale started off through the orchard without delay. Her mare's long tail switched the tall grasses as they slowly walked through the orchard, stirring up the rich fragrances of the earth.

"And with you, my Lady...Shale," called Cinda. She planned to take her time walking back through the orchard. She looked around, hoping to see the new stable hand. He told her he would be bringing the mare. Surely he would not leave the mare alone in the orchard.

"Sheare," she called. No one answered. She swept the orchard again with her eyes, but did not see him. "Sheare," she called once more. *He must have been needed back at the stables.* She sighed in disappointment, but continued her leisurely walk, picking the bright wildflowers as she went.

Sheare watched at the edge of the orchard, hidden in the shadows of the bordering woodland. As soon as he saw Shale riding off alone, he began running away from the settlement. He had another message to deliver.

Shale rode leisurely. The warm sun released the scents of sweet honeysuckle, rich moist earth, and the lush green plants flourishing in the orchard. Beautiful butterflies with myriads of colors, and the melody of birdsong seemed to follow her on her way to meet her love.

In the distance Shale saw another horse approaching. She eased Misty into a gentle canter. Misty shook her head up and down uneasily. Patting her neck, Shale sought to reassure her, "It is only Avian."

Although she obeyed, the mare would not relax. Shale could feel the unrelenting tension of her muscles and slowed to a walk. Carefully, she studied the nearing rider. It was not Avian. This rider sat his mount in an arrogant manner. It seemed to Shale that he barely had control of the animal.

She had seen this elf somewhere before. *At the Festival of Golden Leaves. He was the one who bumped my leg.* She shivered, remembering the cold look in his eyes when she had cried out with pain, almost as if he had enjoyed causing it. She thought of turning back, but she could not ride hard, and he would overtake her. Avian would arrive soon.

"Greetings, my lady. Come, your husband awaits you," Sollen announced.

"You have seen Avian?" Shale questioned him. The gnawing doubt was growing into alarm. "What brings you to Cambria Forest, my lord?"

"The hunt, of course. My brothers hunt your woodlands this day," Sollen responded courteously.

"Why are you not with them, then?" Shale pressed him.

"As I have said, my lady. I have come on behalf of your husband, for he would have you join us." The stallion pawed the ground impatiently and Sollen shifted in his saddle.

Shale frowned. The animal was restless, high strung and ill tempered by its behavior. Her mare shook her head and backed away. "Avian will meet me here."

"That was his intention, but he has been called away to the hunt." Sollen's eyes grew more menacing.

"Very well. I will come, but watch your mount."

"He is magnificent, is he not? Rare bloodlines such as you have never seen, I am sure, although you are quite familiar with horses are you not?"

"I have ridden before, yes. This mare is also a fine animal, therefore keep your stallion in order," Shale replied, never taking her eyes off the white stallion.

"Do not fear, my lady. I have him firmly under my control." Sollen looked at her smugly.

Shale knew better, but said nothing. Sollen allowed his stallion to move alongside her. The stallion arched his neck and reached out quickly to nip at the mare. Shale guided Misty as far from him as possible, but they were next to a deep ravine and Sollen had left her little room to ride.

"My lord, please move your stallion over. I barely have room to ride," Shale explained.

"I know who you are, cousin. You would be wise to accompany me to my kingdom, for only there will you be safe." Sollen's smile was anything but comforting.

Shale glanced at him. "I have no cousins."

"Indeed, you have five. I know who your father is." Sollen studied her closely. "For your baby's sake, you must come with me."

The stallion grew more excited, and Sollen did nothing to calm him. He strayed closer to the mare.

"I am quite safe with my husband, and we would all be safer if you would rein in your mount. He is far too aggressive," Shale spoke firmly. She closely watched the great white horse moving ever nearer.

Impatiently, Sollen pulled the reins sharply. The infuriated stallion whipped around with amazing speed. It leapt into the air and released a vicious kick.

Shale's mare, taught to protect a rider, turned its body into the kick. One enormous white hoof struck the mare's shoulder and threw her off balance. Shale doubled over her saddle and clung tightly to it. The mare's hind hooves found no earth beneath them. Misty scrambled with her hooves and flung herself upward to regain her footing. Falling to her knees instead, she neighed in alarm, and fought to keep herself and her rider from tumbling over and over down the steep slope. Rocks and soil avalanched with them. Suddenly the mare's swift descent stopped as she slammed into a large boulder. The force of the hit took Misty totally by surprise and knocked her breath from her body. She lay still—gasping, trying to breathe in, and listening for a sound from her rider.

Shale saw the large boulder looming upon them and quickly flung herself from the mare. She lay twelve feet away, trying to bring air into her own lungs. A fierce pain ripped through her. She felt her thoughts leaving her, and clutched her abdomen tightly.

Sollen jerked hard on the bit and reined the stallion in sharply. Cursing, he peered over the edge down into the steep ravine. A shower of small rocks was still sliding down, sending clouds of dust into the air. He could not see Shale or the mare. The stallion paced and kicked angrily beneath him. Sollen could feel the energy building in the horse. Its muscles grew more and more tense. The mare's screams had excited it further.

Sollen found a sloping area and forced the stallion to ease down the ravine. At the bottom he turned the stallion back to where Shale had fallen. Dust still hung in the air, marking the spot. He peered through it and saw a movement nearly two thirds of the way down the ravine. The mare lay near a large boulder. She raised her head and nickered pitifully. Sollen gripped the reins tighter as the enraged stallion reared and pawed the air with its hooves. It screamed, and the shrill sound echoed off the ravine. The smell of blood reached Sollen. He struggled to keep the crazed creature from charging up the sharp slope to the wounded mare. The sound of rapidly approaching horses drew Sollen's attention. He jerked the reins with the strength of the desperate and beat the stallion with his whip, until the enraged animal turned and raced through the forest.

Avian and Orrie reined in their horses and peered down into the ravine. Orrie saw Shale first. She lay against a tree trunk. Her matted hair fell across her face. "Avian, there!" Orrie cried, and pointed to where she lay.

"Shale! Shale!" Avian called loudly. She did not move.

They leapt from the horses and slid down the ravine to her. Her blue riding gown was covered with a dark stain. "Shale, Shale." Avian knelt beside her.

Before he could speak again, she lifted her head and pulled back part of her gown. She cradled a tiny baby against her skin. "He tried so hard. He tried so hard to breath, to stay with me." Her fingers caressed the tiny face. She turned dazed eyes to her husband. "He tried so hard. I told him how proud you would be, for he was very brave. I told him we loved him."

Avian stared at his son—so tiny, so still.

"He is beautiful," Shale murmured softly. She began to sing softly and rock back and forth.

Avian swallowed hard. He stared in disbelief at his wife and son. Shale was covered in blood. It was on her lips where she had kissed the baby. It matted her bright, silky hair. It smudged her cheek. He looked away and swallowed again, fighting off the nausea. It could not be.

Orrie touched his arm. "Avian, we must move them. We must take them home."

Avian could not speak. He looked about him, but did not see.

Orrie touched his shoulder and shook it. "Avian, we must move now."

Avian looked at his friend blankly. Orrie shook him hard.

Avian pushed Orrie's hands away. He touched Shale's shoulder gently and tried to speak. Finally he choked out, "Let me take him now, Shale." He reached across her to take his son into his arms.

Shale moved, blocking his reach. "Oh, no. I like to hold him. I am keeping him warm." She covered the tiny head with her gown.

A deep sob escaped Avian, and he put his head in his hands. Kneeling there by his wife and son, his shoulders shook with his sobs.

Orrie stood back in horror, watching with unbelieving eyes. He struggled up the steep slope to his horse and returned to them with a soft cloth.

Bending down to Shale, he spoke soothingly. "My lady, here is a warm blanket. Let us wrap your son and warm him by the fire. We will help you to come, too."

Shale stared at the blanket for a moment. Orrie laid it beside her. Tenderly, she lifted the baby from her gown and laid him on the cloth.

Orrie's hands trembled. Carefully, he helped her wrap the cloth around the tiny form and rose to carry him away.

"Be careful," Shale cried. She leaned heavily on Avian and tried to stand.

He gripped her tightly and whispered, "Come. I will help you. We will go home now."

She struggled to see Orrie making his way up the steep ravine away from them. "Be careful!" she called.

Avian pulled her tightly to him and felt the stickiness of blood when she touched his face. He stared into her dazed expression and gripped her arms hard. "Shale, look at me! Look at me!" he shouted.

Shale frowned and struggled to focus on Avian's face. His cheeks were wet with tears. She wiped them with her fingers. The clearness of understanding appeared in her eyes. She clung to him, and her body shook in his arms as she wept.

Orrie gently tucked the tiny body in his pouch and securely fastened it to his saddle. He glanced at his friends and leaned against his horse. He could hardly bear their grief. He must get them home. He did not know much about birthing, but it was obvious Shale had lost a lot of blood.

As soon as the sound of their sobbing eased, he approached them quietly and laid his hand on Avian's shoulder. "We must take her home, Avian, back to your home. To Crystal and your mother."

Avian looked at him with empty eyes. He turned to Shale. He saw the blood on her hair and gown. He saw the pallor of her fair skin. He shook his head hard and spoke, "Shale, we must go home now. Come."

Together, they carried her to the top of the ravine. Shale struggled to free herself from their grasp, and Orrie released her.

"Where is my baby?" she asked frantically. She turned and started down the ravine.

"No!" Avian screamed at her. He grasped her around the waist and pulled her toward the horses.

"Let me go! I must find him! Let me go!" Shale beat her husband's chest.

Orrie stepped quickly to them and shouted calmly, "My lady! My Lady Shale! I have your baby!"

Shale stopped struggling.

"I have him ready to travel, my lady. Remember? We wrapped him in the blanket, you and I," Orrie said soothingly.

"Oh," Shale managed to say. She looked up at the horses.

Quickly Orrie urged, "Avian, mount up and I will hand her to you."

Avian did not move. He still held Shale tightly.

"Avian, can you carry her?" Orrie persisted.

"Yes, yes." Avian shook his head and mounted.

"Here, my lady. Let me help you onto your horse." Orrie lifted Shale up to Avian and he held her securely.

"Come, this way. Let's go home," Orrie urged. He swung up onto his horse quickly and started off rapidly down the path. He wanted to start before Shale began asking for the baby again. He shuddered at the sight of bloody fingerprints on Avian's cheek where she had touched him. He said nothing. There was no way to soften the blow of their tragedy. What if Crystal and the Queen did see the blood first on Avian?

Periodically as they rode, Orrie whistled a signal for help. It appeared Shale had passed out, but Avian still held her securely. The sorrow on his friend's face was nearly unbearable to him. "Please, God. Don't let her die, too." He whistled loudly again.

A few miles later, his whistle was answered and several riders approached them. He was relieved to see Dracy and Jamie among them. Riding ahead, Orrie briefly told them what had happened. Jamie raced away immediately to alert the household of the need for healing care for Shale. The others positioned themselves protectively around the horse bearing Avian and his wife.

Dracy rode close to Avian and said, "I would carry her awhile for you, my friend."

The grim-faced Avian did not reply, but urged his horse at a faster pace. He could feel more blood flowing from his wife.

Reaching the palace, they were greeted with many helping hands. Avian lowered Shale into Jamie's waiting arms and leapt from his horse. Quickly taking her back, Avian ran inside.

Orrie dismounted and carefully removed the pouch carrying his precious passenger. For the first time in his life, he did not look with joy at seeing Crystal.

Avian ran down the hallway, carrying Shale to the room where she had been when she first came to Cambria Forest. It was a flurry of activity. He carefully laid her on the bed.

His mother and an apprentice began caring for her. They removed her bloodsoaked clothing and covered her with warm blankets. Crystal scurried about, preparing herbal cleansing solutions and teas.

Bethany palpated Shale's abdomen and began rubbing vigorously above her navel. Avian was appalled, as he watched more blood and large clots flow from his wife's body.

"Stop!" He exclaimed, pulling his mother's hands away from Shale. "You must stop."

"No, my son. The blood and clots must come out for the bleeding to stop." She turned to Crystal. "Is it ready yet?"

Crystal hurried to her with a kettle of steaming solution. Its fragrance was a welcome contrast to the strange smell of blood.

Bethany dipped a large cloth into the solution. She handed it to Avian and instructed him to begin bathing Shale's face, hands, and arms. Once again, she began massaging Shale's uterus. This time a large clot came forth, with bright red blood following.

"Good. Thank you God," Bethany said quietly. "The bleeding will slow greatly now." Taking the time to quickly assess her son, she said, "Go to your father, now."

"No, I will not leave. Shale...Shale wake up. You are home now. You are safe." He cleansed her face with the pungent solution and she stirred.

She opened her eyes and focused on him. She grasped his shoulders and tried to sit up. "Where is our baby? I want him. I want to hold him." She continued, "Where is he? Let me up. I have to find him. Avian, let me go to him!" Her fingers dug into Avian's shoulders. Her dazed eyes bore into his. "Why will you not help me?"

"Lie down, my daughter. Your baby is being cared for. You must rest now. Rest for him, Shale," Bethany spoke softly, calmly, smoothing back Shale's hair. Shale turned her confused eyes to Bethany, who took the opportunity and turned her from Avian's arms into her own.

"There, rest for awhile, my daughter." Shale released her grip on Avian and sank weakly down onto the pillows. "Crystal has brought you some warm tea to drink. Here, drink this," Bethany spoke slowly, soothingly. She lifted Shale's head so she could drink the dark liquid.

After one sip, Shale turned her head away. "Ughh, it is bitter."

"Drink for me, Shale. It will help stop your bleeding. Here, drink a little more for me. That is good. I know it is bitter to taste, but it will make you strong." Bethany's soothing tone was persuasive and comforting.

Shale made horrid faces, but drank. She raised her hand and pushed the cup away. She was becoming restless again. "Where is my baby? I want him. Where is he?"

Bethany sang quietly, trying not to think about the tiny one lying in the next room. The tea worked quickly. Shale's body relaxed and her mind quieted. Bethany nodded to the apprentice, who began bathing her gently.

Moving to her son, Bethany held him closely in her arms for a long moment. With tear-filled eyes, she said, "My son, you must cleanse yourself and put on new clothing. Then come, lie with your wife and warm her. We must keep her quiet. She must rest, and she will do so better in your arms."

Avian looked again at Shale, now resting on the bed while the maid gave her sips of different teas. Her eyes, not so glazed now, met his and he went to her. Tenderly he brushed back her hair with his hand. Crystal handed him a cup of tea also and he drank it, feeling some life return to him. He rose to leave.

"Do not leave me," Shale murmured.

"For one moment only, my love. I will come and lie beside you." He touched her cheek.

Shale noticed his bloodstained clothes, and her eyes overflowed with tears. The baby, their baby. She reached down, but the precious roundness was gone. Only a feeling of emptiness and an achy cramping remained. Crystal leaned down and hugged her while she cried.

Bethany gently guided her son to the door. "We will watch over her carefully," she promised. "Mercifully, she will sleep soon."

Avian looked at Shale again, and slowly turned down the long hallway as his mother closed the door.

Bethany nodded at the maid, who entered with clean clothes and herbs. She took them and dismissed her. She massaged Shale's womb, then changed and cleansed Shale thoroughly. The bleeding had slowed greatly.

Bethany turned to look as the apprentice gasped. She was cleansing Shale's lower abdomen. On the left side, a large bruise was revealed, a bruise in the imprint of a horse's hoof. Carefully, Bethany palpated the area around the bruise. She whispered instructions to the apprentice for a poultice and left Shale in her skillful care. Crystal had gone to prepare the herbs for bathing the tiny body. Bethany would help her care for the baby, her grandson. Hot tears streamed down her cheeks and her heart broke for her children. *How could such things happen? How, God? And why? Why to them?*

She quietly closed the door behind her. Turning, she saw Crystal in the arms of Orrie. Both of them were weeping. Bethany turned aside to seek the comfort of her husband. She found him with his arms wrapped around his son.

Avian sat with his head in his hands, sobbing. He looked up and rapidly stood as Bethany approached them. "How is she? Will she live? Will she?" His sorrowful eyes sought reassurance in his mother's face.

"With our love and prayers, she will live. She is sleeping now, my son. The flow of blood has lessened greatly." Wearily, Bethany sat next to them. She took Avian's hand in her own. "My heart is breaking for you, my son."

"I promised her I would protect her. That nothing would ever hurt her again." Great sobs shook his body.

His parents encircled him with their arms and their love. They held him closely and their minds bound together in their sorrow.

When they quieted, Avian went to cleanse himself. He could not think. He could not feel. He was numb with grief. In their chambers, he saw the ornate wooden cradle he had made. He ran his hand along its smooth edge. Shale loved ivy, and he had carved ivy leaves across the top and sides. He pounded his hand against the strong oak and ripped his bloodied clothes from his body. He rubbed himself as hard as he could, as if in scrubbing away the scent of blood he could scrub away the reality before him. He thrust his arms into the sleeves of a shirt lying on the chair and threw open the door. The hall echoed with his rapid footsteps. He had to be with Shale.

Bethany moved into her husband's embrace and clung to him. Corey held her closely, laying his head on her soft hair. *It was not real. It could not be. But alas, it was. What had happened?*

Orrie and Crystal came to them. "It is ready, my mother," Crystal quietly said. Her large eyes were red and puffy from weeping.

Bethany took her daughter's hand. Together they went to care for the baby. They bathed him gently in lavender water and pressed soft cloths gently against him to dry his tiny form.

Bethany dressed him in a soft, green gown she had made in anticipation of his arrival near early winter. Gently, she tucked it under him so it did not look so large. Lovingly, she traced his hairline. "Just like Avian's," she whispered.

Crystal brought the soft material she had been embroidering for a baby blanket. She folded it reverently and placed it in the intricately carved chest belonging to her father. There they lay the tiny son of Avian and Shale.

"I have longed to see him. But not like this. Not like this," Crystal sobbed against her mother's shoulder.

Bethany turned from memorizing her grandson's features. "I know. I know. Today our hearts are broken." She folded her loving arms around her daughter, and they wept over the little one they had longed to hold.

"Tell me, Orrie, what has happened?" Corey demanded sternly of the tall, dark-haired elf.

"Avian went to get Shale to ride, but she was not in their chambers or the gardens. Her maid told Avian that she had walked with Shale to meet him by the tall oak tree near the edge of the orchard, as he had directed. Avian told her he knew nothing of this. The maid became very pale, and explained that a stable boy had given her the message to give to Shale. We went immediately to look for her. She was not at the tree, but the tracks of her horse and another were. We followed them, and found where a horse had slipped off the edge of the ravine. She was halfway from the top, leaning against a tree." Orrie closed his eyes, remembering the scene.

"There was another horse and rider? Where were they? Why did they not help her?" Corey demanded.

"There had been a struggle, my lord. The tracks were unclear," Orrie answered, frustrated that he had not studied the scene more carefully. His thought was to bring his friends to safety.

Corey's sharp mind played over the information again. Something was very wrong in his kingdom. "Send for my captain," he ordered.

Orrie bowed and left immediately.

Angrily, Corey paced the floor. *He had grown complacent, thinking Shale was safe now in his family. Instead, he had endangered them all. Bethany had feared it. He had dismissed the idea, being overly confident in the security of his kingdom and of his standing among the other elven kings.*

Orrie returned with the Captain.

"Question all the stable hands. Find the one who sent a message to my son's wife. Imprison him and any others you find suspicious," Corey thundered the order.

He paced into the courtyard—furious with his enemies, furious with himself.

Cautiously, Orrie followed him. "My lord, there will yet be many questions to be answered. I am at your service."

Turning to face the young elf, Corey forced himself to answer calmly, "Thank you, Orrie. Be ever alert to any information you may find. And Orrie, thank you for helping my children."

"They are my friends, my lord," Orrie responded. Touching his heart with his hand he extended it towards King Corey and left to be his eyes and ears about the kingdom.

As he walked, Orrie remembered Avian's empty expression, unable to accept the sight of his wife, covered with blood, holding the tiny body of their son.

He walked on and prayed, "I do not understand, Father God. I know you love us; that you hurt when we hurt. Help us, for we need you. I hurt. My friends' hurt is great, beyond anything I have seen. Please comfort Crystal and her family. Bring your comfort and healing to Shale and Avian. Bind them together in their love for each other.

"Father God, there are enemies among us. Protect and heal. And help us find those responsible quickly. Thank you, Father." Orrie strode confidently toward the stables. God could do this. God would see them through.

He thought again of the tracks where Shale's horse had fallen. Struggling to piece the information together, he focused his mind again. *Yes, it was as if a struggle had taken place. Was it not an accident that she had fallen?* After giving the king's message to the head stable master, Orrie mounted his horse with determination. He must go back and study the area before the tracks were further disturbed. He hoped that in their haste to help Shale they had not scuffed out any answers.

Swiftly, Orrie rode toward the site. He had reached the old oak tree and was turning left when he was hailed by a familiar voice.

"Cameron! The Lord is with us! You have come at time of great need." Orrie leapt from his horse and grasped Cameron's forearms in greeting. "Come with me. I will explain on the way."

Together they studied the tracks at the tree. "Shale's horse was nervous here," Cameron commented.

"Yes, and the other agitated. They talked, and then rode off together," Orrie added.

"The other's horse forced Shale to ride side by side with it. See where she had tried to drop behind?" Cameron continued as they moved quickly along, following the tracks. "Here, the horse began to bump and push Shale's closer to the edge." They continued to follow the trail with grim faces.

"Here, they struggled again. The other rider may have been trying to snatch her from her horse. Perhaps not, but the horses were struggling against each other. Look there. The larger one turned quickly and lashed out with its hind feet. Shale's horse then lost its footing and fell over the edge," Orrie concluded.

"Look at this. The larger horse tried to go down into the ravine. The rider struggled mightily with it. Instead, they descended into the ravine here," Cameron paused, still studying the tracks before him.

"No. These are marks from another horse. See the deeper indentations here, and the chip in the hoof?"

"Come," Cameron urged.

They slid down the steep ravine. The tracks circled around to just below the place where Shale had lain. The horse and rider had stopped within cover of the trees.

"There is no sign showing the rider dismounted," Cameron said.

"He could plainly see her from here, but he did not go to her. There are no tracks leading up," Orrie said coldly. He could not comprehend anyone doing such a thing. Fury filled him. "Why did he not help her? Why would he abandon her?" Orrie spoke angrily.

"There was a hunting party north of here. I saw their tracks when I came through—about ten riders. This rider did not want to be seen." Cameron put his hand on Orrie's shaking shoulder.

"That, or he heard our approach. Coward!" Orrie spat out.

"Do you know who may have been hunting here today?" Cameron asked.

"They could have helped her. He should have gotten help. He left her to die." Orrie's fury burned hot. "She and her baby."

"Who was hunting?" Cameron asked again, not giving Orrie time to dwell on the tragedy. They needed answers.

"I do not know," Orrie answered. "Wait. Crystal said something about Baierl, and that she hoped he would not come for shelter should the weather turn."

They heard a weak nicker. The mare lay exhausted where she had fallen. A wide path in the rocks showed where she had tried to pull herself nearer her rider.

Cameron climbed up to where Shale's fall had stopped. Orrie followed closely. "She stood here against the tree and tried to walk to her mare, but she slid down to the ground instead." There were disturbances in the earth, showing movements on the ground. And blood. Much blood. The earth was dark with it.

Cameron moved to the mare's side and examined her. She had suffered a strong blow to her right shoulder. Areas of hair had been torn from her back.

"An overly aggressive stallion did this. He has nipped her many times. We can take her back with us, but we must travel slowly, for she will be very sore. I think nothing is broken. Orrie, lend me your horse that I may follow the tracks to see where they lead from here. Start back with this mare and I will catch up with you," Cameron said.

"Come with me instead, Cameron. A fresh horse will speed you on, and Avian will need your comfort," Orrie urged him.

"I will not follow far, and then we will return together," Cameron assured. His heart ached for his friends.

Bethany and Crystal entered Shale's chambers and dismissed the apprentice. Shale arose and Crystal gave her sips of tea. "I am so thirsty," Shale said, reaching for more. "It tastes awful, but I am so thirsty." She was drifting off to sleep again.

They cleansed her body again with herbal solutions and were relieved to see that the flow of blood was ever decreasing.

Avian entered as they finished. Crystal encouraged him to eat, but he would not. He stood looking down at Shale's colorless face. Her lips were white.

"Lie beside her and warm her, my son. She needs you. You need each other. I will return and check on you often," his mother assured. Quietly she and Crystal left them.

He slipped beneath the covers and cradled his wife in his arms. She murmured something and settled against him. Her hand rested on her abdomen and he covered it with his own. The smell of blood was gone from her hair, replaced by the fragrance of lavender. He could feel her heart rapidly pulsing through her body as she lay quietly in his arms. Listening to her soft breathing, he relaxed.

Relieved that the bleeding had slowed, he drifted off into an exhausted sleep, disturbed by dreams of Shale crying out to him. She was falling, and he could do nothing to stop it. Startled, he sat upright in the bed, his hand raised to fend off an attacker.

"Peace, my son," his mother whispered. She lifted the coverlets to see if Shale's bleeding had increased again. "Rest, she is doing well."

He lay down again and covered Shale's hand with his own. She did not awaken.

Tears sprang to Bethany's eyes. Their hands were resting where the baby had. Barely able to hold in her sobs, she closed the door and returned to the arms of her husband.

In the early morning, when the mists still covered the woods, Avian slowly awoke beside his wife. For a moment he remembered nothing but the sweet smell of her hair and her warmth against him. Then it came. The heaviness of grief and loss settled down on him as a great weight. He turned his face into her hair and let his tears flow. *Why? Why? She had lost so much already. They had been so happy to be having a child.*

Avian rose up on one elbow to see her face. Still pale, but her lips were pink now. Her breathing was regular. He could feel her heart beating less rapidly this morning.

The door quietly opened, his mother again. Crystal followed with more tea and herbs for bathing. They set these on the table and Crystal left. His mother came to the bed to check Shale's bleeding. Twice in the night he had helped his mother change the heavy cloth pads. Each time there was less blood than before. He began to help his mother again, and Shale opened her eyes. She gave him a brave smile that quickly faded into tears.

"I feel so empty inside, so empty." She laid her hand where their baby had grown within her.

Avian held her while she cried. His mother made tea and set it on the table beside the bed. She nodded at Avian and he heard the door quietly close behind her.

Carefully holding his wife, he eased himself down to lie beside her and gently stroked her hair. After a time, Shale quieted as he held her. Her eyes searched his desperately and found the same pain and love that mirrored her soul.

"I am so sorry," she sobbed.

He drew her head against him. "Hush, hush. It is not your fault."

"I saw the blood. I felt a pressure in me. I did not know. It hurt so much. I wanted to find help. I stood and took a step and he came out, Avian. He just slipped out. I held him and dried him with my hair. I put him inside my gown to be warm. He, he tried so hard to keep breathing. He tried so…hard…" Her body shook with her sobs, and low moans escaped her.

Avian pulled her closer and rocked her back and forth, resting his cheek on her head. He had no words to comfort her, only his tears to mingle with her own.

When Shale slept again, Avian carefully rose. He had many questions, so many. For some he would have to wait. Shale needed rest now. He went out to find his father, and his anger grew.

Avian heard familiar voices when he drew near his father's council room: the captain of the guard, Orrie, his father, and Cameron. When had he come? It did not matter. "What have you found?" he demanded.

"Avian. I am so sorry for your loss," Cameron said.

Avian nodded. "What have you found? I must know!"

Corey rose from his chair. "Sit, my son, and eat."

Avian shook his head but sat at the table with the others.

A large basket filled with assorted fruits and breads was set before him.

"The newest stable hand is missing, my Lord Avian." The captain of the guard informed him. "We are searching for him, even now."

"Orrie and I returned to where Shale fell, and discovered that her mare was besieged by the stallion ridden beside it. The stallion kicked out, forcing the mare over the edge and wounding her," Cameron began.

Avian slammed his fist against the table. "And killing my son! Where is the rider? Why did he not help her?" He paced to the wall and glared at them.

"The coward fled," Orrie answered. "He must have heard us coming."

"Or the hunting party," Cameron added. "His tracks blended with theirs. Only he did not ride with them, but a distance behind them to avoid being seen. And there was another."

"Another?"

"The stallion and its rider fled. Another watched from below the ravine."

"Where do the tracks lead?" Avian demanded.

"Into the southern borders of Robin's Wood."

Though dizzy the first few minutes, Shale was able to sit up the next day. That afternoon Avian carried her to their own chambers.

She caressed his face and spoke softly to him, "Thank you for staying with me. Avian, fill me with yourself. I love you so much. I need you so much."

"My love, we cannot..." he began.

She put her fingers to his lips, "No, I mean with you, your very soul. Your strength, your love, your hope. You are so precious to me."

He moved to wrap himself around her, careful not to touch her bruised abdomen. Holding her, he sought to give her his strength, his love, his hope, anything he could. He wanted to make everything right again. He wanted to help her, to spare her this pain. They clung together, one in their grief.

Two days later the singing was held to mourn the passing of the son of Lord Avian and Lady Shale. The day was overcast as if all nature mourned with them. No gentle breeze carried the fresh fragrance of flowers and forest plants, nor caressed their cheeks soothingly; even the birds were still as the elves gathered for the ceremony. Beneath an old lilac bush a cluster of rabbits lay with their heads resting upon their paws. Cameron noticed this and thought it odd, but this was not a time to ponder the strange behavior of rabbits.

Avian named his son Baley, for his love passed swiftly through their lives. Lovingly, he placed the ornate box in the place of honor, leaned over it and kissed the polished top. Together he and Shale sat with arms entwined, surrounded by their family. The sad, beautiful voices of the elves lamented their loss and they wept freely with their people.

Songs of mourning, of love, and the preciousness of life flowed on into the evening. Avian peered through his tears at his wife. Shale's strength was waning. He drew her up from their couch and tried to turn her toward their room. Shale resisted him. She could not bear to leave the little box sitting before them. Avian took her to it and she bent over it weeping. He kissed the top of the box and waited for Shale to do so. Finally she was able to kiss the smooth wooden surface and allow her husband to surround her in his embrace. That night, Avian lay with Shale and watched her slip into the deep realm of sleep. He wished he could join her there, but he could not.

Rising, he passed through the back garden and entered the stable. His horse neighed a quiet welcome. Patting the soft muzzle, he spoke quietly, "Ready for a ride, my friend? I am in need of one."

Slipping the headpiece over the ears, he mounted in a quick leap and turned toward the woods. The cool bite of the fresh night air helped to clear his head. He could still hear the mournful songs of his people running through his mind. Urging his horse on, he rode faster and faster until he reached the meadow he sought. Even here the stars seemed dim to him. Sitting astride his mount, he studied the heavens.

"Why, God, why? Has she not suffered enough?" Startled by the intensity of his cry through the thin night air, he sat straighter upon his mount. "I promised her I would protect her. I failed. But you, God, why did you not protect her and our son? She is kind and she loves you, Father God. Why did you not help them?"

The horse shifted uneasily beneath him. He rubbed its thick neck to soothe the animal. He longed for comfort for himself. His heart searched for a reason, but there was none. No reason for a tiny baby to die, for his wife to suffer this tragedy.

His anger stirred within him. The still, small voice of peace battled with it. *Trust, he should trust. God loved them, didn't he? Why, then?*

The still voice of peace tugged harder at him. He wanted to trust. It was so hard when the ones he loved hurt, when he hurt, and he could do nothing to stop it.

Trust, came the voice inside him again. He urged his horse to run on wildly through the meadow.

Shale responded well to the loving care of her new family. Two weeks more passed and she grew stronger.

Near suppertime, Crystal came to her. "Shale, will you join us for this meal? I will help you."

"Yes, I would like that," Shale answered. "Where is my husband?" she asked.

"He is with Orrie, father, and Cameron," Crystal softly replied. She did not look at Shale.

"What is it, Crystal? Tell me! What has happened? Avian is leaving isn't he? I cannot bear it, Crystal! Send

Cameron away, send him away!" Shale covered her face with her hands and turned toward the wall.

"Hush, Shale. Do not upset yourself needlessly. Cameron himself brings news of your brother and sister. You want to know about them, do you not?" Crystal soothed.

"That is not all. I feel it in my heart." Shale rocked herself gently where she sat on the edge of the bed.

Crystal knelt beside her and gently brought Shale's hands down to her lap. "We must have hope, Shale. We must trust God to guide us," Crystal tried to comfort her.

"I know He is with me, Crystal. I know He always is, but this is too much. I cannot understand. I cannot." Shale lay on her side and curled her knees up to her body. She hugged her pillow tightly to her chest. "What now, what now?" she cried and could not be comforted. Crystal held her awhile and then left quietly, fighting back her own tears.

"Shale would not come with me, my mother. She fears the news Cameron brings. She fears Avian is leaving," Crystal informed her mother.

"Poor child, my poor child." The queen sighed and looked out over the courtyard. Corey, Avian, Cameron, and Orrie entered the dining room together.

"Where is Shale?" Avian asked.

"She is distraught, my brother," Crystal replied quietly, meeting his eyes.

Avian excused himself from the company and went to her. He paused at their bedside and stared down at her.

She was still pale and weary. Grief bound her, slowed her healing. He was expecting too much of her too soon.

Avian sighed and paced the room. He wanted to know. He needed to know. *Why did she leave without him? Who took her? Did she recognize them? What could she tell him? Why, why did this happen?* He would kill them. Whoever they were, they were his.

Shale opened her eyes. She watched Avian pace back and forth, his brow furrowed, his expression grim. *He wants to know. He needs to know.* She did not want to think about it. She did not want to talk about it.

Cameron was here. Perhaps he could persuade Avian not to go after him. Perhaps he would help. She prayed silently for wisdom, for understanding and courage.

Avian glanced toward the bed. She smiled a tiny smile, and held out her hand to him. He came to her and took her hand. She could feel the tension in him.

"You are not hungry, my love?" Avian asked.

"No, I am troubled because you are troubled," she answered looking into his eyes.

For a moment Avian was quiet, struggling to calm himself for her sake. "Let us not concern ourselves with that tonight. Come and hear of your brother and sister, for Cameron is dining with us."

"I will come," she paused, "and afterward I will tell you what you want to know." Shale's eyes searched his. She did not smile. She did not like what she saw.

Avian took her face in his hands and gently kissed her. His eyes glowed warmly for her. Shale smiled lovingly and kissed him back. She brushed her hair, took her husband's arm, and went with him down the hallway. She knew that anger burned inside him and it frightened her.

After their meal together, they gathered in the chambers of Shale and Avian. Shale sat on the bed with many pillows about her. Crystal sat beside her. The Queen gave her tea and settled on a chair near her two daughters. Avian paced the room while Cameron, Orrie, and Corey waited for her to begin.

"My maid told me that the stable boy had delivered a message from you, my husband," she began.

"Which maid? Which stable boy?" Avian interrupted, questioning her.

Shale swallowed hard. "Cinda. She said the new stable boy," Shale answered.

"The one who is now missing," Avian fumed.

"Peace, my son. Let Shale tell us what happened. Please continue, my daughter," Corey spoke calmly and smiled encouragingly at her.

"The message said I was to meet you at the Old Oak tree because you had errands to do before we left. So I rode there, and..." Shale started to continue.

"Why would you believe such a thing? You know that I wanted to leave together!" Avian burst in again.

Tears slipped down Shale's face. "I do not know. I do not know," she cried. "It is my fault, my fault our baby died." Her shoulders shook with her sobs.

"No, Shale, No." Crystal cried. "You had no reason to doubt the message."

She glared at her brother. "Stop it, Avian. She had no reason to doubt the message."

Avian knelt by Shale and held her. "Forgive me. It is not your fault. I am sorry. My anger is not at you. Who did this? Tell me."

"You will kill him," Shale sobbed. "You cannot."

Avian did not answer, but paced to the door and leaned against it.

Shale forced herself to take several deep breaths. She continued in a shaky voice, "An elven warrior came out of the forest across the meadow toward me. I thought it was you at first, but my mare was restless. He said he was my cousin and had come to warn me not to come to the festival, because they knew who I was. He said he would take me to you."

"Did you know this warrior, Shale? Had you seen him before?" the King gently asked.

"He was at the Festival of Golden Leaves." Looking to Bethany she continued, "He is the one who bumped my chair when I was resting my ankle. Do you remember? His brother had asked me to dance."

Bethany sharply drew a breath and replied, "You are sure?"

"Yes, for he had such cold eyes," Shale answered.

Bethany stared at Shale. "I always believed he intended to bump your chair."

"Who?" Avian demanded.

Bethany turned to her son. "It was Sollen."

Avian straightened and clinched his fists. Orrie stepped to his side and placed his hand on his shoulder.

"Then what happened?" Corey urged.

"We were so near the edge of the ravine. I told him to move over. His stallion would not leave my mare alone, and he could not control it. I told him to move away from me. Finally, he turned his horse away. It became angry. It leapt into the air and kicked out at me. My mare turned and took the brunt of the blow. She slipped off the edge and we fell. I tried to jump away from her, so she would not roll on me. I remember a rock, and sliding and tumbling down the slope. Then I knew no more. I do not know how long I lay there before I awoke. I felt a wetness upon me. I saw all the blood, I hurt..." Unconsciously she covered her abdomen with her hands. "I tried to get up, to go to my mare, and I was dizzy, but I got up and, and my baby..." Shale burst into tears. Avian struck the door with his fist.

Looking up quickly, Shale spoke to him, "I think he meant to help me, Avian, please..."

"Help you?" Avian exploded. "He sat on his horse and watched you lying there! He would have let you die!"

Shale eyes grew large in horror. She sat frozen on her bed. The thought that someone would deliberately try to kill her and her baby was unbelievable.

"Alas, it is true, my lady. We found his tracks and followed them," Orrie responded to her unasked question. "He sat upon his horse for some time, by the look of the tracks. There was no sign that he attempted to reach you or go for help."

Corey cleared his throat and said quietly, "Enough has been said. Let us take counsel."

"Sollen will suffer for what he has done," Avian pledged.

"Please do not shed innocent blood," Shale pled with him.

"Our son was innocent!" Avian burst out. He left the room slamming the door behind him. Orrie hurried out after Avian.

"My daughter," Corey gently spoke, "if you remember anything else that might help us, send word." He patted Shale's hand and turned to leave.

"Do not let Avian go after him, please, my father. Do not let him go," Shale called to him.

"We will take counsel," was the only assurance he gave.

Crystal and Bethany stayed with Shale and tried to comfort her. Crystal made tea for sleep. Shale sipped it, casting anxious glances at the door.

"You know how long counsels can take, my daughter," Bethany reminded her. "They have much to discuss with the news Cameron brought."

"I do not want him to go, my mother. I love him so much. I do not want him to go," Shale's voice rose and she sat upright off her pillows. "I could not bear to lose him. Please, my mother. Do not let him go. Tell him not to go!"

"Here, my child. Lie back. I will talk with him. Lie back now," Bethany soothed in a soft voice, tears streaming down her own face. She nodded quickly at Crystal who added more solution to the tea.

"Drink this, my child. There. Rest now, for me." Quietly she smoothed Shale's hair off her forehead. She sang quietly, hoping to soothe her.

Gradually, Shale relaxed, overcome by fatigue and the effects of the tea. Finally she slept, exhausted in mind, body, and soul.

Avian was not beside her when she awoke. She could not remember if he had come to their bed that night. He would go. She knew he would go.

"Dear God, please let Avian forgive me. Keep him safe; please bring him home to me. Help me to be brave and loving for him. Let us not part with anger between us. Help me to trust him to you. It is so hard to trust. I am so afraid, God. I am so afraid," she prayed through her tears.

She rose and walked to the balcony. She looked out over the beauty of the forest and let the cool, morning air settle over her. She searched her heart for something to be thankful for, something to help her trust.

The dawning light touched the edge of Bethany's herb garden, lighting up the flowers and deepening the shadows among the plants not yet breeched by its warmth. Two small gray rabbits played together there. Piper should be dancing with them. No, Piper and Samuell were far away, but safe.

In a small corner of Shale's heart a flicker of hope began. She murmured a song of thanksgiving and raised her arms to receive the assurance of God's embrace.

Quietly the door opened behind her, and Avian entered their chamber. She turned and greeted him, "Good morning, my love." She smiled warmly at him.

"I must talk with you, Shale," he spoke firmly, as if to a child.

Crossing the room, she went and sat on their bed. "When will you leave, my husband?" she quietly asked.

Startled by the question, Avian studied her face. She did not look away, and her eyes did not question his decision.

"Tomorrow morning. Cameron has already gone. I will travel with my family as I normally would to a festival." He moved to her side. "Are you strong enough to travel? You must go to Bellflower. I need you to be safe."

Taking her hand, he sat beside her and continued. "I have a plan. After cover of darkness tonight, I will take you to meet your protectors, three of my most trusted friends."

"The ones who watched over us when first we were married?" Shale asked him.

"Yes. You will be safe with them." Rubbing his fingers over her hands, he continued detailing his plan, "Your maid will accompany us to the festival, disguised as you. Thereby your departure may be kept secret longer. It is decided."

"Very well. I trust you, Avian," Shale assured him.

"No arguments?" He raised an eyebrow and studied her again.

"None are needed, my husband. I will have Cinda pack as if I were going to the festival." Shale continued looking up into his eyes. She did not want him to distance himself from her. She did not want him to withdraw. "I know you can not come with me this time, my love. I will miss you so."

She looked down at his hand holding hers, and with her other hand caressed his. She looked back up at him and smiled a tremulous smile. "We have not yet been parted." As she spoke she saw him begin to relax.

"I am sorry that I shouted at you last night. Please forgive me." He peered searchingly into her eyes. He detected a brief flash of pain, and then the peacefulness enveloping her settled over her again. He sighed deeply. "I do not blame you."

Her eyes held his and did not waver. "You are mourning deeply, too, my love." Her countenance shone with love for him. "Be at peace. It is forgotten."

He wrapped her in his arms and buried his face in her hair. Together they cried and lay back on the bed, clinging to each other. When their tears had stopped, Avian rose on his elbow and gently brushed her hair back from her face. How could he have hurt her so? He stared into the eyes that mirrored his heart and bent to warm her lips with his. Their kiss was gentle and slow, and she moved into his embrace. Her love flowed over him, and he reluctantly pulled himself away from her.

"Stay. It is all right," Shale urged him. She did not let go of him.

"It is too soon."

"My healer said it is fine." Her eyes were soft and misty.

"You asked my mother!" he exclaimed. His cheeks grew red and warm.

A soft smile grew about her lips and she answered, "Women in love speak of many things. She is wise and she is my mother now, too. Will you hold me? Please?"

Lying back again, Avian held her against him, smelling her soft hair, memorizing everything about her. They lay together a long time, and then Shale pressed her lips to his searchingly.

"You are sure?" he whispered.

Smiling, she touched his lips with her fingers, "They will miss you at breakfast."

Later that afternoon, Avian practiced his skills with the other Cambria Forest competitors. This would be no game for him. *No game at all. I will be ready. I will avenge my son.*

"Peace, Avian!" exclaimed Jamie as he looked up from the ground where Avian had thrown him as they practiced hand-to-hand combat.

Avian shook his head and offered Jamie his hand to assist him up. "I am sorry, my friend." Slapping Jamie's shoulder, he moved on to the archery and knife throwing area.

Jamie looked to Dracy, who shook his head. "Come, we will speak with him."

"Avian! Stop a moment. I would have a word with you," Dracy called to him.

When You Dance with Rabbits

Avian did not respond until he had thrown his knives with all his strength into the center of the target. Striding forth, he retrieved them, then returned to the starting point, giving his friends only part of his attention as he prepared to throw again.

"Avian, you are practicing as if the goblins are upon you. What troubles you?" Dracy persisted.

Avian did not reply but again viciously threw his knives into the center of the target. Retrieving them, he paused by his two friends. "What troubles me? Our enemies do not always come in the form of goblins. Did you not know this?" he said bitterly. He stalked off toward the archery area, remembering his wife's cries as she had dreamed in his arms that morning.

Dracy caught up to him. "You must keep your head clear, Avian. Do not let your emotions put you off your guard. It is not entirely clear who the enemies are yet."

Whirling upon him, Avian challenged, "It is clear who one of them is. He is mine. Beware yourselves if you doubt who your enemies are. Have you more advice for me? No? Good. I have work to do." Not giving them time to respond, he strode off.

Dracy and Jamie conferred among themselves about his safety. Many on their team had gone ahead as spies, saying they preferred to prepare for the games on site. One would contact Cameron.

"And Henicles should be arriving there soon," Jamie added. "Surely, Avian will listen to him."

"We will pray so, Jamie. Would that we could be there with him," Dracy said. Together they walked to the archery area, staying close to their friend.

Later that afternoon Avian returned to find Shale resting. The vest she had worn on the night he had met her lay on the table, the many pockets filled. Looking down at her, he smoothed back her hair from her face and lay down beside her. She moved close to him, laying her head on his shoulder and encircling his chest with her arm.

Avian sighed. Part of him longed to stay with her, to take her to Bellflower himself. Most of him was filled with restlessness and an urgent need to end this. He would not have them living in fear any longer. Sollen would be stopped.

After dining that evening, the family of Corey talked of the festival. Shale chatted with Crystal about their gowns, and teased her about dancing with a certain tall elf. She laughed when they teased Avian, saying that he must do well in the games to show that marriage had not softened him.

Shale felt reassured when Avian laughed with them. He had not smiled in many days.

As they walked together to their chambers, Avian put his arm around her waist, and she smiled up at him. He opened the door and she anxiously watched his face.

Avian looked about the room with wide eyes. Candles burned softly and the scent of warm pine oil reached him. He inhaled deeply. Several small bottles were warming on a stool near the fireplace. He looked down at his wife.

Shale wrapped her arms around his neck and moved closer to him. Wrinkling her nose at him mischievously, she said, "I cannot have my husband participating in the games without a warm, vigorous massage. We have time, my love."

She pulled him over to their bed and unbuttoned his shirt. "Take it off and be seated," she instructed.

Avian smiled to himself while he watched his wife. She stood before the fireplace, picking up each bottle in the collection and placing them in a specific order. His eyes glowed warmly. She amazed him by doing this. Who had told her of this custom?

Whenever possible before a battle, the wives of elven warriors prayed over their husbands as they massaged them. The custom had been attached to the festival games as well. He now prepared himself to be pampered. With a mixture of amusement and sadness, for she seemed so frail, he watched her fuss over the oils as she arranged them on a silver tray.

Shale placed the tray on the small wooden table by their bed and sat next to him. "Relax now and give me your arm," she instructed very seriously.

Trying to match her mood, he held back his smile and extended his arm to her.

Bending his wrist she massaged it with warm, fragrant pine oil. Her thumbs moved in small circles over his wrist and hand. Each of his fingers received the same thorough care.

"Shale, you are tired. It..." he began.

"Shh...Relax. Let me hold your arm. Let it go," her soft voice coaxed.

Avian complied, letting his arm lie limply in her grasp.

Starting with his shoulder she moved down his arm, kneading his strong muscles and praying for strength and accuracy in the use of his weapons. Next, she knelt behind him on their bed and, beginning at his neck, lightly rubbed the length of his back with quick motions. He sighed appreciatively.

Suddenly she stopped. "Lie down on your stomach. I forgot. You are supposed to lie down. There. That is better." A little flustered, she moved closer to him and began again. Continuing the quick, light movements Shale began to pray over him. "Father God, let my husband think clearly and quickly. Let him not be distracted by anything. Give him strength in his mind, body, and spirit."

Massaging now with her thumbs, she moved across his shoulders. "They are very tight, my love. What did you do when you practiced?" she said. Concern edged her voice.

"You heard them teasing me, my love. I must not let them think that marriage has softened me," he teased.

"It has made you better," she confirmed and set her mind on working out the tense areas she found. "Father God, may Avian's perception be sharper than his weapons and his reactions swift and true." She paused a moment to reflect on her actions so far, then commanded, "Take off your leggings, now, my husband."

He began to rise from the bed to do so, but her eager hands stopped him.

"No! Do not rise yet. Here, I will do it," Shale spoke quickly then silently scolded herself for not thinking of this at the beginning.

Avian froze and lay back down, allowing her to tug off his leggings. He fought back a laugh. She was so serious, trying to do this correctly for him.

Shale lifted a small amber jar of mint-scented oil from the tray. She smoothed it onto his legs and feet, praying, "Father God, may Avian stand firmly, trusting you, and return swiftly to me."

Finally, she sat by his head. "Turn over onto your back, my love. Good. Now lay your head here in my lap." Gently, she massaged his temples and forehead with oil of spearmint. "Father God, let no words or feelings deceive my husband. Let him trust wholly in you, for I love him."

When she finished this, she leaned down and kissed his forehead. Avian lay still and she sat watching him. He was so precious to her, so beautiful. *Please do not keep us apart very long, Father God.* Gently, she lifted his head and slipped from beneath it. She lay down beside him, feeling his warmth and strength, listening to him breathe.

A tiny twitch at the corner of his mouth told her he was not at all asleep and she pounced on him, "Avian of Cambria Forest, you are not asleep!" She frowned deeply at him.

"No, but I am so very relaxed and happy that I cannot move." He looked deeply into her loving eyes. "You are wonderful, my love." He smiled then, and gathered her in his arms. "Thank you, Shale. I am ready now, but how I shall miss you."

Chapter 12

No one questioned them riding at night, for they often did. Shale's arms encircled Avian's waist and his hand rested on hers. She rested her cheek against his back and drank in his presence. Her mare followed behind them. They rode on steadily for nearly an hour before they joined Shale's guardians.

"We back tracked many times and I am assured we were not followed," Avian told them.

He held Shale closely and whispered, "I love you forever, and I will be with you soon. Hasten on now. God be with you."

To his friends he said, "Travel safely and swiftly, for you carry my heart." Kissing her once again, he set Shale on her mount and watched them gallop away. "Father God," he prayed, "Guide them and protect them and give them success on their journey. Be with me at the festival, and let the truth be made known." Avian waited, listening until he could hear them no more.

Swiftly, the three guardians led Shale through the night. Under cover of darkness, she let her tears flow freely down her cheeks.

During the many days of riding, Shale tried to concentrate on Cameron's news of Samuell and Piper. They were growing in character, strength and skills. Samuell was boating now and loved the river. Piper's musical skills were excelling, and she delighted in the times she could be playing the harp or flute. It seemed they were happy in their new home.

Soon her thoughts returned to her husband, and she prayed for his safety. "Father God, let Avian think clearly and keep anger from clouding his decisions. I long to be with him again. I miss him so much. Thank you, Father," she finished. *He would be all right. He would come for her soon. Perhaps Samuell and Piper could return with them.*

When Shale and her guardians rode through open spaces, she urged her mare to run faster and faster through the fragrant grasses. It reminded her so much of her home on the farm. She needed the feeling of home, of security and safety.

Dracy rode up beside her and reminded, "My lady, we must keep an even pace each day to travel this long distance. We must pace the horses accordingly."

She slowed her mare to keep pace with them. Despair came crowding back on her and dug its roots into her heart. She ached for her baby. She tried to fight. She sang beautiful songs of the creation of the world. She watched for butterflies and animals to tell Piper about. She thought of things to be thankful for. Still, it held her captive.

One beautiful afternoon they rode into a clearing stretching as far as she could see. The warmth of the sun seemed to be urging her on. Shale gave the mare her head and pulled herself into a crouch behind the saddle. When she had the rhythm of the mare's movements, she rose up, standing on the mare's rump with her arms outstretched. The wind rushed by her, and she felt so alive and free again! It had been a very long time since she had done this. She felt she was back home, in her father's pastures. Dockle rode up beside her and commanded her to slow down.

Regaining her seat, she slowed the mare and he spoke angrily to her. "Avian is my friend and my brother in arms. I promised him to take care of you and deliver you safely. I will do it, if I have to tie you up, I will." He glared at her. "You could not have shouted your identity any louder with words than you just did on horseback."

Shale pulled her hood and cloak about her and made no reply. She did not like Dockle. What was he thinking? Many elves could ride like that.

That night Shale listened intently to the conversation of her guardians as they ate their simple meal. They discussed the lay of the land ahead of them. They planned to turn north along the river, and that would take them close to the trail leading to Robin's Wood.

It is time, Shale thought. She would plead her case. If they persisted in taking her to Bellflower, she would escape from their watchful eyes. Near the river she could do it. She was sure she could.

She waited for an opportunity and began, "I wish for all of us to go to my husband. He needs our help. Here are three of his most trusted friends and warriors, when they should be with him. Let us change our course. Are we not close to the road taking us to Robin's Wood when we round the bend in the river? Let us make haste to Avian, not away from him. He needs your skills with him."

The three stared at her and then exchanged glances with each other. Avian had warned them that she might try this.

"My lady, your husband would be distracted if you were there. He would be concerned for your safety, and we would be guarding you instead of being free to assist him," Jamie reasoned.

"Do you think I am helpless? Do you not see that I am stronger every day?" Shale spoke tersely.

"My lady, were you the greatest warrior of all, your husband would still seek to protect you. He loves you," Dracy quietly reminded her.

Shale sank to the ground. She seethed with frustration. *How could she help Avian when they would not listen?* After much thought, Shale spoke again. "How much farther is it to Bellflower? A week? Two weeks? Why must three of you take me? Cannot one accompany me and two go to my husband?" Her huge eyes pleaded with them to consider her request.

"My lady, we will discuss your request. Go into the tree now and rest. We will ride hard again tomorrow," Dockle said kindly.

Rising, Shale said, "Thank you, and good night." Though exhausted, her step was light as she left the campfire. Surely they would agree.

In the morning, they galloped the horses to the river where they stopped. Dockle spoke to Shale regarding her request from the night before. "My lady, if you agree to come with me without argument, I will send these two on to your husband. Will you do so?"

Shale longed to go to Avian herself, but Dracy had been right. Avian would be distracted if she were there. She must not endanger him. She must go to Bellflower. She would prefer to travel with one of the others, but they knew Avian better and would be better able to help him. "Thank you. I will do as you ask."

Turning to Dracy and Jamie, she urged them, "Make haste, and may God guide you with His great wisdom."

Shale was never comfortable around Dockle. He always seemed haughty to her. The uncomfortable feeling grew, now that Dracy and Jamie had left them. She remembered the look they had exchanged when Dockle had announced that he would take her to Bellflower. *Were they also uncomfortable with this?* As they continued riding, another thought came to her. *He had said that she shouted her identity by standing on the mare's back during their journey. Why would he say that? Other elves rode that way. She had seen them. No one in Cambria Forest knew who she really was, save Avian, and his fam-*

ily. Did Dockle know? How? The stable boy who had given her the false message—who had told him to do that? The uncomfortable feeling became ominous. She must be on her guard. The leather sheath holding her knife rested against her leg above her ankle where she had secured it. She had this and her woodcraft skills. She glanced at Dockle again. He had not spoken since they set out from the others.

Late afternoon, they stopped briefly to water the horses.

Mounting with ease, Dockle spoke, "We will head south now."

"Is Bellflower not to the West?" Shale asked.

"Yes, but we need to go south for a smoother route," he growled at her.

"I do not need a smoother route. I am fine," Shale insisted.

"No arguing. You want to hurry, so I may return to your husband's side, do you not?" Not waiting for an answer, he led to the south.

Shale followed at a slower pace behind him. He dropped back to her.

"Keep up with me," he ordered menacingly.

"I have just watered my horse. I do not want to make her sick," Shale retorted.

"She did not drink that much. Hurry her on. Or is it you who grows weak?" His sneer was unnerving and she did not reply, but urged her mare to a faster pace.

Night came, but Dockle did not allow a fire. She set out bread and cheese, and took hers to her saddle where she sat to eat.

"So, lady," Dockle spoke mockingly, "tonight you will sleep on the ground like the peasant you are. Avian may be deceived by your attempts at royalty. He is a fool. I have had my fill of his arrogant ways. You will be near to him sooner than you think, but you will not see him alive again. He will dance the Presage with me, and I will kill him."

"The Presage is only evil. Do not be deceived by it," Shale spoke with alarm. Seeing the excitement in his eyes at the thought of killing her husband, she knew her words of warning would not be heeded. Her hand shook.

"You would say anything to keep your royal standing." He stood and approached her.

"Avian will not fight you. He does not know the Presage." Shale lay her food down beside her.

"He will learn, because the fool loves you and he will fight for you," Dockle spoke with certain smugness. "Oh, he will learn it, but I have mastered it."

"You are the fool. It will destroy you," Shale cried.

His hand struck hard against her face, knocking her to the ground. "Nothing will destroy me. I will persuade Sollen that I have the right to fight Avian."

Shale gasped. "What has Sollen to do with it?"

"Sollen will rule his father's kingdom soon. He wishes to destroy Avian." He paused considering this. "I must arrive in time to argue my right to fight him. Sadly, I must keep you alive, and drag you along with me, but you will not slow me down, peasant."

The horses moved restlessly and Dockle looked toward them. Shale drew her knife and leapt to her feet.

Dockle spun around and knocked it from her hand. "Did you think I did not see this while you were riding? Fool!" he sneered. He picked it up and tested its weight. He lifted his hand to strike her again, but a strong arm threw him backward.

"What trickery is this, Dockle?" Jamie demanded.

"She is the trickery! Do you not see it? She is a fraud and a threat to our kingdom!" Dockle spat this out like poison and wrenched his arm free of Jamie's grasp.

"Who has filled you with such foolish thoughts?" Jamie persisted.

Shale shouted, "He wants to kill Avian!"

Dockle whipped around and took her by the throat. He held her silver knife above her. His repulsive sneer told her he would kill her now. He raised his arm to thrust the knife into her chest. Shale closed her eyes and cried out to God.

An arrow whizzed past her ear. She heard Dockle swear and the knife drop from his hand. The arrow had pierced his wrist.

Jamie grabbed her arm and pulled her away from Dockle. A strong voice commanded, "Do not move if you value your life." Dracy stepped into the small clearing. "Bind him, Jamie. King Corey will know what he is about, whether we return him dead or alive."

Dockle began to tremble with rage. "You cannot stop it. The kingdom will be taken. The kings are weak, and their enemies draw nigh to them, unknown. I will be rescued and I will kill the fool Avian and you," Dockle spat out.

"Who would want to save a worm like you, Dockle?" Jamie taunted him. "They will probably kill you themselves to prevent you from speaking against them."

"I will never speak against them. The kingdoms will be conquered before you can warn them."

"Ah, yes," Jamie continued, "I see the North Star is nigh. We are less than one day's ride from where King Corey rests this night. And I hear the spiders of Southern Cambria Forest are very hungry this season. To nibble on a tasty yet sour elf may please them, do you not agree, Dracy?"

Shale cried out, "If indeed we are so close, let us hasten there and warn them."

"There is no need of haste, my lady. Dockle is the only enemy about tonight. The borders of Cambria Forest are yet unbreached," Dracy spoke calmly. "Perhaps the spiders are hungry this night. Surely they have gathered here with no firelight, and now the smell of fresh elf blood to draw them. Tie him to that tree."

Jamie pushed the bound Dockle to a slender linden tree and bound him to it. He squeezed Dockle's wrist tightly to produce a fresh scent of blood and moved quickly away from him.

"My lady, walk fifty paces and build a small fire. Stay there and tend it," Dracy nodded behind him to a small clearing in the trees.

Shale hesitated, but his expression was deadly serious.

A skittering sound was heard above them in the trees, then again from farther away.

"It appears the spiders are hungry. How many bites should I allow before I scatter them the first time?" Dracy asked. His eyes glinted with anticipation.

As the little fire produced a small glow of safety, the darkness of night deepened around Dockle. The skittering sounds increased.

"Ah, they are coming already. Maybe three bites? That will not kill him too soon," Jamie suggested. He moved into the shadows with Dracy.

The wind picked up and the skittering grew louder and faster. Dockle raised his head and looked nervously above him.

Movement in the bush beside him made him cry out, "Stop them, stop!"

A large brown spider jumped onto his leg and began to crawl upward. With no response from his captors, Dockle called out anxiously, "I will tell you everything! Save me!"

Again there was no response, only the increasing skittering of the spiders above him. The bush beside him began to shake intermittently and hissing sounds came from it at odd intervals.

In a hushed voice Dracy spoke, "There are so many of them. Do you think we can scatter them enough to spare him?"

Dockle cried out, "Sollen! It is Sollen! He has hired men to come to Cambria Forest and assail the festival. He seeks to overthrow his father, so that he may rule. Free me quickly!"

"When do they arrive, and from where do they come?" Dracy demanded.

Shale moved closer so she would not miss a word of information. They must warn her family.

"They are to attack the last night of the festival. I do not know from where they come." The bush beside Dockle shook much harder. "I do not know. I do not. Only that they will come on horseback and attack late in the night. Please, save me," Dockle pleaded.

"Bring him," Dracy spoke.

The bush shook violently, and Jamie came forth with a smile and began loosening the bonds holding Dockle to the tree. Shoving him forward, they approached Dracy and Shale.

Enraged by their trickery, Dockle spun toward Shale and threw his bound wrists over her head. He pulled the rope hard against her neck. Shale immediately went limp against him and her weight pulled him off balance.

Jamie raced toward them, but the arrow of Dracy was swifter by far. It struck Dockle's back and the thrust of the arrow pushed him forward, knocking him to the ground on top of Shale.

Jamie rolled them over quickly and slashed through the ropes, freeing Shale from the strangling force at her throat. Gasping, she struggled up and ran into the woods.

"My lady, do not fear," Jamie called out. "It is not safe there. Come to the fire. He will harm no one again."

Shale hesitated. Her hands covered her throat. *Whom could she trust? Whom could Avian trust?* These three had guarded them on their wedding trip. Avian counted them as his closest friends. Did Jamie and Dracy desire power, too? Glancing at Dockle's body, she was reassured by the arrow embedded in his back.

"We have been wary of him since the Festival of Golden Leaves. He has grown coldhearted. We followed you, and our fears were realized. Come to the fire and rest, my lady," Jamie urged.

"No, we must hasten to Avian. He cannot even trust his own warriors. He must know this," Shale argued, stepping from the forest.

Dracy retrieved her knife and his arrow. He wiped her knife clean on the grass, and handed it to her. "Jamie will go to him, and I will see you safely to Bellflower, my lady." Seeing the distress in her eyes, he said, "Avian and the King are not unaware of the deceit in their own kingdom. Do you not see? That is the reason for you traveling at this time. It is no longer safe for you to stay in Cambria Forest."

"Can we not ride now?" Shale pled.

Jamie gently reminded her, "My lady, the horses must rest, even if the riders do not. I am less than one day's hard ride from the King. I will travel with all speed as soon as my horse is ready."

Shale saw that they would not budge. She lay down. Her bleeding had started again, but she would not tell them. She turned onto her side and prayed for her husband.

After three hours had passed, they awakened Shale. Weariness was upon her again. The three parted, and each rode toward their destinations with a clear purpose.

As Shale rode with Dracy, doubts began to plague her. *Did others think of her as Dockle did? Did they really think that she had weaseled her way into Avian's life for social standing and a semblance of power? Could they not see how much she loved him? That he was her life?* Shaking her head, she looked up at the stars and the sliver of moon lighting the sky. *It did not matter what others thought. It mattered only that Avian knew how much she loved him and that they were together.* Fighting off the doubt, she set her mind on her husband.

Avian rode back and forth among the travelers, mingling with fellow competitors, and pretending to comfort and encourage his 'wife,' who rode alone in her carriage. As he was again drawing near to the coach, a galloping horse approached him.

"Jamie," he exclaimed, "What news do you bring?"

"My lord, our mission is completed," Jamie called to him. Lowering his voice, Jamie continued, "Slowly, my lord, we must take counsel."

Avian smiled at him. "Well done, Jamie."

They dismounted and walked their horses. Avian spoke jovially and laughed about the competition until the attention drawn by Jamie's arrival was turned elsewhere.

"She is safe. Dockle proved himself evil as we feared. He is dead, but not before giving us precious information. Sollen is behind the Presage, but that is not all," Jamie reported earnestly. He reached out a restraining arm to Avian. "Sollen plans to overthrow his father's rule. That is the reason for the gathering of men at the borders of Cambria Forest. They are to attack on the last night of the festival, after the celebrating is well underway."

"We must warn King Corsac," Avian began. He stopped, noting the look of dread on Jamie's face. "What is it?"

"The Lady Shale bid me hasten to you with this warning. Dockle knew who she is. I do not understand this and I am not asking for explanation, but if Dockle knew this, who else may know? Does this endanger you, my lord?" Jamie asked.

Avian's grim expression deepened. "We may not deceive them with our decoy then." Briefly he studied the coach carrying his "wife."

"We must get word to Cameron quickly." Avian noted the sweat-drenched flanks of Jamie's mount. "I will send another."

"Only give me a fresh horse. I fear we do not know whom to trust. Please, I would go, my friend." Jamie stood unwaveringly before Avian.

Gripping Jamie's shoulder, Avian sighed and nodded. "Take the red gelding. He is swift and steady."

Jamie nodded and took his horse to the master of the herd accompanying them.

Turning at the sound of horse's hooves, Avian faced his father.

"What word, my son?" Corey asked with a false smile spread across his face.

Avian smiled at his father and reported the information Jamie had brought as though it had been wonderful news. "I have sent him to warn Cameron," Avian finished.

Corey sat his mount and considered this information. "I will send a messenger to King Corsac."

"Choose your messenger with care," Avian advised.

His father nodded grimly, and turned his mount toward his guards.

Avian let his thoughts turn completely to his wife. He longed to see the warm glow of love for him in her eyes, to hear her laughter. He ached to hold her in his arms, to feel her soft hair against his skin; to let her fresh, sweet scent fill his senses. He could see her riding away from him. A shadow darkened her heart. Silently, he lifted his heart in prayer for her, proclaiming his love for her—his need for her. Thus, he rode on in deep concentration, and no one dared disturb him.

Chapter 13

Many days of hard riding brought Shale and Dracy to the borders of Bellflower.

"This is a huge wood. How will we find them? You must go to Avian!" Shale looked anxiously around her at the thick forest.

"We will join the main road and blend in with the other travelers, my lady. It should not be far," Dracy assured her.

"Indeed it is not," came a commanding voice. "Who are you and why have you come upon us in such stealth?"

"First make yourself known," Dracy replied calmly.

"No elf need come in secrecy to Bellflower unless his intent is without honesty." An elven warrior accompanied by two others stepped forth from the wood. "I am Bara of Bellflower.

"We have come with all haste and great need of secrecy, for my lady's life is in danger," Dracy explained. "I am Dracy of Cambria Forest and I bring the Lady Shale, wife of Avian, for safe keeping among you."

Bara studied them, and then spoke, "Come. I will hear your story."

They dismounted deeper in the forest and Shale seated herself with her back resting against one of the broad tree trunks. She listened intently to the message her husband had sent through Dracy to the Bellflower elves. From time to time Bara looked toward her. She was growing paler by the moment.

Finally, Dracy came to her. "My lady, Bara has agreed to take you. You will be safe here, my lady. I will make haste to your husband's side."

Tearfully, Shale thanked him. Dracy lifted her upon her mare.

Bara spoke, and one of his warriors hurried away from them.

"I have sent him to make them aware of your coming." He tore off a piece of bread and handed it to Shale.

Her hand shook when she reached for it. Taking a small bite she nodded to Bara, "I am ready."

Exchanging a glance with Dracy, Bara led Shale's mare at a brisk pace through the woods.

Arriving in Bellflower, Bara sent word to the lord and lady of their arrival. Bara led Shale's mare to a warm tent near a sparkling fountain on the east side of the settlement. Easing her off the mare, he assisted her to a bed, where two maidens skilled in healing waited with soothing teas and cleansing waters.

One of the maidens went to the entrance of the tent and called out to a group of children playing by the fountain. "One of you bring more water, please."

"I will!" A clear voice rang out.

"Let me help, too," cried another. Setting down the brown squirrel she was holding, the young maiden dashed after her friend.

The children came rushing into the tent. Each of them carried a silver pitcher filled with fresh water. They set the pitchers on the table by the door.

The smaller child poured clear cool water into a goblet and carried it toward the chamber where Shale lay. She peered through the thin curtain surrounding the bed and gasped. The goblet crashed to the floor and she cried, "Shale! Shale, you have come! I have prayed and prayed for you to come!" Piper raced to the bedside and her expression of joy turned to one of concern.

"Piper!" Shale reached out to hold her sister. They clung tightly to each other until Shale pushed Piper back to look upon her face. "You are well, my sister? Where is Samuell?" Shale could not help blurting out the questions. Tears streamed from her eyes. She held Piper's hand and lay back on the pillow, exhausted.

Bara noted how much alike they looked. No wonder Shale had seemed familiar to him. Drawing the others aside, he warned them, "No one must know this. No one must know their connection."

Approaching the two sisters, he knelt beside Piper. "Piper, even here, as you know, we must be careful. I am grateful for you that she has come, but we must not let others know yet." He looked to Shale for support.

"Yes, Piper. For a while longer we must keep our secrets," Shale confirmed. She reached up and brushed back a strand of Piper's hair.

"I will stay with you," Piper said.

"No, little one, but the lady will be well soon, I am sure," Bara said.

Piper began to cry and Shale sought to soothe her, "I will be staying with you for a long while. We will have many, many days together, Piper. I love you."

"The child is one of our apprentices. It will not be thought unusual for her to be here helping us at her regular times. If it is permitted, you may return tomorrow, Piper," the apprentice offered. Three pairs of eyes turned to Bara.

"We must be very careful," he reminded them. He turned and left, for their tears were becoming his.

Toward evening when the twilight came to be, the Lady Audrey of Bellflower came to Shale. Bara had told them of Shale's flight to them and the loss of her child. Of Samuell and Piper, Audrey was well aware and pleased with their recovery. Now, at last, their sister had come to them for healing of her own.

Audrey peered down at Shale's weary face. She lightly touched Shale's brow and smiled kindly as Shale opened her eyes.

"Welcome to Bellflower, my lady. Long have we awaited your coming." Audrey's smile faded as she spoke further, "The lord Zane and I mourn with you your great loss."

Shale's expression clouded and tears slid down her cheeks.

Audrey's sensitive fingers gently probed Shale's tender abdomen. She took Shale's hands in hers. "We will care for you. Rest now. We would have you be whole and strong again. Take hope, for love awaits you. The love of your family and the love of your husband surround you. Be at peace. When you are stronger, you will dwell with the family of Raina. They wish to make you welcome."

Audrey touched Shale's brow again, and her tired eyes closed. Was this visitor indeed the Lady of Bellflower? Crystal had spoken of her knowledge of healing herbs. Shale had many questions for the lord and lady, but weariness claimed her. She could not ask them now.

The lady conferred with the Healer and quietly left.

Moments later an apprentice came to her bedside and sat down. "My lady, here is medicine for you."

Shale took the mug and sipped the strong tea. She coughed and nearly choked on it.

The apprentice smiled sympathetically. "It is indeed awful, but very effective. Please drink it all."

"What is this?" Shale questioned, forcing down another swallow.

"It is tea made of the hemlock tree. It will cleanse you, and the bleeding will stop when the cleansing is complete. You will regain your strength," the maiden replied. "The cleansing may be painful, but we will help you, my lady. You will go to Raina's family when you are strong enough." Dropping her voice to a whisper the apprentice continued, "Piper lives there."

Shale's large eyes softened at the thought of living with her siblings again. If only Avian were here. "Oh, Lord God, give him your peace and comfort. Make him strong in mind and body. Give him hope in you. Protect him, please," she prayed. She forced herself to finish the bitter tea.

Within an hour's time the cramping began. The apprentice stayed with her and gave her medicines to soothe her. *She had not lied. The cleansing was both physically and emotionally draining,* Shale thought.

The horrible cramping finally stopped sometime in the night. Cool, soothing cloths were used to cleanse her body and their fragrance was refreshing to her soul. Exhausted she slept, dreaming of her husband, and lying safely in his warm arms.

Three days later in the home of Raina, Shale sat watching Samuell and Piper go about their daily routine. They were thriving under Raina's love and care. Samuell and Piper had adjusted well to life in Bellflower.

They don't need me anymore, Shale thought. *Oh, they are happy that I am with them, but they do not need me. They have Raina, and they love her.* Doubts clouded her mind.

What of Avian? Did he need her? He was strong. He needed a strong wife; one his people had confidence in. Was Dockle speaking for all of Cambria Forest when he accused her of striving for social position and wealth? Would Avian come to believe this? Would his family? Would they still love her as their own? She ached to tell them it wasn't true, that she loved them dearly. That was all she wanted. It was all she ever wanted.

Piper skipped to Shale's chair with fresh fruit she had prepared. "I brought your favorites, Shale," she enthused. "Grapes, raspberries, and apples. These apples taste like the ones we had at home. Try them." Piper's bright smile lit her face.

Shale took a slice of apple and crunched into it. Its sweet taste was very pleasing. "Thank you, Piper. It is very good."

"Piper, why don't you take Shale to the garden and show her your herbs," Raina softly said.

"Come, Shale. Come see my garden," Piper coaxed. "I planted it myself. My rabbits do not bother it, either."

Shale rose and stood leaning on Piper's shoulder until the dizziness passed. Piper led her around the corner of the small cottage. "Here it is. This corner is mine. I selected the plants and put them here myself. I have lavender, lemon balm, bee balm, garlic, fox glove, and mint." Piper looked expectantly at her sister.

"It is beautiful, Piper. You have done well," Shale praised her. "No doubt it is well planned both in its beauty and its usefulness."

Four brown rabbits appeared from behind the blackberry bushes next to the garden. They sniffed carefully and hopped nearer to Piper.

Shale watched as Piper danced with the rabbits, just like she had when she was at home on the farm. Now she was far more graceful. How long had it been?

How long since Avian had come to help them escape their home?

With the thought of her beloved husband, her doubts returned to assail her. *After being apart so long, would Avian still love her? Would he want her? Their baby was gone, so tiny, so precious. She could not help her baby. She could not help Avian. She could do nothing, nothing. She was empty and hollow inside.* Rising from her seat on a stump, Shale quietly left the garden.

Samuell stood watching his sisters. He saw the blank expression come over Shale's face like a cloud blocking the rays of the sun. He started to follow her.

Raina gently touched his arm. She quietly spoke, "Give her time, Samuell. Love her with all your heart and show her that love. She will heal, as you have done."

"But she has lost more. She has lost her child and is now apart from her husband. She fears for his life," Samuell anguished. He watched helplessly as Shale wandered away from them.

Raina hugged Samuell tightly. She could not bear to see this pain in her children's eyes, for in her heart Samuell and Piper truly were her children. *We have all longed to have Shale with us. Her coming was to be a great joy to them, Father God. Not like this, not like this.*

She took Samuell's hand and they followed Shale. Raina observed her closely. The dullness of her eyes was haunting. *What tormented her soul?*

Raina approached her and softly spoke, "Shale. Shale, stop and listen to me." Raina gently touched Shale's arm. Shale stopped moving, but did not look at her.

"You are not eating, or sleeping well. You are withdrawing from Samuell and Piper. It troubles them greatly. Please, I fear your grief will overwhelm you. Let us help you. Let us love you," Raina said earnestly.

Shale continued staring blankly into the distance. Her somber face did not change expression.

Raina tightened her grip on Shale's arm and tried again. "Samuell and Piper need you, Shale. Every day they prayed to see you. Seeing you was their hope. Your love helped them to live through their grief. Gradually they have come to embrace life again. Bring them joy, not more sorrow. You are their sister. They need you. They love you. Come back to them, Shale," Raina pleaded.

Shale did not move. She stood there as if her mind were numb to Raina's words.

"Your husband will be coming for you. Bring joy to him, also. Bring yourself to him. Shale, you must live, you must! For all those who love you! Come back from despair. Come back," Raina cried out.

Shale turned empty eyes to her and began walking aimlessly again.

Raina turned to Samuell with wide eyes. "I will bring the Lady Audrey."

Samuell followed Shale. Deep in prayer, he shadowed his sister, "Father God, please heal my sister. Show us what to do. May she know she is loved."

Shale wandered on aimlessly through the beautiful meadow beneath the gold and red leaved trees. She did not see their bright fall colors. She did not reach up to touch them. She did not smell the sweet grasses or bend down to caress the tiny blue and gold flowers growing at her feet. The dappled pattern of shade and light playing upon the ground remained unnoticed before her.

Finally, she collapsed onto the soft grass. She cried out to God in her anguish, "The emptiness engulfs me. I am nothing, only a little puddle on the ground. Lord, what good is a puddle of emptiness?"

Shale curled into a ball. Her breath came in rapid gasps while the tears streamed anew down her face. She heard deep, mournful moans, full and hollow. Where were they coming from? Alarmed, she realized they were coming from deep inside her. She could not stop them. The waves of grief rolled over and through her again and again, until gradually they slowed and became little shuddering sighs.

Samuell sank down at her side. A slender hand gripped his shoulder.

"Peace, Samuell. She is being cleansed in her soul now, expressing great sorrows that she has long held within her," Audrey spoke knowingly. "It must be."

Audrey gazed tenderly at the crumpled form before her and placed her hand on Shale's head. She spoke to Shale's soul, "What can be done with a little puddle of emptiness? In a little puddle, our Father God will mix clay and form you. He is the master potter, a great craftsman and lover of your soul. He will make you beautiful, and fill you with love. He will shape you into a far more loving vessel than you have ever been."

She knelt beside Shale and took her hand. "You must give this love to those near you, for they are in need of your love. Your husband is not deceived by lies. He loves and needs you. You are his life. It is for you he fights. Samuell and Piper have longed for you with aching hearts. You are needed, Shale. Do not give in to despair. Be filled with hope."

Shale turned her tear-streaked face and looked into the wise and loving eyes of Audrey.

"You will smile again, and you will cry again when the sorrow comes to you in memory. Let your tears flow forth now. Mourn, child, and then rise up to comfort those who love you so. Love, Shale. Love."

Audrey nodded to Samuell and stepped back from them.

Samuell's arms reached out and embraced his sister. He held her shaking body close to him. "Shale, come back. I have longed to see you. I need you to be here. I have missed you so very much. Do not leave me again."

Piper flew from Raina's arms to his side and began crying out her love and prayers for her sister. "I need you, Shale. You must tell me of Momma. I need you with me. I love you."

There Shale found herself, in her little puddle on the ground in Bellflower; face tear-streaked, gown damp from her tears, feeling much of the weight lifted and totally, completely exhausted.

Smiling softly, Audrey left the three children of Connor and Shayna under the loving eyes of Raina. When their tears had dwindled to sniffles and sighs, Raina spoke softly to them. Samuell lifted Shale to her feet and helped her to her room. Piper lifted the coverlet and laid it over her sister's shoulders.

Raina put her arm around Piper's slight form and whispered reassuringly, "We will welcome this sleep. Grief is a great burden. Your love will help her, Piper. Now, as Shale has cared for you, you may care for her."

Shale awoke to a quiet house. Sleeping beside her bed lay Piper. In sleep, she looked again the young child Shale had rocked in her arms. Rising carefully from her bed, Shale left the cottage and lay down beneath a great oak tree. She watched the early morning colors appear upon the sky. The weariness of grief still claimed her, and again she let sleep take her from her pain.

Slowly, Shale awakened. Warming suddenly, she startled and then settled into the warmth and strength of her husband. It was as if Avian were lying close to her, wrapping himself around her. Warming her. Comforting her. Giving her his strength, his hope, his love.

Surrounding them both pulsed the love of their families, ever closer, thicker and strong. Shale lay wrapped in that love, letting it soak into her very being. Her thoughts stirred toward Avian and her love for him swelled within her, filling her. She reached out to him and held him tightly to her heart. She thought of his family, how they had made her their own; of Dracy and Jamie risking their lives to save her from Dockle; of the relief and joy in the eyes of Samuell and Piper when they saw her again.

Shale did not open her eyes. She lay very still and let herself feel the softness of the earth beneath her. She breathed deeply the clean scent of the grass and it refreshed her. The sweet scents of flowers mingled with the scents of the woodland surrounding her and grew ever stronger.

Awakening fully, she felt two hands upon her, one small and gentle, the other strong and caring. Samuell and Piper sat keeping watch over her. They were surrounding her with their prayers and love.

Shale opened her eyes and reached for their hands. "Samuell! Piper!" she cried out. "I love you.

The three children of Connor clung to each other. Their eyes shone through their tears. Love and hope, held captive inside them by grief and fear, now cascaded over them.

Samuell burst out in a song of thanksgiving to God. Piper and Shale joined his rich baritone with their sweet voices. Shale rose, and they danced with joy in the meadow beneath the huge oak tree.

Raina heard their song and ran from the cottage. She rejoiced to see them dancing together. She clasped her hands and laughed. Her smile was as bright as the sun. The circle of their dance opened, and they each beckoned her to join them.

When the dancers collapsed upon the soft grass, Raina said, "You have made my heart race with joy! Come! Let us prepare a feast, for today is a day of celebration. Shale has come back to us." Raina eyes glistened, and she hugged Shale tightly.

Samuell and Piper raced toward the cottage to begin their chores.

"Apple cake!" Piper shouted to her brother. "I will make Momma's apple cake!" Her smile flooded her eyes and they sparkled brilliantly.

Samuell loaded his arms with firewood for the baking. "I can taste it already!" he called after Piper.

Shale embraced Raina and said, "Thank you for loving my brother and sister and me. When I feel the emptiness of my loss closing in around me, it floods through me. It leaves me weary to exhaustion."

Raina nodded and tears came to her eyes. "I know. Let God hold you. Rest in his arms and let him carry you through this storm. Remember that you are loved."

"I will," Shale whispered.

Arm in arm, the new friends walked to join the merry preparations in the cottage of Raina, Samuell, Piper, and for a time, Shale. Avian would come for her, and they would all be together again.

Far away, a sweet smile of love and relief came upon the face of Avian. Shale! He saw her dancing with joy beneath a tall oak and felt her love and strength about him. It encircled him and lifted up his soul, carrying him to her. Samuell and Piper and a maiden with dark hair were dancing with her. In his mind, he dwelt there in their joy. Avian bowed his head in thanksgiving to God and blinked back his tears.

The sound of riders rapidly approaching brought him back to the present. The scouts had returned. His smile faded, replaced with a grim line. No one would hurt her again. He would make sure of it.

Chapter 14

Connor observed his two younger nephews working the colts and fillies under his care. They were doing well. He looked up as a rider drew up to the corral. He was not surprised that Sollen had dropped by today. Cameron had arrived, and Sollen's curiosity was aroused.

Sollen. Connor was sure that it was he who had caused Shale's fall and the loss of her child. It was not two moons ago that Sollen had requested Brendell to attend his herds instead of working here. How did he know where Shale was? Who had told him? Were Samuell and Piper also discovered? The questions whirled through his mind as he watched them finish the training lesson. He would send Brendell on a long errand, and together he and Cameron would question Sollen.

Sollen leaned against the corral fence beside him. "Greetings, are my brothers doing well for you?" he inquired cheerfully.

It took all of Connor's strength to be civil. He did not look at Sollen, but remained studying the horses in the corral. "Indeed, they are doing very well. We are making progress. We will be ready when the time comes," Connor remarked. He turned and fixed Sollen with a look promising action.

Sollen met his uncle's steady gaze. "Very good. For the festival is sure to draw many this year," he said eagerly. "We will have the most magnificent exhibition ever seen."

"I think you overestimate me, Sollen," Connor replied.

"Oh, you will not be the only one exhibiting your skills in horsemanship that day," Sollen reminded him.

"I am aware of that. Do you have something special in mind?" Connor queried.

"Oh, yes, but it is a surprise. You will have to wait with the others." Sollen's eyes glowed in anticipation.

After the other workers had gone for the day, Connor began, "Tell me, Sollen, where were you two moons ago?"

Sollen shifted his feet and replied, "Hunting. It was a fine hunt. We brought home many deer for the coming festival," he said easily.

"And did your hunt take you to Cambria Forest?" Connor continued. "I believe you met another lovely creature in the woodlands there."

Sollen looked about them quickly and moved his hand for caution. "It is not safe to speak here," he whispered. Speaking in a normal tone, he said, "We encountered deer, fowl, and a few rabbits, which we left alone. Good quality game is found throughout our forests, my lord. Are you a hunter?"

"At times. Let us go to my home and share a drink for a good day's work is done. You will join us, Sollen?"

It really was no matter of choice as Cameron moved beside Sollen blocking his way. "I am always ready for good company," he agreed amicably.

In Connor's quarters, they sat where they could keep watch out the windows and continued questioning Sollen.

"Your daughter is not safe at Cambria Forest. She...." Sollen began.

"How did you know that she was there? Who told you?" Connor interrupted.

"My older brother fit the pieces of the puzzle together. The lovely visitor to Cambria Forest intrigued him, for she would not dance with him, and then became betrothed of Avian, King Corey's son, at the Festival of the Golden Leaves. The timing seemed right for her to have arrived there according to your account, and he confided his suspicion to me. He was angry that his opponent should have her favor," Sollen paused a moment with his lies, gauging the effect of his words on his uncle, "and learning that she could be his kin, he was concerned for her, as Avian can be crafty."

Connor straightened at this, and Sollen was encouraged in his lying. Cameron's face he could not see.

"Not long ago, I heard there would be a kidnap attempt. I feared for her and went to warn her."

"Who told you this rumor?" Connor demanded.

"Rumors abound, my uncle," Sollen evaded.

"This rumor you took seriously," Cameron pointed out. "Why did it carry more weight?"

"Because I knew of the hunting party. Many were going, and it seemed suspicious to me," Sollen answered smoothly.

"Why would anyone desire to kidnap my daughter?" Connor persisted.

"As you yourself told us, to force you to serve them by teaching the Presage," Sollen answered.

"Who do you know who is interested in that?" Cameron spoke quickly, changing the direction of the conversation.

"There are many who are curious," Sollen began slowly.

"Who is curious enough to kidnap for money or information?" Cameron continued.

Sollen looked down at his hands, then back up at his uncle. "His name is Thad. He is very interested in the ways of the Presage."

"Are your brothers involved?" Connor asked with an anxious tone to his voice.

Sollen sighed and stared at his hands.

"Answer me!" demanded Connor.

"Baierl is. He is not consumed with it, but involved. He was with the hunting party. Brendell idolizes Baierl. I do not know for sure if he is involved. I have tried to keep him busy, leaving little time for other things, when he worked with my horses," Sollen said with mild accusation in his voice.

"What about you? Tell me truly and I may spare your life!" Connor stepped toward him, furious that his own nephews could be involved in the death of his grandson and nearly his daughter.

"No, my lord. I fear the Presage. My father has said it causes men's hearts to change and become cold. I rode alone to warn my cousin, then joined the hunting party when she refused to come with me." Sollen turned large, concerned eyes to Connor.

Before Connor could speak again, Cameron stated, "The lady will accompany her husband and his family here. We will guard her carefully, as should your guards. Ones that can be trusted."

Connor demanded, "Tell us more about those involved." He wanted to know why Sollen had not helped his daughter, why he had allowed her to ride so close to the ravine, why she had fallen. He wanted to know many things, but Cameron's look warned him. He must wait.

"Yes, Sollen, how are they known to one another? What signals do they use? How many are there? What are their plans for the festival?" Cameron fired question after question at him.

Sollen's eyes widened at the anger behind Connor's questions. Anger could work for his purposes, but this Cameron could be dangerous. He asked too many questions—detailed questions.

Sollen gave only vague answers now, insisting he knew little, but would find out what he could.

Cameron released him then, urging him to be cautious, for these were dangerous ones he would be dealing with.

When he was assured that Sollen was far from Connor's home, Cameron expressed his concerns. "I do not trust him. His story does not ring true. Be at peace concerning Avian. He has no deceit in him. Were Sollen that concerned for Shale's safety, he would have helped her. I examined the site with Orrie. The tracks of his horse did not go in the direction of the hunter's, nor did he ever join them. He circled back toward the woodlands below where Shale lay. He saw that she was hurt. What would drive him to leave her? Fear of being discovered by the hunters? Why should he fear them? Perhaps he knew that she could not ride away with him then, or saw Avian and Orrie approach and fled for his life before the coming wrath of Avian. There are many unanswered questions about Sollen. I fear he could be very evil, my friend." Cameron placed a hand of caution on Connor's shoulder.

Connor shook his head and sighed. Sitting down he said, "It was his older brother that I suspected most. How could I have been so deceived? I have said careless things in his hearing. I must be on my guard."

"What things have you said?" Cameron asked quietly.

"Nothing of great importance, just comments about his brothers, the horses, and their training. Things he could use to deceive me if he twists them. I would not have said these had I been more on my guard. He is very deceitful." Connor was thoughtful, and then met Cameron's eyes. "We need a plan. What would you suggest?"

"Continue to let him think he is in your confidence. Show him tiny bits of the Presage to keep him listening. We must gather more information and try to lay a trap before he does. We will use his own trick against him—give him information that he would know no other way. I fear with the arrival of Avian things may intensify. Sollen is jealous of Avian's skill and perhaps of his marriage to your daughter. There will be many here for Sollen to impress in a show of skills between himself and Avian, or you. A battle must not occur. The Presage—it must not happen." Cameron's expression was intense.

"Then Avian must be warned and guarded. He must let me teach him secrets Sollen would not know. I will not see my daughter's world destroyed!" Connor exclaimed.

"We must control our anger, lest it be used against us," Cameron urged.

"Yes. Yes, you are right." Connor slumped in his chair and put his head in his hands. "We must be wise and calm."

The next morning Connor walked toward the stables, deep in thought. As he passed near the woods, he heard a familiar whinny. Rushing to the woodland's edge, he was met by Willow. "Eli has sent you! May God be praised. In my time of need He has provided." Connor spoke soothingly to the mare and stroked her withers. She nuzzled his sleeve and nickered. Her colt stepped out from behind a myrtle bush.

"Ah, Misty, your colt is beautiful," Connor praised her. He reached out his hand and touched the strong neck of the young colt. "You have traveled many miles. Come and I will give fresh water and feed. I will brush you both myself. I have missed you. I am so thankful you have come," Connor whispered.

When his nephews arrived that morning, they were astonished to find Connor brushing the most beautiful mare they had ever seen. Her conformation was magnificent and her wise eyes appraised them thoroughly.

During the next week, Connor began riding his mare early each morning and late each evening. Grateful to Eli for sending them, he thanked God for His perfect timing and protection. Concentrating fully, he performed intricate patterns within the arena of his brother. Sollen watched him, and he knew this. Each day Connor revealed more of his knowledge of the secret dance between man and horse. Little by little, he sought to plant doubt in Sollen's mind concerning his own skills and training.

Sollen watched and measured his uncle's skills against his own. *Yes, Connor, you know much, but you do not have the diary or my stallion. With my skill and my stallion, I will defeat even you, my uncle,"* Sollen proudly assured himself.

Piper leaned against Shale as they rested under the yellow apple tree. Her long hair fell softly across Shale's arm.

"How long your hair is now, Piper. It has grown so much while we were apart." Shale caressed a long strand and began braiding it.

"Your hair has grown long too, Shale. I remember it being so short." Piper was quiet and then spoke again, "Samuell's birthday is coming. Will you help me make a braided belt for him?"

She did not let Shale answer but hurried on, "I need to make it just like Momma did. Oh, Shale, I miss Momma and Papa. I missed you so much. I am so happy you are here with me."

Putting her arms around Shale's neck, Piper crawled into her lap. "No one else really understands." Tears traced a path down her cheeks. "I love to hear you sing the old songs to me at night. I love to hear your laugh. You don't laugh as much anymore. Do you remember how we laughed when Samuell told his stories before bedtime?"

Piper placed her small hands on Shale's cheeks and looked searchingly into her sister's eyes. "I cried for you to come to me for so many nights while we waited for you. I thought you were not happy to see me, Shale."

"Piper." Shale hugged Piper tightly to her while the tears poured down her cheeks. "Oh, Piper, I am so sorry. I have longed for you so. I have missed holding you and listening to your merry laugh. I missed brushing your hair and singing together. I am very happy to be with you. I am sorry that I made you think differently.

I was afraid you didn't need me anymore," she ended quietly.

"Yes, I do!" wailed Piper. "Raina is nice and good to us, but she is not *you*."

Shale held Piper and rocked her back and forth until their tears ceased. "Tell me about the belt you are making," she prompted.

Holding Shale's hand, Piper began. "I have been saving horsetail hairs and purple flax. Please help me, Shale. I cannot make the pattern flow right. It does not look like the one Momma made."

"Go and get your materials. We will see if we can remember together," Shale said eagerly.

"I have them in my bag," Piper enthused. "See, this is how I began, but it does not look right."

Shale held up the weaving and admired the neat beginning, "You have done very well. We will look at the very beginning."

As she unwound Piper's weaving, her fingers seemed to remember. "Here. Does this seem right? At this point, go over with the purple and down two. Now under with the white, then tan and brown."

"Almost," Piper agreed thoughtfully. "Try going over with the tan as you did the purple. What do you think?" Piper asked.

"That is it! See how the purple and tan are raised more than the others? It does look like Momma's pattern," Shale said.

"Thank you! Now I can finish it in time."

"You have beautiful colors collected here, and sturdy materials. It will be a wonderful belt for Samuell."

Piper grinned up at her. "I have more colors, too. I will add them midway of my weaving."

"You are gifted with an ability to blend the colors of nature well, and your weaving is much better than mine when I was a child."

As they worked together, Shale began to take more interest.

"Do you know that when Avian told me what the blue flowers meant, he said 'Remember, Piper gave me blue flowers when we were traveling? She must have known I would love you.' Thank you, Piper." Shale reached over and tickled her.

"I remember," Piper said. A sweet and mischievous smile rested upon her face. "When we were riding, he asked me lots of questions about you."

"He did?" Shale said blushing. "What did he ask?"

"If you were always so bossy," Piper laughed. "I said yes!"

"You did not."

"Oh, yes, I did," giggled Piper. Her green eyes sparkled.

"What else did he ask?"

"He wanted to know your favorite color, how long your hair was before you cut it, what flowers you liked, and," she giggled, "if you could cook anything besides the bread we were always eating. I told him sometimes your cookies were good, and sometimes they all fell apart, so we ate them in a bowl with milk poured on them. He laughed, and so did I."

"Well, when he comes we will have to make him some very good cookies." Shale's face took on a far away look. "I miss him so much, Piper. I love him so."

"I am happy that you married him. He is funny, and I like him very much." Piper, too, gazed off into the distance as if to see a far off place. "Do you think he has seen Papa by now?"

"It is a very long journey. I do not think he has arrived in Robin's Woods yet. We will wait and hope together that we will see them both soon." Shale looked over at Piper's weaving.

"Now, what color will you use?" She hoped to distract Piper from too many questions about Papa and Avian. She herself did not want to think about the danger now. She could not. She needed time alone to think and pray.

"Happy Birthday, Samuell!" Shale smiled. She had made him a shirt and trimmed it to match the belt Piper had given him.

"Try them on, Samuell!" Piper shouted with excitement.

"Yes, and then we will have Piper's apple cake," Raina agreed.

Samuell pulled on his new shirt and wrapped the colorful belt around his waist. He held out his arms and turned to show off his new apparel.

The shirt was almost too small. "You have grown so much, it will not fit you very long." Shale gazed tenderly at him.

"Bara said I am ready for competitions this spring in archery and canoeing. Thank you for the shirt. It reminds me of Momma," Samuell's voice was quiet.

"Yes, but she would have noticed your growth and made it bigger." Shale paused and said, "Momma loved you very much, Samuell. I do, too. Papa's heart was torn when you were not with me. He longed to see you. We will see him soon, and Avian," Shale reminded him.

"I am eager for that meeting."

"Avian said that you would do well in the Cambria Forest competitions. Wait until he sees you now. Samuell, may I canoe with you tomorrow?" At his look of concern, she reassured him. "I am strong enough."

Samuell laughed. "Yes, but have you ever been in a canoe? I do not want to fish you out of the river."

Shale threw an apple at him and pretended to frown crossly.

"Come and eat, Samuell. I helped make the cake. Come see it," Piper called excitedly from the kitchen.

The rest of the evening was full of fun and laughter. Shale observed Samuell and Piper with their friends and felt contented.

If only Avian and Papa were here. She leaned against the doorframe and let her thoughts drift to her husband. They would be nearing Robin's Wood in a few days. "Father God, thank you that you are with them. Protect them, please. Thank you for this happy day."

That night Shale awoke screaming, "No!"

Samuell rushed in with his knife drawn. His wide gray eyes searched the small room. "What is it? What is wrong?"

"Are you bleeding again? Is there pain?" Already, Raina was reaching for Shale's abdomen. Piper stood beside her ready to run at her bidding.

Shale leaned forward and grasped Samuell's shoulders. "Samuell! I saw Avian! The white stallion was charging him, raging at him."

Throwing off the coverlets, she rose from the bed. "We must go to him now. Get the horses ready. I will be dressed in a moment."

"Shale, slow down. We must think first," Samuell urged.

"I do not have time. I must save him," she cried.

"God will protect him better than any of us," Raina reminded them. "We must pray now and trust for his safety."

Shale sat down on her bed and bowed her head. She listened, praying with them and thinking. It was so hard to wait, so hard to trust, now that loss had come to her. Yet she knew that God was there with Avian. He was always with them all.

Raina prayed, "Father God, we pray for Avian. We ask you for protection, for alertness like an eagle, for you to impart your wisdom to him, to increase his skill in battle, and give him the distinct awareness that he is surrounded with love. And for all those gathered here, we ask your great comfort and guidance, hope and peace."

"Thank you," Shale spoke quietly. "I must leave immediately. Samuell, will you come with me?"

A soft glow filled the room. "Indeed, you must go. Samuell also." Audrey did not smile. "Bara will accompany you beyond the borders of Bellflower where Henicles will meet you. Prepare now. The horses are being readied."

"My lady?" Samuell questioned.

"It is as Lord Aaron has told you," Audrey answered. "You will take warning to the elven Kings, for their lives also are in danger. The evil of Sollen is broad. Make haste. Bara awaits you. May the blessings of God and his angels guide and protect you."

Turning to Piper she smiled and said, "Dear child, it is not your time to leave us yet. Be at peace. Your family shall return to you." Touching Piper's head, she left them.

Shale wrapped her arms around Piper. "I will be back soon, with Avian and Papa at my side." Piper hugged her tightly.

Raina then bid Piper to prepare food for the journey. Piper began at once to fill a bag with ripe, red apples and loaves of thick, brown bread.

"You must go. The horses are here." Raina stood in the doorway holding another sack of food. Looking at Shale she added, "There are herbs if needed."

Shale kissed Piper's cheek. "Take care of your new momma, Piper."

Turning to Raina she said, "How can I ever thank you?" As Shale mounted her mare, Raina called out, "Return quickly. We will be in prayer for you all." Her arm rested across Piper's slim shoulders.

Shale and Samuell rode endlessly through the night, determined to reach the large meadow between the river and the forest before nightfall the next day. Bara had guided them a short distance from Bellflower and returned, bidding them God's speed.

Just before dawn, in the twilight of morning, they stopped to water the horses and give them a brief rest. To Shale's surprise Samuell helped her dismount and took their horses to the stream.

He is grown now, she thought to herself. A strange, warm feeling of change flowed through her. Always before she had helped and tended her little brother. Then as he had grown, they did more things together, yet she still tended to his needs more than he to hers.

Now it was different. The realization of Samuell's maturity left her with a sad, yet proud feeling. A time had passed that would not come again, yet it felt right. He was confident, caring, sure of himself and what was important in this life. When he returned with the horses, she said, "Thank you, Samuell. I am very glad you are with me."

Samuell smiled quietly saying, "I would be nowhere else, my sister. Come, we must move on if you are ready."

"I am ready." Shale allowed him to help her mount, and they began the urgent journey again.

Late in the afternoon they stopped briefly, pleased with the distance they had covered. While the horses rested, they ate Raina's good bread and discussed their plan. "We must get close enough for the horses to see our signals and hear us," Shale said.

"We may have to keep moving from spot to spot if our signals draw too much attention from the crowd," Samuell said. Lifting his face to the sky, he watched a hawk circle in the distance.

"I hope we will arrive in time to contact Papa before we must act. Should we ride again now?" Shale was restless with the need to reach Avian. She stood and paced to a nearby beech tree. She picked a leaf from it, and was unconsciously tearing it into tiny pieces.

"We will arrive in time. Try to relax, my sister. Eat your bread: We may not have many opportunities to eat later." He grinned patronizingly at her restlessness.

Throwing down a handful of tattered leaf, Shale turned to him. "I cannot, Samuell."

Seeing his frown, she muttered, "Oh, all right," and ate a bite, stuffing the rest in her pocket.

"I think we should not let anyone know we are there, Shale. Secrecy may be our best weapon. We will draw attention to ourselves if we ask about anyone. Instead, we must quietly listen and observe those about us, so that we will be able to make a wise plan." Samuell studied her face for her reaction.

She considered his words and slowly agreed. "I want to do something, Samuell, but you are right. We need to be aware of all that we can find. We must find Sollen and learn of his plans," she said determinedly. Brushing back a tear she added, "I long for my husband. Let us ride now, Samuell. I am ready."

"In a moment. Let us talk more first. We can try to signal with our hands and with whistles. If that fails, I have my bow. How many shots I can get off before they try to stop me I do not know. But I tell you this. I will not let anyone kill Avian or Papa. I will not." It was his promise to her.

Suddenly, Samuell stood and peered to the west, with his hand shading his eyes.

"What is it?" Shale asked rising to her feet.

"A large gray horse is traveling at great speed toward us. The rider is cloaked in blue. I believe it is Henicles, but let us take no chances. We will hide until we are sure."

In a few minutes, Samuell's eyes assured them it was indeed Henicles. Mounting quickly, they urged their horses on to meet him.

"Greetings, Henicles!" Samuell called out to him. "We ride to Cambria Forest."

"As do I, now that I have found you. Together we will travel for a while, then I must make haste to arrive ahead of you. Greetings, Shale, you are looking well." His smiling face appraised her and he nodded. "Come, let us ride."

Chapter 15

Avian arrived at the practice area early in the morning with Dracy and Jamie at his side. With great intensity he went through each event, never missing a target. He was focused, ready, and deadly serious.

His companions watched closely as more competitors joined them on the practice fields. Fearing an attack, or that Avian would overreact to a situation, they were barely able to practice themselves.

"You will not win with so little effort," Orrie called as he approached them. "Join us, Orrie," Jamie called back. He nodded toward Avian.

Orrie nodded back and sat near Avian, who glanced at him and said, "Protect my sister and mother."

Orrie assured him, "They will not leave my sight."

"Then can you see them now and swiftly fly to their aid?" Avian asked coldly.

Orrie was taken aback, but answered quietly, "They sit now, surrounded by your father's guard, partaking of breakfast, but I will hasten to them." He began to rise.

Avian reached out to stop him. "I am sorry, my friend. My heart is not with me. It dwells in Bellflower. Stay, Orrie. They will not practice if you leave me." He nodded at Dracy and Jamie. "I would not have them embarrass themselves today."

Stretching, Avian lay back on the thick grass and called out to his friends, "Come, warriors of Corey, let us see your skills displayed."

After the first and second events of the tournament were completed, it was apparent to all that Avian, son of Corey, was not himself. There was no joking with him, no lighthearted banter with the competitors or his teammates.

Avian's focus was sharp and intense. He did not miss a shot or allow a competitor an edge. He meant for his enemies to see that he was ready—that the attack on his wife and the death of his son would not be dismissed.

Orrie, though an opponent, stayed beside him as did Dracy and Jamie, ready to intercede, to defuse any situations that arose.

Corey watched his son with grave concern. His skills were sharper than ever. It was his son's heart and mind that concerned him. Could Avian control his anger? To the comments from others, Corey only shook his head or said to close friends, "The loss affects him."

Sollen's eyes glinted in appreciation. He wanted Avian at his best today when he defeated him. *It would be so much sweeter a victory.*

Sollen's anticipation of battling Avian fed his energy. He moved among the competitors, encouraging them and urging them to excel in their events.

This contrast in Sollen's behavior alerted Dracy and Jamie. They set their watchfulness upon him.

At every opportunity Sollen personally challenged Avian. He did not care when Avian defeated him in each event with a sureness that caused the other competitors to draw back at his intensity and determination. For Sollen knew there would be another event that night, and he would be the victor.

At the close of the competitions late that afternoon, Sollen approached Avian with a smile and congratulated him. "Ah, Avian, you have outdone yourself this day! Why did you bother to bring your teammates with you? You truly have ruled this festival alone."

Sollen continued to compliment Avian, until the crowd around them grew thin and Jamie and Dracy were distracted by the talk of others.

"I know of a greater challenge than you have ever faced. It will further test your skills and your very nerve itself. Will you compete with me? Will you take on a new challenge, woodland prince?" Sollen's voice was ripe with challenge and mockery.

Avian did not waver in his resolve. His intense gaze bored into Sollen. Sternly he replied, "I am more than ready, Sollen."

Sollen could barely contain his excitement. "After the beginning of the sixth dance tonight, you will go to the stables, and my groomsman will bring you to my arena." Studying Avian's companions, he added, "Come alone, if you dare."

"I will come." Avian's eyes flashed a dark warning to Sollen.

"Very well." Smothering a laugh, Sollen strode across the yard.

Jamie and Dracy approached rapidly. "What did he say, Avian? What insults does he spew out now?" The two friends cast a concerned glance at Sollen, then each other.

"Nothing worth repeating. Let us go." Avian turned and led them away.

Already the festival goers were gathering in their seats and around the grounds for the showing of the King's horses. Shale shuddered, seeing many small children with their mothers nearby. What would they see today? But they were not too close to the arena. The crowd would thicken and their view should be blocked. Would Sollen even begin the challenge here? Perhaps not with too many to interfere.

Shale and Samuell positioned themselves in strategic areas of the arena—areas where the sounds of their whistles would vibrate around the entire arena and reach the ears of the performing horses. Should volume become necessary, they would be heard.

Samuell was near the gate where the horses and riders would enter the great arena. From his position, he could signal calming, soothing reminders of the horse's earliest training in the meadows of their youth. Hopefully, many of the horses had been trained by their father, or by others using his techniques. With the quickening of memories from their earliest training in trust, and gentleness, Samuell and Shale would seek to overcome the aggressive training of the last years of the horses lives.

That the horses would resist the final commands of the Presage, refusing to perform the moves—from killing—was Shale's hope. The children of Connor had perfected the signals on their journey here. If they must, they would give the mercy whistle to save their loved ones. This would reveal their identity and place their own lives in danger. Shale felt her two hidden blades and nodded at Samuell, assuring him she was ready. There had been no sign of Avian or Papa, and no time to seek them.

As the yearlings entered the arena and performed their skills in unison, the crowd cheered. Murmurs of appreciation for the talents of the trainers and the quality of the horses flowed among those gathered. From his elevated position near his brother, Connor watched the parade of yearlings, as his nephews and groomsmen displayed the fine colts and fillies. His sharp eyes followed the movements of his allies and potential foes as well. Already he had identified three buyers he had dealt with at the farm. Cameron was about gathering information, and Orrie was positioned with Corey's family on the platform nearby. Only Sollen escaped his gaze.

Shale and Samuell closely observed the movements of the colts and fillies before them. At home in the meadow they had trained their charges more thoroughly, but most of the skills were the same in these young ones. In the two-year-olds, they noticed subtle changes in response to given signals. This was more pronounced among the three-year-olds. King Corsac's sons put the young horses through their routines. Where was Papa? Finally, she noticed Samuell glance toward the upper area where the royal family was seated. Papa stood near them, closely observing his pupils, both horse and trainer. Would he fight Sollen? Would Avian?

The four-year-olds came in with riders and performed some very different maneuvers than the ones Shale was familiar with. She glanced at Samuell across the arena. With deep concentration, his eyes followed the subtle commands of the riders and the instant responses of their steeds. He sought Shale's gaze, and met it with a look of grave concern. Her heart pounded within her. Samuell had recognized something. Could they give counter commands? Could they stop the Presage?

Connor turned his attention back to the arena, as a murmur of astonishment and alarm rose from the crowd below him. A large, white stallion had moved into the arena and was charging the full length of it at break neck speed. Seated arrogantly upon him was Sollen. At the center they stopped. The stallion held his regal head high, nodding sharply and prancing to the side. With nostrils flaring and eyes blazing, he pawed the ground impatiently.

Connor admired the impressive conformation but the stallion's persona was alarming, and menace oozed forth from it. Despite the ease with which the animal appeared to respond, Sollen could barely control him.

A large bird landed in the arena and pecked at some grain spilled upon the ground. With a snort, the stallion bore down upon it, every muscle intent upon reaching its prey and stomping it into the ground.

The bird spread its wings and lifted strongly into the air. The stallion screamed in rage. Only with intense concentration was Sollen able to bring him to a standstill. Sollen then lifted his arm in the air, as if he had planned the whole demonstration. A few less knowledgeable folk were fooled and applauded him. Others joined in.

King Corsac had risen to his feet with a gasp at sight of the stallion. Glancing at Connor, he exclaimed, "Sollen assured me this one's training was coming along well, but it is far more ill-tempered than it was 3 years ago." He shook his head in disgust.

"He is not breeding it, is he?" Connor asked with great concern.

"He better not be," his brother responded with a threat in his voice. The two brothers moved from the dais toward the exit area of the arena.

"Sollen!" shouted Corsac.

Sollen looked toward them and excused himself from the horsemen gathered around him. With a triumphant smile, he approached his father. "Isn't he magnificent, father?"

"It is unsafe to have that beast here. You assured me he was improving. He is far worse. If even you cannot tame him, he must be destroyed." Corsac had lowered his voice, but not restrained his anger.

Sollen's smile faded, and in its place a grim line formed. A flash of disgust and anger came into his eyes. "I can control him, Father. Surely even you saw that."

"I saw a rider putting on a good show of being in control. Obviously, you were not. Nor will you ever be. That beast is beyond training. Take it away. I want a full report of your activities on that farm immediately after the festival." Studying the foul creature, Corsac gave his son a piercing look and strode away.

Sollen looked to Connor, who met his gaze with a glare of warning. "There are children here, Sollen! What if one of them had run into the arena? Could you control him then? He is not worth it, Sollen. Your father is right. Remove him immediately." He stood waiting for Sollen to obey.

Sollen stared back in challenge, but eventually turned, flinging orders to the handlers to return the stallion to his farm. Furiously, he stalked away. *They would not stop him. Fools! Can they not see? This stallion was the key to his success in the Presage. He was magnificent. His temperament, mixed with carefully selected mares, would bring him the perfect horses. His father would not fund it now, but enough interest was shown that he could charge a hefty fee for breeding purposes.*

As for his father, he would succeed in overthrowing him and taking his throne. This night it would begin. His allies were aligned on southern Cambria Forest. Ever they approached unhindered to support him. They would arrive, and he would put his plan in place at the festival—a great celebration to crown him king. His eyes took on a faraway look as his thoughts carried him on. He would rule with a firm hand. He would build his kingdom. He would expand trade. He would increase his forces. His horses would be known as the bravest and best throughout the kingdoms.

Tonight he would finish with Avian and return in plenty of time to disqualify his father and claim the throne. Baierl was gone, and his younger brothers would not challenge him. His allies would take care of those still supporting his father. It would be easy. So easy. Everyone saw his abilities. They would support him.

Sollen smiled to himself. *Corey would be at the festival as well, devastated by the loss of his son. It would be the perfect time to claim Crystal as his queen. He would take Corey's kingdom quietly from within. All in due time.*

Chapter 16

After the display of his horses, King Corsac had bid his guests come and dine in the great hall. The large crowd moved slowly away from the arena. After some time, Samuell rejoined Shale, and they blended in among them.

"Where have you been?" Shale demanded of him.

"Peace, my sister. I have been scouting." Pulling Shale to the side of the flowing crowd, he continued. "I went to see the white stallion."

"What were you thinking?" Shale exclaimed.

"Peace. What is worrying you so?" He mischievously tugged at her sleeve. "We must be patient and disguised." He rolled his large gray eyes at her.

She pulled away from his grasp and scowled at him.

"Say, my friend, were not the competitions fierce this year?" Samuell spoke to her.

"Indeed they were." She glanced at him, not amused.

"There, he is gone." Samuell smiled.

"Who?" Shale asked, wanting to toss off her hood and look about.

"A tall elf who watches me. He watches me because she watches me." Samuell appeared delighted with the situation, and indicated with his head a group of pretty maidens, one of whom was looking in their direction.

"Samuell, this is not the time. We are not to draw attention to ourselves." Shale scolded him, looking away from the maidens and pushing against him to go the opposite direction.

"I have done nothing. It is just my natural charm shining through. I cannot help it," he said turning away from the crowd, a large grin upon his face.

"Tell me, Samuell. What else has you in such a fine mood when you should be on your guard?" Shale was both angry and puzzled by her brother's behavior.

"I thought you would never ask." Recognizing the look Shale gave him, he quickly continued, "I overheard Sollen telling one of the stable hands to take the stallion to the 'natural arena,' for there he would be needed tonight, then he turned to his companion and said to bring 'him' after the sixth dance. 'I will fight 'him' tonight.'"

"Avian or Papa?" Shale questioned anxiously, her eyes huge with concern.

Samuell glanced away, then back at her. "I am not sure. Now we only have to find where this natural arena is and go there."

"That should be easy. We will follow them." Shale nodded to their left as four young elves struggled to lead the temperamental stallion away. "Should we tell Papa?"

"There will not be time." Samuell began walking more quickly as two horsemen took their places on either side of the stallion, urging him on his way.

Cameron kept a watchful eye on Avian and Connor as the dancing began. Connor was besieged with those wishing to congratulate him or steal a piece of wisdom or two from him regarding the magnificent performance of the King's horses. He carefully reminded them of all the hard work that had been done before his arrival. Slowly the attention turned to the dancers and musicians, and Connor was free to move about among the throng. Avian as well was receiving congratulations on his triumph at the contests that day. Due to his brooding manner, no one stayed with him very long, save Dracy and Jamie. They settled at a table midway along the dance floor, where his family was clearly visible.

"Go and dance, Jamie. That maiden from Pennsyl can barely take her eyes off you. You must not make her suffer so." Avian teased him, then started in on Dracy.

"What will they say of the warriors of Corey, who break the hearts of defenseless maidens so easily? Go and defend our honor, or seek the one your heart is yearning for. I myself will retire soon to be with my wife. I will present her with a blue flower, for ever she steals my heart." He added this last part, for Charleen and her cousin had come near them.

Standing, he urged the others, "Go, go for the music is merry and I myself am away."

At a nudge from Charleen, Muriel spoke, "My Lord Avian, allow me to attend to your wife, for she was so kind to me at the Festival of Golden Leaves."

Fighting off a caustic remark, Avian replied, "Alas, ladies, my wife remains in mourning and I would be with her. But for your kindness, here are two fine warriors in need of partners for this dance. You will have to excuse their clumsiness, for they are out of practice."

Bowing low, Avian presented Muriel to Jamie and Charleen to Dracy. Muriel eagerly took Jamie's hand, but Charleen stared coldly at them all and stormed away.

To Dracy, Avian said, "Truly, you have saved me just now. Your duty is done for the night."

"Be wary. She will probably ambush you on the stairway." Dracy smiled to a maiden nearby and left Avian to himself.

Good. The fourth song was ending. He would leave soon. He was ready. Taking an apple from the refreshment table, he took a bite and was pleased with its sweet flavor.

He turned, and the taste died on his tongue. A family playing with their baby blocked his path. The mother held a flower to the baby's nose. The father laughed with delight when his daughter snatched the flower from her mother's hand. The infant quickly turned her head to him and he scooped her up in his arms.

Avian felt the emptiness of loss steal into him again. His son had known the sweetness of flowers only through the delight they gave to his mother. His son had known his father's love only by the gentle pressure of Avian's hands upon him where he rested in Shale's womb, and by the muffled sound of Avian's voice drifting to him there. Avian clenched his fists. It had all been taken from him. He would not lift his son into his arms when he came running with a look of pure joy on his sweet face. He would not take him for his first horse ride or teach him to shoot an arrow. He would never hear his son's laughter.

Unbidden, he felt the love of Shale encircle him, startling him from his dark thoughts. He struggled to keep his mind closed to her. He must not be distracted from his quest. Sollen's arrogance would hurt no one else. He would pay with his own life. Avian turned and strode determinedly into the darkness.

Cameron nodded to Connor, who excused himself and departed from the celebration. Silently, the two watched Avian leave with his guide, then waited.

In a few minutes their patience was rewarded. Ten burly, disheveled men appeared from the wooded area to their left. They urged their horses in the direction Avian had been taken. Cameron signaled the elvish warriors who promptly surrounded them. Seeing no hope of winning a skirmish, the men surrendered their weapons in fear of the elves, and were secured in the prison.

"Sollen and 20 of his followers left just before Avian," Cameron informed Connor.

Connor nodded and lifted his thoughts in prayer. They set their horses in pursuit. Avian rode beside the silent guide, feeling the warmth of Shale's presence seeking to envelope him again. He took a deep breath and steeled himself against it.

Mentally, he reviewed the skills Samuell had taught him during their stay in Pennsyl. He had urged Samuell to teach him so that he might gather information concerning their family, and to impress Shale. The time they spent together had been rewarding in many ways. Now he would use this knowledge to defeat Sollen in battle.

"Thank you, Father God, for you knew that I would need this knowledge. Be with me now. Give me your strength, quicken my senses, give me insight into my opponent's ways, and protect me that I may return to those I love." Looking up into the starry sky, Avian finished his prayer and steeled himself for what lay ahead.

At the natural arena, four elves tried to saddle the white stallion. He was restless and vicious, biting and kicking at them.

"No one but Sollen can do anything with him, yet he insists we prepare this wretch," growled one of them.

During the disturbance, two cloaked and hooded figures slipped into the area surrounding the arena. Moving into the shadows without detection, they stopped and surveyed the view before them. Samuell pointed to the grooming area adjacent to the arena wall. Shale would take her place there. She nodded in agreement.

Samuell continued to study the landscape before him. The cliff walls were steep, but craggy, with small ledges bearing scraggly shrubs. No one within the arena could scale the walls of the cliffs, for they appeared smooth at that point. *From out here, though...* He considered a possible path up to a slightly larger shrub. It should hide him well.

Both Shale and Samuell pushed themselves further into the shadows as a large group of riders entered. Sollen was leading them, joking and showing off his discovery of this natural arena. Samuell knew he had been pumping them full of stories of his skill on horseback all evening. They were fools to believe him.

Shale gripped Samuell's hand tightly and bit her lip. She did not want to shed innocent blood. She did not. She wanted him to know how badly he had hurt her, how he had killed her son and nearly she herself. She wanted..."Oh, God, forgive me. I want him to die for what he did; for all he took from me." Involuntarily she took a step forward.

Samuell positioned himself in front of her and pushed her back against the cliff wall. "No, Shale," he barely whispered into her ear. She was shaking and he could feel her tears against his hand. "Peace, peace. God is here. He will help us."

She quieted and stood stone still. "I will not let him kill Avian."

"No one will let him kill Avian," Samuell assured her. Peering deeply into her eyes he made her focus on him. "Shale, can you do this? Can you give the signals? Can you stay hidden? If you cannot, this is already over. I need you now. Avian needs you. Are you with me? Are you here?"

Shaking her head, Shale cleared her thoughts and looked into her brother's eyes. When had he become mature and commanding? "Yes, Samuell. I am ready."

"You are sure?"

She glared at him and shoved his hand from her shoulder. "I am sure."

"We move with the next distraction. Where will you move to get to your position?"

Quickly, she scanned the landscape again and pointed.

Samuell nodded at her, squeezed her arm and swiftly moved to the cliff wall.

Shale watched as Sollen attempted to mount the irritated stallion. As they scuffled, she raced silently to the next shadow and the next. More horses arrived, and she raced to the grooming area and blended into the tack and baskets piled there.

Glancing up, she saw Samuell directly across from her amidst some water barrels. He held her attention with his eyes. Putting his finger to his lips, he nodded toward the entrance.

Turning her head to see, she pulled air deeply into her lungs and froze. It was the cruel man that had come to the farm and argued with her father the day before her mother died. She looked back at Samuell questioningly. His grim expression confirmed her own thoughts. *Had this man killed their mother?*

She turned to watch as more horses arrived. *Avian!* Tearing her eyes off him, she looked to Samuell, who motioned down with his hands. She ducked lower and fixed her eyes on her husband, following his movement through the crowd.

Sollen stared about him with disappointment. He had expected many more to attend. *It does not matter,* he told himself. *Before this night is over I will take the throne of my father and no one will survive who defies me.*

From his seat on the contentious stallion, Sollen smiled broadly and welcomed those gathered. "Tonight, you will witness not one, but two demonstrations of the magic of the dance, the Presage. You will see its majesty, its beauty unfold before your very eyes, and you will yearn to be part of it. You can be, for you can attain the ability to move so intricately with your horse as to master the dance." He nodded toward a crude man who was now on a large horse from the farm. "Come, let us begin."

The two horses entered the arena side by side, the white stallion side-stepping to get nearer to the other horse. Sollen urged him to the opposite side of the arena by the cliff walls.

At the sound of a bell the two charged each other. Sollen dodged a swift blow from the man's rod and turned his mount to charge again. Stepping to the side, the stallion whipped in and out of the man's reach, allowing Sollen to land a sharp strike across his shoulders.

Avian watched intently, making note of Sollen's movements, the stallion's reactions to them and the positions of attack he used to unleash his weapons.

Shale stayed hidden, focusing on her husband. He was intently studying Sollen. That was good. An air of confidence and determination surrounded him. She wanted to run to him, to beg him not to fight, but it would serve no purpose, save to break his concentration. She must be still. She must wait. She must trust him to God.

"Please, Father God. Please protect him. Give him skill and wisdom and foreknowledge of Sollen's attacks. I don't understand your ways, Father God. But I know you are right here with us. Help him. I will trust you." She lowered her head and fought back the tears.

Her attention was drawn back to the arena by a shout from the onlookers. Sollen had landed a strong blow, and the rider had fallen from his mount. The crude man scrambled in the dust and regained his feet. It did not help him.

The stallion was on him in a second, knocking him to the ground. Whirling to kick at the man, the horse gave him the moment he needed to run for the gate. He almost made it—had his foot on the gate—when the crazed horse bit into his back and pulled him down. It reared up over the man, flailing its sharp hooves, and then crashed down onto his legs. Again it reared and struck down at its prey. The sound of shattering bone filled the air, and the man screamed.

This energized the stallion. It spun around and gathered its hind legs to kick out at the injured man. Two groomsmen grabbed his tattered shirt and pulled him under the gate. The stallion kicked the gate and whirled around, screaming in fury. The rider upon his back appeared equally crazed.

Shouts and screams rising from the onlookers caught Sollen's attention, bringing him out of his trance. Some sought to help the man, and some were quickly fleeing the madness. Others stared in shock at Sollen trying to control the infuriated beast. Sollen managed to move him toward the center of the arena, where the stallion reared and pawed at the air about him.

Calling to the onlookers, Sollen sought to gain their enthusiasm. "Do not leave, my friends. We have only had a small demonstration, an unfortunate one. There is so much more for you to see." Many helped the man into a cart and left with him to seek aid. Few remained to see more.

Shale looked to Samuell. He shook his head in dismay and disbelief. It had not worked. Their signals had no affect whatsoever on the crazed stallion. Shale realized that even the mercy whistle would not have stopped him. There was nothing they could do.

A mile away Brendell approached by the shorter path to the natural arena. His friend, Thad, had been missing for an evening and a day now. With the festival ongoing, he would not have abandoned their team. Coming this way saved Brendel time and gave him the opportunity to look for signs of Thad or the cause of his delay.

Uneasiness came upon Brendell as he neared the second training arena. An offensive heaviness clung to the air about him. His horse neighed uneasily, then shied beneath him.

Dismounting, Brendell spoke calmly to his mount. Near the arena he recoiled from the putrid smell exuding toward him. He covered his nose and mouth with his arm in an attempt to lessen the repulsive smell and continued. The heaviness in the air pressed in, as if to suffocate him.

He opened the gate and entered the arena. He saw nothing unusual at first. Many hoof prints covered the dirt floor. Two horses, moving rapidly, by the stride and slide of the prints. Nothing unusual there. Here one had reared and kicked at the other. His attention was drawn to the corner near the storage area by a shiny round object in the dirt. Thad's jewel. Chunks of dirt were lying about it, as if torn from the ground. Two feet away something indiscernible lay crumpled on the ground, partially hidden by the water trough. He approached it cautiously. The stench of death grew stronger, drowning his sensitive being and repelling him momentarily.

Brendell cried out and scrambled backwards. A severely trampled body lay before him. Collapsing to his knees, he put his head in his hands and cried out in grief and horror. Thad. It had to be Thad. He was assigned chores the day he was absent from the festival; his jewel found by the body. No. Not Thad.

The stallion had done this. It would not be here without Sollen. Why had he not stopped it?

Sollen. Sollen could not have done this. Could he? No. No. It was impossible to think. He could not. He would not.

Flashes of remembrance came to Brendel's mind: Sollen furious at their father, nearly out of control. Sollen hiding a smirk when news had come to them of the loss of Avian's son. The flash of hatred when Avian arrived at the festival, despite his great loss. Sollen treating others as if they were nothing unless they served his purposes.

Realization came to Brendel's battered mind. The brutality of the Presage was before him, and his very being reeled from the revelation of its evil. The total disregard for life struck Brendell with the force of a strong yearling's kick. The Presage had taken Sollen. His brother hungered for innocent blood.

Where was he now? The thought struck Brendell as a blow. He must get to the natural arena. Where was Baierl, his oldest brother? His concern increased, as he realized he had not seen him since breakfast. No, it was Avian Sollen wanted now. He must be stopped. Brendell rode with all speed, his mount eager to leave the stench of death behind.

Approaching the arena, Brendell saw the guards Sollen had hired at the gate facing the arena. He must be cautious to get past them. Slowing his horse, he rode up to them. "I did not miss it, did I?" he said, giving them a sly grin.

Shale gasped when she saw Avian preparing to enter the arena. Each mount was a powerful animal. She knew her husband to be an amazing rider, but he knew not even the subtlest commands for this encounter. His disadvantage was unfathomable. Sollen wore a sneer of smug distain across his fair face. The look in his eyes was sickening, his hate of Avian apparent.

"You have had time to observe our ritual. I have graciously given you one of our more advanced horses for combat. Be aware, son of Corey, this fight is to the death. Are you ready?" Sollen's voice rose in excitement.

Those remaining were silent, awaiting Avian's response. Fixing his opponent with a steely stare, Avian spoke in a cold voice, "I am more ready than you will ever know." To the observers he commanded, "No one may interfere."

"No one will interfere," Sollen mocked. "No one will need too."

"Is this the scheming of weakness? There is no victory in this," a stern voice spat out. "This is not a fight worthy of the Presage. Your opponent is untrained."

Connor strode forth from the shadows. "Where is the challenge, Sollen?" Connor's strong voice commanded attention. "Surely you show no love for the beauty of the dance, where horse and rider move as one in such intricate pattern it cannot be described, only experienced. Surely you have hungered for this, Sollen?"

Connor's piercing eyes never left Sollen's. "If you think yourself so alive, so skilled, then choose an opponent who can dance well with you. Choose one who thrills with the movement, who lives to command a willing, intelligent horse through the perfect steps of the perfect dance. I alone can truly dance that dance with you. You know this, Sollen. Does it frighten you? No? Then fight me."

"He is mine. I will fight him!" Avian demanded.

The intensity and determination in Avian's voice and the fire in his eyes caused Connor to reconsider for an instant. *No, even with his natural abilities and sharp skills Avian could fall; and yet, how much skill did Sollen really have? He had shown little in his exhibition match.*

Overconfident, under trained, Sollen had been sloppy in his form. Maybe...

"I have accepted his challenge! I will fight him!" Avian was adamant. He moved his mount forward.

"Wait!" Connor commanded. "There is treachery here." Studying Avian he saw total concentration, total control.

Across the arena, Sollen seethed with anger. *How dare Connor interfere with his plans? How dare he challenge him, Sollen, soon to be king?*

"I will fight you, Uncle, after I am finished with this fool." Sollen advanced his steed toward them.

"Will you not give us time to see that our equipment is ready? Would you cheat in this also?" Connor demanded.

"Dismount, Avian. Watch me carefully, my hands and feet and legs," Connor instructed.

"I am ready. Do not interfere," Avian responded, trying to move away from Connor's grasp.

"Very well, but this horse will not obey your commands, my son." Connor spoke with a certainty that made Avian stop. "Use mine."

At Connor's sharp whistle a beautiful mare approached from the shadows. Her very motion was full of power and grace; her eyes calm and intelligent.

Sollen straightened in his saddle. She was magnificent. He would spare her, and she would bring him many fine foals. He must be careful not to damage her too much. "Do what pleases you." Sollen's eyes narrowed menacingly. "It will not matter."

Avian dismounted and ran his hand down the mare's strong neck. She was the same mare he had seen with Eli that night so long ago, when he had gone to the farm to attain information. Now sleek and muscular, she was the most magnificent horse he had ever seen. She turned and nuzzled his neck.

"She knows you," Connor spoke with surprise. "That is good. You have her favor." Then he spoke to Avian, directly in his mind. "She knows the Presage, but only in defense of you will she kill."

"So, you have come to help me in my time of need. I thank you," Avian spoke in wonder to the mare. Taking his weapons from the other horse, he mounted and faced Sollen.

"Watch his eyes and hands. Do not let him spin his horse to kick at you. My horse will not betray you. God be with you, my son." Connor gripped Avian's forearm and sprinted from the arena.

From his vantage point partially hidden by a shrub on the cliff wall, Samuell's heart flooded with relief. He had seen the commands given to the horse that Sollen had selected for Avian. It would have been disastrous. Pride and joy filled Samuell's heart while he watched his father. Now Avian would have a chance!

Again, Samuell scanned the surrounding area. The two guards had not moved. The remaining spectators were gripping the railing in suspense. All but one, the cruel man who had killed their mother. Where was he?

Below Samuell the two riders commanded their horses. As they circled each other warily, Sollen taunted

Avian, "Come, woodland prince, show me your skills—what little you know of horses."

Avian made the first move. Spinning to the left, he landed a blow across Sollen's shoulder blades with his rod. In response Sollen's mount kicked out at the mare, which dodged it with a quick sidestep.

Controlling his fury, Sollen nodded at Avian and charged. He swung his horse around in a complete circle with amazing speed and agility, but his blow did not find its mark. The mare had expertly countered the move with a sideways leap.

Sollen did not relent in his attack. Urging his horse forward, he turned his rod and held it like a spear. Avian knocked it from his hand, as his mare whirled away and kicked at the stallion.

Undaunted, Sollen began maneuvering his mount back and forth as he approached Avian. "Your beautiful wife will be grieving. She will need someone to console her." His sneer was ugly.

Avian did not respond. He felt the mare tense beneath him. Which way would she jump this time? As if in answer to his thoughts, the mare sidestepped three paces to the right and paused, intently watching the approaching horse. Avian thought quickly. *Had Samuell taught him this? No.* He waited, never taking his eyes off Sollen.

With a flick of Sollen's reins, the stallion reared and walked toward Avian, its front hooves pawing the air. The mare snorted, but stood her ground. Avian relaxed his grip on the reins. He would let her make the counter movements. Again the mare tensed under him, then ran forward with tiny steps, leapt into the air and kicked hard at the stallion. The blow struck his right flank. Enraged, it shrieked at the mare.

Sollen was infuriated. Galloping around the arena, he took a flagpole from its slot and charged at Avian. Impulsively, Avian signaled his mount and the horse backed up three paces and set itself to counter the blow. Gripping his rod, Avian awaited the attack. The sounds of rod clashing with pole and horses hitting each other filled the air.

Shale cringed and stifled her cry. Where was Samuell? She signaled calming commands, but the horses did not heed them, so entrenched in the battle were they.

Brendell watched in horror as the depravity of his brother was revealed to him. He could see Thad in Avian's place; could feel him tremble with uncertainty as Sollen moved from the semblance of practice to all out attack. Thad had nowhere to flee. He had fought back as best he could, but to no avail.

Brendell raced to the side of the arena and climbed atop the shelter for the horses. The guards laughed, thinking he wanted a better view and turned back to the tension of the battle.

Again and again, Avian and Sollen countered each other, blows occasionally making a strike. Suddenly, the stallion spun away and turned to make another pass. Avian awaited the clash, firmly gripping his rod. At the last second, Sollen dropped low in the saddle and thrust the pole up into Avian's side, nearly knocking him off. The stallion kicked out, forcing the mare to rear and dodge away, dislodging Avian from his seat. As Avian fell, the two guards pinned Connor and Cameron against the gate, knives at their throats. A cloth was tied tightly over Connor's mouth to prevent him from signaling the mare.

Bouncing up, Avian whistled for his mount. Each time she sought to reach him, Sollen and his stallion cut her off, beating and kicking her. Finally, she stood to the back of the arena, pawing the ground and waiting.

In anticipation Sollen cried out, "Now beg for your life, but I will not grant it. Mourn for your wife, for she will be mine, and I will give her strong babies that will live."

Swiftly in one motion, Brendell drew his arrows and let them fly. The two guards fell to the ground dead. Leaping from the shelter, Brendell raced toward his uncle and Cameron. He must free them quickly.

From his perch on the ledge above, Samuell leaned forward in alarm as the whirr of arrows pierced the air. Seeing the two guards fall below him, he watched in amazement as another elf raced to his father, freeing him. *Who was this? No matter—he was helping them.* Samuell was torn between reaching his father and maintaining his position. From here he could hit any target easily. He forced himself to wait. Avian was not safe yet.

Avian did not move as Sollen urged the stallion forward with intricate movements. Quickly he memorized the pattern. It was very similar to one of the basic patterns Samuell had shown him. As the stallion neared, Avian could see its crazed eyes. It was no longer obeying Sollen.

Avian forced himself to wait. *Just a little closer... closer...Now!* Avian reached out quickly as the stallion moved to the left. Grasping the mane, he swung himself around and up, kicking out strongly at Sollen. He caught him on the chin and chest, jolting him out of the saddle to the sandy floor of the arena.

Quickly on his feet again, Avian braced himself for Sollen's charge. Sollen put his shoulder hard into Avian's chest. Rolling backward, Avian pulled Sollen with him and flipped him over into the sand. Both warriors were quickly on their feet again, facing each other.

Brendel's shout filled the arena, his voice rising with terror at what he saw, "Behind you! Sollen!"

The pounding of charging hooves filled his ears and Sollen, confident in his abilities, turned, fully expecting the stallion to slow for him to mount and fulfill his desire in the fullness of the Presage. The dark glow of certainty fled Sollen's eyes, and confusion, followed by terror, replaced it in rapid succession.

Flailing front hooves raised high above him crashed down. The stallion was blinded with fury. Riders were on the ground, and he attacked violently, never hesitating.

Sollen fell to the arena floor with a look of disbelief and horror on his face. Avian reached out for Sollen, but was driven back repeatedly as the great horse flung its hind quarters around, and lashed out wickedly with its back hooves. Again and again, the stallion raised sharp hooves, and trampled the one beneath them. In a matter of seconds, Sollen was dead.

Raising its great head and tossing it up and down over the body of Sollen, the beast gave a snort and finally backed away. Head held high, ears shifting back and forth, it stood until it saw movement in the arena. Screaming, it raced toward Avian.

Connor whistled to his mare. The animal raced across the arena to him. Leaping upon her back, Connor sped for Avian. Drawing the stallion's attention by bumping him, he signaled calming signs and gave the mercy whistle again.

Move, Papa! Move! Samuell silently pleaded. One shot. He needed one clear shot.

Hesitantly, the large horse shook his head and pawed the ground in front of him. Trotting side to side, it looked to Connor, then Avian where he stood motionless in the arena. Abruptly, the stallion screamed and charged Avian.

The whirr of arrows ripped the air and Avian dove, rolling for cover. The tall, white stallion reared and flailed the air with his hooves, then fell screaming to the dust. Two arrows pierced his chest.

Connor halted and looked about. *Whose arrows had pierced the great horse?* Only Avian, Cameron, and Brendell, who stood staring at the body of his brother, remained. The others had fled. He straightened in his saddle as a hooded elf raced into the arena. The hood fell back, revealing long, strawberry blonde hair. Hearing the sweet voice of his daughter calling out her husband's name, Connor did not move to intercept her. Now a second hooded elf approached him lithely from the far wall.

"Papa!" the elf cried out.

Connor jumped from his mare and ran to his son. He pushed back the hood to fully see his face. "Samuell! Samuell, my son." Connor cried with great joy.

Avian stared with disbelief at the face of his wife as she flew into his arms. "You are here. But how?"

Shale did not answer, but smothered him with kisses. He held her tightly to him, and as he did, he felt it. Strength and health flowed through her.

"Quickly," Cameron called loudly, "We are not safe here."

Avian looked toward Cameron, then down at Shale. "Come quickly. We must flee." Clutching each other tightly, they hurried to Cameron.

Gripping the reins of his own horse, Avian leapt up and extended his arm to Shale. Lithely, she jumped and he drew her up behind him. Reaching her arms around him, she leaned close to him and lay her head against his strong back.

Quietly, Connor spoke to his nephew. "Come, Brendell. We must seek your father."

Brendell lifted the body of his brother and walked to Connor. Raising sorrowful eyes, he said, "I did not believe he would kill, but he would have. He would have. I found the body of Thad. He had been trampled to death."

"I am sorry." Connor stepped closer to help Brendell. He found Samuell beside him, and together they took the battered body from Brendell's arms. "Brendell, take the blanket from your horse and spread it on the ground for us. Brendell."

Dazed with confusion and despair, Brendell slowly moved to obey. Carefully, they lay the mutilated body of Sollen onto the blanket and solemnly folded it over him. Lifting it gently, they secured the body onto one of the waiting horses.

While Connor spoke with Brendell, Avian moved his horse away from the others and whispered, "Shale, I am taking you away to a safe place."

"No, Avian. I want to stay with you. I need to be with you. I am not afraid." She spoke firmly to him, her warm breath against his neck.

"Shale, I will not..." he began.

"I must stay with you. We must face this together." Her voice was strong and determined.

Pausing, he thought of her in the woodlands of her homeland, the night they had fled. She had been strong and determined that night. He felt the strength of her arms encircling him. She was strong. He felt it in her spirit, as well as her body.

The others were leaving. He turned his horse to follow them. Shale tightened her grip on him, again letting her head rest against his back. She was singing a prayer for them. He placed his hand over hers.

"Brendell, come with me. We must ride ahead to your father. He must hear this from us. There must be no more harm done this night." Connor looked with compassion on his nephew's sorrowful face.

Brendell urged his horse to a faster pace. He must trust his brother's body to those with him. Turning to Connor, he spoke with great concern, "I have not seen Baierl since breakfast today."

"We will find him, Brendell. I, too, have not seen him. That may be good. We will not lose hope." To himself, he wondered how far Sollen's insanity had gone.

Brendell met his uncle's gaze. "My father knew nothing of this. He only wished to raise the horses. Baierl turned from it early on, warning us it was but a tired ritual from an evil time."

He paused and looked away. Bravely meeting Connor's eyes once more, he continued, "We were blind to Sollen's depravity. We wanted the skills of a renowned horse master, Piperel and I. That is all. I swear it." His sorrowful eyes held no lies.

They approached the stables from the rear, for the festival celebration was in full swing.

"I will summon my father and send a trusted messenger to guide Corey and his family to the safety of their lodgings." Brendell strode off without waiting for Connor's reply. At the outskirts of the celebration, he sent a messenger to his father and another to King Corey.

Looking to King Corsac, Corey gathered his family and took them to the security of their lodgings, within the confines of King Corsac's dwelling. Orrie accompanied them, eager for word of Avian.

King Corsac met Brendell and Connor, noting their grim expressions. He looked questioningly to them, concern and annoyance mingled on his face.

"I must speak with you privately, my father." Brendell spoke with a calm authority his father did not know his youngest son possessed.

Nodding, Corsac led them to his chambers and dismissed the guards to the hallway.

Connor remained standing beside Brendell as he spoke with his father.

"I have found the body of Thad, my father. He was trampled to death in one of Sollen's practice arenas," Brendell began.

His father's face mirrored the grimness of his son.

"It was the Presage. It was Sollen," Brendell continued.

"It could not be. No." Corsac rose from his chair and looked to Connor, who met his gaze grimly.

"Father, I saw it. I saw the patterns in the earth. I witnessed Sollen doing the same to Avian." Brendell paused, letting this sink in.

Corsac collapsed back into his chair. "Avian, is he...?"

"No, my father. Avian lives." Brendell answered, dreading what he must say next.

"Sollen must be punished. He..." Corsac began.

"Sollen was beyond that, my father. He was consumed. He was intent upon grinding Avian's body into the ground as he did Thad's. By his own hand, Sollen is dead, my father. The great horse killed him before we could stop it."

Corsac stared in disbelief at Brendell. Slowly he covered his face with his hands.

"Brendell saved the lives of Avian and me tonight, my brother." Connor spoke quietly, feeling the grief of his brother. "We have moved Corey and his family to safety, lest problems arise here, for some of Sollen's supporters fled before the end."

"How could this happen? How? He was always headstrong, but to kill his own people..." Corsac's sentence faded as he slipped into thought.

"Alas, the evil plans of my brother will yet be revealed, I fear. Where is...?" Brendell was interrupted as the chamber door burst open.

Queen Nieril, followed closely by Charleen and Piperel, strode into the room.

"Why have you summoned us in the middle of the dancing? Piperel was about to dance with..." the queen began. Piperel rolled his eyes in protest.

"Be quiet! That is of no importance!" he thundered, looking with disgust at his wife. "I have allowed you to bluster about, enamored with yourself, for too long!" Slamming his hands down against the table he demanded, "Where are your sons?"

"Corsac, I hardly think you need..." she began.

"Yes, you hardly think. Where are your sons?" Corsac thundered again, staring her down. The silence in the room hung heavily between them.

Alarmed, Brendell resumed his question, "Baierl, has anyone seen him today?" He looked up into Connor's eyes, fear growing inside him. "Have you seen him?" The near panic in his voice startled them all.

"He is with a maid from Pennsyl. He left this morning. Why he would miss the competitions, I don't know," Piperel answered, avoiding the grim look of his father.

"You are sure?" Brendell pushed on.

"That is what Sollen told me. I saw Baierl leaving with some others this morning, but he did not answer my inquiry—only waved as he rode off." Piperel responded earnestly. "What is wrong, Brendell? Father?"

"Yes, what is going on? I want to return to dancing and…" Charleen began.

"You will speak when you are acknowledged!" her father thundered angrily.

"Sit down, all of you, for a great grief has come to us." His voice wavered briefly. When they were seated he continued. "Sollen has brought great sadness and shame upon us. Go to your rooms, my Queen and my daughter. Weep for your loss and pray for the death of the evil that overcame his mind. He was overcome to the point of murdering his own people." Corsac rose and slammed his hands onto the tabletop as he spoke.

Slowly, he looked up and found the eyes of Nieril. "Justice is done, for the evil he sought has taken him from us. Sollen is dead."

Anguished cries arose from his family as the shock of loss struck them. Nieril tumbled forward, and Piperil eased her back against her chair. Gently taking his wife's arm, Corsac helped her rise and steady herself upon Piperel's arm. The same he did with his daughter. Charleen clung to him in her grief. He held her and patted her back, then gently turned her into Brendell's arms.

"I will return. I must be with my family." Corsac said. He took his wife's other arm and led them from the room.

Connor spoke to the guards in the hallway concerning the arrival of the rest of his party with Sollen's body.

He returned to his seat. "Where are the rest?"

"Avian is escorting Shale to his family's chambers. He will join us soon," Cameron said.

Corsac and his sons returned. Seeing Cameron had joined them, he spoke to Piperel, "King Corey is in his chambers. Bring him and those he chooses to our council."

Nodding to Cameron, he paced the stone floor where his father had paced before him. Stopping by Brendell, he embraced his youngest son and together they wept for the loss of Sollen and the horror that was now upon them.

Piperel returned, bringing Corey, Avian, Samuell, and Orrie. They paused in the doorway, observing Corsac and his son, then quietly went to their places around the council table.

Turning to his sons, Corsac continued, "Your brother, Baierl, is safe. He and a third of our warriors, along with a third of Corey's warriors, are guarding our borders from invaders—evil men summoned by Sollen to overtake my kingdom and place Sollen on the throne."

"No, my father!" Brendell burst out.

"Never could this be. Sollen could not do…" Piperel stopped as his father held up his hand for silence.

"He can, and he has. Alas, we did not know the darkness that clouded Sollen's mind." Corsac sank heavily into his chair.

Looking to Connor, he continued, "I would not at first believe the message sent by King Corey. They had captured a follower of Sollen's from their own realm. Under fear of death the traitor confessed all. My brother and Cameron explained to me the plan of attack. As a precaution, we have sent our warriors." He looked around the table. "More followers have escaped, fleeing from where Sollen was killed. Our warriors will trap them like flies. I have sent messengers to alert our warriors to hold any seeking to leave or enter the borders of Cambria Forest." Covering his face with his hands for a moment, Corsac gathered himself and stood.

With a voice of authority he addressed Corey, "Come, King Corey, we must speak with our people and announce the doom and punishment for the Presage."

In the Great Hall, the two Elven Kings stood with dignity and authority before their people. The music ceased, and all eyes turned to them. Anyone who had doubted the authority of the kings ceased doubting as Corsac proclaimed a unified ban on the teaching and performance of the Presage, with penalty of imprisonment and forfeiture of all horses and property. Then he announced the death of Sollen and Thad. Carefully he clarified that Thad was an innocent victim.

"Not so my son, Sollen. His mind was taken by the blood lust of the Presage." Pausing, Corsac looked over the crowd gathered before him. "Sollen was trampled to death by the demon stallion, while seeking to kill one of his own people."

Astonished murmurs and cries arose from those gathered before them.

King Corsac raised his hand for silence, but could not speak.

Corey stepped forward and placed his hand solidly on Corsac's shoulder. "I stand with King Corsac on this matter. Firmly we stand together. The Presage is wholly evil. Using the enticement of pride and power, it steals hearts of valor, turning them to selfishness and blood lust. I have seen the evil it brings. I am seeing it now before my very eyes. It turns brother against brother. It kills husbands, wives, and children. Use your skills to protect your loved ones and your friends. Do not destroy them one by one for a game of evil."

Corsac stepped forward and spoke again, "My people, people of Corey, our kin, there is unrest on the borders of this great forest. Our combined warriors are there already, and more will be sent. All of you, go to places of safety, for there will be no further celebrating this night."

The Captain of the Guard came forward from Corsac's side and announced in a loud voice. "All warriors make ready for battle and present yourselves to your captains immediately."

The Elven Kings rode out at the head of their united armies to defend Cambria Forest. Avian rode beside his father for a time, then dropped back among the warriors. The oppressive weight of evil was near. It sought those dear to him. He could feel its malice hovering in the very air about them. Cowering in the shadows of the wood it watched, biding its time, looking for the opportunity to strike.

Intently, Avian focused on the evil. Where was its focal point? Whom did it stalk? Samuell? Connor? The kings? Creases formed on his forehead as Avian strove to discern this. His head lifted as he realized it. The evil did not center on one person. It did not care, for in harming one, the others would be hurt. It hated them all.

Avian looked to Dracy and dropped from his saddle, joining the warriors marching about him. Immediately, Dracy mounted the horse and rode on.

Blending into the woods, Avian waited, intently focused upon the woodland sounds around him. All his senses trained on the woods. He listened for the sound of a startled bird, a broken twig, a rustle of leaves or grass; he sought the scent of sweat, of fear, a crushed flower, anything to guide his focus to the evil.

Blending into the shadows of the forest, Avian waited, intent upon the sounds around him. There. Movement through the brush. Whoever this enemy was, his woodcraft was skillful. With great stealth, Avian moved quickly toward his prey.

He strained to hear subtle sounds of movement—the intake of breath, the creak of wood, the spring of plant pushed aside, the soft squish of moss.

Ahead now, moving rapidly forward. A foot print in the soft earth. Swaying grasses, a bent branch. Avian pursued his enemy relentlessly.

Beyond them was a ridge covered with low growing bushes. Avian's warriors would pass below it. Avian rushed forward silently, and then froze.

Near. Very near. His hair prickled on the back of his neck. He did not breathe. The heaviness of evil oppressed him. His warriors would be moving into the area under the ridge now.

A sign, Avian prayed. *Show me where he is.* Avian's eyes grew large as he heard the soft, swift sound of an arrow plucked from its quiver and threaded onto the bowstring. He threw himself sideways into a large man kneeling and aiming into the warriors below him.

Avian bounded to his feet, his knives appearing in his hands. His opponent faced him with a litheness surprising in a man of his size. Facing each other, Avian saw the cruel way the man's mouth formed its sneer. The cold deadly stare in his eyes was meant to chill the blood of his opponent.

This was the man they had sought. The one who had killed Shale's mother, the one who had hunted them through the wilderness to Pennsyl. The one who watched as his son died, hoping to see Shale die as well.

The cruel sneer turned to a horrid smile as the man watched recognition dawn upon Avian's face. "You are not in my plan to kill today, elf, but I will not waste the opportunity."

"You kill like the coward you are. Innocents unknowing of your presence." Avian's eyes did not flinch. They did not widen in fear or apprehension. He stood focused, intent, unmoved by the man. It would end here.

They circled one another in the small space, each looking for a sign of weakness in the other, for a moment of distraction to attack.

A glint came into Avian's eyes. His opponent favored his right leg slightly with any shift to the left. He held his knife in the ancient grip of an elvish warrior. Avian glanced down, allowing his opponent an opening.

The man rushed Avian, hoping to overpower him with a shove and stab maneuver. Avian rolled and placed his feet into the man's midsection, flipping him over and onto the uneven ground of the sloping ridge.

Angrily the man regained his feet. The quickness of this elf infuriated him. They circled each other again, but this time the man was forced to step to the left each time on the uneven ground. His eyes did not leave Avian. Snorting in frustration, he devised another plan. The elf would not expect him to move to his weaker side. His prey was eluding him while he delayed here. He must end this interruption. Faking a move to the left, he shifted right, thrusting his blade with all his strength.

Avian closed the circle, pivoted to his left, and thrust his knife through the man's shoulder as he slashed at the air where Avian had been a half second ago. Unbelieving eyes looked out from the cruel face as the man rolled over the edge of the ridge onto the ground below. He moved no more.

Connor, Samuell, and Cameron rushed to Avian's side as he slid down the ridge. Connor knelt by the body, and pushed back the headband revealing elvish ears and blonde hair beneath a wig of black drawn back at the nape of the neck.

Connor did not speak.

"Who is he, father?" Samuell asked quietly, breaking the silence.

Cameron interrupted them. "Put him on my horse. We must take his body with us. It must be shown to our enemies, and then they will surrender."

Samuell drew his blanket from the saddle and laid it out to wrap the body.

"Do not wrap the body, Samuell. We are at war, and our enemies must see that their leader is slain," Cameron instructed.

Samuell fell backwards from the blow as his father spun and fired. The arrow whizzed past him, embedding into the heart of their foe. The raised hand, gripping a gleaming knife, collapsed to the ground.

Samuell looked up into the eyes of his father. Connor pulled him to his feet and embraced him.

King Corsac rushed to them. "Are you harmed?"

Connor nodded toward the body.

Corsac looked upon his foe and said, "Dagnir. Long has he sought to harm our family. I prayed he would never find you, Connor."

"Who is he, father?" Samuell asked. He had to know. "Did he...did he kill Momma?"

Connor squeezed Samuell tighter.

"He will kill no more." Looking to Samuell, Corsac continued, "He worked for our grandfather for many years. When Grandfather perished, he sought an inheritance, but was instead banished for his love of the Presage. Since that day, he has borne ill will toward our families, and we have tracked his movements until three years ago when he escaped our watch."

Turning to his captains, he commanded, "Take him to our enemies and dump his body before them. They will disperse. Pursue them to the edge of the borders of our lands and maintain our parameters. We will await word from you here."

Two days later word arrived that the enemies were routed, abandoning the war at the death of their leader. Many had even cheered at his death, for he was a cruel master and had held many of them in allegiance through threats of violence to their families.

Leaving guards at the borders, the armies of King Corey and King Corsac returned to Robin's Wood and peace settled about them again.

On the third day of their return from battle, continuation of the festival began. Connor sat with Shale and Avian as they watched Samuell best two archers in the final competition of the morning. Connor turned to look behind him as a small hand touched his shoulder.

"Piper!" he cried, springing to his feet and gathering her up in his arms. Tears flowed gratefully down his cheeks as he kissed her face, and swung her around in his arms. "Piper, it is really you." He hugged her to himself again, then asked, "How have you come to me?"

"My mother brought me to you, Papa! See?" Piper pointed beyond the crowd of observers to a dark haired elvish maiden watching them with tears streaming down her face.

"Raina!" Shale cried. She rushed past him to embrace her. Raina dropped the woven basket she was holding and embraced Shale. The basket wobbled and tipped. Piper's cherished doll spilled out. Quickly, Raina stooped and picked up the doll, carefully dusting its dress. Tenderly, she tucked it back into the basket, and arm in arm with Shale approached them.

Piper wiggled from her father's arms when they neared them and, taking Raina's hand, extended it to her father. "Papa, this is my momma. She brought me to you. She is wonderful." Piper beamed up at him.

Slowly, he took Raina's hand. She quickly bowed and, searching his eyes, spoke to him, "Thank you, my lord, for the honor of caring for your children has been mine, and I am grateful."

Returning her gaze, Connor struggled to answer, "My deepest thanks to you, my lady. I am at a loss for words." He drew back from her and looked to Shale for help.

"Come and sit with us. Samuell is winning the archery contest. You must watch him," Shale invited.

Eagerness appeared on Raina's face, but she covered it quickly with a small smile. "I do not wish to interfere, Shale. Your family needs time together." She turned to go.

Seeing Piper's face fall, Connor spoke quickly, "Please, join us. It would be our honor to have you."

Raina studied him briefly and nodded.

"Raina, this is Avian." Shale smiled.

"We welcome you, Raina. Thank you for caring for my wife in her time of need." Avian spoke warmly. Shale pointed to Samuell on the contest field preparing to take a shot.

"Come, Papa, I cannot see my brother," Piper said, tugging on her father's arm. They moved to stand beside Shale and Raina. Piper clung tightly to Connor's hand until Samuell's arrow soared to the center of the target. Jumping up and down, she cheered loudly, then grasped the hands of her father and Raina in excitement as Samuell prepared for his next shot.

Connor sought to quiet his heart as he watched his son competing and felt the warmness of Piper's small hand encircled in his own. His family was together again. Grateful tears threatened to spill down his cheeks.

Raina turned to look at him with compassion in her eyes. She gave him a soft smile of understanding and turned back to the competition.

It had upset him greatly to hear Piper call someone else 'momma.' He missed Shayna so much. She should be here with them, but she was not. He drew a deep breath and focused on Samuell as he released his arrow and it sped toward the target.

Center again! Samuell ducked his head as the Cambria Forest archers descended on him. His face radiated his joy as they congratulated him heartily.

Avian squeezed Shale's shoulders gently and left to join the celebration. Soon he returned with Samuell who was grinning jubilantly.

Piper rushed to her brother, shrieking with delight. Joy bloomed across Samuell's face. He scooped her up and began swinging her around in a circle until she screeched for mercy.

"Where is Raina? Did she come? Tell me and I will let you go," he demanded.

"She is here! She is here!" Piper cried.

"I do not believe you, little one," Samuell answered. He held her snugly in his grasp.

"There, there with Papa and Shale," she gasped, out of breath from laughing.

Samuell set her down and strode toward the laughing group waiting to congratulate him.

"Well done, my son!" Connor smiled into Samuell's dancing eyes and gripped his forearms firmly.

"That is wonderful, Samuell. I knew you could win." Shale beamed at him as she slipped her arm around Avian.

Raina stood back watching them, her eyes sparkling with pride.

Released by his father, Samuell stepped to Raina. "Mother, you have come. Now we are truly all together." Samuell hugged her tightly. "Thank you for coming."

"I am happy to see you safe and well, my son." Raina smiled sweetly and caressed Samuell's hair.

Connor turned and walked away.

Raina nodded to Samuell and looked in his father's direction.

Samuell turned and followed Connor. "What is it, Papa? What is wrong?"

"She is not your mother."

Samuell gripped his father's arms. His intense grey eyes penetrated into Connor's. "No, my father, and I will never forget the love of my mother. Be assured of that. But, Papa, Raina has been as a mother to me and to Piper for nearly two years in Bellflower. She cared for us with her whole heart, Papa. She truly loves us. I do not know what would have become of us if not for her." He paused and brushed a wayward strand of hair from his forehead. "I tried not to love her. I kept pretending it was only a game Piper and I were playing. We had word from Lord Cale that you were safe and sent your love. Then we heard nothing, and Raina's love slipped into our hearts." He paused and stared out over the meadow. "I was afraid, Papa."

"I am sorry, Samuell. I could not risk being followed if I came to you. I am sorry to have grieved you so." Connor gripped Samuell's forearms again and stared deeply into his eyes. "So many nights I wept for you and prayed for your comfort and safety. Prayed that someone loving and kind would be caring for you."

"Your prayers were answered, Papa. There she is." Together they watched Raina walking quietly with the others. A sweet smile lit her face as Piper bounced among them, chattering in amazement at all she saw.

Connor swallowed twice and cleared his throat. "I must thank her. Perhaps she would join us for the feast tonight. You would like that, would you not?" He grinned mischievously. "She can tell me all about your escapades in Bellflower." He released Samuell's arms with a squeeze.

"Escapades? I was always very well behaved. It was Piper who was the problem." Samuell dodged his father's playful slap on the shoulder and smiled, delighted that he had made him laugh.

Raina agreed to join Connor and his family for the feast. She was happy to be with all of the children, and to finally meet Avian and their father. All of the stories Samuell and Piper had told her were true, and more so. She felt, in a way, that she already knew each one of them. Yet, her heart did not fully rejoice, for she knew that her presence reminded Connor of the loss of his wife, and the time he had been forced to be away from his family. For many years she, too, had dealt with the sadness of loss, for her husband had died in battle with her brother many years before. Seeing Connor studying her, she gave him a tremulous smile.

The music began and Samuell arose instantly from his seat.

"Dance with me, Samuell," Piper cried.

"Oh no, Piper. This dance is for me," Connor responded quickly. He extended his hand with a gracious bow. Samuell's distraction with the maidens seated around them had not escaped him.

Samuell smiled his thanks and turned, only to find the object of his attention being drawn to the dance floor with another. Turning to Raina he bowed and offered his hand, "May I have this dance, my mother?"

Raina glanced quickly at Connor for his reaction.

He stood smiling at them with Piper holding tightly to his arm. "After you, my lady." He bowed and extended his arm for them to pass.

The evening passed quickly. As the tables were being filled with blue, white, and yellow flowers, those mingling among the celebrating throng moved to find their partners for this celebrated dance.

For Avian and Shale no movement was necessary, for they had not left one another for a moment. Orrie stood next to them holding Crystal's hand securely in his own. Corey stood behind Bethany with his hands resting on her shoulders. The dance floor would be full tonight, as each heart was reminded of the preciousness of life and love.

Raina moved to the refreshment tables and chose a cup of sweet wine. She found a spot where she could see the dance floor clearly and she watched eagerly, waiting to see Shale twirl by, safe at last in Avian's arms.

Surprisingly, Jamie stood near Muriel who, away from Charleen, showed herself to be an intelligent and compassionate maiden.

Charleen, subdued, sat with her mother, apparently chastened by the realization of her selfishness and the knowledge that life is to be cherished. The captain of her father's guard did not escape her gaze. Before, she had allowed herself to see him only as a lowly opponent for verbal sparring. Now as she was coming to realize the true lowliness of her behavior, she recalled times spent with him. Times when he had seen her at her best and worst, yet thought no less of her. *He should think less of me for I have been despicable*, she thought as she studied him. At that moment he turned and smiled at her. Hesitantly, she smiled back, and then looked down at her hands folded in her lap. She was startled by the tears springing to her eyes.

The music began, and she lifted her head. She watched, amazed, as her parents began the dance, each holding out a blue flower for the other. She could not remember her mother ever looking so young. Having cast off the cloak of bitterness and greed that bound her soul, she was absolutely radiant. The eyes of her parents never left each other as they moved among the ever growing throng of dancers.

Charleen started when a reassuring voice broke into her thoughts.

"My lady, will you join me in this dance?" The tall captain held out his hand for hers. Smiling shyly, Charleen accepted his hand. Her eyes sparkled through her tears.

Connor and Samuell stood together on the fringes of the crowd, while Shale and Avian moved past them, lost in the magic of the dance and the glow of love in each other's eyes. Piper laughed with the other young maidens, her arms laden with fragrant blossoms to shower upon any new couple proclaiming their betrothal.

Samuell nudged his father and, without turning toward him, whispered, "We have been espied, my father."

Glancing down at Samuell in mock horror followed by a charming smile, Connor replied, "Retreat or charge?"

"I am told that if one does not wish to dance with them, one may sit with them and partake of refreshments, while discerning one's strategic course of action," Samuell replied, continuing to apprise the maidens standing near Raina. She watched them with amusement shining in her green eyes.

Connor nodded graciously to them and spoke to his son. "I see it is too late for you to discern wisely in this situation, as you have already been affected. I have never heard you utter such a sentence in your entire life." He studied Samuell's smitten face. "How old are you now, my son?" he asked sternly.

Samuell opened his mouth to reply with mild indignation, but his father spoke first. "You seat them. I will bring refreshments. Your beautiful mother would never forgive me if I should fail in the task of socializing her son." With that he started off toward the maidens, Samuell close on his heel, displaying a dashing grin.

After introducing himself, Samuell seated the maidens and waved for Dracy to join them. Raina watched with a pleased smile on her face.

Connor spoke softly into her ear, startling her. "Will you join me, my lady, in the task of socializing my son? I fear it will be too much for me alone."

She turned large, green eyes to study Connor and saw an openness there that had eluded them earlier. "My Lord Connor, I would be honored, though I fear the lad has not neglected this area of his training." She smiled and nodded at Samuell, who was already entertaining the group with one of his tales.

"Ah, yes, his mother would be pleased. Let us gather refreshments for them and see that he remembers his manners." Smiling down at her, Connor gently took her arm and escorted her toward the refreshment tables.

When You Dance with Rabbits

Avian held Shale closely while they danced, his head resting lightly on hers, feeling the softness of her hair against his cheek. From time to time he closed his eyes, breathing in the sweetness of her scent, feeling the warmth of her against him. Opening his eyes again, he whispered, "There, my love, look with me upon a sight we have longed to see."

Shale lifted her eyes to his and followed his gaze into the sea of dancers. In rhythm with the music the dancers parted, and she saw Crystal, two blue flowers in hand, wrapped in Orrie's arms. At the edge of the dance floor, Piper was poised, barely able to contain herself, waiting to shower them with armloads of fragrant blossoms.

With a gentle laugh, Avian drew Shale's attention back to him. She met his eyes and smiled radiantly at him. They were now on the edge of the dance area merging with the beautiful gardens. Looking intently into her eyes, Avian turned, drawing her with him onto the walkway between rows upon rows of blue flowers.

"I wanted to pick my own for you this night." He tenderly tucked three tiny blue roses into the braid of her hair.

Shale, in turn, selected a very large blue one and presented it to him. He tucked it securely in his belt. She took his hands and kissed each palm.

Encircling each other's waist, they walked together through the fragrant gardens on the pathway to their chambers. The sounds of music faded behind them, but were replaced by the music in their hearts.

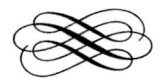

One year later, Shale sat on their bed contentedly nursing their baby. Avian gently laid his head on her shoulder, and gazed down at their robust son. Intent upon his feeding, the baby nursed eagerly and looked up at them. A sweet peace enveloped them, wrapping them in the warmth of love.

Shale felt such joy rise in her heart that she felt it would surely burst. She leaned her head lovingly against her husband and caressed her baby's small hand, feeling his tiny fingers curl around hers.

For a while they rested together, absorbing the warmth of their love as a family. Eventually, the baby pulled away from his feeding, now more interested in his father's voice and face. He kicked his little legs and reached up to grasp Avian's nose.

Lifting him gently from Shale's lap, Avian spoke to his son, delighting in his bright eyes and waving hands. Shale settled back against the pillows, smiling affectionately at the sight of her husband carrying his son to the window, talking all the way. Holding him securely against his shoulder, Avian patted his back and began telling a story of a lost little rabbit seeking his way home through the wilderness. Turning, he looked at his wife, his eyes full of love and promise.

To order additional copies of

When You Dance with Rabbits

Have your credit card ready and call:

1-877-421-READ (7323)

or please visit our web site at
www.pleasantword.com

Also available at:
www.amazon.com
and
www.barnesandnoble.com

Printed in the United States
52924LVS00001B/1-69